The
ANGELS'
SHARE

The
ANGELS'
SHARE

ELLEN CROSBY

Minotaur Books
New York

First published in the United States by Minotaur Books, an imprint of St. Martin's Publishing Group

www.minotaurbooks.com

Library of Congress Cataloging-in-Publication Data

Names: Crosby, Ellen, 1953– author.
Title: The angels' share / Ellen Crosby.
Description: First edition. | New York : Minotaur Books, 2019. |
Series: Wine country mysteries ; 10
Identifiers: LCCN 2019032232 | ISBN 9781250164858 (hardcover) |
ISBN 9781250164865 (ebook)
Subjects: LCSH: Montgomery, Lucie (Fictitious character)—Fiction. |
Murder—Investigation—Fiction. | GSAFD: Mystery fiction.
Classification: LCC PS3603.R668 A85 2019 | DDC 813/.6—dc23
LC record available at https://lccn.loc.gov/2019032232

Our books may be purchased in bulk for promotional, educational, or business use. Please contact your local bookseller or the Macmillan Corporate and Premium Sales Department at 1-800-221-7945, extension 5442, or by email at MacmillanSpecialMarkets@macmillan.com.

First Edition: November 2019

10 9 8 7 6 5 4 3 2 1

For Rick Tagg
With thanks and love for twelve years of educating me about
the business of grape growing and winemaking, for answering
my many questions with good-hearted patience and humor,
and for plying me with fine Virginia wine.

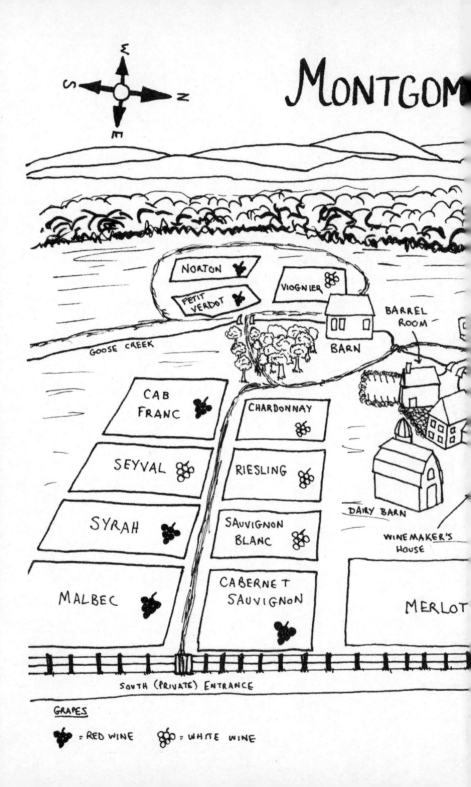

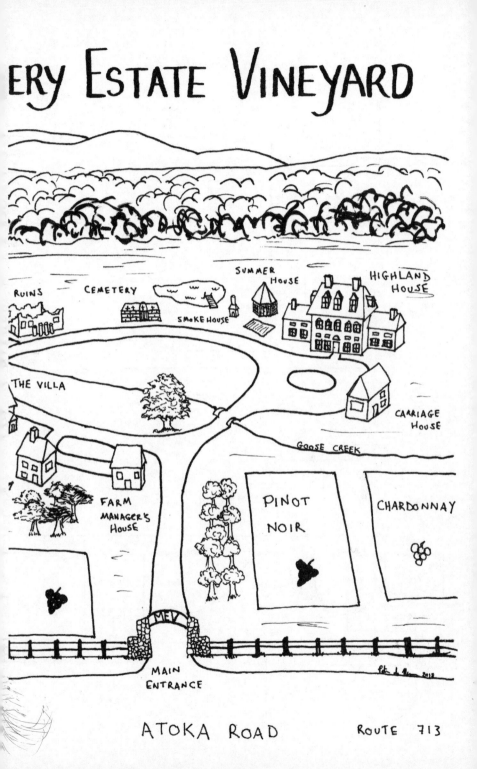

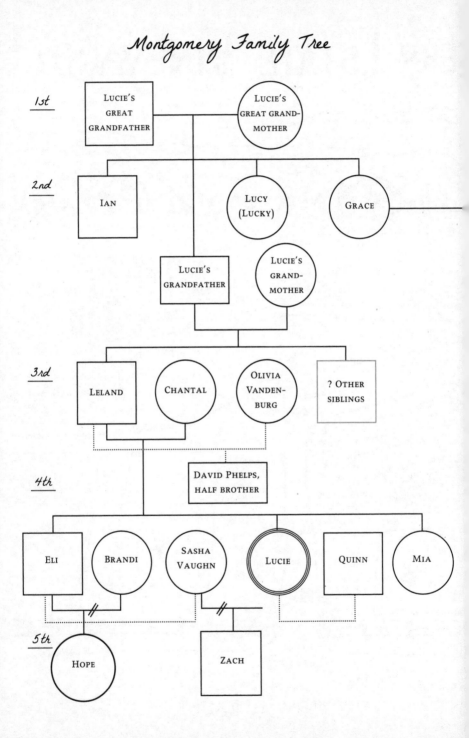

Montgomery Family Tree

1st — Lucie's Great Grandfather — Lucie's Great Grandmother

2nd — Ian — Lucy (Lucky) — Grace

Lucie's Grandfather — Lucie's Grandmother

3rd — Leland — Chantal — Olivia Vandenburg — ? Other Siblings

4th — David Phelps, Half Brother

Eli — Brandi — Sasha Vaughn — Lucie — Quinn — Mia

5th — Hope — Zach

Avery Family Tree

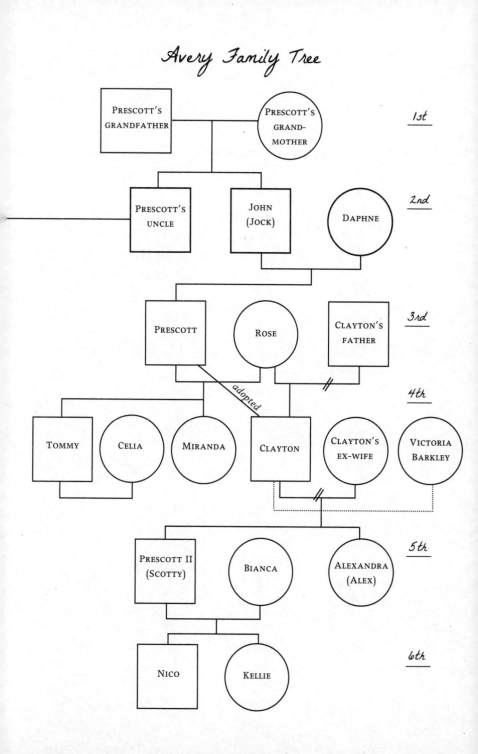

What's past is prologue.

—WILLIAM SHAKESPEARE, *The Tempest*

Today relatively little Madeira is drunk in the U.S. Americans seem to want light, quick-drinking wines, and Madeira, which is heavy and must be sipped and savored at leisure, is like daytime baseball: a wonderful institution, made for the spirit of another age. Really fine Madeiras are today the Edsels of the wine world: a handful of fanatics hoard them and talk about them, but most people have never tasted one, let alone bought one.

—JOHN HAILMAN, *Thomas Jefferson on Wine*

The
ANGELS'
SHARE

One

Vintage Madeira is the color of old blood.

A nearly indestructible wine, it improves almost magically with fire and heat. Once upon a time the value of a barrel of Madeira was determined by the number of voyages it made secured in the holds of cargo ships that crisscrossed the oceans. Thomas Jefferson famously used to send his Madeira back to sea—to African ports or the distant Indies—if he decided there were not enough destination stamps on the barrels he'd ordered.

No other wine in the world requires at least half a century to fully mature or can live for two centuries and remain so potent and wonderfully drinkable. To taste Madeira—really old Madeira—is to taste history.

"I have a proposition for you, Lucie." Prescott Avery's pleasant baritone, breath hot with alcohol, was low in my ear even though no one else was around. Somehow he had managed to whisk me away from party crowds, rooms filled with laughter and chatter, the clink of china and glasses, and the beguiling beat of a samba.

"I thought we could discuss it over a glass of one of my old Malmseys," he added.

Malmsey is the best Madeira in the world. Sweet, made from the malvasia grape, it comes from Madeira itself, a mountainous Portuguese island off the coast of North Africa with a reputation as a place of eternal spring.

No one turned down Prescott Avery, even though he always managed to make it seem as if he were doing you a favor when, in reality, you'd find out later it was the other way around. He meant to charm and flirt with me—I already knew that—but in five years, he'd be a century old. This was the harmless seduction of a sweet old man with hearing aids and a cane.

We were at an after-Thanksgiving neighborhood party in his magnificent home, alone in an opulently furnished room filled with museum-worthy art and bookcases lined with leather-covered books, no doubt all rare volumes or first editions. A fire flickered in a fireplace surrounded by an elaborately carved mantel of cream-colored Italian marble. My brain was already buzzy with alcohol, two deliciously lethal Caipirinhas that I had drunk too quickly in the past few hours. If Prescott wanted to make some kind of deal with me, I wanted to be clear-headed and have my wits about me.

"I'd love to try your Malmsey," I said. "Maybe I could come by one day next week. Now that harvest is over and we've finished most of our cellar work, things have finally quieted down at the vineyard."

Prescott made a tsk-tsk sound with his tongue. "Actually, my dear, I was thinking about right now."

I didn't want to do this *now*. "What about the party? We really shouldn't leave . . ."

He gave me a coy wink, cutting off my protests. "Nonsense. It's my party, isn't it? Besides, we won't be gone long."

It wasn't actually his party. Prescott Avery II, his grandson, whom the family called Scotty, and Scotty's Brazilian wife, Bianca, were hosting their annual Saturday-after-Thanksgiving celebration, a traditional feijoada dinner for about a hundred friends and neighbors. Normally the get-together was Atoka's laid-back antidote to leftover turkey, cranberry sauce, and stuffing, with its Brazilian comfort food menu of black bean and pork stew, garlic rice, fried manioc, collard greens, and sliced oranges. It was served with caipirinhas, Brazil's potent national drink of muddled lime and a sugarcane hard liquor called cachaça. This year Prescott had insisted the gathering be held at Hawthorne, his home—or "the Castle" as everyone called it—rather than at Scotty and Bianca's magnificent horse farm just down the road. And this year the vibe was anything but laid back.

A few caipirinhas in and word had gone around that Prescott had insisted that everyone in the family spend the night at the Castle so he could convene a board of directors meeting first thing the following morning at which he planned to share news about the future of Avery Communications. It didn't take a genius to figure out what was on his mind. For the last three years Prescott had watched his stepson Clayton relinquish his role as publisher of the *Washington Tribune* to his two grandchildren, Scotty and Alexandra. He had also witnessed their increasingly public feud over how the newspaper should be run. Clayton, caught up in an ugly divorce, had done little to tamp down or even discourage the bickering between his son and daughter until it had finally disintegrated into two warring camps at the *Trib*. This afternoon Alex and Scotty were barely speaking to each other and when they did, they were icily civil.

Maybe Prescott just wanted to get away from the taut-as-a-violin-string tension among his family, and needed an accomplice. Plus he had piqued my interest: what proposition?

"This must be important if you want to discuss it right now," I said.

He didn't bite. "Then let's go, shall we? We can take the elevator. It will be easier for both of us."

He indicated my cane with the tip of his. Mine was utilitarian, the consequence of a near-fatal automobile accident ten years ago and doctors who said I'd never walk again. His, crystal with a beautiful antique silver handle engraved with his family crest, was merely an aid to help with balance, though he often joked that it was his magic wand. He slipped his free hand under my elbow. His grip was surprisingly strong.

"Where are we going?" I asked.

"My wine cellar. I thought you might like to see it since the little renovation was finished last month."

Ah, the hook. I'd visited Prescott's wine cellar before, though more often I'd seen photographs of it in the pages of glossy lifestyle or shelter magazines. "Wine by Design: The Twenty Most Beautiful Wine Cellars in the World" or "The

Largest Private Wine Collections in America You'll Never
See."

"I would."

"Excellent. We'll be back before anyone misses us."

I doubted that. Clayton, Scotty, Bianca, and Alex had all
been keeping an eagle eye on Prescott this afternoon, no doubt
wondering about the news he planned to announce tomorrow
morning. Our departure would not go unnoticed.

"What about Quinn? Why don't I go find him?" I said. "I
know he'd love to join us."

Quinn Santori, my fiancé, was also the winemaker at my
vineyard. If I got a private tour of Prescott's newly renovated
wine cellar without him, I'd never hear the end of it.

Prescott drew my hand through his arm and patted it.
"Oh, he'll give you up for a few minutes, my dear," he said in
a reassuring voice. "Besides, you're the one I want to talk to.
Only you, Lucie." He laid an index finger over his lips like we
were conspirators. I could read the message in his eyes.

Don't tell anyone.

He led me down a long corridor lined with more paintings
in ornate gilded or carved wooden frames that I knew for a
fact were original Old Masters. Classical bronzes and marble
sculptures that had once graced temples, palaces, and gardens
in ancient Greece, Italy, or somewhere in the Middle East were
subtly lit and so beautiful they took my breath away.

Then there was Hawthorne Castle itself, an honest-to-
goodness castle with turrets, towers, crenellated walls—even
a portcullis leading to an inner courtyard with a multi-tiered
fountain in the center—built by Prescott's father, Jock, in

the 1800s as homage to his British wife, Lady Daphne, so she would not be homesick for her beloved England. Hawthorne also possessed a knight in a full suit of armor that stood guard in the foyer, a small garden maze modeled after Henry VIII's maze at Hampton Court Palace, an orangerie, servants' quarters, three swimming pools, a bowling alley, and dozens of formal rooms for entertaining where hand-woven silk and wool carpets from Morocco, Iran, China, and Turkey covered floors with elaborate inlaid borders of exotic wood. In total, the Castle had sixty rooms, including fifteen bedrooms, along with three Tudor-style guest cottages. In addition to the art on the walls, the high-coffered ceilings were painted with murals of hunting scenes and pastoral landscapes or cherubs and creatures from mythology; the intricate woodwork had been carved by craftsmen Jock had flown in from Italy.

"I'm sure you must never get tired of seeing these beautiful things," I said. "I know I wouldn't."

"I don't," he said, "but to be honest, acquiring them is what really interests me. It's more about the thrill of the hunt, if you know what I mean. Learning the provenance of each item—about the artist, the owners—traveling the world to find something so rare and exquisite, so sought after . . ." His voice trailed off.

Only to give it all away.

People in Middleburg and Atoka still talked about it. How shortly before Rose Avery, Prescott's beloved wife, died five years ago, the two of them had signed the Caritas Commitment, a philanthropic promise drawn up by some of the world's most influential billionaires, to give away the majority of their wealth as a legacy, a way of giving back for the very good fortune they had enjoyed in their lifetime. Already Prescott and Rose had bequeathed many paintings and sculptures in the Avery art collection to important galleries and museums upon their deaths, adding to donations made by Jock and Daphne. What remained after those bequests were fulfilled—more art, furniture, jewelry, books, carpets—would be sold at auction with the proceeds going to charities the Averys supported— most of it to the Miranda Foundation, named for their late daughter.

"I think it's incredibly generous that you've committed to giving it to charity," I said. "I can't imagine how you could do that—let go of everything."

"It was Rosie's idea. She was the driving force in setting up the Caritas Commitment, you know. My Rosie always said that we are merely temporary stewards of our good fortune." His hand swept the length of the hall. "All these things belong in a place where anyone can see them. Where *everyone* can see them . . . My God, we have a Picasso in one of the guest powder rooms because there was no place else to hang it."

He chuckled at the irony of a Picasso in a bathroom. We reached the elevator and he pushed the call button. Like everything else in the house it had its own fascinating history: originally commissioned in France to be installed as the first elevator in the Senate wing of the U.S. Capitol, Congress changed its mercurial mind while Hawthorne was being built and Jock had snapped it up instead.

The elevator gave a faint whine as it descended from one of the upper floors and stopped on the main floor. Prescott pulled the outer door aside and the inner door slid open.

He gestured to me, ever the courtly Southern gentleman. "After you, my dear."

I stepped in and saw my reflection in the dusky glass of an antique mirror on the back wall, my features accentuated in the slightly distorted reflection. Dark brown hair pulled back in a French braid, my favorite pearl drop earrings that had been my mother's, hollowed cheeks, eyes with smudged circles underneath since we had been hard at work in the vineyard right up until Thanksgiving this year and I still hadn't caught up on sleep.

Prescott's eyes met mine in the mirror and I knew that he had been studying me. What did he want to talk about that we couldn't have discussed upstairs?

It still surprised me to realize that he and I were distantly related. My great-aunt Grace had married Prescott's uncle, joining the Montgomery and Avery families together three generations ago. I had been named for Grace's sister Lucy, who the family had nicknamed Lucky, because of her carefree joie de vivre and uncanny good fortune. Like the time she gave a girlfriend her ticket to sail home from London so she could stay behind and continue an affair with a married man, who happened to be a count. The ship was the *Titanic*.

We reached the lower level and the elevator stopped with a tiny jolt. This time Prescott opened the inner door and the exterior door slid open. We stepped into another corridor; sharply cooler and lit by flickering gas wall sconces. More art hung on the walls: paintings that were darker, surrealistic. Macabre. I thought I recognized Salvador Dalí, Goya, and Andy Warhol. Originals, all of them.

I looked away from a bloody severed head being held up

by a gruesome-looking demon and said, "What else is down here besides your wine cellar?"

His lips curved in a small smile. "The bowling alley, the Italian marble swimming pool, storage rooms for the chairs and tables when we have our big parties, holiday decorations . . . that sort of thing. And, of course, my archives."

Prescott's collection of documents and memorabilia dating from the earliest days of the country—particularly anything belonging to the Founding Fathers who were Virginians—was probably the most extensive in the world outside of the Library of Congress. Leland, my late father, had also been a historian and collector of documents and first editions on early Virginia history, and occasionally had sold some of his precious books and papers to Prescott when he needed money—usually to pay gambling debts.

We walked by a door with an old-fashioned dead bolt and a padlock.

"What's behind that door?" I asked.

Prescott's smile widened. "The dungeon. No castle would be complete without one."

My stomach tightened. Was he serious, or merely teasing me?

"I thought that was just talk," I said. "Kids trying to scare other kids, especially at Halloween."

"So I've heard, but it's part of the mystique of Hawthorne," he said. "I certainly wouldn't want to discourage the idea. Would you?"

He hadn't said yes or no. "I suppose not. Especially considering the cheerful art collection that's on display down here."

He chuckled as we turned another corner. "I like to think we have very catholic taste in art. A little of everything."

I had now completely lost my bearings. The wine cellar, I knew, extended underground well beyond the Castle walls. Reportedly it contained twenty thousand bottles and was so extensive Prescott's sommelier used a golf cart to traverse its many aisles. Supposedly every bottle had been chosen because it was one of the best, and there were no fillers. The value was somewhere in the millions of dollars.

We stopped in front of another door that looked sturdy and unyielding, from an era when the Castle occupants might have needed to reinforce every entrance, ensuring they were protected from potential enemies. Ironically next to the door was a state-of-the-art keypad that flickered to life when Prescott touched it and keyed in a code. I was standing near enough to see it flash on the display before disintegrating into a set of asterisks: HTWSSTKS.

Probably a mnemonic for a phrase that meant something to him. A series of heavy clicks sounded, as tumblers fell into the right places and the door silently swung open.

Once again Prescott indicated that I should go first.

I hesitated, a flash of panic in case the moment I walked through the doorway he'd key in his "Close Sesame" passcode, abandoning me inside. He had sidestepped the question about the dungeon, just as he had avoided telling me why he'd brought me here. But of course nothing of the sort happened and he followed me into the room.

Dim lights brightened automatically as though we were in a theater at the end of a performance. It was all I could do not to gasp. The "little renovation" had transformed the tasting room from a 1920s jazzy Prohibition-era hideaway with Tiffany lamps, lighted mirrored shelves filled with crystal glasses, acres of marqueted paneling, and a plush, comfortable sofa with matching chairs surrounding a tiled fireplace into an austere room of carved stone that reminded me of a medieval French château. White pendant lights hung from the vaulted barrel ceiling and in the alcoves, twinkling like stars. Rows of wine bottles lying in clear Lucite wine racks so they looked as if they were floating formed an undulating wall that separated the bar from a seating area. An arched door had been left ajar so I could see into the wine cellar itself where row upon row of dark, gleaming bottles lined the walls until they vanished into the inky blackness. If there had been music playing, I would have expected a Gregorian chant.

"So, do you like it?" Prescott asked. "All the stone was quarried here on the property. I brought in master stonemasons to do all the work . . . *master* stonemasons. The best."

Prescott only worked with the best of the best.

"It's . . . spectacular. Nothing at all like the way it looked before."

More art hung on the walls—this time instead of paintings there were black-and-white photographs taken by some of the world's most renowned photographers and photojournalists. I made a quick tour, reading names and captions: Henri Cartier-Bresson, Alfred Stieglitz, Diane Arbus, Robert Capa, Edward Steichen, Ansel Adams. I stopped in front of the lone exception: an oil painting of a beautiful young woman in a blue-and-white gown, her red cape strewn on what appeared to be a throne next to the sea. Two men—one elderly, one young—and a horned creature that looked like a devil, surrounded her.

I was still staring at it when Prescott said in a sharp voice, "Take a seat, Lucie, won't you? The sofa's very comfortable."

I stole one more quick glance at the painting and read the small plaque attached to the bottom of the frame. *FERDINAND COURTING MIRANDA,* WILLIAM HOGARTH, CIRCA 1735.

Miranda. Rose and Prescott's daughter's name.

"Lucie," Prescott said again. "Do sit down."

I turned around, flustered, as if he'd caught me spying or eavesdropping. He was standing behind the bar where a bottle of Madeira, a decanter filled with dark, ruby wine, and two crystal tulip-shaped glasses sat on a silver tray. Just how far in advance had he planned this meeting? It obviously hadn't been a spontaneous idea.

"I see I've been expected," I said. "It looks like your Malmsey was already waiting for us."

Now he was the one who looked chagrined. His smile was half guilt, half guile. "I spoke to my sommelier earlier and asked him to decant our wine. He's new, but so far, so good."

"Is he here? In the wine cellar?"

"No, he's upstairs helping at the party. It's just you and me down here."

I'm sure he didn't mean to sound menacing, but a small shiver went up my spine. I walked over and sank into the sofa, which was covered in a concrete-colored fabric. It enveloped me like a pillow and felt like the softest cashmere.

I slipped my phone out of my pocket and checked the strength of the signal. One bar and then no bars. No way to let Quinn know where I was. Damn. I already regretted not insisting that he join us.

"I heard you have a new laboratory," I said. "Maybe you could show it to me?"

"Some other time I'd be happy to," he said in a silky voice

that let me know he knew a distraction when he heard one. "It's quite amazing. I funded the technology at Cal for nuclear resonance testing, which allows one to analyze the contents of a bottle of wine without opening it and disrupting the aging process. Very useful if you're checking for fakes." He picked up the tray. "Relax, Lucie, darling. I promise I'll have you back upstairs in no time. I just wanted us to have a little privacy, is all."

He walked over and set the tray on a glass-topped coffee table with a base that looked like a fiery blue geode. I thought he would join me on the sofa, but he settled into a black-and-white zebra-striped barrel chair directly across from me. He leaned over and poured our Madeira.

There are wines, beers, and spirits that pair well with food. Vintage Madeira is not one of them. It is to be drunk for the pure pleasure of drinking it—savored on its own—a drink for when you're in a reflective mood.

"You're drinking thirty-two-year-old Malmsey," Prescott went on. "The grapes were picked in your birth year. I thought you might like to taste something of the history of what was happening in the world the year you were born."

On the one hand his thoughtfulness touched me—any winemaker knows there is a particular magic to drinking a wine attached to a significant date. On the other hand, I was feeling more and more like a trapped insect that was slowly being spun into the web of a very clever spider. Prescott's business prowess was legendary. I was being set up for something he really wanted.

"How kind," I said. "Thank you."

He handed me my glass and picked up his own. "To many more birthdays."

"To your health. And your centenary in five years."

We sipped our wine and he leaned back and closed his eyes. "Do you taste that velvety honeyed richness?" he asked after a moment. "The trademark of a vintage Malmsey . . . rich, sweet. The aromas of butterscotch, cocoa, and coffee that can fill a room."

Madeira is the drink of a bygone era, generally considered the beverage of an older person. It must be sipped and enjoyed in an unhurried, leisurely way. Most people my age have probably never tasted it, but Madeira's fascinating history had intrigued Quinn and me enough that we were experimenting with making our own at the vineyard. Every summer for the past few years, we hauled three old whiskey barrels filled with Seyval Blanc mixed with brandy outside and left them on the metal roof of the barrel room where the temperature could easily soar into triple digits. And last year we stored one of the barrels in our attic during July and August, just to see what would happen to the taste.

Prescott seemed content to savor his Malmsey in silence, so I, too, settled deeper into the sofa and drank mine. Finally he said in a rich drawl, "I'm sure you've been wondering why I invited you here."

"The thought did cross my mind."

He grinned. "I'm about to make you an offer you can't refuse."

Which meant he intended to make sure I *didn't* turn him down. I sat up straighter, on full alert.

"I see. And what offer would that be?"

"I want to buy the Madeira your great-uncle Ian bought

back in the 1920s. I'm sure you know what I'm talking about. My family has been trying to purchase it from yours for nearly a century. Ian wouldn't sell it and neither would any of your kin, including your daddy. But I'm an old man now, Lucie. I want those bottles." He shifted so he was sitting on the edge of his chair and fixed his eyes on mine. "Name your price. I will pay it. *Anything.* Surely it can't mean as much to you, to your generation, as it means to me."

"I'm sorry—"

He cut me off. "I mean it, Lucie. Do not turn me down. Any price. Whatever you want." He added, as if to soften his words, "After all, we are related, you know. You'd still be keeping it in the family."

I set my glass on the glass-topped geode. "What I was about to say was that I have no idea what you're talking about. *What* Madeira?"

For a moment he looked stunned. Then he burst out laughing. "I must need new hearing aids. I thought you said you don't know what I'm talking about, but you're just pulling my leg, darlin'. You're not serious."

"I'm absolutely serious," I said. "If my father knew about some old bottles of Madeira as you said, I wouldn't be surprised if he either drank them or sold them to someone he owed money to. You knew Leland. He wouldn't—couldn't—hold on to something that precious or valuable. He always needed cash to finance his gambling habits. The vineyard was a financial ruin when I inherited it, if you remember."

But he was focused on the wine, not my father's wayward behavior. "You know *nothing* about that Madeira? You're quite sure?"

I nodded. "How did Ian Montgomery get hold of one-hundred-year-old bottles of Madeira?"

Prescott almost didn't need to tell me. Ian was my namesake Lucky's brother, a gambler and a risk-taker like my father had been. However, unlike my father—and gifted with the same good fortune Lucky had—everything Ian touched turned to gold.

Before he could answer, I took a guess. "He won them in a bet."

"Close," Prescott said. "And these days they're not one-hundred-year-old bottles, either. They date from 1809, which makes them—"

I finished his sentence. "Over two hundred years old. My God, Prescott, are *you* serious?"

"James Madison was our fourth president and the city of Washington, D.C., had just been founded a few years earlier." He leaned back and crossed one slim leg over the other, reaching for his cane and playing with the engraved silver handle. "As to how Ian acquired the Madeira, I probably don't need to tell you that he was a Prohibition bootlegger working with The Man in the Green Hat."

That much I already knew: George Cassiday, an unemployed veteran from World War I, more famously known as The Man in the Green Hat, had literally set up shop in the U.S. Capitol, first in the Cannon House Office Building and later, after the police caught him, moving to the Russell Building on the Senate side, providing a steady supply of alcohol to members of Congress that went on for years. I'd heard stories that Ian worked with Cassiday, often carrying suitcases of booze directly to the offices of congressmen and senators.

So while Congress was busy telling the rest of the country drinking was illegal and immoral, they were awash in the stuff themselves.

I nodded and Prescott went on. "What was less well known was that while Cassiday had his hideaway offices in the basement of these buildings, Ian knew all the secret places in the warren of passageways and underground tunnels that linked every House and Senate office building to the Capitol just like he knew the back of his hand."

He set down the cane and picked up the decanter of Madeira, pouring some more into my glass before filling his own. "What happened was that Ian got scammed by a fellow who owed money to the Mob, promising to take a shipment of some top French vintages, all premier cru wines, off the guy's hands. Ian paid him, the man vanished, and then Ian discovered the wine had been stored in a closed-off tunnel near a boiler room. Everything was undrinkable."

"Except the Madeira?"

Prescott held up a finger. *Not so fast.*

"The Madeira had already been there," he said. "Two cases of it. Twenty-four bottles. All nailed shut, never opened. Hidden in the recesses of that tunnel, but far enough from the boiler that it wasn't destroyed the way the wine was. When Ian finally got a look at the bottles, the labels told him everything. The Madeira had been imported via Baltimore for a congressional ceremony to toast the anniversary of the signing of the Declaration of Independence on July 4. President Madison was supposed to be there."

I caught my breath. "Then those bottles would be quite valuable."

He arched an eyebrow. "Indeed."

"So who owned the Madeira? Not the guy who sold Ian the spoiled wine, apparently."

Prescott gave an elaborate shrug. "It didn't matter. Finders keepers, as far as Ian was concerned. Payback for buying the cases of cooked wine. Besides, it was Prohibition. Whoever originally owned it was probably long dead and the Madeira had been forgotten about. Why it wasn't drunk in 1809 . . ." Another shrug. "Who knows? Anyway, Ian decided to keep it for himself since he knew the value was only going to increase. After he died, everyone else in your family hung on to it as well. No one wanted to sell."

That didn't sound like my family at all. Why had we kept Ian's Madeira for another almost-century? And, more important, why didn't I know anything about it? There was something Prescott wasn't telling me. Why couldn't he have asked me about this upstairs? What was up with the cloak-and-dagger secrecy?

"I'm sorry," I said. "I really wish I could help you, but I can't. I never knew anything about these bottles."

"What a pity," he said. I couldn't tell if he was angry or merely regretful. "Did you know that a few years ago Christie's sold two bottles of 1795 Madeira for ten thousand dollars apiece? Do you have any idea what your bottles could be worth to the right person?" Before I could answer, he added, "I just happen to be the right person, Lucie. I'll pay you more than that."

I did the math. He was talking about a crazy amount of money. "Why?"

"Because I have just acquired a unique treasure that can

only be unveiled with that Madeira. And for another even more important reason I can't discuss. At least not yet."

"And why is that?"

He reached for his crystal-and-silver cane once again and stood up. "Come. I'll give you a tiny hint. However, first you must give me your word that you won't say anything to anyone about what you're about to see."

"All right."

He waved the tip of his cane at me as an admonishment and a rebuke. "Lucie, I'm absolutely serious about this—it's not some lark. You must promise or this conversation is over."

Startled, I said, "I promise."

"Good." He lowered the cane. "Then you may follow me."

Two

followed Prescott over to the arched entrance that led to his wine cellar. Maybe he was going to show me one of his many fabulous vintages or another priceless Madeira. Instead he stopped in front of a bookcase that was next to the Hogarth painting.

To my surprise, Prescott swung it out as if it were hinged to the wall and he was opening the cover of a book. Underneath was another keypad. Once again he pressed buttons for the code, though this time I wasn't fast enough to see what it was. With a click the bookcase slid to one side, revealing a door behind it. Another click and the door slid open. Just as with the tasting room, motion sensor lights in the room brightened.

"After you," he said, as if it were the most normal thing in the world.

For a second time I calmed my nerves, wondering if he might lock me in this secret room until I remembered the location of a priceless cache of Madeira, which he claimed had been in my family for three generations. But he followed me in, just as he had done before, and the door slid shut behind us with another smooth click.

The room was windowless, just like the tasting room, but this time I felt claustrophobic. Where were we? It seemed like a private shrine or a place that was sacred to Prescott. Sacred . . . and secretive.

The walls were painted a luminous green. Cream-colored pilasters with painted veins made to look like marble were spaced along the walls every few feet, their gilded capitals gleaming in the glow of underlights. The black-and-white marble-tiled floor looked like a giant checkerboard. The most prominent item was an antique carved desk, which sat on top of three steps as if on an altar. On the desk three candles in a silver candelabra were placed next to a large open book. I walked up for a closer look. A Bible with an old-fashioned silver compass and carpenter's square lying across it was open to the Song of Solomon from the Psalms. Love poems. The most sensuous verses in the entire Bible.

Let him kiss me with the kisses of his mouth—for your love is more delightful than wine.

There was something familiar about the compass and square, placed as they were on the Bible. It took a minute before I remembered what it was: these were the symbols of a Freemason. On either side of the desk were two identical heraldic flags of red crosses on white shields. A crusader's cross. The shield of the Knights Templar.

I looked around the room. A life-sized oil painting of George Washington wearing an apron decorated with Masonic symbols hung on one wall. On the opposite wall an antique wall clock in the shape of a triangle ticked slowly. On either side were swords with beautifully decorated hilts. Masonic symbols again. A leather apron with another compass, carpenter's square, and the letter *G* stitched with beautifully colored beads hung in an alcove. On either side of it were two columns, each with a globe where the capital would be: a black globe seemed to represent the heavens; the other was earth.

This room *was* a shrine.

"You're a Freemason," I said to Prescott. "And a member of the Knights Templar."

"I am," he said. "I have been for over seventy years. You didn't know?"

I shook my head. "I didn't think anyone who was a Mason spoke much about it. You're rather secretive."

My father had never become a Freemason for one fundamental reason that I recalled: Masons had to believe in God or something called a "Higher Power." Leland thought God, or any kind of Supreme Being for that matter, was a lot of hogwash. And he believed that when you died, you died.

"We're not a cult," Prescott said in a dry voice. "In spite of what some people believe."

I nodded and tried to keep my face expressionless. Maybe not a cult, but what I did know about the Masons, or thought I did, was that it was a male-only organization where members greeted each other with secret handshakes, dressed up in elaborate garb for ritual-filled ceremonies that dated back to Biblical times, and never, ever talked about what they did at their meetings.

"Do you meet in this room?" I asked.

"Good Lord, no. This is most definitely not a Masonic lodge. We don't meet in anyone's home."

"Then why are we here?" I asked. "Why am *I* here?"

"Because there is something I want you to see. I've not even told my family about it yet." For a moment a pained look flashed across his face. "I'll only get reprimanded for spending—or should I say, 'wasting'—what Clayton seems to believe is his money. His inheritance. You see, my stepson doesn't share my penchant for continuing to collect rare and beautiful things. My grandchildren aren't especially happy about it, either." He tapped the side of his head. "They think I'm starting to lose it."

For Prescott Avery, billionaire philanthropist, the man who controlled one of the largest media empires in the United States, who had everything he wanted in life, it was an astonishing, breathtaking admission. Why was he saying this now?

And why was he telling me?

"What do you mean?"

"That I'm chasing—what does Clayton call them—'unicorns' that are more the stuff of myth and legend than real, tangible things."

"Such as?"

Prescott gave me a knowing smile and a shrewd look, as if he'd caught himself telling tales out of school to the wrong person. "Sorry, darlin', I'm not trying to involve you in family politics. Just a bit of venting, is all. I shouldn't have 'fessed up about any of that. Be a good girl and forget about it, okay?"

If anyone else had asked me to "be a good girl" I would not have let it pass. Besides, I wanted to know what, exactly, were the unicorns he was chasing. Instead I said, "I know about families and money, Prescott."

"So you do," Prescott said. "But you've come through it well. I only hope the same will be true for me and mine."

After Leland died, my brother Eli and I finally threw a pair of dice to decide who got the vineyard, the farm, and Highland House, our home. He'd wanted to sell it and get his money. I wanted to keep our land and the farm since it had been in the family for more than two centuries. As our lawyer said while trying to get us to quit our wrangling and settle things before the money all went up in smoke for legal fees, "Blood is thicker than water, but money is thicker than blood."

Wasn't it the truth?

I thought of the warring factions between Alex and Scotty at the *Washington Tribune*. My best friend, Kit Noland, ran the *Trib*'s Loudoun County bureau in Leesburg, the next town over from Middleburg, so she didn't work in the Washington newsroom. She'd told me more than once that if she had to be in D.C. these days she'd rather put out her eyes with hot pokers.

"Come," Prescott said. "As I promised, you're the first person to see this since it was delivered Wednesday morning. The day before Thanksgiving."

He was standing next to what I assumed was a painting hanging on the wall, except that a black cloth covered it. I'd noticed it as soon as I walked into the room.

He removed the cloth with care, but like a magician revealing a special trick, he waved it with a flourish. "What do you think?"

I was expecting something related to the Masons, so it took a moment to realize what it was:

In Congress, July 4, 1776. The Unanimous Declaration of the thirteen united States of America.

I caught my breath. "It's the Declaration of Independence. How in the world did you get this? Isn't it supposed to be in the National Archives?"

He flashed a smile, looking well pleased with himself. "Don't worry, the original—the Matlack Declaration, to give it its proper name—is still in the National Archives in Washington, under lock and key with full-time guards and maximum security. But this . . ." He waved an expansive hand. "What you're looking at is an extremely rare copy that was given to James Madison in the fall of 1776. November 12, to be precise. There's a date on the back."

Given to James Madison, who had been the president the year Ian's cases of Madeira were bottled.

"As you can see, this copy is handwritten, not printed," Prescott added. "By none other than Thomas Jefferson, the man who was asked by the Continental Congress to compose the original document." He placed both hands on the silver handle of his cane and leaned closer to me. "Jefferson wrote out another copy of the Declaration of Independence, added the signers' signatures in his own handwriting, and gave the document to James Madison. Which makes this copy priceless."

I stepped closer to examine the document. Under the low light, it was difficult to make out the words in the elegant script, but I could still read what was written and a shiver ran through me.

We hold these truths to be self-evident, that all men are created equal, that they are endowed by their Creator with certain unalienable Rights, that among these are Life, Liberty and the pursuit of Happiness.

I looked up at Prescott. "Where in the world did you get this?"

"It was discovered in a box of documents in a farmhouse in Iowa by a real estate agent who was going through the owner's possessions. Looking for items to sell and what to throw away. The provenance has been traced to James Madison as the original recipient and handwriting experts at Monticello have authenticated Jefferson's handwriting."

Now I knew why he'd said it was priceless.

"Have you ever looked at the signatures on the Declaration of Independence?" he asked.

I had a fuzzy memory of studying the document and who the signers were in a high school U.S. history class. "I can't name them all, if that's what you're asking."

He shook his head. "I'm not talking about who *did* sign it. I'm asking if you know which famous Founding Father did *not*."

I dredged up my knowledge of the Continental Congress and a hot summer in Philadelphia. Thomas Jefferson had drafted the document, as Prescott just said. So what was he getting at?

I took a guess. "James Madison didn't sign it?"

"Exactly. Madison—who drafted the Constitution—didn't go to Philadelphia during the summer of 1776 while the Declaration of Independence was being drawn up, nor did he sign it," Prescott said. "But as I'm sure you know, Madison and Jefferson were great friends. And, of course, Monticello, Jefferson's home, and Montpelier, Madison's home, were not far from each other."

"So Thomas Jefferson gave James Madison a copy because he didn't attend the Continental Congress," I said.

Prescott nodded. "That makes this document only the third handwritten parchment copy of the Declaration of Independence in existence. The other two are the Matlack copy in the National Archives and a second, known as the Sussex Declaration. That copy was discovered in England a few years ago in the West Sussex Record Office, where it had been languishing for nearly two hundred years. It had been a gift to the third Duke of Richmond, who had been a big supporter of the American side during the Revolution.'"

He waited for me to take that in. "The Sussex Declaration was written horizontally and the names of the signers were copied out in a different order—not by state—by whoever hand-wrote the document," he said. "However, the Jefferson Declaration, as I'm calling it, was written in exactly the same vertical format as the copy that was signed in Philadelphia and it's the same size. The difference is that Jefferson signed everyone's name. They weren't original signatures."

I turned back to look at the rows of signatures.

"Have a closer look, Lucie," Prescott said. "Do you notice anything unusual? About the signatures, I mean."

I squinted and after a moment, I said, "Well, it's clear they were all written by the same person. And . . . John Hancock's signature, which is usually the biggest, is quite small."

"Very observant." Prescott sounded approving. "Do you notice whose signature is the biggest in this version?"

I squinted again. "Thomas Jefferson's."

He cackled. "Hilarious, isn't it? A little inside joke, because Hancock's signature was so big in the original document. He said he signed it like that so the king of England would be sure to be able to read it. But in this copy, my copy, Jefferson got the last laugh."

"Prescott, this really is an incredible document," I said. "The ink has faded a lot less than the copy in the Archives."

"It has. I also acquired a collection of letters written by Dolley Madison to her husband, as well as others written to her during the War of 1812. The ink on those letters is equally well preserved. And I acquired a rare copy of the diary of Paul Jennings, one of the Madisons' trusted White House slaves. It was the first White House memoir ever published."

Things were starting to make sense. "Does this copy of the Declaration of Independence have anything to do with the Madeira that Ian found and Leland supposedly still has hidden away? You want it because James Madison was meant to drink a toast to the signing of the Declaration in 1809—am I right? Those could have been the very bottles."

"You're mostly right," he said. "I want to drink those bottles of Madeira at a special party I'm planning for my brother Masons on December 14, just before the Miranda Foundation's holiday gala."

"You want to *drink* it?"

"Not all of it, but why not drink a few bottles? Even accounting for the angels' share, there will be enough for everyone to have a small glass as a toast."

In spite of myself, I smiled. The angels' share was the amount of alcohol or spirits lost to evaporation in drinks like cognac, whiskey, Madeira, or wine—anything that aged in barrels or casks. The story went that the angels drank the alcohol that evaporated through the porous oak because it rightfully belonged to them. For me it always conjured images of rowdy, bacchanalian parties with drunken angels tripping over their celestial gowns and knocking against each other's wings as they cavorted in heaven.

"That Madeira is also priceless," I said. "Regardless of how much the angels drank."

"That's exactly the point." He threw me a look as if drinking it were the most logical thing to do. "Lucie, there are two weeks until the fourteenth. I'll do anything you need to help you find those bottles."

"Even if there were two years, I wouldn't know where to begin to look. It's not hidden under a bed or in a closet, you know. And I've been through the attic and Leland's wine cellar in the basement."

"Maybe your father left a clue in the documents he kept in his safe-deposit box."

"*What* safe-deposit box?"

"Good Lord," he said, exasperated. "Don't tell me you didn't know about that, either?"

I folded my arms across my chest and gave him a stony look, waiting for him to go on. If I spoke, I would scream or cry or yell. How many more secrets did my father still have that would pop up out of the blue and bite me?

Prescott let out a long breath as if he was weary of explaining so many things about my father that I should have already known. "Leland kept a safe-deposit box at Blue Ridge Federal. I assumed you would have emptied it out when he died. He kept items there . . . things he didn't want anyone to see."

"You mean, things he didn't want my mother to see." My voice rose. I was hurt, but I was angry, too.

I thought—*hoped*—by now we'd straightened everything out, learned everything there was to know about my complicated, flawed father. Gambling debts. Loans. Everything had come down on me like a house of bricks after Leland died. And then there had been the son he never told us about, David Phelps, my biracial half-brother, whom I'd met only a few months ago.

"Lucie." Prescott's eyes were filled with sympathy. "I'm sorry. I don't wish to hurt you, my dear. But your father came across something—a letter—while he was doing some research about the Jamestown Settlement. He wasn't sure what it was, so he brought it to me. At the time, I had no clue what it meant, either."

"Go on." At least he wasn't talking about documents referring to another affair or another child Leland had fathered.

Prescott pointed to the Declaration of Independence. "Now I do know what your father's letter meant, thanks to this."

I was growing irritated and tired of his riddles. "What are you talking about? What does the Declaration of Independence have to do with Jamestown and a letter my father found?"

"More than you might think," he said with an enigmatic smile. "I've been doing some research of my own, studying the Declaration of Independence and how Thomas Jefferson chose the wording, the language he used. And, for that matter, the language James Madison used in drafting the Constitution."

"I'm lost, Prescott."

He held up his hands, urging me to have patience. "Since the founding of our country there has been a mystery surrounding these documents—a lost treasure that would explain many things and would also possibly answer one of the most tantalizing puzzles of the last four hundred years. Quite by accident your father stumbled upon a valuable piece of the puzzle concerning what really happened to that lost treasure. Thanks to Leland Montgomery, I believe I have now found the final clue to its whereabouts. Or at least I hope so."

He gave me a triumphant smile.

I'd had too much to drink. Prescott was talking in circles about some mysterious lost treasure, a puzzle my father knew about, and finding clues to its whereabouts. Maybe. That my father was involved already made me suspicious. Leland was a sucker for every bad deal, every con, every get-rich-quick scam that was out there. Had Prescott gone down the rabbit hole with him?

"What clue would that be? To what mystery, what lost treasure?"

"Why, my dear, you don't think I'm going to tell you, do you? For one thing, I'm not quite ready. There's one more thing I need to take care of. For another, it's far too dangerous." There was a twinkle in his eye. He was enjoying this.

"How is it dangerous?"

"There is a reason this secret has remained hidden, buried for nearly four centuries," he said. "There are powerful individuals who do not want it to be revealed."

"But you're going to defy them? In spite of the danger?" Maybe he was pulling my leg.

"Don't mock me, Lucie. Or underestimate me. It's about the thrill of the hunt, as I've told you. And this has been the thrill of a lifetime." He smiled. "Besides, I am an old man and I am wealthy. There is nothing anyone can do to intimidate me anymore. As the proverb goes, 'Truth is the daughter of time, not of authority.' It's time to shine a light on what has been hidden in the darkness for so long. I intend to be the one who does it."

"Yes, but if you're only going to tell your Masonic brothers at this special party—where you were hoping to drink the Madeira—doesn't that mean it's still going to be a secret? Since the Masons are a secretive organization?"

He chuckled. "A very astute observation. My Masonic brothers deserve to be the first to know for a lot of reasons. Some will be upset. Others, I hope, will be intrigued. But eventually everything needs to come out in the open and I will see that it does, all in good time. In the meantime you must give me your word—once again—that you will keep this conversation strictly between the two of us. Do you understand? *Tell no one.*"

"Prescott—"

"Your *word*, Lucie." His lighthearted demeanor was gone.

"All right, you have my word."

"Good." He sounded mollified. "Now you may go. But I'll be calling on you because we must find that Madeira. In the meantime . . ." Once again he laid a finger over his lips. "Silence."

As if by magic, the hidden door in the wall slid open.

I fled.

Three

t was cooler in the hall, as if someone had opened an outside door and let in a blast of frigid November air.

Which way had Prescott and I come? Which way back to the elevator?

I turned left. I hadn't gone more than half a dozen steps before I realized I didn't recognize the paintings on the walls. Especially the one in front of me, though it wasn't a painting. It was a rectangle of fabric, displayed under a piece of glass. Old and fragile, it was an unusual shade of dull coppery red with a skull and crossbones stitched on it. If it hadn't been so old, the fabric would have shimmered as if it were shot with gold. The edges were tattered and small holes were scattered through it. Bullet holes. The ragged edges were from wind-blown years atop a ship's mast.

What was Prescott doing with a pirate's flag? I read the small placard below it.

Rare Jolly Roger flag captured from the pirate ship Black Fortune *off the coast of North Africa in 1790. A red flag meant no mercy shown to captives.*

Another rush of cold air like icy fingers caressed the back of my neck. It was time to get out of here. I turned and walked quickly in the other direction, this time passing art I remembered and the padlocked door to the room Prescott hinted might really be a dungeon.

The elevator was waiting, just as we'd left it. But the moment I stepped inside, I knew a woman had been in this carriage and taken this elevator while Prescott and I had been together in his wine cellar and that secret room. Years ago when I was living in France recovering from my accident I took a job at the Perfume Museum in Grasse where my nose for recognizing the notes of a perfume and the *sillage*—the lingering scent trail the wearer leaves behind—had improved quite a lot. It was a talent that came in handy for a winemaker: I could usually correctly identify almost every aroma and note in a particular bottle of wine.

This perfume was strong and heady, evoking dusty Middle Eastern bazaars or Scheherazade spinning tales for a thousand and one nights. The scents of cardamom, lavender, and sandalwood. Something as strong and spicy as incense. I would know it immediately if I met the wearer.

Who was she and what was she doing downstairs? Why hadn't I run into her?

The elevator deposited me in the upstairs hallway. The laughter and chatter were muted now; I must have been in Prescott's wine cellar for longer than I realized and guests must be starting to leave. Through one of the large mullioned windows in the study where Prescott and I had spoken earlier, the afternoon sunshine had faded. Dusky gray light was turning the bushes, trees, and sculptures in the garden into smudged shadows.

I was right; the rooms were less crowded, though there were still a lot of people here. Most of them were either in the dining room finishing the ramekins of Bianca's sinfully rich homemade flan that had been served for dessert, or sitting on sofas and chairs pulled up around the fireplace in the drawing room watching the University of Virginia wallop Virginia Tech in football on the big-screen television above the mantel.

I finally found Quinn. Actually, he found me and pulled me into a corner. He was holding a mug of black coffee, though I could still smell caipirinhas on his breath.

"Where have you been?" he asked in a low voice. "The party's winding down. I'm ready to get out of Dodge. I ran into Alex and Scotty having it out in the butler's pantry when I was looking for you. It was getting ugly. Those two shouldn't be around sharp knives in the same room."

"I was with Prescott in his wine cellar," I said. "I'll tell you all about it at home."

"You were in Prescott's wine cellar? Without me?" His voice rose and he looked as upset as I knew he would be.

"Shh. Someone will hear you."

"No wonder you didn't answer my texts."

"I would have if I could have, but I didn't get them. There's almost no service down there." I reached into my pocket for my phone. "Damn. My phone. It's gone."

"Did you leave it in the wine cellar?"

I nodded. "It probably fell out when I pulled it out to try to text you. Prescott's still down there. I need to go back and get it."

"I'm coming with you." He set down the coffee mug on a nearby table and followed me out of the room. "Let's get it and then we can say our good-byes. Although I don't know what happened to the family. They all seem to have disappeared."

"It's a big house. Come on; let's do this before Prescott leaves the wine cellar. Though I did happen to notice the code he used to open the door."

There was no one in the long art-filled corridor except two waitresses collecting empty plates and glasses from rooms wherever people had left them as Quinn and I hurried back to the elevator. It was still waiting on the main floor, but the strong scent of perfume had dissipated.

"Can you imagine living in a place like this?" Quinn asked as the carriage gave a slight jolt and we started down to the basement. "Of course it won't be the Averys' home once Prescott is gone."

"What do you mean?"

"I spent some time with Grant while you were downstairs with Prescott. He wasn't shy about discussing the family financial situation. One too many caipirinhas, I think." We stepped out of the elevator. "Which way? This looks like a maze."

"Straight ahead. Don't worry; I'll know if we're going in the right direction because of the art on the walls and whether we pass the dungeon. What did Grant say?"

"Dungeon?"

"Yep. What about Grant?"

Grant Lowry was the *Washington Tribune*'s managing editor. My friend Kit Noland thought he walked on water. He was what she called an old-school journalist—tough, demanding, rolled-up shirtsleeves, unbuttoned top collar button and loosened tie, someone who looked like he'd answer to "chief" or "boss" and still remembered the newsroom when it was noisy and smoke-filled, before computers, the internet, and cell phones turned it into a place as silent as a morgue. What made him so beloved by his reporters—in spite of being as tough as old boots and expecting his reporters to be the best of the best—was the knowledge that he would literally go to jail for any of them if it meant protecting his people and their sources.

I didn't think he was especially good-looking—longish gray hair tousled and generally in need of a haircut, sharp hawk-like features, and the kind of tanned, weather-beaten face that, as the saying went, "looked like a couple of miles of bad road." But he was brilliant, charismatic, and charming with an undeniable rugged sex appeal. Prescott had hired him when he was still running the *Trib*. Now Grant was dealing with the fallout of the feud between Scotty and Alex.

"According to Grant," Quinn said, "once the family gives away their money thanks to the do-gooder promise Prescott and Rose made, there won't be much left in the piggy bank. They're probably not going to be able to hang on to Hawthorne and most of their other properties. The *Trib* is hemorrhaging money and so are enough of their other newspapers that they've been robbing Peter to pay Paul."

He stopped walking. "What's with these paintings? Cannibalism, dismembered babies, and . . . Jesus, what are those two people doing with that goat? Is that what I think it is?"

"Come on." I tugged on his arm. "It is, but we need to get to the wine cellar. It's just around the corner."

I dragged him with me and he followed, though he was still eyeing the art. "Some people have the weirdest taste," he said. "And fetishes. This stuff looks like porn."

"I'm sure they're all original paintings worth a fortune. We just don't have the artistic sensibility to appreciate them."

"Okay by me."

"Just because your taste runs to Elvis-on-velvet . . ."

He grinned and slung an arm around my shoulder, pulling me to him and kissing my hair. "Anything wrong with that?"

"Damn."

"What?"

"The door to the wine cellar is shut. Maybe I should knock to see if Prescott is still in there."

He wasn't.

Quinn shrugged. "Didn't you say you saw him type in the code to unlock the door?"

"I did."

"Well, then?"

I frowned.

"What?" he said. "You're not breaking and entering, you know, if you just want to get your phone."

"It feels wrong. He wears hearing aids, you know. Maybe he didn't hear us knocking."

He sighed. "How about this? What if I call you and we can hear your phone ringing? If he's there, he'll hear that and I bet he'll answer. If he doesn't pick up, at least we'll know the phone's still in there and he's probably gone. Would you feel better?"

"I suppose so."

He dialed my number and we put our ears against the thick door like a pair of amateur spies. Quinn leaned over and stole a quick kiss. I kissed him back. From inside the room I heard the faint sound of the ringtone I used for him.

He nodded. "It's there. Go ahead, Light-Fingered Lucie. Open the vault. Supposedly the wine in there is worth millions."

"Funny. Real funny." I punched in the code I remembered from watching Prescott, reciting the letters as I typed. "HTWSSTKS. Does that mean anything to you?"

"Hot . . . was sticks? Hat was stuck? Hot wish sticks?" He shook his head. "Nope."

Just as before I heard a series of clicks and the door swung open like the entrance to Aladdin's Cave.

"It should be right there in the sofa cushions," I said as we stepped inside. "What the—?"

An overpowering smell of honey, butterscotch, cocoa, and coffee filled the room.

"That smells like Madeira," I said. "Prescott's Malmsey. Something's happened . . . something's wrong."

Quinn sprinted across the room to the sofa and armchair where Prescott and I had been seated less than an hour ago. He stopped and looked up. His face told me all I needed to know.

I reached him seconds later and we both knelt down. Prescott lay on the floor, his frail body crumpled so he was partially on his side, one arm flung above his head as if trying to protect his face, the other stretched out like he was reaching for something. Blood pooled under his head and there was a partial bloody handprint on the edge of the glass-topped coffee table. His glass of Malmsey had broken into two pieces—the stem and the goblet—and lay on the floor. The decanter had toppled over and most of the contents had spilled out. Odd, because decanters with their wide bases, which allow the liquid to breathe and open up, usually don't accidentally tip over. My glass, however, was exactly where I'd left it. The tableau bothered me. Something wasn't right.

Otherwise, though, sweet, viscous Madeira was everywhere in puddles and spreading liquid tentacles. It had even mixed in with Prescott's blood. I swallowed and prayed I wouldn't throw up.

My chest felt like it might explode. "We have to get help right away."

But I knew we were too late even before Quinn leaned down, listening to Prescott's heart and touching his fingers to find a pulse. He straightened up and shook his head.

"He's dead, sweetheart. He must have tripped and hit his head on the table. Or maybe he had a heart attack . . . I don't know. A doctor will figure it out."

My eyes filled with tears. "I should have stayed with him. If I'd been here, I could have gotten help, maybe saved his life."

"Lucie." Quinn's voice was gentle, but urgent. "There's nothing you can do now and you don't know that it would have been different if you had been with him. We still need to get someone down here. Clayton or someone else in the family. They're going to need to make arrangements, take care of the bod—take care of Prescott."

"Right." I felt numb. *I should have stayed should have stayed should have stayed.*

"I'll wait here, be with him. You go back upstairs and find someone." He gave me a small nudge. "Go on, honey. The party's breaking up so more people will have left. It will be easier to handle everything discreetly. I'm sure the family will want to keep this news private for a while before they have to make an announcement."

I nodded. The death of philanthropist and media billionaire Prescott Avery would make not only local and national news, it would make international news.

This time when I left the wine cellar I knew which way to go in the maze of corridors to get back to the elevator. With Prescott gone, Clayton was now the head of the Avery family. He was the person I needed to find first.

If I hadn't been so focused on looking for him, I probably wouldn't have collided—almost literally—with Kit's husband Bobby Noland who was deep in conversation with Dr. Winston Churchill Turnbull. I turned the corner into the dining room and didn't see them standing next to the French doors, which had been thrown open to accommodate the many party guests.

Bobby grabbed my arm to keep me from crashing into him and Win. "Whoa, Lucie. Where's the fire? What's going on?"

Bobby was a senior detective with the Loudoun County Sheriff's Office and Win was our newest medical examiner who, at age seventy-four, had recently returned from a year of volunteering at a military hospital in Iraq. It was only a matter of time before the two of them ended up downstairs, not as guests of the Averys, but because of who they were and what had happened.

"Lucie." Win's expression was kind but concerned. "What is it?"

Bobby gave me a sharp-eyed look. He and I had known each other since he was seven and I was five. There wasn't much I could put past him, so I didn't even try.

"I'm looking for Clayton," I said, keeping my voice low. "Prescott had a bad fall in his wine cellar downstairs. It looks like he hit his head on the edge of a glass coffee table . . . there's a lot of blood. I'm afraid he's dead."

Bobby and Win exchanged glances.

"Were you with him when it happened?" Bobby asked.

"No."

"You're sure he's dead?" This from Win.

"Yes."

"Does anybody else know about this?" Bobby said.

"Quinn," I said. "He's there with Prescott now. I was trying to find Clayton when I ran into you."

Another coded look passed between Win and Bobby.

"Look," Bobby said, "you obviously know where this wine cellar is so why don't you take Win there and I'll find Clayton. I'll tell Clay what happened. We'll join you as soon as we can, okay?"

Bobby did this for a living, delivering in person the worst news anyone could hear to unsuspecting family members, letting them know that their loved one wouldn't be coming home anymore because he or she was dead. I didn't know how he could do it again and again: it was an accident . . . the shots were fatal . . . I'm afraid we believe she committed suicide . . . I'm so sorry, my deepest condolences, my sympathy, my prayers to you and your family. Then he had to witness the shock, heartbreak, and grief.

Now he was watching me, waiting for an answer. "Are you all right, Lucie?"

"I'm . . . fine." Which was a lie. I hadn't realized I'd been gripping my cane handle so tight my knuckles were white, but I'd had no idea what I was going to say to Clayton other than blurt out the truth: Prescott is dead. Thank God Bobby was handling it; he would be far better at finding the proper words of consolation.

"Thank you for doing this," I added.

He nodded. "No problem. And later on, you can fill me in on what happened before Prescott hit his head." Bobby wore his no-nonsense cop face. "Because I'm sure there is more to the story."

Prescott had made me promise I would keep our conversation to myself. He didn't want his family to know about his purchase of James Madison's priceless copy of the Declaration of Independence, penned by his good friend Thomas Jefferson, along with other valuable documents pertaining to Madison and his wife, Dolley. But now Prescott was dead and Bobby would be asking me officially, not out of prurient curiosity.

How much was I going to tell him? He clearly wanted to know what I was doing in Prescott's private cellar and why Quinn was there.

Did I have to explain about Ian Montgomery's ill-gotten Madeira and Prescott's hints about possibly discovering the answer to a puzzle that would reveal the whereabouts of a spectacular lost treasure? That he believed he was venturing into potentially dangerous territory if he shared what he knew? Wouldn't Bobby twirl a finger next to his temple and give me one of those are-you-out-of-your-ever-lovin'-mind looks?

Hadn't *I* wanted to twirl a finger next to my temple and ask Prescott the same thing?

Across from us Clayton Avery strolled into the dining room. Victoria Barkley, his girlfriend, hung on one arm discussing something that seemed to consume Clay's interest. The two of them had their heads together like a pair of conspirators, Clay nodding as she spoke.

"Don't turn around," I said to Bobby, "but Clayton and Victoria just showed up. They're by themselves. And in their own world."

Victoria was Clayton's latest significant other, although rumors abounded this afternoon that they were about to officially announce their engagement. They'd met a few months ago at a party at the Russian embassy after Prescott loaned two paintings—a Kandinsky and a Chagall—for a special exhibit on Russian artists at the National Gallery of Art that Victoria, a museum curator, had organized. She and Clayton had been inseparable ever since.

Everyone in Atoka drew the obvious stereotypical conclusions since Victoria was an attractive blonde with the willowy figure of a fashion model, closer in age to Scotty and Alex than she was to Clayton. Sexy, hot blonde makes older man feel young and virile again. Younger woman—some would say "gold digger"—finds boyfriend to indulge her love of couturier clothes, expensive jewelry, and sailing trips to Greece and skiing holidays in Switzerland.

Bobby's head swiveled around until he found Clay and Victoria. Then he turned back to me. He knew I'd ducked answering him and he knew I knew it.

"See you downstairs," he said. "I'll go tell Clay."

Four

For a man in his midseventies, Win Turnbull had the spry agility of someone at least twenty years younger. I walk fast enough with my cane, but I can no longer run since my accident and that terrifies me. Win slowed his pace as soon as he realized I was having trouble keeping up—and apologized. I hated that he had to do that.

"Don't worry," I said. "I'm working on getting faster."

"I know you are," he said. "You've got grit, Lucie."

When Win had been in Iraq, he had performed what he called "meatball surgery" under appalling conditions, reattaching limbs where possible and amputating them when there was no more hope. Sometimes on children. He'd seen plenty of grit.

"Thank you for that."

I led him to the elevator, the basement, and down the maze of corridors. I caught his startled look as he took in the unusual art, but unlike Quinn he didn't comment. Nor did he say anything when we walked into Prescott's wine cellar with its opulent medieval French château decor and, through the arched doorway, the rows of wine racks with bottles of rare vintages that stretched into the darkness.

Quinn got up from the sofa where he'd been keeping vigil with Prescott, looking surprised at seeing Win instead of Clayton.

"Hey, Doc," he said. "Over here."

"Bobby is going to tell Clayton what happened and bring him down here," I said.

Quinn nodded and moved out of the way so Win could kneel beside Prescott.

"Rigor hasn't set in," Win said after a moment. "It hasn't been very long since the time of death. Lucie, tell me what happened when you were with him."

I gave him a rough timeline, explaining that Prescott had invited me for a glass of Madeira to discuss purchasing some of my wine. When we were finished he wanted to stay in the wine cellar for a while, so I went back upstairs to the party.

It wasn't the whole truth, but it seemed to me there was no point bringing up the tour of Prescott's secret shrine that paid homage to his Masonic beliefs. He'd hit his head here in the wine cellar, so why mention the other room?

"Was he drunk?" Win asked.

"No."

"You're certain? There's alcohol on his breath. Rather potent, in fact."

"If he was drunk, I didn't realize it," I said. "Actually, he seemed quite lucid. What happened, Win?"

"Possibly a heart attack or a stroke. I'll know after I do the autopsy. It looks like he tried to reach for the table after he hit his head. If he was conscious I'm surprised he didn't try to call for help."

"There's no cell phone service down here," I said. "He wouldn't have been able to reach anyone."

"Speaking of cell phones." Quinn fished my phone out of his pocket and handed it to me. Win watched the exchange.

"We came back when I realized I'd lost my phone," I told him. "If Quinn and I hadn't shown up when we did, it might have been a long time before someone thought to look for Prescott down here."

"Why is that?"

"Because he didn't want anyone to know he'd invited me to his wine cellar," I said and realized belatedly it sounded as bad as I thought it did. "Didn't want his family to know, that is."

That sounded even worse. It was time to shut up.

"Oh?" Win's eyebrows went up. "Why not?"

"There was talk at the party that he was convening a meeting of the Avery Communications board of directors to-morrow morning, most likely to announce plans to sell the *Washington Tribune,* as well as several other Avery Communications newspapers that were losing money."

Win gave me another arched eyebrow look, but before he could reply we heard voices in the hallway. He stood up. "That must be Bobby and Clayton."

"It sounds like more than just the two of them," Quinn said.

He was right. Clayton and Bobby entered the room first, followed by Scotty, Bianca, Alex, and Kellie, Scotty and Bianca's twenty-one year-old daughter.

It was hard to read the expressions on everyone's faces.

Shock? Grief? *Relief?* There would be no meeting tomorrow to discuss selling the *Trib* or any of the other newspapers owned by Avery Communications. The timing of Prescott's death had been convenient, even prescient, for anyone in the family who didn't want to sell.

And that, frankly, was everyone named Avery who had just walked into this room. All of them were on the board of directors, including Kellie and her older brother. So were Clayton's ex-wife and Celia, Tommy Avery's widow, whom Prescott had appointed to be the executive director of the Miranda Foundation after Tommy died.

Bobby's eyes zeroed in on Win's and I caught the imperceptible shake of Win's head. *Don't let them look. It's bad.*

Bobby put a restraining hand on Clay's arm. "This is not going to be easy, Clay," he said. "You don't have to see him this way if you don't want to. Or any of you, for that matter. There's no need for an I.D."

Alex's eyes flashed. "I want to see him."

"Sweetheart," Clayton said in a cautioning voice, "Bobby just warned us this was going to be difficult. Let me do this."

"*Dad.*" Alex put all the weight into that word that said *don't stop me and don't patronize me.* "I can handle it."

Scotty put his arms around Bianca's and Kellie's shoulders. "Maybe you two don't want to see him. Remember him as he was."

I had been watching Kellie, who had started shaking, a sure sign she was about to burst into tears. She was doing her best to hold it together but after Scotty spoke her face crumpled and she let out a ragged sob, burying her head on his shoulder.

"Poor Pop-Pop. Someone should have been here with him. He shouldn't have been alone." Her voice choked with grief and I flinched. That someone could—should—have been me.

Scotty transferred his distraught daughter to his wife's arms. Bianca moved Kellie away from the rest of us, murmuring consoling words in Portuguese in her daughter's ear.

"Dad," Scotty said, "the three of us should do this. We have to."

Quinn and I exchanged glances and he jerked his head sideways, indicating the door. I nodded. We stepped outside into the cool, fresh air of the corridor, away from the mingled smells of Madeira and death, allowing them privacy for their sad task. I closed my eyes and waited for what I knew would come: their shocked, anguished reactions to Prescott's body lying in a pool of blood. Even Alex let out an unvarnished cry of grief.

After a moment of respectful silence Win and Bobby took over, talking them through what came next. Eventually I heard Clayton say, "There's a door around the corner that opens out to a driveway. It's sheltered and it's near the orangerie. The ambulance or whoever comes can use that entrance to transport Pres—ah, his body—to the . . . ah, morgue. There's a private back road so no one needs to see any vehicles come or go. I'll show you where it is. I'd like to keep this quiet as long as possible."

"Dad." Alex sounded patient but firm. "Word *is* going to get out. You know that. Nothing stays a secret around here. Everybody in Middleburg and Atoka was at Hawthorne this afternoon and there are still a few folks upstairs who haven't left. Victoria's handling them but she has to make up a story about why none of us are there to say good-bye. The family—us—we need to be the ones to control what's said about how Grandpop died. Grant's already driving back to D.C. to the newsroom because it's going to be a bombshell when this gets out."

"Are you serious?" Scotty, irate, cut her off. "Did you send Grant to D.C. without telling me?"

"Of course I did. Who do you want to handle it, Scott? The overnight shift on Thanksgiving weekend? The newsroom's probably full of interns, for God's sake." Her words crackled with sarcasm. "Everyone who could take the holiday off did take it off. It's supposed to be a slow news cycle. We're down to a skeleton crew. Use some common sense."

Scotty and Alex were yin and yang, dark and light— except they didn't complement each other, didn't fit neatly and seamlessly together to make a whole. Instead they were opposites that repelled rather than attracted. He was dark-haired, dark-eyed, the responsible son. The stoic eldest child, stepping up to the plate to help his father at the newspaper, majoring in journalism at Columbia and eventually taking Clay's place as publisher, knowing his father never wanted the job. Alex was flighty, mercurial, blond and fair-skinned, frivolous, carefree. Spending money she didn't have and marrying men she quickly tired of. A career in New York as a writer for the now-defunct *Village Voice* after studying English lit at Brown. A writer of plays and poetry, her latest project was a cathartic tell-all memoir—if rumors were to be believed—that the family managed to make sure didn't see the light of day. Instead she was brought back to D.C.—thanks to Prescott—as co-publisher of the *Washington Tribune* alongside her brother.

The Avery family version of rehab, meant to help her settle down and keep her close to home. It hadn't taken long before the fireworks between her and Scotty started and people began using words like *dysfunctional* and *toxic* to describe the working environment at the *Trib*.

"That's enough, you two," Clayton admonished them in a sharp voice. "Stop squabbling and show some respect."

"We should go," I said to Quinn. "We don't belong here."

A shocked silence from the wine cellar followed my remarks and then a murmured conversation. Quinn and I exchanged looks. My voice had carried; they had forgotten about us standing outside the door, unintentionally overhearing their vitriol and that argument.

Quick footsteps and Clayton appeared in the doorway. "Lucie, Quinn—sorry, we didn't realize you were still here. Please join us for a moment. There are a couple of things we'd like to discuss with you."

"Of course."

Quinn and I exchanged knowing glances and followed Clayton into the wine cellar.

The rest of them were no longer standing next to Prescott's body, which had been moved to the sofa; his face now respectfully covered by Scotty's blazer. They had migrated to the bar where Scotty had opened a bottle of red and was pouring it into wineglasses. Cumulatively this afternoon we had all probably drunk enough to float an ocean liner. More alcohol in such a volatile atmosphere seemed like it might be tossing a match into a tinderbox—but who was I to say?

Scotty held up the bottle. "You'll have some, Lucie and Quinn, won't you? In memoriam? Bobby, Win, you, too?"

It was hard to say no.

"Dad." Scotty turned to Clayton. "You should give the toast."

Clayton raised his glass. "To Prescott Warren Avery, who lived a long and full life. May you now be with those you loved most—Rose, Miranda, and Tommy. God bless."

There was silence while we drank. By unspoken agreement something had changed in the family chemistry and it seemed as if the Averys had closed ranks after their argument. I knew what was coming next, why Clay had called Quinn and me back into the room.

We knew too much.

Quinn and I were the sole source of any potential leak concerning Prescott's death. The only ones who knew exactly what had happened, outside of Bobby, Win, and the family. Bobby and Win got a special exemption; we did not.

"I am so sorry you two had to be the ones to discover Prescott the way you did," Clayton said in a smooth, take-charge voice. "I know it must have been a terrible shock. You did the right thing getting Bobby and Win down here. But I must ask you both—in fact, I must insist—that you respect our family's privacy by not revealing how you found Prescott. That you leave him his dignity."

Quinn nodded and I said, "We understand."

"The announcement for public consumption will be that Prescott died in his sleep," Clayton went on. "A heart attack, a peaceful death. In the bosom of his family, finally joining his beloved Rose." He looked from Quinn to me. "Is my meaning clear?"

"Crystal," I said.

"There is no need to . . . embarrass . . . him or us with any tawdry details," Scotty said. "We appreciate your discretion."

"And I know we can count on you both," Clayton said. He turned and faced Bobby and Win. "I'm asking the same courtesy of you as well. I see no need for an autopsy, do you, Win?"

Win set down his wineglass. "You don't want to know the cause of death?"

"He was ninety-five," Clayton said. "Does it really matter whether he had a heart attack or a stroke—or maybe he tripped after perhaps imbibing a little too much alcohol at a party in his own home?"

"If that's your wish," Win said.

"It is."

"Lucie and Quinn," Clay said, "you don't need to stay any longer while we handle . . . everything. Thank you again for what you did here."

We were being dismissed.

"Our condolences once again," I said. "If there's anything we can do . . ."

"Thank you, but we're fine. We'll be fine," Alex said. It was the first time she'd spoken since we walked into the room.

"We'll see ourselves out," Quinn said.

There was silence as we left. I couldn't wait to get out of there. Halfway across the room the tip of my cane came down on something that crunched as though I'd just broken it. I froze.

"What the—?" Quinn said.

Before either of us could pick it up, Bobby came over and got it. A small—and now destroyed—hearing aid.

"This must be Prescott's." He held it up so everyone at the bar could see it.

"It is," Clayton said. "It must have fallen out when he tripped . . . or after he collapsed."

"Wait a minute." I looked around the room. "Where's his crystal cane . . . his magic wand? It should be here somewhere, too."

"Maybe it rolled under the sofa," Scotty said.

Bobby went over and checked. "Nope. At least I don't see it."

"We'll find it," Clayton said. "It has to be here somewhere."

His eyes met mine. I knew then that he was aware of Prescott's Masonic shrine—how could he not know?—and the hidden door in the wall. It was the last place I'd seen Prescott when he was still alive. Maybe he'd dropped the cane in there and that was probably what Clayton was thinking.

For now neither he nor anyone else knew that I'd been in that room, nor the secret Prescott didn't want any of them to know about. I wanted to keep it that way, though I had the uneasy feeling Clayton might have already figured out that I knew something.

"We should be going," Quinn said. "Good-bye, every-one . . . and, again, our condolences."

On my way out, I couldn't resist one more glance at the bookcase behind which the door to Prescott's Masonic shrine was located. If you didn't know a secret door was there, you'd never guess. My glance fell on the Hogarth painting next to it, *Ferdinand Courting Miranda*. It was askew. Could Prescott have flailed about and knocked into it before he fell?

Quinn tugged my arm. "Let's get out of here," he said under his breath.

We didn't speak until we were back at the elevator and well out of earshot of everyone in the wine cellar.

Quinn said it first. "What the hell just happened in there?"

"I don't know," I said. "But something's wrong and it has to do with Prescott's death. His family is covering up a secret." The elevator door slid open and Quinn opened the inner door so we could step in.

As the door closed I added, "Whatever it is, we're now co-conspirators. Except we don't know to what."

Five

Kit Noland met Quinn and me as we stepped out of the elevator. She was already dressed for Christmas in hunter-green wool trousers and a cherry-red turtleneck. A necklace with tiny chili pepper lights occasionally winked red and green. The holiday outfit didn't go with her all-business demeanor. She was holding a mug of black coffee and she'd clicked off party mode.

"Grant told me before he left for the newsroom that Prescott was found dead downstairs in his wine cellar," she said as the elevator door closed behind us. "They're trying to keep it quiet so no one at the party finds out."

She was speaking a mile a minute, already in overdrive. Writing the story in her head. I knew from experience that she was looking for the lede. Once she got that—figured out how or where to begin—she told me that the piece more or less wrote itself.

I was nodding as she spoke, but my mind was racing, too.

Would anyone in the media care that I had been the last person to talk to Prescott before he died? Hopefully not. Prescott had left too big an imprint on everything he'd touched, the empire he'd built, for anyone to bother with a minor detail like me.

"I know Bobby's there because I can't find either him or Win Turnbull. Why were you two down there? What's going on?"

Already Kit knew about Prescott from Grant Lowry and he had found out from Alex. As they say, three can keep a secret if two are dead. The Averys were never going to be able to contain this news and certainly not spin it the way they wanted to, that Prescott died peacefully at home in his sleep surrounded by his family. Instead, I could just imagine the headlines: *Billionaire Philanthropist and Media Mogul Prescott Avery Dies Alone at His Own Party.*

"You're going to have to talk to someone in the family," I said. "They want to handle this."

She looked taken aback. "Oh," she said. "I see. A gag order, huh?"

"I didn't say that."

"You didn't need to. Either way, that shouldn't include talking to me."

"They didn't give us a list," I said.

"I guess I'd better call Grant and let him know. And see what I can worm out of my husband once he shows up . . . though it probably won't be much. I love him to death, but he doesn't cut me any breaks." Her eyes narrowed. "Was there something suspicious about Prescott's death? Is that the reason you're not supposed to talk about it?"

Quinn and I exchanged glances.

"It's probably better if you ask Bobby or Clay your questions," Quinn said. "We ought to be getting home."

"I'll take that as a yes," she said, giving him a sharp nod. "Look, the optics are already bad, Prescott dying at his own party on Thanksgiving weekend. Not talking about it is only going to make things worse."

"I doubt Prescott was thinking about the optics when he died," Quinn said.

"You know perfectly well what I mean." She glared at him and then turned to me. "Never mind, then. Luce, talk to me. Whatever happened, the Averys' own newspaper needs to report the story honestly."

I hesitated. "I, uh . . . think you should ask Clay, Kit."

She shot me a look of dismay. I wasn't going to help her, either.

"Prescott Avery's death is already going to be a big story. If there's something weird or odd about the way he died, it's going to turn into a soap opera drama. And if you were downstairs, you know something."

"We sort of got an ultimatum," I said. "They want to do all the talking."

"As bad as that?" She was mad.

"I'm sorry," I said. "Look, can I ask you something?"

"Yeah, sure. Shoot. I'll answer you if I can." Still pissed off.

She finished her coffee and set the mug down on a windowsill ledge with a sharp click. Outside the window, the gardens and sprawling terraces were now unsubstantial dark shapes on a darker landscape.

"How many people knew Prescott was probably going to

announce that he wanted to sell the *Trib* at tomorrow's board meeting?"

She looked surprised by the question. Then she exploded. "Are you kidding me? Every newsroom in the world leaks like a damn sieve and we're no different. Everyone and his grand-mother knew about that rumor. It's all anyone was talking about this afternoon—at least among the Tribbies who were at the party." She paused as the puzzle pieces slid into place. "So there *is* something to Prescott's death, isn't there?"

I remained mute, but by now she knew as well as I did: *How convenient for those who didn't want to sell that Prescott died before that meeting.* In other words, a lot of people who'd been at today's feijoada wouldn't be unhappy that Prescott Avery could no longer force a sale of the *Washington Tribune*.

A waitress walked past the three of us, picked up Kit's cof-fee mug, and nodded, a polite smile on her face that said we were overstaying our welcome. The party was over.

I felt Quinn's hand on the small of my back. "Time to go," he said.

"Wait." Kit held up her hand. "At least tell me what you were doing down there. I'm sure there's no gag order on that."

Quinn flashed me a warning look. "Prescott invited me downstairs because he wanted to buy some of our wine," I said, dodging her real question. "I'm sure now the deal is off, so it doesn't matter anymore. And I accidentally left my phone in the wine cellar so Quinn and I went back to get it."

"You were the ones who found him. And he was already dead." She spoke like these were established facts, not ques-tions requiring answers.

I nodded. "I came upstairs to find Clay, but I ran into

Bobby and Win first," I said. "We left after the family showed up. I'm sure Clay can tell you everything else that you need to know."

"Like cause of death, which would be useful information." She pulled her phone out of her trouser pocket and pushed a button. Speed dial. "I'll ask him when I see him. And thanks for at least telling me that."

As Quinn and I walked down the hallway I heard her say, "Grant. Talk to me. What the hell is going on? Who's lowering the cone of silence on Prescott's death—Clay or Scotty?"

Quinn gave me a sideways look and shook his head.

"I can't lie," I said when we were out of earshot. "You know that. Certainly not to Kit. When we're together it's like our minds meld. If I hadn't told her, she would have just sucked the information out of my brain like she always does. I can do the same with her. Besides, do you honestly believe the Averys are going to be able to keep what really happened out of the press? Their *own* newspaper? Kit wouldn't stand for publishing a false story and neither would Grant. The *Washington Tribune* wins Pulitzers every year because of their tenacious, honest reporting. Not even Prescott Avery is going to get a break."

"We shouldn't be in the middle of this."

"We *are* in the middle of this. We found Prescott and I was the last person to be with him before he died."

"Lucie, Quinn. I didn't realize you were still here."

We froze. Neither of us had noticed Victoria Barkley, who was striding down the hall toward us, a startled expression on her face.

Had she overheard our conversation? Had any of the staff

overheard us? I flashed a quick smile and hoped I didn't look as if she'd discovered us stealing the family silver.

Victoria's cheeks were bright pink and her shoulder-length blond hair, which had been in a stylish updo the last time I saw her, was tousled and windblown, as if she'd just been outside.

I relaxed. She didn't look as if she'd been paying attention to what we were saying. Maybe because, like a lot of party guests, she was a bit drunk. Or maybe because she was preoccupied with what was going on downstairs while she was still up here. As if she read my thoughts about her disheveled appearance, she pulled a couple of hairpins from her hair and used them to tuck the loose strands back into place.

"I was saying good-bye to what I thought were the last of our guests," she said. "It's quite cold outside now. And windy."

"We were just leaving." Quinn sounded apologetic. "And we can see ourselves out. No need to trouble you."

Victoria knew about Prescott. Clay would have told her and she had been on her way to the elevator to join the others in the wine cellar when she stumbled upon us.

"Nonsense." She still seemed rattled. "Of course I'll walk you to the door."

Our silence was awkward as she retraced her steps and led Quinn and me to the elegant foyer. From one of the alcoves, the armored knight seemed to watch us through slitted eyeholes.

What were Quinn and I going to say? *Thanks for a great party? Condolences on the death of your fiancé's stepfather?* Nothing at all?

Surely she realized we had been downstairs with Prescott. She had been with Clayton before Bobby brought him downstairs. She would *know*.

"If there's anything we can do," I said, "please don't hesitate to ask."

Her eyes flickered understanding and I was glad we weren't going to keep up the charade that nothing had happened.

"And, uh, about Kellie." Quinn held out his hands, palms up. I knew Kellie's raw grief and tears had unnerved him. Any woman's tears unnerved him. I'd learned that from experience. "Please tell her she doesn't need to come to work tomorrow . . . actually, not to show up until she's ready. Let her know to take all the time she needs, could you?"

That was sweet; I was glad he'd been the one to say it.

Last spring Kellie had told her parents that if she didn't take a year off from her studies at Harvard she would have a nervous breakdown. Scotty wanted her to stick it out—Averys weren't quitters—but Bianca had prevailed, worried about her daughter's mental health, so the compromise had been that Kellie would stay home for one year as long as she returned to school and graduated the following year.

Though Scotty wanted her to spend what would have been her senior year in the *Trib*'s newsroom learning the family business, Kellie showed up at our vineyard to ask for a job as a cellar rat. We weren't looking for anyone, but Quinn hired her on the spot. She was terrific—smart, capable, with good instincts. Francesca Merchant, who ran our tasting room, managed to cajole her into pouring wine and doing tastings on the weekend. Our clients loved her. Despite the fact Scotty and Bianca had never said anything to either Quinn or me, we knew their daughter's employment choice for her gap year hadn't gone down well at home. What they didn't know was that Kellie had no intention of returning to Harvard. She wanted to go to France and study winemaking.

She'd been plying Quinn and me with so many questions, asking our advice, that one evening after everyone had left for the day I asked her if that's what was going on. Her eyes grew wide.

"Please," she'd said, "promise me you won't tell my parents. I think my father would disown me if he knew. I'm supposed to go into the family business, become a journalist, not a winemaker."

"Of course Quinn and I won't say anything. But you're going to have to tell them sooner or later," I'd said.

"I know. I'll do it. But not right now."

And we'd left it at that.

"I'll let Kellie know that you said she should take time off," Victoria was saying. "This is going to be . . ."

She, too, seemed to be struggling for words. Finally she said, "Difficult."

Especially if you lie about what happened.

I smiled and said, "The Averys are tough. I think that's one trait both our families share."

Victoria looked puzzled. "Both which families?"

"The Averys and the Montgomerys," I said.

"Are you implying that you're . . . related?"

"That's right," I said. "In fact, Prescott brought it up it up this afternoon."

"How did this happen?" Victoria looked as if I'd just told her the Averys were related to direct descendants of Jack the Ripper.

"A couple of generations ago a Montgomery married an Avery."

For a split second I thought she looked relieved. "So you're not *close* relatives."

"I can't even do the math to figure out how many times removed we are."

She smiled and I realized she *was* relieved.

Prescott hadn't been dead more than a couple of hours. Was Victoria worried about relatives like us—known and unknown—coming out of the woodwork to find out whether we might benefit from his will and substantial wealth?

Quinn touched my elbow. "Sweetheart."

"I know."

Victoria walked over to the door and started to open it.

"Wait," I said.

She turned around and this time her annoyance and impatience were obvious. Even Quinn frowned at me.

"What is it?" he said.

Prescott's crystal cane with its elegant family crest engraved on the silver handle—his magic wand—stood propped in an umbrella stand that was part of an antique mahogany hall rack.

"That's Prescott's cane," I said. "How did it get here?"

Victoria's eyes went to the cane and she waved a hand, unfazed. "That cane? He always left it here so he could take it when he went out. It was one of his favorites."

It seemed strange to hear her speak of Prescott in the past tense.

"But he was using it today," I said. "He had it when we went downstairs. He even joked about taking the elevator because we both use canes."

Victoria shook her head. "He had more than one silver-and-crystal cane, Lucie. Believe me, Prescott was quite the collector. And that included beautiful and expensive canes like this one."

She was reading from Clayton's playbook; that was obvious. What had Prescott told me earlier? *They think I'm chasing unicorns, spending their inheritance with the things I collect.* That's why he'd sworn me to secrecy about the Jefferson copy of the Declaration of Independence and the other items he'd purchased.

"I should have realized there was more than one," I said, "except the one he was using was so unusual."

Victoria shrugged. "Prescott was always searching for . . . something unique, one of a kind. An object with a mythical story behind its origin, a provenance that gave you goose bumps imagining its history. He wanted to find things that no one else possessed, be the first to own something fabulous and a true treasure."

She didn't say the word *unicorn.*

But as a museum curator, Victoria lived in the art world and she understood collectors and their quest, their passion, to own objects that were unique. Because they *had* to have it. For a brief moment, she sounded wistful. *The thrill of the hunt.* That's what Prescott had said. When he finally got whatever it was he had been chasing, it was almost anticlimactic.

I could feel Quinn stirring, growing more impatient beside me.

"Sweetheart, we *really* should go," he said in a firm voice. "Victoria, we're so sorry for your loss. A death in the family is always difficult, but it's especially tough during the holiday season."

Quinn's words seemed to move her and she leaned in to give him a kiss on the cheek. "Thank you for that," she said. She turned to me. "You, too, Lucie."

"One final thing," I said.

"Yes?"

"I couldn't help noticing your perfume. It's so unusual. What is it?"

She looked startled, but then she extended her forearm so I could catch the scent on the inside of her wrist. "Today's the first time I've worn it. It's by a new French designer. Forgive my pronunciation but it's called *Je Ne Regrette Rien*."

I bent to smell the fragrance on the inside of her wrist. "It's lovely."

"Thank you."

We stepped outside and the door closed behind us.

It was the same perfume I'd smelled in the elevator earlier this evening. Had Victoria gone downstairs to talk to Prescott just before he died?

And if she had, why?

Six

The Averys had hired local kids to take care of valet parking for their party, driving guests' cars from the Castle entrance to an adjacent meadow. Since we were the last to leave except for Kit, Bobby, and Win, our navy-blue Jeep was parked out front and the keys were in the ignition. Win's vintage wood-paneled station wagon and the SUV that belonged to Bobby and Kit were there as well. And the kids were gone.

Quinn opened the passenger door and helped me in.

"Are you going to tell me what's going on?" he asked after he climbed into the driver's seat. "What that last conversation was all about, you asking Victoria about her perfume? *I Regret Nothing.* What kind of name is that?"

"It's the name of a song. Edith Piaf's signature song, actually."

"Edith who?"

"Edith Piaf. She was a French cabaret singer in the 1940s

and '50s. She had one of those voices that makes you think of Montmartre and smoke-filled clubs where everyone drinks whiskey or absinthe. My mother used to play her music all the time."

"Why did you ask Victoria about her perfume?"

"I smelled it in the elevator when I took it back to the main floor the first time I left Prescott," I said. "The funny thing is, I didn't have to call the elevator to the basement. It was already waiting. So either she took it downstairs for some reason, or she took it to one of the upper floors and when she was finished, she sent it back to the basement."

"Huh. Maybe she went upstairs to, you know, powder her nose. Or use the bathroom."

"First of all, no woman powders her nose anymore. Second, if she did go upstairs, don't you think it's odd the elevator was waiting in the basement?"

"Well, then, whatever it is you do with your makeup when you need to fix something. And, like you said, she could have sent it back downstairs after she used it."

"Except people don't usually do that."

"So what are you saying?"

"That it's more likely she took it downstairs."

"And did what?"

"Unless she wanted to go swimming or bowling or get something out of the storage rooms, I'd say she wanted to talk to Prescott," I said.

"You didn't run into her."

"No, but you saw what a maze it's like down there. Maybe she wanted to wait until I left."

"So she waited somewhere out of sight until you were gone

and then went to see Prescott?" He paused. "Don't you think that sounds a bit far-fetched?"

It did.

"Maybe," I said. "But I'm certain she used the elevator."

"Right. Okay, suppose she did go to see Prescott. Do you think she was with him when he fell?"

"If she was, you'd think that she would have gone for help. Since she didn't, I'd say he was still alive, still fine," I said. "The two of them chatted, she left, and then he fell and hit his head."

Quinn started the Jeep. "Okay, she waited downstairs until you were gone, had a quick word with Prescott about something, and then she left? It couldn't have taken long if you saw her upstairs with Clayton, right?"

"Yes . . . I suppose . . . or maybe you *are* right. Maybe she didn't go down there." My what-ifs were seeming more and more implausible.

He turned onto the dirt-and-gravel road that wound around a wooded hill leading from Hawthorne to Route 50, the main east-west highway. This far west of Washington, D.C., it was called Mosby's Highway in honor of Colonel John Singleton Mosby, the Confederate rebel who was also known as the Gray Ghost. After the highway sliced through the top of Virginia, it continued due west, practically a straight arrow across the country passing through small towns in America's heartland until it ended in Sacramento, California, three thousand miles from where it began in Ocean City, Maryland.

There were days when I wondered what would happen if Quinn and I stayed on Route 50, instead of taking the turn-off for home, if we kept driving until we reached California.

Maybe continue a bit farther until we arrived at the Pacific Ocean.

"Hey." Quinn said. "Are you still with me?"

"Yes. Sorry. Just thinking."

A nearly full moon was starting to rise on the horizon and in the pale silver wash of light, I could see him frowning. He looked as if he were trying to work out the logistics of who had been where when Prescott died.

"Why couldn't Victoria have waited to talk to Prescott until after the party?" he asked. "What was so urgent, so important? Assuming she did go see him."

I yawned. The caipirinhas, the Madeira, and the warmth of the heat from the car radiator were making me drowsy. "Maybe she was upset that she and Clay didn't get to announce their engagement at the party. I suspect Prescott might have ruined their moment with his own announcement about a family board meeting in the morning. You said yourself that Scotty and Alex were so angry they shouldn't be around sharp knives. Not the time to break out the champagne and celebrate an upcoming wedding."

"So maybe she'd had a few too many caipirinhas and she went downstairs to talk to Prescott without Clay there?"

"Look, Kit said the rumor going around the *Trib* staff at the party was that Prescott wanted to sell the paper, along with some of the other newspapers that belong to Avery Communications. And Grant told you the Averys are in such financial trouble that once they auction off the art, jewelry, and furniture that was promised in the Caritas Commitment, they're not going to be able to hang on to Hawthorne. A lot of this news and new information seemed to bubble to the surface this afternoon," I said. "Victoria knows the art world better than any of the family because of what she does for a living. Maybe she wanted to appeal to Prescott without any of them around, ask him not to completely dismantle the incredible art collection they owned, not throw the baby out with the bathwater. A few caipirinhas can make anybody bolder, more reckless."

"I don't know," he said. "Taking on a cagey old lion like Prescott wouldn't be her best idea. Say Victoria did manage to get down to the wine cellar and back upstairs in time for you to see her in the dining room with Clay—she's pretty fit. But as Clay's future wife, Prescott's decision to sell is going to affect her financially as well. I've heard that she thought she was marrying Daddy Warbucks."

I smiled. "Well, by now she knows she's not."

We had reached Mosby's Highway. Like the Averys' private road, it, too, was dark and deserted. Over the next week or so, folks would decorate their homes for the holidays. There would be lights woven through bushes and trees and along rooflines, Christmas trees placed so they could be seen through living room windows, sweet tableaus of a happy, festive season, reindeer sparkling on front lawns, and an inflatable snowman or a Santa with spotlights on them to brighten the road.

We drove through the village of Upperville in silence. By the time Quinn turned onto Atoka Road, I was still going around in circles. He slowed for the turn onto Sycamore Lane at the entrance to the vineyard.

"If Victoria had been there when Prescott fell, I don't think

she would have left him, said nothing when she got back upstairs, and let him bleed to death," I added.

"Unless," he said with a shrug.

"Unless what?"

He didn't reply until we reached the fork in Sycamore Lane
where the two-hundred-year-old tree that had given the road
its name was now cleaved in half after lightning had struck
it a few years ago. Quinn's headlights caught the ivy that
had grown over the jagged trunk and some of the now-bare
branches that still lived. He turned right toward the house.

"Unless she deliberately pushed him."

"My God," I said, "I hope you're wrong. That's murder."

Murder. The word hung between us in the frigid November air as it if were encased in a frozen speech bubble.

WE WERE BOTH STUFFED too full of black beans, pork,
and flan and buzzed from caipirinhas to have dinner or another drink, so Quinn made a fire in fireplace in the parlor
and we ended up on opposite ends of the sofa with our feet
up—Quinn reading *The Wild Vine,* about the discovery of the
Norton grape, by Todd Kliman, until he dozed off, and me en-
grossed in an Ian Rutledge mystery by Charles Todd.

A couple of logs collapsed on each other, sending a noisy
spray of sparks up the chimney. Quinn stirred and woke up.

"Welcome back," I said.

"I wasn't sleeping. Just resting my eyes." He sat up and
swung his feet onto the carpet. "Another log or should we let
it die down?"

"We're both tired," I said. "Why don't we let it die and then go to bed? It won't take long."

"It's only eight-thirty. I'm hungry." He gave me an evil grin. "How about a piece of your pumpkin pie?"

"I will explode if I eat another bite today."

He got up. "I'll bring a big slice and two forks."

He returned with the pie a few minutes later and set the plate on the coffee table. "Would you like a glass of Madeira? Goes perfect with your pie."

Madeira. I couldn't. At least not tonight.

"I'd rather have a glass of Riesling. There's a chilled bottle of ours in the wine refrigerator. Riesling goes with pumpkin pie and it's not as heavy as Madeira."

We were one of the few Virginia vineyards that made Riesling. It was a difficult grape to grow here and our wine always sold out, but we'd kept back a few bottles from our last vintage to drink at home.

"Okay." He gave me a puzzled look. "I'll get it."

When he came back with the two glasses of wine, we moved to the floor, piling up throw pillows to lounge against as we sat cross-legged in front of the fire.

"Have you gone off Madeira?" He passed me a fork. "You looked like I'd suggested drinking rat poison when I brought it up."

I coughed and a piece of pie went down the wrong way. When I finally caught my breath I said, "It's not that."

He waited.

"I had a glass of thirty-two-year-old Malmsey with Prescott this afternoon when we were together in his wine cellar. He knew it was bottled the year I was born, which was why he served it," I said. "That wine was amazing."

I couldn't tell whether he was impressed or envious. Or both. "Why did he lure you away from a great party to have a glass of thirty-two-year-old Malmsey? Just the two of you."

I told him about the two-hundred-and-ten-year-old cases of Madeira that Prescott said he was certain my family still owned. And about how after Ian Montgomery had found them in the tunnels under the U.S. Capitol during Prohibition and had hung on to them once he realized their provenance and value.

"You've got to be kidding me," Quinn said. "Even one bottle of that wine would be worth a fortune today."

"If we still owned it. And, yes, Prescott told me just how much it would be worth—and that he was willing to pay even more to have Ian's Madeira."

Quinn let out a long, low whistle. "You think it's gone? Do you think Leland sold it?"

I shrugged. "Or drank it."

"He would do something like that, wouldn't he?"

"He would."

Quinn got up and picked up the fireplace poker, stirring the fire, which had burned down to glowing embers. "What made Prescott bring this up today, all of a sudden? And why the super-secret negotiation? Unless he wanted to show off his wine cellar, remind you what a serious collector he was."

He put the poker back in its stand and sat down across from me again. "I've only seen one other wine cellar like that one in my lifetime and it was in a fourteenth-century château in Bordeaux after a Chinese investor bought it and completely restored it. No expense spared."

"Prescott said all the stone had been quarried on his property. I don't think he spared any expense, either."

There was one small bite of pie left. Quinn pushed the plate over to me. "Finish it."

I did.

"You didn't answer my question," he said. "Why today?"

Prescott was dead. Was it really necessary for me to keep his secret now? From Quinn? Was I still bound by my promise not to say anything about the Jefferson copy of the Declaration of Independence he'd just acquired? I knew why he didn't want his family to know: they thought he was a spendthrift chasing frivolous purchases. His unicorns. But as soon as Clay walked into that special Masonic shrine next to the wine cellar, he'd know about Prescott's latest acquisition.

Besides, now it belonged to Clay—unless it was one of the items to be sold as part of the Caritas Commitment.

I told Quinn everything. About Prescott's Masonic hideaway and how he'd wanted to drink the Madeira when he unveiled his copy of the Declaration of Independence to his brother Masons.

"I don't know much about the Freemasons," he said when I was done. "Except they're a men-only club and sometimes they dress up in weird costumes that remind you of Halloween. And they have special ceremonies that no one can talk about."

"I don't know much, either, but Prescott says there's a lot more to being a Mason than the secret handshakes and the unusual costumes. They do quite a lot of charity work," I said.

"Well, I suppose it fits that Prescott wants to present the Declaration of Independence to his Mason brotherhood in a special ceremony and toast it with Leland's Madeira."

"Which we don't have."

"Prescott's sure the labels say the Madeira was supposed to be drunk by James Madison on the Fourth of July at the Capitol?"

I nodded.

"And you really have no idea where it is, what happened to it?"

"We don't have it," I said again. "I never heard of it before today. That's why I'm sure it's gone. Leland never could hang on to anything of value. He was always selling things to pay off his gambling debts. Besides, we would have found it by now, don't you think?"

"Probably. But damn. I would have given anything to taste two-hundred-year-old Madeira. Not to mention how much money those cases would be worth."

"Two hundred and ten years. Even if we found the wine, Clayton's not going to buy it. The deal's off," I said. "Prescott told me Leland had a safe-deposit box at Blue Ridge Federal. He thought maybe he might have left a clue there about where he hid the Madeira."

Quinn's eyebrows went up. "You cleaned out his safe-deposit box after he died. There wasn't much in it, as I recall."

I drank the last of my Riesling. "Prescott hinted there was a second safe-deposit box. Where Leland kept . . . private stuff. Things he didn't want my mother knowing about."

Maybe there had been more affairs and more children

we weren't aware of. Maybe Leland had robbed a bank and stashed the cash there. With my father you never knew.

"If there was another safe-deposit box," Quinn said, "you would have known about it by now. Somebody would have said something at the bank, don't you think? Seth Hannah is one of the Romeos and he's practically an uncle to you, Eli, and Mia. It's a neighborhood bank and you know everyone there."

Seth Hannah was the president of Blue Ridge Federal and Quinn was probably right. We would have known about a second safe-deposit box by now. Seth would have told us.

Quinn got up and pulled me to my feet. "The fire's out. Why don't you go upstairs and get ready for bed? You've had a hell of a day. I'll clean up here and join you in a few minutes."

He caressed my face with the back of his hand. "Let's try to forget about all this, sweetheart. At least for tonight. Okay?"

I nodded.

But later that night I awoke, bolting upright in bed, my heart pounding hard against my rib cage. Downstairs the grandfather clock's rich chime sounded three times as Prescott's last words came back to me. He'd said he was on the verge of uncovering a four-hundred-year-old secret that powerful people didn't want known and my father had provided an important clue that had led Prescott to his discovery.

And for his safety—as well as mine—I couldn't tell anyone about our conversation. Because whatever this mysterious secret was, anyone who knew about it was in danger.

Now I guess that included me.

Seven

Overnight the temperature dropped below freezing so that by the time Quinn and I went downstairs for breakfast, the lawn and gardens were covered in a fine coat of hoarfrost that shimmered and gleamed as if the landscape had been shined to a high polish. In the pale morning sunlight, the straw-colored ornamental grasses looked diamond-tipped.

Prescott Avery's death was the number-one story on the Sunday morning NPR news show. Quinn and I listened as he made coffee and I cut slices of my future sister-in-law's homemade pumpkin spice bread and put them in the toaster.

The local reporter who covered the story gave a straightforward account of how Prescott had collapsed at his home and was found by family members a short time later. He had been hosting an annual neighborhood Thanksgiving weekend party and had left to get something in his wine cellar when the tragedy occurred. Dr. Winston Churchill Turnbull, a Loudoun

County medical examiner who happened to be a guest at the party, pronounced the ninety-five-year-old Mr. Avery dead at the scene.

The toaster dinged and Quinn poured our coffees. As usual he had brewed it strong enough to fuel one of the spaceships that resupplied the International Space Station. I got out butter and a jar of my homemade strawberry jam from the refrigerator and brought the toast over to a scarred-up oak trestle table where for generations my family had sat to discuss, opine, argue, comfort, laugh, cry, and eat. If I looked closely enough, I could still see Eli's algebra homework and a perfect circle where Leland had smacked down a quarter one night as a family bet, both imprinted in the soft wood.

"At least your name didn't come up in that story," Quinn said. "So it seems you're off the hook."

"Thank goodness. And I guess that's a more or less accurate description of what happened."

It was obviously a slow news day—Thanksgiving weekend, after all—because after the live report, the show's host replayed a clip from an eight-year-old piece about the group of billionaires that had met in Aspen, Colorado, that spring to establish the Caritas Commitment. It was followed by a full-length interview with Prescott recorded thirty years ago when he turned sixty-five as part of a series of leadership interviews with highly successful, creative entrepreneurs called "Perspectives on Life." How had Prescott achieved his business and financial success? What habits had he cultivated that had helped him the most? What stoked his creativity? What advice did he have for the next generation?

Finally, as the interview was about to wrap up, the reporter had asked Prescott about his retirement plans. Prescott swore, which was bleeped out.

Then he said, "Are you kidding? Who said anything about retiring? I have too many things to do, too many projects and ideas in my mind to slow down now. Hell, son, I'm just starting the third half of my life." He laughed. "I don't plan on quitting for a long time."

"Last question, Mr. Avery: Any regrets about decisions you've made over the years? Anything you'd do differently?"

There was a pause before Prescott said in a pained voice, "No regrets about any decisions I've made—just lessons learned that made me who I am today. But I do have two great sorrows: the deaths of my son and daughter. My deepest personal regret is that their time on earth was cut too short. But as to regrets about my business decisions, or would I change anything— no, none. I regret nothing."

Quinn's eyes met mine. *Je ne regrette rien*. Victoria's perfume.

"I know," I said. "Life's just full of little ironies sometimes, isn't it?"

AS USUAL THE *WASHINGTON Tribune* lay on our doorstep, courtesy of one of the workers who got it for us every morning from the faded, weather-beaten *Tribune* mailbox at the entrance to the vineyard and drove it to our front door. I picked it up as Quinn and I left the house just before ten o'clock and brought it with us in the Jeep.

Quinn's plans for the rest of the morning were to take one of the ATVs out to the field to examine—for at least the fourth time—the diseased vines in the Merlot block that we'd discovered during harvest. I wanted to talk to Frankie Merchant about our plans for the annual "Christmas in Middleburg" celebration next weekend. It was one of the town's biggest events of the year, three days of festivities that included tree-lighting, caroling, the Goose Creek Hunt's well-loved Hunt and Hounds Review, a parade, and Breakfast with Santa at the community charter school. If other years were anything to go by, the town would probably swell to over ten thousand with people from D.C., Maryland, and other parts of Virginia arriving—if the weather cooperated. Since Middleburg's population as of the last census totaled 851 and in Atoka you could practically count the number of residents on the fingers and toes of the mayor and the three members of the town council—okay, truth be told, Atoka had sixty-four residents—it was a huge influx of visitors for us.

On the drive from the house to the winery, I read Quinn an abbreviated version of the *Trib*'s story about Prescott's death. As Kit promised, it was their headline and her byline was on it.

PRESCOTT AVERY, PATRIARCH OF INFLUENTIAL MEDIA AND NEWSPAPER DYNASTY, OWNER OF *WASHINGTON TRIBUNE,* DEAD AT AGE 95.

"Okay . . . she writes that the cause of death is still unclear, but apparently Mr. Avery became unwell at a party he was hosting for friends and neighbors at his home on Saturday afternoon and collapsed at approximately five P.M. downstairs in his wine cellar." I looked up. "She must have gotten the time of death from Bobby or Win."

"Anything in there about you finding him?"

I skimmed the rest of the story. "Nope. Win Turnbull, local medical examiner, pronounced him dead at the scene. Blah, blah, blah . . . nothing we don't know. No funeral plans have been made so far, but in lieu of flowers the family requests that donations be made to the Miranda Foundation."

"Looks like they abandoned that plan to claim he died in his sleep," Quinn said.

"What difference would it make, anyway?"

"Beats me. Maybe Clay is hoping nothing leaks out about the family being pissed off at Prescott for supposedly wanting to sell the *Trib*. It doesn't look so good now that he's dead."

"You can't keep a secret like that," I said. "Word is going to get out sooner or later."

"Maybe Clay was hoping for later."

I refolded the paper. "I think we should send a donation to the Miranda Foundation."

He nodded. "Did your parents know her? Miranda, I mean. How old was she when she died?"

Five years ago Quinn had moved to Virginia from California when my father hired him just before he died. Even if Quinn lived in Atoka for another fifty years, folks would still say that he was "from away." No one expected him to understand the convoluted and intertwined history, genealogy, and backstory of Southern families like mine and the Averys who had lived on the land we owned since before the country was founded. Although to Quinn's credit, he was becoming

assimilated enough that once or twice I had heard him referring to the crew as "y'all" or its Southern plural "all y'all."

"Leland knew Miranda," I told him, "but she died before
he and my mother were married. She was in her mid-twenties.
Everyone was shocked because it was so unexpected. She was
perfectly fine, then a week later she was gone."

"It must have nearly killed Prescott and Rose to lose both
their children within a couple of years of each other," he
said.

"I'm not sure which was a worse tragedy," I said. "Miranda
came down with the flu one winter and within days she had
pneumonia. Then she got an infection that turned into sepsis.
By the time they got her to the hospital it was too late."

"Someone at the party yesterday was talking about the
motorcycle accident that killed Tommy. He was speeding and
he'd been drinking. No helmet."

"His blood alcohol was one-point-four," I said. "The family
was in Nantucket, the last day of a summer vacation. The police said he had been doing seventy when he took a turn on a
winding beach road and spun out on a patch of sand. Flipped
over multiple times and broke his neck and back. Tommy was
the apple of his father's eye, the golden boy, the heir apparent," I said. "His death just about destroyed Prescott. Celia
had had a miscarriage a few months earlier and hadn't been
able to get pregnant, so there would never be an heir to carry
on the family name, either."

Quinn pulled into the parking lot behind the ivy-covered
building my mother had designed, where we sold wine, held
tastings, and hosted many of our events, parties, and musical
evenings. She had named it the Villa and wanted it to look

like one of the graceful old homes she remembered from her childhood in France rather than a boxy commercial building.

Already this morning smoke was curling out of the chimney. That would be Frankie's doing; her car was in the parking lot. On cold days like this, we kept a fire burning in the enormous stone fireplace using firewood the workers collected all year, mostly old or dead trees from the property.

Quinn parked the Jeep and said, "I can't imagine how awful it must have been for Prescott."

"Rose still had Clayton, who was her son from a previous marriage, so he was a comfort to her," I said. "But Prescott felt as if he had no one. He and Clayton never really got along—different temperaments, Clayton with his dark hair and dark skin like his Italian father instead of a blond, blue-eyed Ralph Lauren model like Miranda and Tommy. I think both Clay and Prescott tried for Rose's sake, but any effort they made fell apart after she died. It was as though Prescott resented Clay for living when his own son was dead."

"No one can live up to a saint," Quinn said. "A person who's been crystalized in amber and remains perfect for all time. You're just punishing someone for not being who you want them to be. Or need them to be. I feel sorry for Clay."

"So do I. Plus he gave up his own career—he wanted to be a landscape architect, since no one expected him to go into the family news business. He took over Tommy's job as assistant publisher until Prescott retired and ran the place until handing the reins over to Scotty. Until the family brought Alex in, that is."

"I wonder how Clay feels now that Prescott's gone," Quinn said. "Maybe he's relieved. Can't say I'd blame him."

I stole a quick, worried look at him. Quinn had never known his own father, who had walked out on his mother before Quinn was born. It was a prickly subject.

"I don't know," I said. "Prescott was a force of nature and he could be cantankerous. I think it must have been difficult for anyone to live with him—with the exception of Rose. He adored her and she felt the same way about him. My mother said it was as if they lived in their own little world and nobody mattered but each other. On the one hand it was very sweet, a real, romantic love story. But she also said they were so self-absorbed that any affection or attention they gave their children was almost an afterthought. Funny, but I think Clay picked up that diffidence even though he and Prescott aren't blood relatives, which is why Alex turned into such a rebel and Scotty's just . . . so intense. Clay's wife couldn't cope with it. Plus she had Rose to live up to. So they split up."

"Rose died the summer I arrived here when you were still in France," Quinn said. "I remember your father stopping by the barrel room on his way to the funeral. It was the first time I'd seen him in a three-piece suit. He was driving into Washington since the service was at National Cathedral. He went to the cemetery, too, over in Leesburg."

"Union Cemetery," I said. "That's where the Avery family plot is. Rose was a good person, except she had a blind spot when it came to Prescott. After she was gone it was as though he'd lost his compass. He told me yesterday that his family thought he was spending too much money on expensive purchases, like the copy of the Declaration of Independence. Which makes sense if they're as broke as Grant hinted they were——he shouldn't be buying priceless historical documents."

It also probably explained why Prescott told me not to mention to anyone what he'd done. By now, of course, Clay would have discovered the Declaration if he had checked out Prescott's Masonic shrine.

"It's always hard to believe folks as rich as the Averys could have money problems," Quinn said as we got out of the Jeep.

"It happened to us," I said. "Although we didn't have that kind of money."

"Maybe not, but you still managed to dig out of a deep hole."

"I never want that to happen again. Ever."

Not sleeping at night, wondering and worrying how we were going to pay the crew. No money to fix the air-conditioning system in the house when it conked out during the hottest August on record. Selling family heirlooms one by one, a slow painful trickle. Buying more time at Blue Ridge Federal not to foreclose on the farm. Trying to keep up a cool, calm, unworried façade when we were just about at rock bottom.

"It won't happen again." He kissed me. "I won't be long. I want to take another look at those vines while there's still no snow on the ground. We really ought to rip them out and start over. Replant in the spring."

I wished he hadn't said that.

"Come on, you know I don't want to do that. My parents planted those vines almost thirty years ago. They're the oldest vines we own. They may not have been producing much, but the wine was amazing. Maybe we can regraft them. Or save them somehow."

"Sweetheart—"

"Can we talk about this another time?"

I had one more idea, but I hadn't brought it up with him yet. He probably wouldn't go for it.

"Sure." He gave in and I was glad we were ending the discussion before it turned into another argument. "I'm going to stop by the barrel room to check on the tanks Antonio was supposed to clean after I'm done in the field. I'll meet you in the Villa after that."

I nodded and he dropped another kiss on my hair. "I love you," he said and then he was gone.

FRANKIE MERCHANT LOOKED UP from behind the long S-shaped bar where she was untangling a string of Christmas lights when I walked into the Villa a moment later. A green plastic storage box with its red lid leaning against it was full of more lights. They, too, looked like a nest of snakes.

"I saw you and Quinn in the parking lot, so I put the kettle on. I could use a cup of tea to warm up and I thought you'd like one, too."

It was hard to heat the enormous vaulted-ceiling room in winter to a comfortable temperature. A fire in the fireplace took some of the edge off. Behind the bar, the staff used space heaters. But it still got chilly, especially if you spent the afternoon here pouring wine for guests.

"I'd love some tea. Thanks."

Frankie took off her glasses and used them as a headband to sweep a strand of strawberry-blond hair off her face. "I called the Averys this morning. Got the maid and asked if I could talk to Kellie even though I knew she wasn't coming in to work," she said. "She told me what happened yesterday. I didn't know you and Quinn were the ones who found Prescott."

I nodded. "How did she sound?"

Frankie came around from behind the bar and walked over to the fireplace, standing with her back to it, hands behind her. "Brokenhearted."

"She was devastated yesterday."

"Poor kid. I think she was closer to him than she is to Scotty or Clay."

"Quinn told her not to come to work until she's ready. She's probably going to need a few days off."

Frankie's eyes clouded. "I don't mean to sound selfish but I hope she's not going to stay away too long. This week is going to be crazy with everything we've got going on."

"Come on, we'll manage. We always do."

"I know." She sighed. "The water's probably hot. I'll get our tea. I brought in a holiday-spiced tea from Fortnum & Mason. An early Christmas gift from a girlfriend who just got back from London."

"Sounds lovely. I'll take a look at those lights."

"I wonder who put them away last year and got them in such a mess." She stuck her hands on her hips like an irritated schoolteacher about to scold a student who'd forgotten the homework again.

"Me, I think. Sorry. We had an event coming up right after

New Year's and I seem to remember we were rushing to get all the decorations taken down."

"Oh." She looked nonplussed. "Well . . . in that case, they're all yours."

Frankie ran the day-to-day operations of the retail end of our business, plus she planned all of our social events with the skill and precision of a general organizing a multifront military campaign. For years I'd taken care of everything by myself as my mother had done, but it finally got to be too much and I'd hired Frankie. Eventually, as we grew, the work got to be too much for her as well so we'd hired a staff—an assistant tasting room manager, a bookkeeper, and two elderly women who took care of social media, advertising, and filling orders. But Frankie was still the commander who supervised everyone else.

She disappeared into the kitchen and I brought the lights over to two leather sofas that faced each other across from the fireplace. Mosby, the vineyard barn cat and champion mouser, who mostly appeared in winter when it was cold outside and food was harder to find, lay flattened like a gray velvet rug in front of the crackling blaze. He opened one sea-green eye and blinked at me before going back to sleep. I sat down on one of the sofas and laid the lights out on a large oak coffee table. They were a mess, all right.

Frankie returned carrying a tray with our tea and a plate of Christmas cookies.

"How's it going with the untangling?" She sat down across from me.

"Slow."

She handed me a mug of tea. "I made cardboard holders to

wrap the lights around just so they wouldn't end up like this. I found them in the bottom of the box. Maybe this year you might try using them."

"Noted."

She grinned. "Have a cookie. I baked these last night, trying out recipes for our holiday cookie exchange. I couldn't sleep so I got up and made cookies."

Frankie was an insomniac with OCD tendencies. If she wasn't baking she'd be vacuuming her immaculate basement or alphabetizing her spices.

I bit into a cookie that tasted of tart lemon. "These are delicious. So's the tea."

"Cocoa nibs, clementine, and Christmas spices in the tea. Lemon curd in the cookies."

A log popped and hissed and the fire collapsed slightly. Mosby rolled over, ignoring it. Frankie got up, took a log from a bundle of firewood that was stacked in a copper bucket, and put it on the fire.

"When do you want to put the decorations up?" I asked.

She had been planning our holiday events since Labor Day; we'd both agreed that with the ugly state of politics in Washington, the general malaise in the country, and the depressing headlines in the news, we wanted a simple, old-fashioned holiday and the theme would be "Home for Christmas."

A cookie swap. A tree-decorating party where folks could string cranberries and popcorn to make garlands. A night of caroling. We would serve wassail and mulled wine, and since we were opening the first bottles of our Madeira for Christmas, Frankie wanted to make Madeira cakes and mince pies.

We were also collecting nonperishable items for the food

pantry in Leesburg and toys and winter coats for the homeless shelter. Eli, Sasha, Quinn, and I had decided to forgo giving gifts to each other and spend the money instead on food, toys, and coats for the local charities.

"I thought I'd start decorating tomorrow. You and Quinn are still getting the tree and the pine garland on Tuesday, right?" Frankie asked. She licked lemon curd off her fingers. "I'll take care of the wreaths. This year I'm using grapevines to make them."

"I don't know how you can outdo what you did last year. Those wreaths were gorgeous," I said. "And yes, to the tree and garland on Tuesday. We're also getting the tree for the house. Eli and Sasha are going by Seely's tomorrow with the kids to pick out their tree—it'll be their first one as a new family, plus they're in the new house, so they're making a big deal of it for Hope and Zach. Noah said he'll send a truck by with all three trees on Wednesday."

"A nursery that delivers. Nice."

I reached for another cookie. "Montgomery Estate Vine-yard is probably their best customer in two counties. My family has been buying plants from Seely's Garden Center since Noah's father opened the place fifty years ago."

"It's your first Christmas together, too," Frankie said. "You and Quinn. Any special plans?"

"Quinn's always been sort of a minimalist about Christmas. And you know me, I go overboard decorating the house, trim-ming the tree, holiday baking, Christmas music . . . all of it, just like you do. I think we'll have to see how this works out."

"I was hoping he'd play Santa when we have the tree-trimming party. I've got the suit and beard. You think he'll go for it? I already got Eli to agree to dress up when he plays the piano for our caroling night."

If my brother hadn't been an architect, he would have been a concert pianist. Once upon a time he had considered applying to Juilliard.

"Eli is a natural ham. He'll do anything. As for Quinn as Santa Claus . . . I don't know. I'd love to be around when you ask him," I said.

"Actually, I thought you could do that."

"Me? Why me?"

"Who else? Come on, he's less likely to turn you down. Please?"

She gave me her sunniest smile.

"All right." I relented. "He's coming by after he examines the diseased vines in the Merlot block and checks some things in the barrel room. By the way, we gave everyone the day off. That includes you. I hope you're not planning to stick around and work all day."

"It's quiet. I thought I'd get a head start on things for next week. Especially since I'll be one person short without Kellie."

The front door opened and closed. It was too soon for Quinn to have finished in the vineyard. I turned around to tell whoever it was that we were closed.

It was Bobby Noland and he wasn't here to buy wine.

"I saw the Jeep in the parking lot as I was driving over to your house," he said. "So I took a guess you and Quinn might be here."

"Quinn's either in the vineyard or the barrel room," I said. "He'll be here shortly. Is something wrong?"

Bobby was wearing a pair of jeans and work boots. An

open-necked plaid flannel shirt under a navy blazer. As he walked over to us, I caught a glimpse of his shield attached to his belt underneath the blazer. This was not a social call. He was here on business.

He glanced at Frankie, who immediately got up and said, "I think I'll get the rest of the Christmas decorations from the storage room, if you two don't mind."

She started to leave and then, gracious as always, said, "Bobby, there's spiced tea in the teapot and homemade cookies. Can I get you a mug?"

He held up a hand. "I'm tempted, Frankie, but I'm trying not to put on my usual Christmas fifteen pounds. I already got a head start with what I ate for Thanksgiving."

She smiled and left the room.

"Mind if I take a seat?" he asked.

"Of course not," I said as he sat across from me. "What's going on?"

"There's news," he said. "A new development. When B. J. Hunt was preparing Prescott's body for the funeral, he noticed some bruises that didn't look consistent with that fall Prescott took, so he asked me to come by and take a look. We're opening a new investigation into the death of Prescott Avery. He didn't fall and hit his head. Someone struck him and the blow killed him, although Win gets the last word on what exactly did happen."

I felt the air leave the room. "What are you saying? That Prescott was murdered? In his own home?"

He nodded. "That's exactly what I'm saying."

Eight

Murder. I already had an idea who might have been downstairs yesterday while Prescott and I were talking together in his wine cellar. Quinn and I had discussed the subject at length.

Victoria Barkley, Clayton's almost-fiancée.

If I said something to Bobby, she would zoom to the top spot on his list of suspects. But if she were a legitimate suspect, he needed to know. If I said nothing, it was obstructing a murder investigation.

"I can already tell by the look on your face that you're not surprised, Lucie," Bobby said. "What do you know?"

If any other detective except Bobby had been sitting here, he or she wouldn't have made that statement. But Bobby and I knew each other practically as well as brother and sister and there was no conning him.

I told him about noticing the scent of a perfume I didn't

recognize in the elevator after I left Prescott. And then realizing it belonged to Victoria as Quinn and I said good-bye last night.

"She might have gone upstairs to use the bathroom or get something in her bedroom, and then sent the elevator back to the basement as a courtesy because she knew Prescott was down there." I felt as if I were apologizing. "All I know is that when I stepped inside, there was a distinct scent of a perfume that I couldn't identify. And when Quinn and I said good-bye to Victoria yesterday, I recognized her perfume as the one I smelled in the elevator. So I asked her about it. She said it was new and that she was wearing it for the first time. It's called *Je Ne Regrette Rien*. French for 'I regret nothing.'"

Unlike me, Bobby had a great poker face. I couldn't tell if my news surprised him or not.

"You have that good a nose for perfume, do you?" He sounded skeptical.

I would bet my life I was right about this. That I recognized the *sillage*—the lingering scent—of this particular perfume after the wearer had left the small jewel of an elevator. It was distinct and anything but subtle. Telling Bobby about it put Victoria Barkley's life under his microscope and I knew it. I wasn't going to make anything up.

"I worked at the Perfume Museum in Grasse when I lived in France and spent a lot of time learning and identifying different fragrances, in case you've forgotten. Grasse, by the way, is the perfume capital of France. So, yes, I do have a good nose for perfume," I said, letting my irritation show that he could be so dismissive. "Also for wine."

"Okay. Point taken."

"Thank you."

He seemed to be considering what I'd just told him. "Well, if she didn't go upstairs and send the elevator back to the basement after she returned to the main floor, then someone wearing that perfume—possibly Victoria Barkley—took it downstairs."

"It's possible someone else was wearing the same perfume," I said, "but somehow I don't think anyone but Victoria— almost a member of the family—would have used the elevator."

"Okay," he said. "Say you're right. What else is in that basement? Saying it was Victoria who went down there, maybe she needed to get something for the party."

"Actually, I asked Prescott what else was on that floor as we were walking to his wine cellar," I said. "Besides his cave, his archives are there, along with storage rooms, a swimming pool, and a bowling alley. He joked that there was also a dungeon."

"Any idea how long you and Prescott were down there? Or what time you two left the party? You came and found me and Win around quarter to five. I heard one of the clocks chime and happened to check my watch."

"It was light outside when we went downstairs and dusk when I came back by myself. They hadn't served dessert before we left and by the time I came back people were leaving. I don't know. Maybe half an hour? Forty-five minutes?"

Bobby looked up from his notes. "What were you doing down there, anyway?"

Here it was.

"Prescott invited me to join him in his wine cellar because he wanted me to try a glass of Malmsey. Actually he insisted."

Bobby's face blanked so I said, "It's a very good brand of Madeira. Quite expensive. Made from special grapes—Malmsey—on the island of Madeira. He opened a bottle from the year I was born."

Bobby waited.

My tea had gone cold, but I drank it anyway and cradled the mug in both hands. "He also said he had a proposition for me. He told me that my family owned a cache of very old Madeira—bottles that were over two hundred years old—and he wanted to buy them. I told him I had no idea what he was talking about and that was sort of the end of it."

"Sort of?"

I looked into the bottom of my mug as if the answer might lie in the tea leaves of Frankie's fragrant Christmas spiced tea. "The end of the discussion about buying the Madeira. Inviting me downstairs to try the Malmsey was his way of enticing me—in private—to sell him the wine. He offered to pay any price for it, whatever I wanted."

"Could have been worth a lot of money to you."

"Bobby, Leland probably drank the damn wine. Or sold it to pay gambling debts, as I told Prescott. I never knew anything about it." I glared at him as a log caved in and the fire hissed next to us.

"Okay, sorry. But there was something else besides the Madeira." A statement, not a question.

I placed my mug on the coffee table. "Did you know Prescott was a Mason?" I asked.

"I did."

It was Bobby's business to know everything about everyone, so his answer probably shouldn't have surprised me.

"I didn't know," I said and got up to put another log on the fire. "After we talked about the Madeira he brought me into another room. The door was behind the bookcase in his tasting room. When it opened and we went inside, it looked like some kind of Masonic shrine. There were engraved swords, a Bible with a compass and a carpenter's square lying on it, the flags of the Knights Templar, a painting of George Washington in his Masonic apron in front of the Capitol . . . things like that."

I brushed grit off my hands and sat down across from him again. "I had a feeling it was a privilege to be invited to see that room."

"Why did he show it to you?"

I told him about Prescott's copy of the Declaration of Independence.

"It was handwritten by Thomas Jefferson and it's priceless," I said. "I have no idea what Prescott paid for it. It's only the third documented copy of the Declaration handwritten on parchment in existence."

Bobby set his pen down on top of his notebook. He hadn't written down anything I'd said about what Prescott had told me about the Declaration of Independence. To me that meant Bobby was looking for something else.

"Does this have anything to do with why he invited you to his wine cellar?" he asked.

"Leland's Madeira—if it exists—has a label on the bottles that said it was intended for a special Fourth of July ceremony at the Capitol. Attended by President James Madison."

"And?"

"I know this is going to sound weird."

"You'd be surprised how much weird I hear every day. Try me."

"Prescott claimed he was on the verge of uncovering a four-hundred-year-old secret and somehow the Jefferson Dec- laration, as he called it, led him to the last clue. He wanted to present what he discovered—or was about to discover—to his brother Masons at a private party the night of the Miranda Foundation holiday gala in two weeks," I said. "They were going to drink some of the Madeira as a toast."

"A four-hundred-year-old secret, huh? Any idea what it was?"

I could tell he wasn't buying this. He still wore that poker face.

"Of course not," I said. "He also said powerful people didn't want this . . . thing . . . to be found out. And that tell- ing me any more than he already had was dangerous."

Even to my own ears, my somewhat rambling explanation of a long-hidden secret whose discovery would set in motion dangerous repercussions sounded like something out of *Na- tional Treasure*. Or another Indiana Jones movie. Fascinating and engrossing, but totally made-up.

"Dangerous for who?" Bobby asked.

"Me. And, presumably, him."

"Do you think he was in a rational state of mind when he was telling you this? How much did you two have to drink when you were downstairs together?"

"A small glass of Madeira. He wasn't drunk, if that's what you're asking. Look, I know it sounds a little out-there, but he was dead serious."

"Good choice of words." His face cracked into a small smile.

"You know what I mean."

"I heard you asked Kit who among the guests yesterday knew that Prescott might have had plans to sell the *Washington Tribune*," he said.

Complete change of subject. He thought Prescott's buried treasure, or whatever it was, wasn't relevant to his murder. He was definitely looking elsewhere.

"That's right," I said. "I did ask her about that."

"Had you already discussed this subject with Prescott when you were alone with him?"

"No. It was none of my business."

"Did Prescott bring it up? Did he mention anything about someone in his family being angry or upset about this rumor?"

"No, Prescott didn't bring it up, but yes, he told me members of his family were upset with him. It wasn't about selling the *Trib,* though."

"What was it about?"

"Buying things like the Declaration of Independence. Collecting rare and beautiful paintings or sculptures or historical items, as he and Rose had always done. He swore me to secrecy about the purchase of the Declaration," I said. "He especially didn't want his family finding out."

"Why not?"

"He said Clay told him he was wasting money on frivolous purchases. That he was spending Clay's inheritance."

"Prescott said Clay told him he was spending Clay's inheritance? He used those words?"

I tried to remember exactly what Prescott had said. "He said Clay called his purchases 'unicorns' because they were so rare and precious. Clay said Prescott was 'wasting' money buying these things."

"Did he mention whether anyone else in the family shared that point of view?" Bobby asked.

We were really getting into it. Yesterday nearly one hundred friends and neighbors had been at an after-Thanksgiving party at Hawthorne, an annual event we all looked forward to. Today I was being asked to rat out who might be a murderer among us—specifically, among Prescott's family. I got why Bobby was doing this, but I didn't like it.

"Bobby, I feel like a traitor."

"Lucie, if you don't tell me what you know, you could be obstructing a murder investigation. I need to find out who murdered Prescott Avery. There were more than a hundred people at that party yesterday and most of them had been drinking. Before we found out Prescott's death wasn't an accident or from natural causes, the family had people in to clean Hawthorne from top to bottom—including the wine cellar. So any evidence we might have found was destroyed or thrown out." Bobby sounded mad. "If you know something, you need to tell me about it."

"I know."

"So who else in the family thought Prescott was spending their inheritance?" He held up his fingers and made quotation marks around *their inheritance*.

I took a deep breath. "He mentioned Scotty and Alex. He said the two of them thought he was . . . 'starting to lose it,' was how he put it."

"Like he needed to be reined in on his spending?"

"I don't know. Actually I interpreted it that they were

implying that he could be talked into spending money without understanding what he was really doing. He wasn't at all happy about that."

Bobby nodded. "Did they say anything about power of attorney or guardianship?"

"No, it didn't get that far. Besides, Prescott was as sharp as a tack. You know that."

"What about his grandchildren? Kellie, for instance. She works here," he said. "Did she ever mention anything about trouble between her parents and Prescott?"

"Not to me."

"Anything else you can tell me?"

"Nope. But I do have a question."

"What?"

"Did you ever find Prescott's cane?"

"Clayton found it. He said it was underneath some shelves in the wine cellar. Why do you ask?"

"Did you know Prescott has more than one crystal cane with a silver handle on it?"

"I do. How do *you* know that?"

"I saw a cane that looked just like the one he was using in the hall rack by the front door when Quinn and I were leaving. Victoria told me Prescott owned several silver-and-crystal canes. She said he collected them."

"I see." Bobby leaned back against the sofa and closed his notebook. He crossed one leg over the other. "Other than Victoria possibly being downstairs when you and Prescott were there, did you hear anything or see anyone else? The staff, maybe?"

"No one," I said. "Who did you have in mind? Do you think Clay went with her?"

Bobby shrugged. "You tell me. They were both upstairs by the time you ran into Win and me. Besides the elevator, there are stairs between the main floor and the lower level. Also a door that leads to the side garden."

"What are you saying?"

"How long do you think it took you to get from Prescott's wine cellar upstairs to the dining room?" His eyes strayed to my cane, which was propped against the sofa. He hadn't said anything outright but I knew what he was thinking: it would take me longer than someone who had two good feet. Someone who could sprint, or run.

"I got lost. So maybe five minutes. Ten?"

"Okay," he said. "Thanks."

"Can I ask you something?"

"Sure. Not sure I can answer, though."

"How was Prescott killed?"

Bobby's jaw twitched. I wasn't certain he was going to answer me. "B. J. Hunt found an injury—to the head—that wasn't consistent with the fall Prescott took. He was struck by something."

I thought of Prescott, fragile, nearly a century old. "What was it?" I said, my voice rising. "How could someone hit an old man like that?"

"It was a blunt object. So far we haven't found it, so the killer probably took it with him. Or her. And got rid of it."

"How are you going to find out who did this?"

"The same way any detective does. Ask a lot of questions. Connect the dots. I've told you this before, but a killer always takes something from the scene of the crime and always leaves something behind. Locard's exchange principle, it's called. It works every time. I just need to find out what those things are." He sounded grim. "And I will."

As much as I didn't want to believe it, it seemed to me the dots connected into a big circle around the Avery family. One of them—or maybe more than one—was guilty of murder.

"Speaking of asking questions," Bobby went on, "Quinn was downstairs with Prescott before we arrived. I need to talk to him as well."

My heart sank. Quinn had overheard Scotty and Alex arguing about Prescott's possible plan to sell the *Trib*. Quinn's comment to me had been that neither of them should have been around sharp knives. And now Bobby was going to talk to him and ask what he knew.

"You're in luck," I said, as the front door opened. "He's here right now."

I KNEW BOBBY WANTED to talk to Quinn in private, so I left them and joined Frankie, who was in the middle of getting the Christmas decorations out of the storage room. I found her sorting through a box of ornaments.

"I think I'm going to borrow a few of these to use as decorations on the wreaths," she said, ringing a tiny silver bell. "Okay by you?"

"Of course it is."

She closed her hand around the bell to silence it. "Prescott Avery was murdered," she said.

"How do you know?"

She pulled out her phone, tapped a couple of times, and held it up for me to see. "Because of this."

It was a news aggregator app. There were links to at least half a dozen stories by different news organizations: ABC, Fox, MSNBC, CNN, *The New York Times, People,* and the *Washington Tribune.* All of them with roughly the same headline, except for one New York tabloid that read *Suburban Shocker in Wealthy Virginia Horse and Hunt Country: Multibillionaire Prescott Avery Killed in Cold Blood at Party in His Own Home.*

"Oh, God. What an awful headline."

"Is that why Bobby is here?"

I nodded.

"Why would he think you know anything?" she asked.

"Because in addition to Quinn and me finding Prescott, I was the last person to see him alive. Except for the killer, of course."

"I didn't know that." She looked worried. "Who do you think did it?"

"I don't know. Bobby seems to be zeroing in on the family."

"I heard there were about a hundred people at that party yesterday. It could have been anyone."

"Not necessarily."

"What do you mean?"

"It had to be someone with a motive."

"There were plenty of guests who had excellent motives," she said. "Tribbies who didn't want Prescott selling the newspaper out from under them, for example."

"Good Lord, where did you hear *that*?"

"Where else?" She raised an eyebrow. "The General Store. The Romeos were there this morning having their regular kaffeeklatsch."

The Romeos—which stood for Retired Old Men Eating

Out—were also retired old men drinking out, whether it was coffee every morning at the General Store or happy hour at one of the many restaurants and watering holes throughout Loudoun County. Between them they managed to eavesdrop on, and subsequently vacuum up, every conversation and tidbit of information about the goings-on in our county they could find. They then reported their news—some would call it gossip—to Thelma Johnson, the octogenarian owner of the General Store and All-Around Queen Bee of Information. Filtered through Thelma's reality, which consisted of daytime soap operas and her beloved Ouija board, she in turn disseminated what she learned faster than it could make its way around the internet.

My father had been a Romeo. Clay Avery was one as well. Accuracy wasn't always important in the Romeos' information-collecting process. Speed was.

"What were they saying?" I picked up a box labeled CHANTAL'S ORNAMENTS and took off the lid. My mother's collection of beautiful vintage glass ornaments—Santas, a partridge in a pear tree, a drummer boy, striped candy canes, colored balls. She had brought them with her from France.

"Well, of course, no one knew then that Prescott had been murdered," she said. "They were talking about the board meeting he intended to convene today—and that it was sort of convenient he was dead so there would be no talk of selling the *Trib*."

I closed the box and set it down. "I assume Clay wasn't there for this discussion."

"Good Lord, no! No one would have breathed a word about it if he had been," Frankie said.

I shook my head in disbelief. "Yesterday we were at Hawthorne celebrating the beginning of the holiday season. Today the entire family is suspected of murder—the death of a ninety-five-year-old man who was the head of the family," I said. "How did it come to this?"

QUINN FOUND FRANKIE AND me as we were carrying the last of the decorations out of the storage room. He picked up a box that had FRAGILE! WINE BOTTLES! written on it in red marker.

"Bobby's about to leave," he said. "You want all these things moved into the tasting room, Frankie?"

"Yes, please."

"How did it go?" I asked him when Frankie was out of earshot.

He gave me a look as if he'd just sold his soul to the devil. "I had to tell him about the conversation I overheard yesterday between Alex and Scotty in the butler's pantry. The one where Scotty said he'd do whatever it took to keep Prescott from selling the *Trib*."

"Oh, God. He probably didn't mean that literally yesterday. Today it sounds . . ." I didn't want to say what it sounded like.

"I know."

Bobby was finishing a call on his mobile as Quinn and I walked back into the tasting room. He had his back to us but I heard him say, "Yeah, I'm talking to him next. Right. Bye."

He turned around, looking grim, eyeing the three of us but focusing on Quinn and me. "I'd better get going. If you two think of anything else . . ."

"We'll let you know," Quinn said.

"I hope it's someone none of us knew," I said.

"Whoever it is knew the Masonic code on the keypad to get into the wine cellar," Bobby said.

I blinked and said, "What Masonic code?"

He flipped open his notebook and read to us. "HTWSSTKS. It stands for 'Hiram, Tyrian, Widow's Son, Sent to King Solomon.' It's in every Masonic temple in the world and on a lot of Masonic gravestones."

So HTWSSTKS wasn't *Hot Wish Sticks*. Quinn and I exchanged glances.

"Who is Hiram?" Quinn asked. "And why was he sent to King Solomon?"

I got out my phone and searched. "Hiram Abiff was the Grand Architect of the Temple of Solomon, which was built as the final resting place of the Ark of the Covenant. He was murdered by three men in the temple one night for refusing to divulge secrets about how the temple was built that only he knew as a master stonemason."

"That's right," Bobby said. "For the Masons, Hiram's kind of their hero. He represents honor and loyalty because he died rather than giving up their secrets."

"The Ark of the Covenant," Quinn said. "The gold box where the Ten Commandments were kept? The stone tablets God supposedly gave Moses?"

"That's right," Bobby said.

"Probably the most sought-after treasure in the world," Frankie spoke up. "Solomon's Temple was destroyed when the Babylonians destroyed Jerusalem, in the fifth century B.C., if I remember my Catholic school Biblical history correctly. The

Ark disappeared and was never seen again. To this day people are still looking for it."

"It's been a while since the fifth century B.C.," Bobby said. "But it makes a good movie or a good story, that someone might have found another clue about where it is."

"So those letters, which every Mason in the world knows, were the code to Prescott's wine cellar?" I asked. "I wonder why he bothered with a secret code if it was that easy to figure out."

"For the same reason millions of people still use one-two-three-four as their home security code," Bobby said. "Or, if they're really creative, their birth month and date. Because it's easy to remember and they feel better about having an extra layer of security." He shoved his phone in his pocket. "I'd better get going. I'll see you guys later."

After he left, the three of us looked at each other. Frankie said it first.

"I wonder who did it."

"Don't we all?" Quinn said.

Any ideas?" she asked.

My eyes slid to Quinn. "Not me," he said.

I shook my head. "I don't even want to think about it."

"It wasn't someone in the family," Frankie said in a firm voice that convinced nobody. "I'll bet you anything it was a Tribbie."

Nine

The lights were on in the carriage house where my brother Eli had his architectural studio when Quinn and I pulled into the driveway after we finished helping Frankie carry the boxes of Christmas decorations into the tasting room.

"I swear they're like mushrooms," Quinn told me on the ride home. I was relieved we weren't talking about Bobby, Prescott, or a murder. "They multiply in the dark in that storeroom. I'm sure there were more this year than last year."

"Oh, come on," I said, laughing. "Don't be a Grinch. Frankie loves Christmas as much as I do. Maybe we get a bit carried away, but the house and the Villa look so beautiful and festive when they're decorated, don't you think? Especially if it's a white Christmas."

He grinned. "You're talking to a California boy. I used to go surfing on Christmas Day. And Californians are mostly into lights. On everything. Buildings, palm trees, you name it, we light it up. It's like fairyland. Or Disneyland."

"Speaking of lights, Eli's working. I thought I might drop by and have a quick chat with him," I said as we climbed out of the Jeep.

"Does this have to do with what Prescott told you yesterday?" Quinn asked. "You want to ask him if he knows about the missing cases of Madeira?"

"Yes."

He gave me a reflective look. "That was a *yes, but*. Yes, but what?"

Somehow he always knew when I was holding back. "I want to know if he knew about the second safe-deposit box Prescott said Leland had rented. The one where he kept his secrets from my mother."

Quinn placed his hands on my shoulders and looked down into my eyes as if he could see clear through into my soul. "I'll go see about dinner. Take all the time you need, sweetheart."

There are days when I'm on my knees in gratitude for this man who understands me so well. I know with every fiber of my being that he will always be there when I need him. Even if I don't ask. Like right now.

"Why don't you come with me?" I reached for his hands and twined my fingers through his. "I don't want us to have any secrets from each other. Whatever Leland did, whatever secrets he kept, I want you to know about it, too."

"You're sure?"

"I am."

"Then let's go talk to Eli."

Eli yelled, "It's open," when I knocked on his studio door a moment later.

He was hunched over his drafting table, staring at a laptop that sat on top of a sheaf of drawings. Two coffee mugs were pushed into a corner. I TURN COFFEE INTO ARCHITECTURE and WORLD'S OKAYEST ARCHITECT. The coffeepot, which sat in a coffeemaker on a table behind him, was empty and the light switched off. His dark hair looked like it hadn't seen a comb recently and he was unshaven, wearing a faded Virginia Tech sweatshirt and old jeans.

As usual, a long, low table on one side of the room was piled with rolled drawings that looked like an incoming tide. The current architectural model he was building for a client—a beautiful, precise, miniature reproduction, as was his style—reminded me of Fallingwater. I could still smell the glue he'd used. Before the cold weather had set in, he'd bought an electric fireplace, plugged it into the wall, and designed and built bookcases on either side to match the mantel and surround so it looked as if it had always been there. Now the fireplace was turned on, taking the chill off the drafty room with its wall of windows where large doors had once been.

He looked up and stretched, swiveling in his chair so he was facing Quinn and me. "Hey," he said, yawning, "what's up?"

"We just finished talking to Bobby Noland," I said. "Did you know Prescott Avery was murdered yesterday?"

When Eli was busy working on a project for a client, he could be oblivious to everything.

He didn't know. "Jesus. Are you serious? Who did it?"

"If Bobby knew the answer to that, he wouldn't have had to question us."

Eli laced his hands behind his head and yawned again. "Don't be a wise-ass, Luce. Let me rephrase. Does he think you know who did it?"

I avoided looking at Quinn. The answer to that was "maybe," but I didn't want to admit it to Eli. I'd pointed enough arrows at Victoria Barkley based on nothing more than the scent of her perfume.

I said, "No," as Quinn said, "He wanted to know what we knew."

"So which is it?" My brother looked from me to Quinn, reading both our expressions like open books. "Wait a minute, did this happen at the party? Somebody killed Prescott at his own party?"

Quinn nodded.

"We were there yesterday," I said. "I was the last person he talked to before it happened. Well, next to last. And Quinn and I found him."

"Jesus," Eli said again and picked up a mug. He examined what was in it, took a sip, and set it down like the contents were radioactive. "I'm sorry Sasha and I didn't make it, but we had a couple of friends lined up to move her furniture out of her place and bring it to the house. But considering a murderer was lurking around Hawthorne Castle, I think I'm glad we didn't go. Someone really killed Prescott—a ninety-five-year-old guy? Who would do that?"

"Bobby is zeroing in on the family. Everyone seems to have a motive and it's mostly related to money," I said.

My brother's eyes flashed and we stared at each other. "Sounds familiar," he said.

"Let's not go there. What's past is past."

"Someone hit him over the head in his wine cellar," Quinn said. "We found him on the floor. Lucie forgot her phone down there so we went back to get it. By the time we arrived we were too late, so there was nothing we could do. He was already dead."

"Prescott Avery. He was a multibillionaire. He had everything. And Hawthorne . . ." Eli shook his head in wonderment. "That place is incredible. Any architect would have killed to be on the team that designed it. Not literally, I mean." He paused. "You guys want some coffee? I can make a fresh pot. Grab a seat. Pull up those stools over there."

"We'll pass on coffee," I said. "But thanks, anyway."

Quinn dragged two high-backed stools across the room so the three of us were sitting around Eli's drafting table.

"I hope you won't have to stay here too late," I said.

"I have a deadline to show a client drawings first thing tomorrow. It will take as long as it takes," he said. "So what brings you guys here? Something besides Prescott."

"Two things," I told him. "I don't want to hold you up since you're busy, but yesterday afternoon Prescott told me Leland had a safe-deposit box."

"Which we cleaned out," Eli said right away. "Car titles, will, marriage license, my selective service card, for some reason. His and Mom's birth certificates. The usual stuff."

"Not that one. *Another* safe-deposit box. Where he kept things he didn't want Mom to know about."

In the poignant silence that followed, I knew my brother was thinking the same thing that had gone through my mind. *What more could our father have hidden that we never knew about?*

But more important was this: *did we want to find out after all this time?* They say the heart can't hurt if the head doesn't know. Did we *want* to know?

My brother gave me a wary look. "Where is this safe-deposit box?"

"Apparently at Blue Ridge Federal."

"You'd think Seth would have told us about it."

I nodded. "You'd think."

"You could just leave it alone," Quinn said. "It's been five years. Maybe it might be better to let sleeping dogs lie."

"I'm for leaving it alone. Let this dog keep lying, like Quinn said," Eli said. "Besides, we never found a second key when we sorted through all his stuff."

"Well, if the safe-deposit box was secret, then he would have hidden the key, wouldn't he?" I said. "And he wouldn't have told anyone about it."

"Apparently no one in the family. But he did tell Prescott Avery, it seems." Eli fiddled with his mechanical pencil, spinning it like a dial in a board game or the hands of a clock gone crazy. There was an acid edge to his voice. He wasn't enjoying this conversation. Eli liked stability. Order. Predictability. Leland had popped up in our lives again like a jack-in-the-box at the end of the music when you were sure the spring was broken and nothing would happen.

"I know you, Luce. You're the one who did the DNA test and found out about David," he went on. "Now you want to find this key. And if you do, then you want to check out the safe-deposit box. Am I right?"

I shrugged. "Now that I know about it, I suppose I do. I don't want any of Leland's ghosts to haunt me. Or any of us. Besides, Prescott seems to think . . . *seemed* to think . . . Leland might have left be a clue about the old cases of Madeira in that safe-deposit box."

Eli's face went blank. "What old cases of Madeira?"

Quinn and I exchanged looks. "Sorry," I said. "That was thing number two. I should have told you about the Madeira first."

"Told me what?"

When I was finished, my brother shook his head. "Look, if there was any booze lying around the house, especially something that valuable, you know as well as I do that Leland either drank it or sold it. Besides, where would it be that we haven't already looked?"

"If there is a safe-deposit box and Leland left something—a clue or a letter—about the Madeira, it's still there and it's not going anywhere," Quinn said. "You don't have to do anything about it right this minute, Lucie. No one's putting a gun to your head to find out . . . especially if it's too upsetting right now."

He meant too upsetting to Eli. And because of other stressful things like Prescott's murder and the busyness of the upcoming holidays.

I started to protest when what he said about putting a gun to my head made a missing puzzle piece slot into place with a neat click.

"I know where the key might be." My mouth felt dry.

"Quinn just said something that made me realize where it might be hidden. Where I believe it *is* hidden."

"What did I just say?" Quinn said. "Where's the key?"

"What was the one place that Leland made absolutely sure was off-limits to all of us?"

Eli's eyes widened. "His gun cabinet."

My father's gun cabinet was a beautiful hand-carved piece of furniture, not a utilitarian box where he kept his weapons. He was a collector as well as a hunter and he had supervised every detail of the work done by the Amish cabinetmakers that built it. It sat in his former office—now the library—and, though I am neither a hunter nor a collector, I had left it where it was.

"You think the key's there?" Quinn asked.

"Why not?" I said. "It could be behind something, attached to the top of a drawer or the back of the cabinet itself."

"We never found a key there before now," Eli said.

"Because we weren't looking for one. Especially one that was probably deliberately hidden."

"I suppose you want to check it out," he said. "Like right now."

"I do. You want to come?"

"You know I do. If you're going to look for it, I'm not sitting here on my hands."

I caught Quinn's eye. There was a glint of excitement in his.

"Okay," I said. "Let's go."

THERE WAS NO SECRET about where Leland kept the key to the gun cabinet itself. On the top of the ledge of the door to the library. Too high for the fingers of a child—Eli, Mia, and me when we were little, and now Hope and Zach—to reach. As for the ammunition drawers, they could only be unlocked with a special code on a built-in dial. I had found the code with the original bill from the woodworking company. Fortunately Leland had never changed it.

Eli got the key to the gun cabinet. Quinn brought a bottle of red—a Pomerol—and three wineglasses from the dining room. Once the cabinet and the ammunition drawers were unlocked, the three of us started to examine every surface.

"Do you think it's behind the gun rack?" Quinn said. "Do we need to take out all of the rifles and long guns?"

"If we do, Leland had to do it as well," I said. "I don't think he would make this hiding place so complicated or inaccessible."

"*If* he hid it here," Eli said. "And *if* he was still using that safe-deposit box when he died."

"Oh, ye of little faith," I said. "Seek and ye shall find. Believe and it shall happen."

"Shut. Up."

"I found it."

"You did not."

"I did." I held up a small envelope and opened the Velcro fastening, sliding out two keys with long notched shanks. The number 57 was stamped into them. "These are safe-deposit box keys, all right."

"Where was the little envelope?" Quinn asked.

"Here."

In a narrow drawer where Leland had kept a multi-tool

and some cleaning rods, I'd discovered the envelope taped to the inside top of the drawer.

Eli shook his head in disgust. "Wonder if he kept anything else, more stuff he didn't want us to know about?"

The bitterness in his voice told me he still hadn't forgiven Leland. For a lot of things.

"Does it matter anymore?" I asked.

Eli picked up his wineglass and drank, his eyes clouded and his mood darker than it had been before we started this. He was Leland's son and the eldest child. Leland, who had never wanted his children to call him Dad or Daddy or Papa, hadn't done any of the father/son things with Eli that would have forged a bond between them, brought them close together, never taught him practical things like how to tie a tie properly or throw a football, never passed on knowledge that would have smoothed a rocky adolescence. Instead he let Eli fend for himself, tag along with other boys whose dads coached their Little League teams or were the Scoutmasters or took them to D.C. to watch the Nationals or the Capitals or the Wizards play.

Then a few months ago, my supposedly innocuous DNA test had led to the discovery of another son Leland had fathered. What we didn't know and might never know, since David's birth mother didn't want to have anything to do with the child she gave up for adoption, was whether Leland had known about David. Eli said for David's sake he hoped Leland never had a clue. Ignorance would be preferable to not caring, being abandoned.

"I suppose none of it matters now," Eli said and my heart ached for him because I knew he was lying and it did matter.

I touched his arm. "Why don't I call Seth Hannah tomorrow and make an appointment to stop by Blue Ridge Federal and see what this is all about? I'll let you know what happens, okay?"

"Do you want me to come?"

"Nah, you've got clients and work to do. It's quiet at the vineyard so I'll go."

"I'm still for letting sleeping dogs lie, Luce. But you and I are different that way. You're more like Mom. You wear that same suit of armor she wore. She managed to put up with all of Leland's crap and still be an amazing, loving mother. I don't know how she did it. So go ahead and find out."

I nodded because I couldn't speak.

He gave me a one-armed brother hug and dropped a kiss on top of my head, something he almost never did.

"Good luck," he said, his voice roughened with emotion. "But be careful. When Leland's involved, you're playing with fire. I'd just hate to see you get burned." He turned to leave, then seemed to think better of it and turned around to face me. "Again."

And then he was gone for good.

Ten

Thanksgiving is the only holiday when we eat food we never eat any other time of year. It's also the only American holiday based entirely around everyone in the country dining on almost the exact same meal at almost the exact same time. And it is the annual lament of my cousin Dominique Gosselin, who owns the Michelin-starred Goose Creek Inn, that this national gastronomic eat-a-thon revolves around food that is neither healthy nor good for us.

I tended to agree with her about some of the more calorie-laden, artery-clogging food—candied yams with marshmallow topping being at the top of my list—but my most enduring memory of Thanksgiving is not food, but something my French mother said to me when I was a little girl.

"It is so uniquely American, *ma chérie,* for a country to give thanks once a year for its good fortune, its bounty and many resources, and to remember its origins," she'd said. "We have no such holiday in France to express our gratitude for the beauty and richness of our land, for freedom, liberty, and justice, for friends, neighbors, and family, and for living in a country blessed with peace. I *love* Thanksgiving and I love that the very first Thanksgiving took place here in Virginia at Jamestown."

And so did I. The warmth and good cheer as the holidays began, when it was not quite winter but definitely the waning days of fall, always tugged at my heartstrings. Harvest was over. A season was beginning that would be filled with parties, gift-giving, tree-decorating, caroling, peace on earth and goodwill to men, a new year and a fresh start. Leaves had been raked, trees were bare, and the vineyard had gone dormant for the year. My mother loved it when our house was full of guests, so we always hosted Thanksgiving for the rest of the family and any neighbors and friends who she'd learned would otherwise be alone that day. I remember when she would start baking and preparing everything the week before so the house had smelled of cinnamon, cloves, allspice, and nutmeg for days. When she brought home the turkey—always a freshly killed turkey from a local farm in Upperville—it had been a big occasion.

Tonight, after all the drama and tension of the past twenty-four hours, I wanted to eat Thanksgiving leftovers for dinner, comfort food that would be sure to induce a tryptophan drowsiness, send me off to sleep with no nightmares of bloody murders or bank vaults filled with long-buried secrets.

Quinn and I got bowls and platters out of the refrigerator, heating up casseroles and my family's version of mashed potatoes—mixed with celeriac for a little zing—along with the last of my homemade orange-cranberry sauce. The envelope with the safe-deposit box keys in it was still in my pocket and every so often as I leaned against the counter I could feel it dig into my hipbone.

We ate in the kitchen, though I dimmed the lights and lit the candles we'd used in the dining room on Thursday. Quinn poured more of the Pomerol we'd opened earlier into our wineglasses.

We touched glasses and I said, "Happy End-of-Thanksgiving."

"Happy End-of-Thanksgiving."

He passed me the platter of turkey and speared a couple of pieces of dark meat for himself.

"Those Merlot vines in the south block don't look good," he said. "I know how you feel about trying to keep them, but I really think it would be better in the long run to tear them out, wait the three years until the new vines start producing, and start over."

He saw my unhappy look in the flickering candlelight and brushed the top of my hand with his fingers. "I know you don't want to do that and I understand your reason, sweetheart. But it doesn't make financial sense to spend the time and money to see if we can salvage vines that are that far gone. Plus we need to keep the disease from spreading."

Usually I was the one making the exact same arguments he was making. Time and money. Not sentiment. Of course he was right. But ripping out those particular vines would be like tearing out the heart of the vineyard and there was a psychological cost to that, at least for me. They were the very first vines my parents had planted and I suppose I thought they would always thrive, always produce good—even excellent—

wine as they grew older. They would serve as a connection between the past and the present.

"What if we got some help?" I said. "There's a woman living down in Charlottesville who advises a number of vineyards when they've got problems like ours. Not just in Virginia but also in California and overseas. She's supposed to be a miracle worker."

"Are you talking about Josephine Wilde?" he asked through a mouthful of turkey.

I nodded. "Josie Wilde. I've only heard great things about her."

"And I've heard she's not taking on new clients because she's got more work than she can handle," he said. "Plus she's very particular about who she'll work with. She expects you to do exactly what she says if you sign on with her."

"To have someone with her expertise helping us, I'd be willing to do anything," I said. "What about you?"

He bristled. "I don't want someone else taking over the running of this vineyard."

"Because you'd be outnumbered by women?"

He gave me a mock outraged look. "I can handle that. I'm very secure in my masculinity."

I grinned. "Then it's settled. I'd be willing to put my faith one hundred percent in what she says. I've seen her reports. She puts together a big, thick notebook that's an exhaustive, comprehensive examination of every aspect of the grapes, vines, and soil. She uses drones to take aerial shots so she can show you exactly what's going on in every single block of grapevines. Plus she does a row-by-row calculation of the canopy of each block to determine how much shade a particular row will cast on the next one, depending on the geography of the terrain."

Quinn whistled softly. "Sounds like you've been thinking of contacting her for a while."

"I think our wine is getting better and better. Why not make it great?"

"I'd like to meet her first," he said, "before we decide."

"Oh-ho," I said. "You've got this the wrong way around, my darling. She would want to meet *us* first before *she* decides if she's willing to take us on. And apparently just getting that first meeting is a huge step. Then we'd have to have a compelling, intriguing reason for her to say yes because, as you said, she already has a full plate with her current clients, her research, and her travel schedule."

Quinn squinted at me. "Do you want to call her and sweet-talk her or should I?"

"I'll do it," I said. "Not that I don't think you aren't utterly charming, especially when you want to be, but—"

"Don't finish that sentence," he said. "And you call Ms. Plays-Hard-to-Get."

IT DIDN'T TAKE LONG to clean up after dinner. He washed, I dried.

"I thought I might have a cigar tonight," he said. "You mind?"

House rules: no smelly cigars indoors. He smoked on the veranda, or elsewhere depending on the weather.

"Of course not," I said, "except it's chilly out."

"It's also a really clear night. The wind this afternoon blew away the clouds so I thought I'd do a bit of stargazing. Want to come?"

Of all the things I'd learned about my fiancé over the years, the one that surprised me the most was his love of astronomy. The first summer Quinn came to Montgomery Estate Vineyard, he'd asked my father for permission to set up a telescope in our backyard next to our old summerhouse because it sat on the crest of a hill. There the unobstructed view of rolling hills, checkerboard fields, and horse farms below and the star-studded night sky above went on for miles, all the way to the distant Blue Ridge Mountains.

Later it was our practice, especially on warm evenings, to take the last of the dinner wine and two glasses outside where we sat in Adirondack chairs that overlooked the valley and he would explain to me the stars, planets, comets, meteor showers, and other celestial objects that appeared in the nighttime sky at that time of year. Then he would set up his telescope and point out everything to me, until I grew to look forward to our nocturnal stargazing sessions as much as he did.

"I'll come with you," I said. "What are we looking for tonight?"

"Jupiter," he said. "Did I read you that article in *Sky & Telescope* a few months ago about the twelve new moons they just found?"

I nodded. "What about it?"

"Come on," he said, "let's get our coats and I'll tell you."

We brought flashlights with red filters over the lights so we wouldn't ruin our night vision. The Adirondack chairs were cold—it would feel like sitting on a large block of ice—so I got two heavy quilts out of the summerhouse and bundled up in mine while he set up the telescope and smoked his cigar, its tip glowing like an orange mini-moon in the quiet darkness.

"I found Jupiter," he said. "Come on over and take a look. Tonight you can really see the Galilean moons so clearly."

Quinn had told me long ago that Jupiter's four biggest moons, which collectively were named after their discoverer Galileo Galilei, were eventually named Io, Europa, Ganymede, and Callisto, after the lovers of the Greek god Zeus—a small irony since the ancient Romans worshipped Jupiter as their equivalent of Zeus.

I got up and dragged my quilt over to the telescope like it was a royal robe. "What about the twelve new moons? Can you see them?"

"They're tiny," he said. "Maybe as small as a mile or two wide. More like 'moonlets.' They're probably the result of collisions and what was left over after the giant planets formed."

"You mean like space debris?" I bent down and looked through the eyepiece and there it was. Jupiter, the largest planet in the solar system, a dazzling, non-twinkling silvery star. "How many moons are there in all now?"

"Seventy-nine, counting the new ones," he said. "They're thinking of naming one them Valetudo. It's sort of an odd duck, an outlier because it's orbiting an outer belt of moons that are traveling retrograde around Jupiter."

"Valetudo. What an odd name. Who was he—or she? Another Greek god?" I leaned down and looked at Jupiter one more time. Quinn had told me that it was the fourth brightest object in the sky after the sun, moon, and Venus. Mostly made up of gas, two and a half times larger than all the other planets in the solar system combined. First discovered by the

Babylonians in the seventh or eighth century B.C. Now just a bright silver disk the size of a small bead through the lens of the telescope.

"You're almost right," Quinn said. "Valetudo was the Roman goddess of health and hygiene, plus she was the great-granddaughter of Jupiter, who, of course, was Zeus to the Greeks. Anyway, Valetudo fits with all the other names since the IAU requires Jupiter's moons to have mythological names that relate to . . . well, Jupiter. Valetudo may not be around long," he added. "Since it's going the wrong way, it might end up colliding with one of the other moons."

"The International Astronomical Union is that strict about controlling the naming of moons?"

He nodded. "They're strict about controlling the naming of any astronomical object. There has to be some order, some system," he said. "And they're not all named after characters from mythology. Uranus's moons have names of characters from Shakespeare and Alexander Pope. All twenty-seven of them."

"I think Shakespearean moons sounds so poetic."

He relit his cigar and the tip glowed again. "That's why they picked poetic names. Titania and Oberon were the fairy king and queen in *A Midsummer Night's Dream*. Most of the other names came from *The Tempest,* which is also all about magic." He started ticking them off on the fingers of his non-cigar hand. "Miranda, Caliban, Prospero, Ferdinand . . . I forget the others, but there were seven in all."

"Miranda and Ferdinand were characters in *The Tempest*?"

"That's right. Why?"

"I saw a painting in Prescott's wine cellar the other day. It

was called *Ferdinand Courting Miranda*. The artist was someone named William Hogarth."

"I saw that painting, too," he said. "The old man in the
painting was Prospero and the ugly creature was Caliban,
Prospero's slave and a witch's son. I thought it seemed odd
among all those black-and-white photographs that were hanging on the wall."

"That's what I thought, too," I said. "Do you know anything about the plot of *The Tempest*?"

"Actually, I do. After I found out about the IAU and the
naming thing I bought a copy of Shakespeare's plays so I
could figure out who all the characters were."

He had brought the book with him when he moved his
otherwise spartan collection of possessions into my house
after we got engaged.

"Miranda was the daughter of Prospero, who was a magician, and Ferdinand was the duke's son who wanted to marry
her. The duke was sailing back to his country after attending
a wedding when Prospero used his magic to shipwreck their
boat so it ended up on the island where he and Miranda were
living." He paused. "Hey, you don't seem interested in this."

"Sorry, I am. But I'm still thinking about that painting."

"What about it?"

"It covered a hidden keypad. When Prescott moved it aside
and keyed in the code, the bookcase next to the painting slid
to one side and there was a door behind it."

"To that Masonic room you told me about?"

"Yup. Do you know what was even more odd about that
painting?"

"Besides covering a keypad that opened a door to a secret room? Not really."

"It was a copy."

"So?"

"The Averys don't collect copies. They collect originals."

"Maybe they loaned the original to an art gallery and Prescott hung a copy there as a placeholder."

It was possible. "Maybe."

"You don't seem convinced and you look like you're freezing. Go on, I'll pack up the telescope and meet you in the house," he said. "Besides, I've got to finish smoking my stinky cigar."

I blew him a kiss and started to leave. "Hey," I said and he turned around. "Would you mind if I borrow your copy of *The Complete Works of William Shakespeare*?"

"It's our copy now," he said. "Of course not."

I'd made space for his books on the library bookshelves when he'd moved in, plus he kept other books, as I did, on a bookshelf in the little sitting room off our bedroom that had once been my mother's office. The Shakespeare was in the library. I found it and sat down on the sofa, opening it to the table of contents. The comedies were listed before the tragedies and *The Tempest* was the very first play. I found a more detailed summary of the play than the one Quinn had given me after a quick search on my phone.

Prospero, a magician, conjured up a storm at sea in order to cause a shipwreck that would bring a king and his entourage sailing from Africa home to Italy to the island where he lived with his beautiful daughter Miranda. It was a story of revenge and control—through magic—but in the end all worked out well. Ferdinand, the king's son, would marry Miranda and everyone would return to Italy together. There hadn't been a shipwreck after all—more of Prospero's magic—and Prospero, who had lived on the island for years among his vast collection of magic books, was willing to give up his library to return to civilization. The play ended with him asking the other characters and the audience to forgive the mischief he'd caused.

Prescott and Rose's daughter had been named Miranda and Prescott had always referred to his crystal cane as his magic wand. Were they just coincidences or did Prescott consider himself a magician of some sort who could control others? Had he and Rose named Miranda after the beautiful young woman in *The Tempest*?

Maybe they just liked the name. Maybe I was reading too much into this and there was nothing at all special concerning Prescott and Shakespeare's play.

Somehow, though, I couldn't shake the feeling that there was a connection somewhere. It was no accident the Hogarth painting—a copy, no less—hung in his wine cellar and that it was tied to his secret Masonic room. But how did it relate to his daughter who died more than thirty years ago?

Because I also had a feeling the answer had something to do with Prescott's secret, his lost treasure. And more than ever, I wanted to know what it was.

Eleven

As soon as Blue Ridge Federal Bank opened on Monday morning, I planned to call Seth Hannah, its president, and ask him for a meeting to talk about the envelope with Leland's mysterious safe-deposit box keys. Not only was Seth a Romeo who'd been a good friend of my father's, but also he had gone out of his way to help me after Leland died when I discovered Leland had put up the vineyard as collateral for a loan and fallen behind in paying it back. Seth had cut me some slack on the loan because he didn't want to see me lose the vineyard and the house and I'd been grateful. What I couldn't understand was why he hadn't told me about the other safe-deposit box.

"If your father had another safe-deposit box at Blue Ridge Federal, I can't figure out why you wouldn't have received a notification that it existed," Quinn said, echoing my thoughts. We were sitting at the kitchen table eating breakfast. "Things like that don't slip between the cracks. At a government office maybe—they lose paperwork all the time—but not a bank."

"That's not entirely true. What about The Urn?" I asked. "Banks lose paperwork, at least Blue Ridge Federal does."

Quinn stopped buttering a slice of toasted baguette to consider the plight of The Urn. "Well, that's kind of an unusual case, don't you think?"

"It contains the cremated remains of a human being." I gave him an indignant look. "How do you lose the documents for a person?"

"Okay. Fair enough. Maybe the same thing happened to your father's safe-deposit box and that's the explanation."

"Maybe."

Whoever had left a brass cremation urn containing the ashes of their beloved dearly departed in the vault of Blue Ridge Federal years ago, he or she had never returned to claim it and the paperwork either vanished or had been misplaced. Over the years—and there had been many—it had become part of the nightly ritual for whoever was locking up and setting alarms at the bank to wish The Urn sweet dreams. It was even considered bad luck to forget to say good night to it, prompting a number of superstitious beliefs to become part of the urban legend of The Urn's mystique.

"What makes everyone so sure The Urn contains the ashes of a person?" Quinn asked. "What if it's someone's dog? Or cat? Or, since this is horse and hunt country, why not a horse?"

I frowned at him. "I don't know. We've always assumed it's a person. The whole town has. At this point, how could you tell, even if you opened it up to check, whether it was a horse or a person . . . oh, jeez, why did you bring that up? Now I'm not going to be able to stop wondering about it."

He added homemade strawberry jam to his buttered baguette. "I'm sorry. I didn't mean to burst your bubble. I feel like I've just told you Santa Claus isn't real and doesn't live at the North Pole."

"Speaking of Santa Claus," I said, "there's something I need to talk to you about."

"Oh, yeah?"

"Frankie was wondering . . ."

The security alarm panel beeped that someone had opened and closed the front door and a moment later, Eli appeared in the kitchen, bundled up in a navy pea coat with a roll of architectural drawings under one arm. He also had our copy of the *Washington Tribune*.

"Here's your paper," he said. "Wait until you read the article on Prescott." He set it down on the kitchen table open to the front page with its banner headlines.

TRIBUNE OWNER PRESCOTT AVERY'S DEATH
NOW CONSIDERED MURDER.
LOUDOUN COUNTY SHERIFF'S OFFICE OPENS INVESTIGATION.

Grant Lowry had written the story, rather than assigning it to one of his reporters. Quinn picked up the newspaper.

"Want some coffee before you have to meet your client?" I asked Eli. He looked tired and there were raccoon-like circles under his eyes. From an upstairs window I'd seen the lights on in the carriage house when Quinn and I had gone to bed last night.

"Who made it?" My brother thought Quinn's coffee tasted like road tar.

"Me."

"Sure, I'll take a quick cup."

I got up to get it for him. He set his drawings on the counter and shrugged out of his coat, throwing himself into the chair next to Quinn.

"Anybody eating that last piece of Sasha's pumpkin spice bread?" he asked.

"You are," Quinn said. "Grant says the Sheriff's Office has got no one in custody yet and they're keeping all options open."

"I guess he doesn't want to put it in print that Prescott's family members are among the chief suspects," Eli said as I handed him his coffee. "Thanks, Luce. Pass the butter, please? Can I borrow your knife?"

I gave him my knife and the butter. "Did you have breakfast?"

"A bowl of cereal from a pink box that had a unicorn on it. I think Sasha bought it for Hope."

I took my seat. "No one has been accused of anything. Innocent until proven guilty. And the *Tribune* is not a tabloid. Why should they jump all over the gossipy accounts that there's a family feud? They have an obligation to report the facts."

"The facts are that there is a family feud," Eli said.

"Which may not have anything to do with Prescott's death," I said.

Quinn tapped his finger on Grant's newspaper story. "I wonder how the *Trib* is going to play this."

"Straight, honest reporting. They have to," I said. "Or their reporters are going to boycott, maybe even quit. Kit will quit, for sure. She won't stand for her newspaper whitewashing a crime or covering it up."

"Who do you think did it?" Eli asked. "Since you two were at the party and you're the ones who found Prescott."

"I don't know," I said. "There were over a hundred people there and everyone had been drinking. But as Bobby always says, you need to look for someone who had a motive. In this case, you're talking about a lot of people. Aside from the family who had a big financial stake in Prescott not selling the *Trib,* there were a lot of Tribbies there who felt the same way."

"And one of those Tribbies felt upset or angry enough to kill Prescott?" Eli raised an eyebrow. "Really?"

"I don't know. Maybe after a couple of caipirinhas," I said. "It could have been a conversation that escalated, got out of hand. Which would mean it wasn't premeditated."

"I don't think it makes sense for anyone in the family to have done it," Quinn said.

"Why not?" I asked.

"Think about it. Would any of them—Clay, Scotty, Alex, Bianca—be so coldhearted as to murder Prescott right under the noses of their guests? Isn't that pretty risky, having all those potential witnesses? It would be so much easier to do it when no one was there. An overdose of sleeping pills or the wrong medication, instead of hitting him over the head. Who could prove something like that wasn't an accident?"

"You're forgetting Victoria," I said. "She lives there, even though she and Clay aren't married. Yet."

"Same principle applies to her."

"Except if it was someone in the family, it would reduce the number of suspects from about a hundred to five," Eli said.

"I think Quinn's got a point," I said. "The fact that it did happen at the party makes a case for why it probably *wasn't* a member of the family."

"So we're back to square one," Eli said. "Who did it?"

"Beats me," Quinn said. "I don't envy Bobby. He's got a personal as well as a professional stake in this one since Kit works for the *Trib*."

"I guess we'll just have to wait and see," I said.

SETH HANNAH'S SECRETARY SAID he was busy when I called at 9:01, so I asked if she would give him a message. Eli was gone, off to meet his client. I knew he didn't want to be around for this phone call, but he did ask me to let him know how it went and what happened when I went to see Seth.

"Please tell Seth I'm calling about my father's safe-deposit box," I said to the secretary. "And that I'd like to talk to him about it. In person."

"Mr. Hannah is tied up in meetings today and his calendar is quite full for the rest of the week," she said.

"I discovered the existence of this safe-deposit box by accident," I said in a calm voice. "Last night. I also have the keys. I thought Mr. Hannah might be able to explain why he kept it a secret all these years since my father passed away."

"I see." Now she sounded flustered. "Can you hold for a moment, please?"

Ten seconds later she was back on the phone. "Mr. Hannah asked if you could come by at ten o'clock. This morning."

"Absolutely. No problem. I'll be there," I said and she hung up.

"What was that all about?" Quinn asked.

"Seth Hannah suddenly became 'unbusy' when I pushed his secretary on why no one at the bank ever told me about Leland's safe-deposit box. He'll see me at ten."

"Great," he said. "By the way, you were going to ask me something before Eli walked in. Something about Frankie."

Would you dress up as Santa Claus for the Christmas party?

"It can wait. I'd better get moving or I'll be late for my appointment with Seth."

"If you say so." Quinn looked me over. I was still wearing the sweatshirt and sweatpants I'd slept in. "Are you going dressed like that?"

"Probably not."

"You'd better change, then."

BLUE RIDGE FEDERAL BANK was located on the corner of Washington and North Liberty Streets in Middleburg, a town that had been founded in 1787 by Leven Powell, who named many of the streets for the Founding Fathers because they were his friends. Washington Street—named for George— was our main street and divided the north- and south-named streets like Hamilton, Madison, Jay, and Marshall. We had a single traffic light a block from the bank at the intersection of Washington and Madison. Less than a mile on either side of that light you were already outside what we called Middleburg's "corporate limits." Not exactly a blink-and-you'll-miss-it town, but we liked it just as it was, with its pretty art galleries and antiques stores, charming cafes and restaurants, and little specialty shops whose owners knew everyone who walked through their door.

There had been a bank on the corner of Washington and North Liberty since 1835; originally it was the People's Bank of Middleburg. When Blue Ridge Federal bought the national historic trust building after PBM went out of business, they retained the beautiful architectural features like the PBM medallions—intertwined gilt and royal-blue letters on a cream-colored background—on either side of the arched entrance, the gas lanterns, and the tiled mosaic floor of the PBM logo flanked by two rampant lions in the outside foyer. Inside, with its black-and-white tiled floors, wrought-iron and marble tellers' windows, high ceilings, and carved woodwork, it was the kind of elegant, imposing place you trusted to keep your money safe.

The tellers' windows were located in a row on the main floor. The vault was at the back, a large old-fashioned behemoth of steel, copper, and concrete with a stainless steel wheel like a ship's wheel on the exterior and complicated gears and moving parts on the inside that resembled the workings of an intricately designed watch.

A couple of tellers waved at me as I walked in and said hello. I waved back and pointed a finger toward the ceiling. The office of the president was on the second floor. There was a small elevator behind the staircase, but I took the sweeping circular staircase instead because I am stubborn and I will always challenge myself not to take the easy way and give in to my disability.

Seth's secretary, a motherly woman who had streaked her

short silver hair with neon purple, was sitting at a desk outside his office when I showed up at precisely ten o'clock.

"I like the purple," I said.

She grinned. "I did it on a dare from my grandson. But I'm going to let it grow out."

"Really?"

She gestured to the closed door with SETH HANNAH, PRESIDENT stenciled on it in gold. "He thinks I'm still dressed up for Halloween." She stood up. "I'll let him know you're here."

A moment later she came out and held the door open. "Please go through."

Seth Hannah was a small, compact man with a silver-gray pompadour smoothed back in a way that always made me think of a fox. He had a broad, high-domed forehead, dark intelligent eyes behind horn-rimmed glasses, and a good poker face, as any of the Romeos who played cards with him knew only too well. It was a real asset for a banker and that's what I was getting right now.

"Lucie, my dear. How nice to see you." He came around from behind his desk and took one of my hands in both of his. "I heard the news about you being with Prescott Saturday afternoon when he . . . passed, God rest his soul. It must have been a terrible shock. What can I offer you? A cup of coffee, tea, or a glass of water? Please . . . please. Have a seat."

He ushered me over to a pair of club chairs covered in royal-blue crushed velvet and settled me into one of them. His office always reminded me of an English gentlemen's club. Dark paneled walls, an oil painting of the bank's founder with a handlebar mustache and bushy sideburns, heavy, dark furniture, and an enormous vase filled with roses and mums in the colors of autumn sitting on a low sideboard. Inside I knew he kept top-shelf bottles of liquor that he brought out for special visitors and challenging situations. But not at ten in the morning.

"Water would be great," I said. My mouth already felt parched.

He pressed a button on the multiline telephone on his desk and said, "Could we have some water, please?"

He sat in the other club chair as his secretary knocked on the door and walked in, carrying a silver tray with a pitcher and two glasses on it. She set it on a small table between us and said, "Please let me know if you need anything else."

Seth poured two glasses of water and placed mine on a drink coaster with the Blue Ridge Federal logo—the hazy blue mountains as a backdrop for the bank's name in bold black letters—printed on it. He leaned back in his chair and crossed one leg over the other.

"What can I do for you, darling?"

He already knew about the safe-deposit box keys. He was fishing. My guess was he wanted to know how much I knew before he tipped his hand.

I pulled the little envelope out of my pocket, opened it, and dumped the keys on the table. "You can tell me about these."

He picked up one of them and turned it over, studying it. "It's one of ours, all right."

"Come on, Seth." My anger flared. "Are you really going to make me play twenty questions? Prescott told me about this safe-deposit box just before he died. I had no idea about it until Saturday."

His eyes flickered. "Where did you get these keys? From Prescott?"

"Leland hid them. We found the envelope in his gun cabinet last night. Taped to the top of the drawer where he kept his cleaning tools."

"We?"

"Quinn, Eli, and me."

He steepled his fingers. "What do you want to know, Lucie?"

"Why didn't you tell me about it? Especially after Leland died. I was executrix of his estate."

"I was waiting for you to come to me and ask," he said. "Your father was adamant that no one was to know about the existence of this box unless he himself had told them."

"He was *dead*. When did you think he was going to tell me? Maybe communicate through Thelma Johnson's Ouija board? Why didn't *you* tell me?"

Seth shook his head. "His instructions were clear. I honored them. He said *no one*. After he passed—which was a shock, as I don't need to tell you—I was in a bit of a quandary. Lee was dead and I promised him I'd keep his secret. So what was I doing to do?"

He shrugged and answered his own question. "I decided to wait and see if you came forward with the keys. After about eighteen months when you didn't appear to know anything about the safe-deposit box, I had someone drill it open. Then I emptied it and removed the signature card and paperwork from the files that showed your father as the sole owner."

He sat back and folded his hands together in his lap. I wondered how many bank regulations he had violated by taking matters into his own hands.

"In other words you did what you did so none of your employees, or perhaps an auditor, would be able to find any record to prove Leland's safe-deposit box existed."

He flushed but he said in a steady voice, "That is correct. There were no other signatories on that card, Lucie. None. Only your father."

"Did you destroy the contents of the box?"

"Good God, of course not. That would have been wrong."

Unlike opening someone's safe-deposit box without notifying their next of kin.

"So obviously you know what was in that box," I said. "It wouldn't happen to be some very old bottles of Madeira, would it? Or information about where they might be located?"

"What—Madeira? Lord, no, there were no bottles of anything." He looked genuinely surprised. "As for information about their location, I couldn't say."

The Madeira itself wasn't here. What a letdown. Though I think I would have been surprised if it had been. Prescott said there were cases, not bottles. That still didn't mean Leland hadn't left information about where they were hidden.

"What was in it, then?" I asked.

"Papers. Documents, I presume."

"You presume?"

"They were in an envelope. I never opened it. It wasn't mine to open." He waved an admonishing finger at me. "Lucie, my advice to you is not to open it, either. Your father didn't tell you about that safe-deposit box for a reason. You're asking for trouble if you stir things up after all this time."

"Stir what things up?" Prescott had said nearly the same thing. "What kind of trouble?"

"I'm not joking about this. Your father—and you know what an avid historian he was—told me he came across something in his research that would have been better left undisturbed. He sat right here in my office—exactly where you're sitting now—and told me over a couple of Bourbons one afternoon. We decided it was best to lock those papers up. Put them away. I didn't realize he'd spoken to Prescott about it."

I squirmed in my chair, wishing he hadn't told me about that conversation with Leland. *Exactly where you're sitting right now.* Drinking Bourbon. That was Leland, all right.

"Why didn't he just destroy them and be done with it?"

"I don't know. I believe he intended to figure out what the best way to handle them would be." Seth held out his hands, palms up. "But he never got the chance, did he?"

"Do you know if the papers have anything to do with the Freemasons?"

Seth had been reaching for his water glass. His hand shook, spilling water on his suit jacket, giving him away. He set the glass down, pulled out his breast pocket handkerchief and dabbed at a small water spot on the sleeve of his gray pinstriped suit.

I pushed him. "I'm right, aren't I? Did my father tell you that?"

"He might have hinted at it."

"Aren't you on the board of the Miranda Foundation?"

"I'm on the board, but I'm not a Mason," he said. "What made you ask about them just now? Did Prescott say something about them?"

Seth hadn't been straight with me. I didn't need to tell him everything. "Not really. Just hinted at something."

If Seth realized I was lying, he let it go. "And now Prescott's dead, too. Murdered."

"The Sheriff's Office seems to be looking for someone who was upset that Prescott wanted to sell the *Washington Tribune*," I said. "I think Bobby believes that was probably the motive for killing him, to stop him from proceeding with the sale. And that's why they're focusing on the family. They've got the best motive, even though they're not the only ones who would be upset. A lot of people could be out of jobs."

"Then let the Sheriff's Office do its work, Lucie. And forget about this thing," Seth said in a firm voice. "I wouldn't mention anything about it to anyone, if I were you."

"I'm not really sure what 'this thing' is." I finished my water and set the glass down. "According to Prescott, there's a good chance Leland left some information about the location of several cases of Madeira that would be over two hundred years old by now and quite valuable. I'd like whatever was in that safe-deposit box, please. I'm sure there are fees involved since no one paid for renting the box or for you storing the contents these last five years."

Seth stood up. "There are no fees. I handled this matter myself. President's prerogative." He walked around to his desk and sat down in his high-backed leather chair.

He swiveled his chair around so it was blocking my view. I heard the creak of a door opening, which would be the cabinet behind his desk, and then silence. And finally the metallic sound of a latch unlocking.

"You kept everything *here*? In your private safe?" I asked.

When he swung his chair around again so he was facing

me, he was holding a large envelope, big enough to contain legal-sized papers.

"I did what your father asked me do to," he said. "The problem was that he still had the keys to the safe-deposit box and I had no way of getting them from you without betraying him."

He came back and set the envelope on the table between us. The edges were tattered and the envelope looked worn and a bit grimy. I left it where it was, but I put the keys back in the small safe-deposit box envelope, secured the Velcro flap, and slid it over to him. He didn't pick it up, either.

"How are the Masons related to the Miranda Foundation?" I asked him.

He looked surprised, but he answered readily enough. "The Masons—specifically Prescott's lodge—have been very generous in helping the Miranda Foundation with its work."

"In what way? What, exactly, do Masons do besides hold secret meetings and dress up in costumes and have secret handshakes?"

Seth's face cracked into a small smile. "I'm not a Mason so I can't tell you much, but I do know their stated purpose is this: to make good men better. They're a philanthropic group and they do a lot of charitable work, much of it behind the scenes and without fanfare. Did you know, for example, that the Masons and the Miranda Foundation recently bought three homes in Loudoun County and are in the process of renovating them with adaptive features so that they can become homes for adults with special needs? Once the construction work is done, we're going to turn them over to a nonprofit foundation that already has many established group homes."

"What a wonderful thing to do. No, I didn't know about it."

"Which is how the Masons like it," he said. "They don't broadcast what they do. And the Miranda Foundation respects that."

"I see."

"A lot of people think they're some kind of cabal out to control governments and that they have dark motives for what they do, an agenda with a world vision—and an even darker history," he said. "Which is supposed to explain why they're so secretive."

"You don't believe that?"

"The men I know who are Masons are good people. So, no, I don't believe it." He sat back in his chair again. "Tell me about those bottles of Madeira. What made you think they'd be here?"

I told him what Prescott had told me. "It was the first time I'd ever heard of them," I said. "Leland's safe-deposit box is my last hope for finding out if he left any information about where the bottles might be. According to Prescott, they would be worth a lot of money."

"Would you be willing to let me know if you find something about that wine?"

"I would." I reached for the envelope. "Thanks for this, Seth."

"Sweetheart, I'm not sure you should be thanking me. Your pa didn't ask me to keep these documents locked up for no reason. I don't feel quite right about handing them over, though I know they're legally yours."

"I can handle this," I said. "Don't worry."

He shook his head. "I do worry. And I feel like a damn Cassandra."

We locked eyes. Cassandra, the Greek goddess who had been given the gift of prophecy by her lover Apollo until she went back on her promise to do as he wished. Her punishment was the curse of never being believed even though she spoke the truth.

"I promise. I'll be *fine*," I said.

He didn't reply. But he did give me a you'll-be-sorry look.

Twelve

Prescott Avery had warned me that the secret he was on the verge of revealing was too dangerous to share; my father, who had provided him with a key clue to its existence, had gone to great lengths to make sure no one except Prescott had known about his second safe-deposit box. Plus Leland had even persuaded Seth Hannah to not only violate bank regulations but also turn a blind eye to the fact that removing my father's papers from his safe-deposit box and storing them in his private safe was just plain wrong.

Five years ago when I came home from France for Leland's funeral, it had hit me like a physical blow the first time I walked into his office at home and saw his desk strewn with papers and bills, his favorite coffee mug with the Montgomery family crest stenciled on it next to his computer, and the beautiful lapis-and-silver Montblanc fountain pen my mother had given him lying there as if he'd gotten up for a moment and intended to be right back. I found more reminders throughout the house of just how abruptly his life had been inter-rupted—a half-read biography of Robert E. Lee open on his nightstand, the remembered scent of Floris's JF, his favorite cologne, on a tweed blazer draped over a chair, a scribbled phone number on a pad next to the telephone in the kitchen for the garage in Aldie where he got his truck repaired and a price quote with five exclamation marks next to it.

He wasn't done with living. He expected to have more time.

Whatever was in this envelope was also probably only part of a story, something Leland had left for safekeeping and to which he intended to return. Seth had said as much.

But my biggest hope—and the reason I really wanted to know what it contained—was that he'd left a clue to where he'd stored the Madeira. The kind of money Prescott had been talking about could be a substantial financial cushion, something to give us breathing room in the lean years. But would opening this envelope be like opening Pandora's box?

Even if it was, I was still going to do it.

I waited until I got back to the Jeep to unwind the thread around the clasps so I could slide out the papers. A blast of arctic wind rocked the car until it shook. The sky had turned lead-colored and it felt cold and raw enough to snow, though there was none in the forecast. I started the engine, put on the heater, and pulled out the contents of the envelope.

I went through everything twice—first, quickly, and then, because I didn't understand what I was looking at, more slowly. That second time it was clear Leland had left no clues about the whereabouts of the Madeira. Nothing. Zero. *Rien. Nada.* I pounded the steering wheel in frustration. Prescott had been wrong and I'd been counting on him being right. Damn.

As to what I found, none of it made sense or seemed related to the other papers in the packet. Though there were two fragile pamphlets that were possibly of some monetary value—that was something. The first, published in London in 1625, was called *A true reportory of the wracke, and redemption of Sir Thomas Gates Knight; upon, and from the Ilands of the Bermudas . . . July 15. 1610.* The second had been published in London in 1613. It, too, appeared to be a description of a shipwreck that involved the island of Bermuda: *A Plaine Description of the Barmudas, also called Sommer Islands With the Manner of their Discoverie, anno. 1609 by the shipwrack and admirable deliverance of Sir Thomas Gates and Sir George Sommers by Silvester Jourdain.*

There were three more items. An original document, a letter written on August 23, 1814, by someone named Hobson Banks, with a return address in the St. Louis district of Middleburg, a part of town that had been an African-American community. Leland had put the letter in a page protector. The handwriting was difficult to decipher and the spelling and grammar were poor, but it was written to an unnamed woman—Dear Madam—and discussed the author's success at getting "the preschus package" safely from the President's House to a place of safekeeping located where President Madison did meet President Washington. "I am certin," he wrote, "that Pres. Jefferson wood aprove."

In the last paragraph he inquired whether she had received any news on the success of the other mission carried out by the gentlemen from New York in which his friend Paul Jennings had been of some assistance. Banks concluded by wishing her well and praying that God would protect her and the president in this terrible time of war, promising to return as soon as he was able to do so. It was signed, "Your humble servint, Hobson Banks."

By the time I finished reading, I was sure the letter had been written to Dolley Madison, First Lady and wife of President James Madison. Madison had been president during the War of 1812, fought between Britain and America, but more important, in August of 1814, the month this letter was written and as the war still raged, British troops had marched into Washington, D.C., burning not only the White House and the Capitol, but torching much of the city. Had Hobson Banks removed something from the White House—known in those days as the President's House—for safekeeping at Dolley's request? Was he the slave who had managed to flee the city before the British arrived with the Gilbert Stuart portrait of George Washington that Dolley had so famously cut out of the frame?

So what, if anything, did Hobson Banks's letter have to do with Prescott owning a copy of the Declaration of Independence that Jefferson had written out for James Madison?

I put the letter aside and examined the last two items. Both were grainy photocopies of newspaper photos, one dated 1938, and the second 1992. I looked at the newer photo of three men and a young woman standing around what looked like an archeological excavation site. One of the men was Prescott Avery; the two others were members of the Colonial Williamsburg Foundation. The young woman, who appeared to be in her early twenties, was identified as Josephine Wilde, a doctoral student in geology at The College of William & Mary and a researcher at the Jamestown Settlement.

Small world—it was the same Josie Wilde I wanted to talk to and ask if we could hire her to help us with our grapes.

The caption under the photo read:

An archeological excavation undertaken by the Colonial Williamsburg Foundation in conjunction with Historic Jamestowne in November has reached the conclusion that "Francis Bacon's Vault" is not and was never located in the area excavated at the northwest quadrant of Bruton Parish Church. This excavation lays to rest— permanently—centuries of speculation about its existence.

The 1938 photo showed four men standing around what was apparently the same location.

Church officials at Bruton Parish in Colonial Williamsburg have recently uncovered the foundation for the first brick church built on this site, which was completed in 1683. With an influx of students from The College of William & Mary (founded in 1693), and the relocation of the Virginia capital from Jamestown to Williamsburg after a fire destroyed much of the settlement in 1699, a new church, which is the present-day church, was built in 1715.

Two of the four men identified in the photo were from Bruton Parish Church; the third was a member of the Rockefeller

Foundation, which had provided the funding to restore Colonial Williamsburg. The fourth man was Jock Avery, Prescott's father. Very small world.

Why would two generations of Averys be present at two different excavations more than fifty years apart on the grounds of Bruton Parish? I'd been a student at William & Mary a dozen years ago and I'd never heard of "Francis Bacon's Vault"—probably because, according to the 1992 story, it never existed.

And what of this "shipwrack" in 1609 that led to the discovery of Bermuda? I pulled out my phone and did a quick search, landing on someone's blog page.

In 1609 a flotilla of ships set out from Plymouth, England, for Jamestown, Virginia, to bring more settlers and needed supplies to the new English colony. During a storm at sea, the flagship Sea Venture, *a brand-new ship on its maiden voyage, was blown off course. Because it was leaking badly, the captain deliberately wrecked it on the island of Bermuda where the approximately 150 survivors spent nine months building two smaller ships with local wood and remnants from the wreckage. After setting sail almost a year after their arrival in Bermuda, the new ships, named* Patience *and* Deliverance, *arrived in Jamestown only to discover that most of the settlers from the other ships had died. This dark period in Jamestown's history became known as the Starving Time. It is widely believed that the story of the* Sea Venture's *wreck on Bermuda was the basis for William Shakespeare's play* The Tempest.

I sat back, my mind reeling. Shakespeare's play *The Tempest,* Bruton Parish Church in Williamsburg, the Jamestown Settlement, and James Madison were somehow all related to whatever my father and Prescott were searching for. *Something dangerous.* Two-hundred-year-old Madeira—that James Madison was to have drunk—was also part of this puzzle, according to Prescott. And there was a chance that it all had something to do with a secret society.

I had no idea what Leland and Prescott were looking for. No clue how to put this puzzle together.

But it intrigued me and I meant to try.

A CAR PULLED UP next to me and the driver, a woman, pointed a finger at my car and raised her eyebrows, the universal gesture for *are you leaving this parking place anytime soon or are you just going to sit there and text?* I was so rattled after what I'd just read that I nodded, indicated I was leaving, and angled out of my spot. She zipped in behind me as I pulled out.

I was driving in the wrong direction, away from home, but I kept going. By the time I turned left onto Highway 15, known as James Madison's Highway—an irony that wasn't lost on me—I knew I was heading for Leesburg. It was the county seat for Loudoun County, a town with colonial roots, older than Middleburg by thirty years. It was also where the Declaration of Independence and the Constitution had been sent for safekeeping during the War of 1812. Had Presidents Washington and Madison met somewhere in Leesburg? I didn't know, but it was definitely possible.

Right now, though, I had a different destination in mind: Union Cemetery, where I planned to visit Miranda Avery's grave and to see where Prescott Avery would soon be buried.

Were Miranda's death thirty years ago and Prescott's murder two days ago related? I didn't think so, at least not right now, but it seemed to me there was some link connecting the two of them. I just couldn't figure out what it was.

The Avery family had its own gated memorial in the middle of what was a historic burial ground that had been established in the mid eighteen hundreds a few years before the Civil War. Although anyone might have thought differently, its name—*Union* Cemetery—didn't imply that it was a burial site for Union soldiers. Instead the name came from the united decision of a group of local churches to create a cemetery open to all denominations and faiths on land that, in those days, was on the far outskirts of Leesburg. Now the town had grown up around it.

It was a peaceful, pretty place surrounded by pre–Civil War trees and lanes that wound past rows and rows of weathered granite gravestones. A Confederate War Memorial, where Confederate and Union flags were set out on Memorial Day and Veterans Day, stood at one end. A thirty-foot-tall granite column, which had been designed for a public building in Washington, D.C., had been installed in the 1890s after the builders rejected it when they discovered that it was imperfectly cut. A few years later, a sweet little sandstone chapel was also built on the cemetery grounds.

The Avery obelisk, one of the tallest with a distinctive Celtic cross on top, wasn't difficult to find. I drove through the main entrance and immediately saw it on a bluff practically in the middle of the cemetery. Jock Avery, it was said, had used the Italian stonemasons who worked on his home to carve the four-sided obelisk's intricate design and the cross. The family name, which had been embellished with gold, glittered in the bleached-out light on this blustery December afternoon.

The wrought-iron gate to the Avery graveyard unlatched with a complaining creak and I let myself inside. At least half a dozen headstones surrounded the obelisk and there was space for more members of the family when their time came. I found Tommy's and Miranda's markers next to their mother's and wondered if Prescott would be laid to rest beside Rose or whether he and Rose had decided they would be on either side of their beloved children. So far it looked as if there were no plans to prepare for Prescott's casket to be interred here. But if it snowed and the ground froze, the family would have to wait anyway. Plus the Loudoun County Sheriff's Office still had to release Prescott's body. The funeral would take place after that.

The unpolished gray granite headstone of Prescott and Rose's son Tommy was poignant in its stark simplicity. Underneath his name and dates of birth and death, was one word: BELOVED. My mother had told me his parents' grief had known no bounds; it had nearly destroyed Prescott. Tommy had been young, handsome, carefree, the anointed heir, but also a reckless daredevil. Clayton had never been able to fill the void left by his tragic death. How soul-destroying could it be to realize that, whatever he did, Clay could never be as good, as smart, as popular, as *beloved* as his half-brother in the eyes of his stepfather?

Not only that, Prescott didn't like Victoria, Clayton's

almost-fiancée, and he had most likely been about to sell the newspaper Clay had sacrificed his own career to run, once again demonstrating to his family and the world that Prescott himself still ran the show. For Clayton that final decision to publicly undermine him must have been humiliating. Was it possible he'd been so angry he confronted Prescott downstairs in the wine cellar on Saturday and . . . ?

The wind buffeted me again and I moved from Tommy's marker to Rose's and Miranda's headstones, which were also simple unpolished granite stones. On Rose's, the newest and least worn, was written: I WOULD NOT WISH ANY COMPANION IN THE WORLD BUT YOU. And on Miranda's was poetry: WE ARE SUCH STUFF AS DREAMS ARE MADE ON AND OUR LITTLE LIFE IS ROUNDED WITH A SLEEP.

I pulled out my phone and turned my back to the wind, looking up both epitaphs. Shakespeare. *The Tempest.*

Again. What was it about that play that Prescott Avery had chosen lines from it to eulogize his wife and daughter? It had also been important to my father, who had locked up copies of two diaries from survivors of the shipwrecked *Sea Venture* in a safe-deposit box—supposedly the play had been based on their stories.

I was done here; I'd found what I'd come for. Quick prayers for Rose, Miranda, and Tommy and then I headed back to the Jeep. A few flakes of snow swirled down from the flat, white sky, melting as they landed on the tops of headstones. The weather report hadn't mentioned snow. I started the engine and my phone rang. A number flashed on the display with *Clayton Avery* above it. An electric current went through me as if I'd been caught taking something that wasn't mine. Clay couldn't possibly know I was parked in front of his mother's and half-brother's and sister's graves at Union Cemetery.

Could he?

I answered the call, hoping I sounded perfectly normal.

"Lucie, Clay Avery. Hope I didn't catch you in the middle of something."

I let out a relieved breath. "No, not at all. I'm over in Leesburg finishing up an errand."

"Great, as long as you're out—and you'd practically be driving by here anyway if you're heading home from Leesburg—I wanted to ask if you would stop by the house. There's something we need to discuss. It's rather urgent."

I knew where this was going. First, I wouldn't "practically" be driving by Hawthorne Castle. Second, Clay wanted to talk about my conversation with Prescott just before he died. We didn't need to discuss it; he wanted me to tell him what had gone on.

"What's this about, Clay?"

"Let's save it for when we meet," he said, brushing off the question. "How about in half an hour? Could you be here then? Come by for a drink or coffee."

"I . . . sure."

"Great," he said. "See you soon."

I had already told Bobby about my conversation with Prescott over a glass of Madeira in his wine cellar just before he died. But that was after it was determined he hadn't died of natural causes as everyone had assumed.

Telling Clayton was a different matter. For one thing, he was high on Bobby's list of suspects, fitting the bill perfectly with motive, means, and opportunity. And killing Prescott in plain sight of more than a hundred party guests, meaning there were so many potential suspects, had been a brilliant, if cruel, move. *If* Clayton had done it.

Maybe he hadn't. What if he, like Prescott, wanted to buy Leland's cache of 1809 Madeira and that's why he wanted me to stop by? Too bad I was no nearer to knowing where those bottles were today than I had been on Saturday.

I called Quinn as I put on my signal for Mosby's Highway at the roundabout where it met Highway 15 and told him I was stopping by Hawthorne and why. Quinn was still out in the vineyard trying to figure out what to do about the diseased Merlot vines.

He sounded preoccupied. "Don't worry about when you get home. Persia already made dinner. All we have to do is heat it up."

"What's for dinner?"

"You even have to ask?" he said. "Turkey casserole."

Comfort food. Again. After this day, I'd welcome it.

"Sounds good to me," I said. "See you soon."

But first I had a meeting—a command performance, actually—with Clayton Avery, who was very likely on the top of Bobby's suspect list for the murder of his stepfather, Prescott Avery.

Thirteen

I wasn't expecting to see the black ribbon twined through the wrought-iron gates at the entrance to Hawthorne Castle and wondered who had been responsible for that poignant detail. Somehow I guessed it might be Bianca. Alex and Scotty would be busy at the *Trib* and Victoria would be with Clay, probably organizing the wake and funeral.

A tan-and-gold Loudoun County Sheriff's Office cruiser sat in the driveway in front of the gates, blocking my way. I stopped and the deputy got out of his car and came over. I rolled down the window, gave him my name when he asked, and told him I was expected. He went back to his car and a moment later, backed out of the way so I could pass by.

The Averys' elderly housekeeper opened the door when I rang the bell. She gave me the ghost of a smile and invited me in. The sadness in her eyes spoke volumes: that Prescott's death was as hard for her as if she'd lost a member of her own family, not just her employer.

"Mr. Clayton is expecting you," she said, taking my coat. "He's in the library."

"I know where it is," I said. "Thank you."

Prescott had always been Mr. Avery to the staff at Hawthorne. Even after he was gone, Clayton was still Mr. Clayton. Somehow I reckoned he'd change that pretty soon.

The big house was eerily silent, as though still getting used to the loss of its owner. End-of-day light through the windows of the rooms on each side of the hallway cast long pale streaks that reminded me of icicles on the oak floors and Persian carpets. The library was at the back of the Castle, its windows looking out on the terraced gardens and the fairy tale–like glass orangerie where the family had hosted so many parties and celebrations over the years.

Clayton stood in front of a fireplace, his profile limned by the flickering light of a cheerful blaze, a drink glass in one hand and the other resting against the mantel like he needed it to prop him up. He seemed unaware that I was standing in the doorway, so I knocked on the doorjamb and he started before turning around.

"Lucie." He looked like hell. Not grief-stricken, but anguished. Exhausted. "Thanks for coming by. Can I get you a drink? I was just about to refresh mine. What would you like? We've got everything, including wine, if you prefer."

"No drink, but I'll take a glass of water, thanks."

The antique wooden bar cart was across the room and the only surface without a vase of flowers sitting on it because it was already crowded with crystal decanters and bottles of alcohol.

Clay held up his glass, stared at it, and shrugged. "Okay,

if you're sure. Come in. Have a seat." He gestured to a burnt-orange chesterfield sofa on one side of the fireplace. "Sparkling or still?"

"Sparkling, please. The flowers are lovely, Clay," I said. "So many tributes. Have you been able to make any arrangements?"

I didn't want to say *yet*.

He put ice in a glass and opened a bottle of sparkling water. "No." He filled the glass and brought it over to me. "The Sheriff's Office still hasn't released the . . . Prescott. I hope they do it soon. We need closure."

"Hunt's Funeral Home is taking care of everything?"

He nodded. "The wake will be at Hunt's and the funeral will be at National Cathedral in D.C. The interment will be in our family plot in Union Cemetery."

The Averys had always gone to Trinity Episcopal Church in Upperville. Prescott had been a member of the church's vestry, the lay governing board, and Clay and Scotty had served as lectors over the years.

Clay poured himself a hefty serving of what looked like Scotch out of a crystal decanter and sat down in a leather club chair across from me.

"Why did you choose National Cathedral, rather than Trinity, if you don't mind me asking?" I said.

Clay looked astonished. "Are you kidding me? Prescott chose it. He planned his entire funeral, everything from the hymns and the readings to the eulogists. I'm surprised he didn't write them himself and hand them out. The only person he asked from the family was his granddaughter, Kellie. The others are friends, business colleagues. Apparently he called them all up and got their commitments." He drank his Scotch. "Of course he always had to be in control. Of everything."

His bitterness was palpable. I sipped my water and nodded. This might be more than Clay's second Scotch of the day and it seemed to be darkening his mood. He swirled the ice cubes in his glass and the noise sounded like breaking glass. We were done with small talk. He was going to get down to brass tacks, ask me about my conversation with Prescott.

Find out what I knew.

He crossed one leg over the other and our eyes met. "It's a hell of a situation," he said. "Murder."

I hadn't expected him to be quite that direct.

"Any idea who did it?" I asked.

"Oh, come on, Lucie. You know as well as I do I'm the number-one suspect, followed by Scotty and Alex." His voice was filled with scorn and anger. "Not necessarily in that order."

"Did you do it?"

He shot right back at me. "Do you think I did?"

Did I? I hesitated and he pounced.

"You think I killed him? Really?"

"No, I . . ."

"Why don't you tell me what the two of you were doing downstairs in his wine cellar on Saturday?" Harsh. Still angry.

Here it was. Maybe we could trade information. Maybe he knew something about what Prescott planned to reveal to his Masonic lodge before the Miranda Foundation's gala in two weeks. The answer to the secret, the whereabouts of the lost treasure he and Leland had been searching for.

I also could have said, "None of your damn business."

"Well?" he said.

"If you asked me to come by because you needed someone to vent your anger on, you should have told me, Clay. I could have saved us both some trouble." I stood up. "I'll see myself out."

He looked stunned, then penitent. "Lucie, I'm sorry. I'm just under so much stress right now. Please don't take it personally and please don't go. Please. Have a seat. And I'd really like to know what you and Prescott talked about on Saturday."

I sat. "According to Prescott, my family owns several cases of Madeira that date back to 1809," I said. "Prescott tried to buy them from my father, who wouldn't sell, and apparently Jock tried to buy them from my great-uncle, who also wanted to keep them. So Prescott asked me if I'd sell them to him."

"And what did you say?"

"I told him I had no idea what he was talking about. I never heard of any Madeira."

"How much did he offer you?"

"He told me to name my price."

Clay groaned. "Look, Lucie, even if you do find that wine, the deal is off, okay? Why did Prescott want those bottles? I mean, why now?"

"He wanted to drink them as a toast at a special party for his Masonic brothers the night of the gala."

"What special party?"

When I hesitated again, he said, "Come on, Lucie. What special party?"

"He . . . found something, or was on the verge of finding something, that he wanted to celebrate that night. Something . . . significant. He said it was a 'dangerous' secret."

Clayton looked like he wanted to throw his glass across the room. "Jesus. Not again."

"What do you mean?"

"My stepfather may have been one of the most astute businessmen I ever met, plus he understood the newspaper business like no one else, but he chased after every damn unicorn that came down the road."

Unicorn. The same word Prescott had used. A mythological creature that didn't exist.

Clay got up and walked over to the bar cart. For a moment I thought he was going to top off his Scotch again. Instead he came back to his chair and sat down, elbows on his knees, leaning toward me like he was going to let me in on a secret.

"Look," he said.

Whenever someone started a sentence with "look" and used that tone of voice, I've learned that what comes next is going to be an explanation they need you to believe, a con, or a lie.

I waited.

"Prescott had an almost childlike fascination with finding things that were supposed to be unfindable. Things that might not even exist. He loved the chase, the hunt. The more elusive the better. Money was no object."

The thrill of the hunt. Prescott had said *that* to me as well. Once he found what he'd been seeking, possessing it was almost anticlimactic.

"You mean, like Leland's Madeira?" I asked.

"Not exactly. Did he ever tell you about our so-called ancestor?" Clayton set his glass on a side table and used his fingers to make quotation marks. "Henry Every, the pirate?"

I thought of the Jolly Roger flag I'd seen in the corridor as I was leaving Prescott's wine cellar the other day. "No," I said.

"Henry was one of our less illustrious ancestors—Every, Avery, you just had to change the *E* to an *A*—who also happened to be the richest pirate who ever lived. He pillaged and plundered in the Atlantic and Indian Oceans in the late 1600s and dabbled in the slave trade as well. In his day he was known as the 'King of Pirates,'" Clay said. "His ship was called the *Fancy*. Great name, isn't it?"

He didn't wait for my answer, nor did he seem to need one. "What made him so famous—or infamous—was that Every pulled off the biggest pirate heist in history, attacking a fleet of ships from India on their way to the annual pilgrimage in Mecca," he went on. "The stories of how he and his men tortured their victims and raped the women before they killed them would make your skin crawl, Lucie. When it was over, there was a price on Every's head—everyone in the world wanted to find him—and he disappeared. Forever. Word was that he was hiding out somewhere in the Atlantic colonies, maybe the Caribbean islands or maybe even Virginia. And he took his share of the treasure with him."

Clay sat back in his chair, eyes hooded, watching my reaction to his macabre tale. My heart thumped against my chest. Now I understood why Prescott owned the red Jolly Roger flag that hung on the wall next to his wine cellar. It was from a pirate ship that had plundered a century later, but one that showed no mercy for its victims, just like his ancestor Henry Every had done.

"What happened to the treasure?" I asked, although I could guess what he was going to say.

"Some people believe it's still out there somewhere. Prescott was one of them," he said in a grim voice. "Do you have any idea how much money he spent tracking down historians, descendants of Henry, traveling to England and Africa and India and all the places Henry supposedly lived to see if he could figure out where that treasure might be?"

"I'm guessing the answer is a lot."

"Damn right, a lot. Too much." He picked up his glass and stared into it before drinking. When he looked up he said, "Would you care for some more water?"

"No, thanks."

"I think I'll have another Scotch." He got up and went over to the bar cart.

It was none of my business to dissuade him, so I didn't. But before he got too much further in his cups I said, "I suspect you must have realized that Prescott showed me the copy of the Declaration of Independence he'd just bought on Saturday."

He turned around. "I noticed you looking at the bookcase while we were downstairs together in the wine cellar. So I figured you'd been in his Masonic sanctum sanctorum. It's a privilege, Lucie. Not many people get the honor." I couldn't tell if he was being serious or sarcastic. "And then when I saw the Declaration and all the other items he'd bought, James and Dolley Madison's letters, that slave's memoir . . ." He shrugged. "Well, what of it?"

"There seemed to be something about those items that was especially important to him," I said. "I had a feeling it was relevant to whatever he was going to share with his Masonic brothers the night of the gala."

Clay gave a short laugh. "And you think he confided in me?"

"Did he?"

"Of course not. The only thing he told me right before everyone arrived for the feijoada was that he was going to sell the *Tribune* and half a dozen other papers that he said were in trouble."

"You had no idea before that?"

"No." He returned to his chair.

"That must have been rough."

He gave me a look filled with irony and anger.

"I'm sorry," I said.

"We argued, of course. He told me right here in this room." He glanced over at the fireplace and I could just imagine the two of them, voices raised, shouting at each other. "I said if we needed money for the family business, he should sell some of the acquisitions he and my mother had made over the years and we could use the money to shore up the *Trib*. He was wrong to give up on our family's flagship newspaper."

"And?"

"He said 'absolutely not' to selling any of the art or sculptures because everything was going to be sold on behalf of his and my mother's charities once he died, most of it to benefit the Miranda Foundation. He and my mother had already signed the Caritas Commitment along with so many other billionaires." He paused and added, "But as I reminded him, it was only a pledge, not a binding legal commitment. It wasn't like he'd set up an irrevocable trust. Though even those can be undone if you have a smart enough lawyer."

"In other words, now that he's gone you don't have to go

through with the Caritas Commitment, even though he and Rose signed the pledge?"

"Not according to my lawyers." There was a gleam in his eyes—satisfaction? triumph?—before they narrowed. "However it does complicate matters as far as Bobby Noland's concerned. I'm sure you can guess why."

"It gives you a motive for murder?"

"The best," he said, with a grim smile. "So now that you know that piece of information, tell me. Do you think I killed him?"

A shiver went down my spine. Was he teasing or dead serious?

"You mean, do I believe I'm sitting here by myself in a room with a murderer?"

"That's another way of putting it."

I said, "No," in a faint voice that didn't convince either of us.

"Lucie," he said, "I didn't do it."

"Who did?"

"I don't know. But it wasn't Scotty or Alex, either. I'd bet my life on that."

"An angry Tribbie?"

"Perhaps. Whoever it was, that person was a friend. A guest at our party. Someone we invited into our home. That's pretty hard to stomach," he said. "And speaking of guests, can I just point out that you were the last person to see Prescott?"

I said in an even voice, "The person who killed him was the last person to see him. What motive would I possibly have?"

"I don't know," he said. "You tell me."

"None at all."

"It's not pleasant being accused of something you didn't do, is it?" he said. "Especially when we're talking about murder."

"Point taken."

"Prescott and I didn't always see eye to eye, but I respected him. And I didn't kill him." Clay stirred in his chair and glanced out the window. My gaze followed him.

The orangerie was outlined in white fairy lights that had winked on sometime during our conversation. They reflected off the glass against the dark periwinkle sky and made the little building look even more like an enchanted cottage in the midst of the woods.

"I'm talking too much and it's getting dark," he said. "I should let you get home. I hope you understand about the Madeira, Lucie. I really can't keep the deal Prescott made with you."

"It's not a problem, because I don't have the Madeira. Though I wish I did," I said. "Can I ask *you* something now?"

"I suppose so."

"Why was Prescott so fascinated with Shakespeare's play *The Tempest*?"

He looked stunned. "How the hell did you know about that?"

"Your half-sister was named Miranda. The copy of the painting in his wine cellar was from the play—and Prescott only owned originals." I took a deep breath. "Also the epitaphs on your mother's and Miranda's gravestones are lines from the play."

"Jesus," he said, bristling. "You've been doing some digging, Lucie. What's going on here?"

It didn't sound like a compliment. "Can you tell me why he was so interested in the play?"

"I already did," he said, still annoyed. "Prescott thought he was goddamned Prospero. The exiled Duke of Milan, living on an island with Miranda, his beautiful daughter, and a library of books that were all about magic. His damned cane was his magic wand. And like Prospero, he believed he had the power to control all things, to make people do his bidding. He *believed* in magic and believed he possessed magical abilities."

I was pushing my luck, but I asked anyway. "What about the historical basis for the play, the wreck of the *Sea Venture* when it was on its way to Jamestown? That was very real."

Clay gave me an impatient look. "Of course it was real, and of course that intrigued him. He went to Bermuda and Jamestown and donated a pile of money to the Jamestown archeological project to do research on the *Sea Venture* and what happened during the year those people spent in Bermuda. That's why you'll find Bermuda coral at the Jamestown Settlement today. Plus Jock was good friends with Henry and Emily Folger when they were in the process of getting their library built on Capitol Hill back in the 1920s. Jock donated money and helped with getting building permits, which were a nightmare since Henry had been sneaky in buying up lots two blocks behind the Capitol and directly behind the Jefferson Building of the Library of Congress. Prescott kept up the family relationship with the library—the Folger Library, I mean—plus he was on their board. As a result he had carte blanche to do as much original source research about the history of that play as he wanted."

"So part of his interest relates to the *Sea Venture* and Jamestown," I said.

"He was also a huge collector of anything to do with Shakespeare." Another shrug. "He owns three copies of the First Folio. Paid a king's ransom for them."

"I didn't know that."

"They're supposed to be given to the Folger Library now that he's dead," Clay said.

"That's very generous."

Clay stood up. A not-too-subtle cue that we were done.

I stood as well. "I should go."

"I'll see you out."

"No need," I said. "I know the way. Clay, if there's anything my family can do . . ."

"There is."

I waited.

"Lucie, I don't know what you think you're doing or what you're looking for, but you should drop it. There's no *there* there. Prescott could sell ice to Eskimos; he was such a charmer and he apparently has you believing a crazy-ass story about a fantastic discovery he was gonna make, some deep dark secret he was on the verge of uncovering—a lost treasure. Forget it, okay?" He twirled his finger next to his ear. "Prescott had been losing his grasp on reality for a while now, but you couldn't talk to him about it without a huge blowup. Whatever he told you, I'm sure he believed it, but the truth is, it's all a fantasy. Save yourself some grief. And me, too, okay?"

I said okay and he seemed relieved.

"What do you mean by 'and me, too'?" I asked.

"I told you. I've already been talking to our lawyers," he said. "I'm sorry Prescott's gone, but at least he didn't get to go through with his plan to sell everything out from under us, especially the *Tribune*. I'm sure we can make a case for him being not entirely of sound mind before he died. It'll make it easier to make changes in promises and commitments that the family can no longer afford to keep."

He was talking about the Caritas Commitment.

"I see," I said.

I left him standing by the fire with his drink, just as I'd found him half an hour ago. Whatever Clay said just now, I didn't doubt the veracity of what Prescott had told me on Saturday. I believed him for the simple reason that my father had been searching for the same thing Prescott was and Clay didn't know that. Even though Leland was known for chasing rainbows and throwing his money away on lost causes, there was something different about this time.

Now all I needed to do was figure out what the two of them were searching for.

Because I thought it was real.

Fourteen

High beams momentarily blinded me as a car swung around a corner of the private road that led from Mosby's Highway to Hawthorne Castle. The driver had been barreling down the middle of the gravel-and-dirt road like he or she owned it. I swerved hard and ended up on the rutted shoulder, slamming on my brakes to avoid plowing into a stand of hollies and white pines.

In my rearview mirror, I saw brake lights followed by taillights as the other car backed up until it was alongside the Jeep. A window powered down, so I lowered mine. Scotty Avery wore a stricken expression as he recognized me and apparently realized how near he had been to causing a head-on collision.

"Lucie, I'm so sorry. I wasn't expecting anyone to be coming down from the big house and I'm late, so I was in a rush to get home. My head is somewhere else lately, but that's no excuse."

"It's okay," I said, though I was shaken by what had almost happened. "No harm done."

Relief flooded his face. "Thank God. Need some help getting unstuck?"

"No, thanks. The Jeep drives like a tank. I'll be fine."

"That's good." He gave me a curious look. "What brings you here?"

"Your father asked me to drop by."

"Ah."

His profile was faintly illuminated by the lights from the console of his gold Lexus SUV. Just like his father, the strain of the last two days appeared to be getting to him and he looked exhausted. If I'd met him a few seconds earlier as he roared around that curve, he knew just as I did that one of us would probably be calling 911 now instead of having this conversation. If we were lucky.

"Everything okay with you and Pop?" he asked. I could hear the thrum of tension in his voice.

He wasn't going to ask directly, but he wanted to know why Clayton had summoned me to Hawthorne Castle. There was no reason not to tell him at least part of the truth.

"He wanted to know what your grandfather and I talked about when he invited me down to his wine cellar the day of the party," I said. "I told him that he asked if I'd sell him some wine. Unfortunately we no longer have it."

"Oh." He seemed relieved it was something as innocuous as buying wine. I wasn't about to get into the rest of it.

"How are you doing, Scott? I know you and Bianca and the kids must be going through hell right now."

His face cracked into an are-you-kidding-me ironic smile.

"Nico went back to Brown yesterday, we figured it was best for him to try to get back to normal, but Kellie's in tough shape. I probably don't need to tell you that Alex, Dad, and I are in the crosshairs of the Loudoun County Sheriff's Office's investigation. They think one of us killed my grandfather." He shook his head as if he were trying to clear his mind or wake up from a bad dream. "Plus apparently someone overheard Alex and me arguing on Saturday. I said some things I didn't really mean."

I was glad he didn't know it was Quinn who'd stumbled onto their argument. He had said it sounded vicious. On both sides.

"Don't worry," I said. "Bobby will get to the bottom of it. He knows how to sort out the difference between the truth and someone blowing off steam."

"Let's hope so." He didn't sound optimistic.

"Do you have any idea who did it?" I asked. "I'm still stunned."

"Me, too," he said. "As for who did it? Nope, not a clue. I can tell you it wasn't me. My grandfather and my father didn't get along, but Pop isn't capable of murdering anybody. I'm sure of that."

I brought up the obvious omission. "What about Alex?"

He blew out a breath. "Alex. Jeez, I don't know. She's hot tempered and fickle, and you'd have to be living in a cave not to know she and I don't get along. We only talk on an as-needed basis."

Apparently Prescott's murder didn't qualify as an as-needed basis for a conversation. Plus he hadn't answered my question nor said he didn't think his sister was a murderer.

"That's got to be tough, working together every day," I said.

"It wasn't my idea." His voice hardened. "I didn't get a say in that decision. Grandpop figured it would be easier to keep her in line if she was back here rather than up in New York. After her third marriage fell apart, she decided to start shopping around a tell-all memoir. She said she nearly had an agent lined up, plus she was sweet-talking some publisher." He shook his head in disgust. "With Alex that's code for she's sleeping with him."

"I heard about the memoir," I said.

"Are you kidding me? *Everybody* heard about it. And I'm not just talking about the Romeos and their morning kaffee-klatsch at the General Store. There was a piece about her in the goddamn *Post*. Of course they were only too happy to run a story about a scandal involving the Averys. You probably saw the piece. After Alex finished dragging her husbands through the mud, she was going to start on our family and all of our supposed hidden secrets about how we acquired our money and the newspapers."

I had read the gossipy story in the *Post*, but Scotty wasn't finished venting his anger. "She made us sound like a bunch of thugs. Mafiosi. It sent Grandpop into orbit. Hence the order to come home. He said there was nothing dishonest about the way the Averys had earned their money and there was no story to tell."

He stopped talking and shook his head as if he was remembering an ugly family scene.

"I'm sorry."

His laughter held no mirth. "You and me both. You know

what's ironic? No one—none of us, Pop, Alex, my kids—is an Avery by blood. Grandpop adopted my father after Grandma Rose married him and Pop changed his last name to Avery," he said. "So this whole thing is just insane."

"Was Alex angry with your grandfather because he made her come back to Virginia?"

Scotty raised an eyebrow. In the washed-out light, he suddenly looked disdainful as if he were pulling up the figurative drawbridge to Hawthorne Castle and the Avery family. "Are you asking if she was angry enough to kill him? Come on, Lucie, you probably know more than I do. You were the last one to see my grandfather alive."

I wasn't sure if he was trying to provoke me or make a not-so-subtle accusation.

"Second to last." I kept my voice even. Hadn't I just said the same thing to Clay?

Scotty stiffened. "There may be no love lost between Alex and me, but I'm not going to trash my sister. Frankly, we'd be more likely to kill each other, especially when we get going about something." He paused. "You know what? Forget I said that. I'm just running my mouth. I didn't mean anything by it."

"Of course."

He revved his car's engine, the noise menacing in the tomb-like night silence. I jumped.

"Sorry, accidentally hit the gas pedal," he said. "And I'd better get home. I'll wait until you're back on the road and make sure you're on your way."

"Thanks, but I'll be fine," I said. "Good luck, Scott."

He nodded without replying and powered up his window. He was upset and I'd hit a nerve, pressing him about his sister. I reversed the Jeep until I was off the shoulder, stuck my hand out the window, waved, and tooted my horn. He honked back and a moment later his taillights disappeared in a spray of gravel.

By the time I got to the turnoff for Mosby's Highway, I wasn't sure what to make of that disquieting whipsaw conversation. I had just spoken to two of the three people Bobby Noland most suspected in the murder of Prescott Avery. Both claimed they didn't do it, but if they had, neither one of them would have confessed their crime to me.

Then there was Alex. Scotty had defended her in a muted way, but he never said outright he was certain she wasn't guilty of murder.

Which still left the question: did Alexandra Avery kill her grandfather on Saturday afternoon under the noses of one hundred people who were upstairs eating and drinking at her family's annual post-Thanksgiving party? Scotty had said she was hot tempered and mercurial and that she and Prescott had argued over her returning to Virginia.

Adding up all of those things, it seemed to me they would move her straight to the top of the list of suspects.

I wondered if Bobby Noland had already reached the same conclusion.

I WAS IN THE middle of putting Persia's turkey casserole in the oven to warm it up when Quinn got home.

He kissed me and said, "Sounds like you had a hell of a day. How did it go with Seth . . . and Clayton? Red or white?"

My meeting at the bank with Seth Hannah seemed as if

it happened weeks ago instead of just this morning. "White. Chardonnay, please."

He walked over to the wine refrigerator, opened it, and started pulling out bottles and scanning labels. "Virginia Chard okay?"

"Great."

He came back with a bottle from Slater Run Vineyards, our down-the-street neighbor. I fixed a salad and made a lemon and olive oil dressing while he warmed up Persia's homemade biscuits.

I told him everything while we ate, starting with my talk with Seth and the documents he'd given me and ending with Clay summoning me to Hawthorne and my unsettling talk with Scotty. Quinn didn't say a word while I spoke. When I was finished the only sounds in the room were the steady tick-tock of the antique pendulum wall clock and the occasional hiss of the gas heat coming through the floor vents.

The under-cabinet rope lights lit the perimeter of the kitchen, giving it a dreamy look against the black void of the windows. My mother's antique silver candelabra and her Waterford candleholders from our Thanksgiving table were still on the table from last night, though the green-, gold-, and rust-colored candles had now nearly burned down to nubs. Their flickering, dwindling light made the room feel as comforting as if we were protected in a cocoon. Added to that was the effect of a couple of glasses of Chardonnay and the lingering warmth and smells from the oven, and I had the disconnected feeling that I had been telling Quinn a story that happened to someone else.

He covered my hands with his. "I hope Bobby finds out

who killed Prescott soon and this ends," he said. "Clay seemed nervous about what you might know and it sounds like Scotty wouldn't let Alex off the hook as a possible suspect for the murder of her grandfather."

"Un-hunh."

He squeezed my hands. "Hey. You're not listening to me. I know that 'un-hunh.' Your mind is a million miles away."

"I am listening. But I'm also thinking about what Prescott said about the mystery he planned to reveal at the Masons meeting before the Miranda Foundation gala. And that it might have something to do with the documents Leland kept in his safe-deposit box."

Quinn withdrew his hands and folded them together, leaning in from across the table. "I think you might want to give Clay a little credit, sweetheart. That he's right about Prescott chasing unicorns or pirate treasure or rainbows. And your father—with all due respect—was notorious for doing the same thing."

"I know," I said, "but this feels different."

"Because?"

"I'm not sure yet."

He sat back, lips pursed together, an expression I knew well. If he opened his mouth, he'd regret whatever flew out, especially if he hadn't thought it through first.

"I'd like to find out what they were looking for, what was so important," I said. "I thought we could start with doing some research to find out more about the documents in Leland's safe-deposit box."

"We?"

"Yes, we. Will you help me? Please?"

"Lucie, Seth and Clay told you to forget about this, and Prescott said whatever he was looking for was dangerous. Even if there is a *there* there."

"How will we know if there's a there there if we don't look?" I said. "And it can't be dangerous because no one knows that Prescott told me anything. Nor does anyone know about Leland's documents. Seth said he never opened that envelope and looked at what was inside."

Quinn worried on his lower lip with his teeth and shook his head as if he wanted to say no. Instead he said, "I don't know about this, sweetheart."

"What harm would there be in doing some internet research? If it's a dead end, we'll stop."

He stared at me for a long time. Finally he said, "What kind of internet research?"

I smiled. He was in.

"First I want to find out what 'Francis Bacon's Vault' is. In four years at William & Mary, I never heard anything about it. Plus Josie Wilde was at the second excavation in the Bruton Parish Church graveyard where people from the Colonial Williamsburg Foundation and someone from the church said the vault never existed. I was going to call her anyway. Now I can ask her about it."

He grunted in agreement and said, "Do you think your father thought this vault existed?"

"I don't know. Maybe. Prescott and Jock must have thought there was something to it for both of them to be present at excavations that were more than fifty years apart. Each looking for the same thing."

Quinn got up and started clearing away our dishes. "This is beginning to sound like looking for pirate treasure."

"Maybe. People do find pirate treasure, you know."

He turned around from the sink and faced me. "You're excited about this. Aren't you?"

"Intrigued. Curious." I stood up and blew out the guttering candles.

"Plus I know how much you love all the Indiana Jones movies."

I made a face at him and said in my haughtiest tone, "Indy was looking for *real* things."

"Yeah, the Holy Grail and the Ark of the Covenant. Which he, of course, found. Both of them."

"You can be such a wet blanket sometimes, you know?"

He threw the dish towel at me. I caught it before it hit its intended target. "I like to think I'm the voice of reason," he said. "It's a good thing we're not telling anyone about this. They'd think we were nuts."

It was a good thing he didn't know what I'd learned from Clayton earlier today: that Prescott had fancied himself a real-life Prospero, the magician from *The Tempest*, believing he had special powers to persuade people to do what he wanted.

I ignored what Quinn had just said about us being nuts and plowed ahead. "Okay, you can look into the letter Hobson Banks wrote Dolley Madison. I think we ought to go on the assumption that the letter in Leland's safe deposit box was the missing puzzle piece that convinced Prescott there was more to find. He said a letter Leland showed him helped him put the whole thing together."

"What whole thing?"

"A lost treasure that has to do with Thomas Jefferson, James Madison, and the Declaration of Independence. And apparently the Jamestown Settlement and Williamsburg are involved in some way. And maybe Shakespeare."

"Must be a hell of a treasure."

He stacked our plates in the dishwasher while I covered what was left of the casserole and put it in the refrigerator.

"Maybe it is," I said.

"I hope you're not going to get too wrapped up in this. It could just be a pig in a poke."

"You still don't believe me."

"It's not you, sweetheart. I'm not sure I believe *them*. Prescott and Leland."

"Well, I do."

He threw up his hands. "Why?"

"Because Leland went to a lot of trouble to hide those documents," I said. "And he got Seth Hannah to go along with him. Plus I don't believe Clay that Prescott was as off his rocker as Clay implied. He was pretty sharp, if you ask me."

"What makes you say that?"

"Clay needs to be able to convince his lawyers that Prescott was starting to lose it," I said. "That he wasn't competent enough mentally to make financial commitments. And he was spending money recklessly. So he's got to make anything Prescott said or did sound loony or off the wall. He's looking at trying to get out of the Caritas Commitment and he doesn't want to sell the *Trib*."

"Okay," Quinn said. "Let's suppose Prescott's right and so was Leland. Now what?"

"I'll see what I can find on Francis Bacon's Vault and you look into the Banks letter. Also someone named Paul Jennings. Banks mentioned Jennings in his letter and Prescott owned a copy of Jennings's memoirs. He was a slave who worked at the White House."

"I suppose you want to do this tonight," he said.

I smiled. "You suppose right."

QUINN GOT HIS LAPTOP from his backpack and poured the last of the dinner wine into our glasses, which we carried into the library. He threw himself onto the sofa, stuffed a throw pillow behind his head, and opened the laptop. I sat across the room at my father's antique partner desk and powered up the desktop computer.

For a while there was no sound but the quiet clicking of computer keys as we searched for answers. Half an hour later, Quinn found what he was looking for, but I felt like Alice who had fallen down the rabbit hole, getting deeper and deeper into secrets, lies, conspiracies, and plots to control the government. At the heart of it, or at least where everything seemed to begin, was Sir Francis Bacon, the English polymath who was a philosopher, scientist, statesman, and author living from the late 1500s to the mid 1600s. He was also a prominent Freemason and a prolific writer.

When I told Quinn, it was going to vindicate his conviction that we were chasing unicorns or looking for the Holy Grail, just like Indiana Jones. I sat back from the computer and my chair creaked. He looked up over the top of his reading glasses.

"What'd you find?" he asked.

"You go first. My story is a bit convoluted."

"Mine isn't much better," he said. "I didn't find anything about Hobson Banks, unfortunately. But, as you said, Paul Jennings was a White House slave who worked for James and Dolley Madison. He wrote his memoir in—wait a minute." He scrolled on his laptop and began reading. "He wrote his memoir, *A Colored Man's Reminiscences of James Madison,* which was published in 1865. By then he'd bought his freedom from Daniel Webster. His real fame came when he was fifteen because he helped Dolley get the eight-foot-tall Gilbert Stuart portrait of George Washington out of the White House before the British burned the place during the War of 1812."

Earlier I had shown Quinn the contents of Leland's envelope, which now lay spread out all over the desk. I picked up the sheet protector containing the letter from Hobson Banks.

"Banks apparently got something out of the White House as well," I said. "He writes about his 'preschus package.' I wonder what it was. Maybe he was the one who took the Declaration of Independence and the Constitution and brought them to Leesburg. They were moved, too, you know, the summer the British burned Washington."

"Nope." Quinn shook his head. "It wasn't him. Hang on."

He clicked a few more times. "The entry about the War of 1812 on the U.S. history website I found says those two documents were stored at the State Department. Clerks bundled them up, shoved them in a book bag, and one of them brought them to Leesburg for safekeeping."

Today the Declaration of Independence and the Constitution were enshrined at the National Archives in specially built glass cases to provide maximum security and guards who would come running, guns pointed at you, if anyone so much as breathed too heavily on the glass. The light in the Rotunda, where they were kept along with the Bill of Rights was so dim you could barely read what was written, but necessary to preserve the pale, faded ink and keep it from vanishing forever from the paper. I tried to imagine both documents being shoved in someone's satchel, slung over a shoulder, and brought to Leesburg, probably on horseback.

I frowned at Quinn. "If it wasn't the Constitution and the Declaration of Independence, what did Hobson Banks carry with him that was so precious?"

"Besides the Gilbert Stuart painting that she gave to two men from New York to take with them after Jennings and the others cut it out of the frame, Dolley also managed to get some of the White House silver out. It also says she removed 'some documents' but not what they were. Maybe Banks took those things—the silver and the documents," he said. "If he did, none of it ever found its way back to the White House."

I couldn't keep the excitement out of my voice. "That's it. That's got to be what Prescott found. Where Banks hid his precious package."

"Do you think Prescott left notes or maybe something on a computer about where it is?"

I couldn't tell if he was being sarcastic or serious.

"If he did, I'll never have a chance to look around his sanctum sanctorum to find out. Definitely not now with the three Averys under suspicion of murder."

"You could tell Clay about it. He might try to have a look."

"Sure, and I could tell him the Tooth Fairy visited me last

night. He'd believe that, too. Clay made certain today that I knew he wouldn't buy Leland's Madeira—presuming we ever found it—and he's not about to get involved in whatever Prescott was looking for. He'd probably think it was just another wild goose chase."

"Point taken." Quinn shoved his reading glasses up so they were on top of his head. "Your turn. What did you find?"

Here it was. Wait 'til he heard what I'd turned up.

"Francis Bacon's Vault—if it really existed—is actually more commonly known as Bruton Vault because it is supposedly located in the graveyard of Bruton Parish Church in Williamsburg. It's the oldest church in Virginia and it's still an actual functioning church, not part of Colonial Williamsburg. My college roommate used to go to services there."

He nodded, impatient. "What's in the vault?"

"Not so fast. There's more to the story before what's in it ended up in Williamsburg." *Before I get to the things you're going to think are completely off the wall.*

He let out a noisy sigh, making sure I knew he wasn't happy.

"I'm telling this my way," I said. "In the proper order."

"All right, do it your way. Knock yourself out."

I made a face at him. "*Supposedly,*" I said emphasizing the word, "a man named Henry Blount, who was a relative of Sir Francis Bacon, brought certain documents from England to the Jamestown Settlement in 1653. Or it could have been 1635. Either way, the cache of documents was kept secret and when Blount got to Virginia he buried them under the Jamestown church. He also changed his name to Nathaniel Bacon. Later he became known as Nathaniel Bacon the Elder."

"Because his son was Nathaniel Bacon the Younger?"

"Not exactly. The younger Nathaniel Bacon was his nephew, not his son, and he was called Nathaniel Bacon the Rebel. The rebellious Bacon burned Jamestown to the ground in 1676."

"Not a nice guy. Do I need to write this down?"

"No, and don't be snippy."

"I'm never snippy. Want a cognac?"

"I'd love a cognac."

He got up and went into the dining room where we kept a collection of liquors and spirits. When he returned, he handed me my snifter and I held it in my hands to warm the alcohol.

"I'm sorry. I'm giving you a hard time," he said.

"It's okay," I said. "But the story gets even more complicated."

"You mean the plot thickens?"

"More like turns to mud."

He sat down on the couch and propped his sock feet up on the coffee table. "So what happened?"

"At some point the documents are moved to Williamsburg," I said. "It could have been because the James River was going to flood and it probably had something to do with plans to move the capital of Virginia from Jamestown to Williamsburg. Other Vault-believers say Bacon's Rebellion was a cover to move the documents out of Jamestown. Whatever the real reason was, no one disputes that they were moved to a large vault built under the tower of the first Bruton Parish Church in Williamsburg."

"There's more than one church?"

"They rebuilt it, and when they did, they moved it. Not

far—just a few yards away. It's still on Duke of Gloucester Street, the main street in Williamsburg."

Quinn sipped his cognac. "So what, exactly, are these secret documents?"

"This is the muddy part."

"Why am I not surprised?"

I turned back to the computer screen for a moment. "No one is exactly sure, but supposedly there is a complete copy of a novel written by Sir Francis Bacon called *New Atlantis*. Also several manuscripts of Shakespeare's plays—except they're in Bacon's handwriting. In other words, they're proof that Sir Francis Bacon—not Shakespeare—wrote Shakespeare." I looked up at him. My heart was pounding in my chest. What if this were true?

"What else?" he said. "You have a funny look on your face."

I hesitated. "I also came across some pretty wacky theories about what else might be in that vault."

"I'm all ears."

He was going to look at me as if I'd grown another head when I told him. "Supposedly there might be secret codes and documents, including a formula for alchemy—turning lead to gold—and that anyone who is able to decipher the documents will have superhuman vision that will allow them to enter the presence of the Superior Gods. Whoever they are."

"If you say so." He looked as if he was trying not to laugh.

"I know," I said. "It sounds nuts, doesn't it?"

He grinned. "Sounds like the kind of thing your father would be looking for. Or the plot of another Indiana Jones movie."

It did.

"The most reasonable—and consistent—theories by people who believe the vault existed claim it definitely contained a copy of *New Atlantis* as well as manuscripts proving Bacon was the author of several of Shakespeare's plays," I said. "Bacon died before *New Atlantis* was published and the novel was never finished, or at least that's what everyone thought. Supposedly, though, he *did* finish it and the vault contains the only copy in existence."

"Why is that such a big deal?"

"Because Bacon describes a Utopia that's actually a blueprint for America. It's the organizational plans for our government, along with instructions for the type of democracy he thought the United States should become. It also happens to be taken directly from the beliefs and ideals of the Freemasons."

"If that's true, then the conspiracy theories about the Masons secretly plotting to control the American government when it was first established are correct, right? And that Francis Bacon was not only behind the plans for setting it up, but the plan for our government was masterminded in England?"

"I guess so," I said. "If it is true, I can see why, as a Freemason, Prescott would be so interested in locating those documents. Leland, too—although his interest would be more for historical reasons."

"And if Shakespeare didn't write Shakespeare," Quinn said, "that would be a bombshell. Those documents would be worth a fortune."

"Wouldn't they?" I nodded. "At least now I understand what Prescott told me."

"What's that?"

"That there are people who don't want these documents ever to be discovered."

"*If* they exist." Quinn still wasn't convinced. "Look at those newspaper articles you showed me proving the Bruton Vault didn't exist."

"Or maybe it *did*," I said. "And someone moved the contents. Again. Just like they were moved from Jamestown to Williamsburg."

"Move them where?"

"To the White House."

"That's crazy."

"I know," I said. "But it would explain what Prescott said about Leland's letter—the Banks letter—giving him an important clue in solving the mystery of where the lost treasure might be."

"True." He still sounded dubious, but at least his interest had perked up. "So these documents—if they exist—aren't in the White House anymore, either."

"That's right. They're not because Hobson Banks removed them on Dolley Madison's instructions. And Prescott had a pretty good idea where they went." I paused and added, "Which he was going to reveal, until someone murdered him."

Fifteen

For the life of me I couldn't figure out what Hobson Banks meant in his letter when he wrote that his "preshus package" was safely hidden away in a place where George Washington and James Madison had met. And that Thomas Jefferson would approve. All three Founding Fathers were Virginians: their estates—Mount Vernon, Montpelier, and Monticello—were now museums. Jefferson and Madison had been neighbors in the Charlottesville area; Washington's home was south of Alexandria overlooking the Potomac River.

So where had Washington and Madison met? At one of their homes? It was probably simpler to figure out where they *hadn't* met. Around here, if you said, "George Washington slept here" it was almost certainly true. Before he began his political and military career, Washington had been a land surveyor in this area and traveled extensively throughout the region.

Quinn had already gone upstairs to bed and I'd promised

him I would join him shortly. But I knew I wouldn't sleep until I did some more internet searching to quiet my racing mind. As a Virginian, my knowledge of those three Founding Fathers was fairly decent—in school we studied Virginia history for a year—but nothing that would make me a *Jeopardy* champion. I also realized I didn't know enough about the relationships they had with each other, something that might provide a clue to where Banks could have hidden his White House package.

What I discovered was that James Madison, author of the Constitution and "Father of the Bill of Rights," had been a close personal advisor to George Washington and that Washington had relied heavily on him because Madison knew more about the Constitution than anyone else. Madison was also close to Thomas Jefferson, helping to get him named as secretary of state during Washington's presidency and serving as Jefferson's campaign manager when he ran for, and won, the presidential election of 1800.

Maybe in return for Madison's help and friendship, Thomas Jefferson had presented him with a handwritten copy of the Declaration of Independence since Madison had neither been present at the Continental Congress in Philadelphia during the summer of 1776 when it was drafted, nor had he signed it. And now Prescott Avery—or his estate—owned that previously unknown piece of history, which I suspected had cost Prescott a small fortune.

What all this meant was that Hobson Banks's documents and the White House silver could be anywhere, though I was reasonably certain he had hidden everything somewhere in Virginia. It seemed likely he had fled D.C., crossing the Potomac River and looking for a safe hiding place in this area, just as the Declaration of Independence and the Constitution had been brought to Leesburg, probably at roughly the same time. Why nothing that Banks had taken with him had ever been returned to the White House was another mystery, unless something had happened to him and his secret died with him.

. If that were true, it was a very good hiding place indeed not to have been discovered for more than two centuries.

So how in the world did I think I was going to find it?

The grandfather clock in the foyer chimed midnight. Quinn had gone to bed more than an hour ago. I shut down the computer and went upstairs, undressing in the dark so I wouldn't wake him and slipping into bed, cuddling up to the warmth of his body.

By the time the grandfather clock chimed one, he rolled over and murmured, "You're so restless. You really ought to try to get some sleep."

"I will," I said. "I'm sorry I woke you."

"C'mere." He pulled me into his arms and kissed me. I kissed him back and before long we were making love, tangled around each other in the sheets. By the second time all my thoughts about centuries-old secrets, plots to control the government, and murder had vanished and all I could think about was what he was doing to me and how much I loved him.

Finally I slept.

I SENT JOSEPHINE WILDE an email while Quinn was making us an omelet for breakfast the next morning and asked if

I might be in touch concerning the possibility of her taking us on as clients. I told her briefly about the problem with our diseased Merlot vines.

My phone dinged that I had email just as we finished cleaning up. I clicked on the mail app and opened it.

"That was fast. Josephine Wilde wrote back," I said.

"What did she say?" Quinn asked.

I held up my phone. Two words. *Call me* and a phone number.

"At least she didn't turn us down," I said.

"Give the lady a call," he said, "before she changes her mind."

I sat down at the kitchen table, tapped on her number, and hit call.

Josie Wilde had a Southern drawl that sounded as if it had been dragged through gravel. She was also no-nonsense and down-to-earth.

"Tell me about your Merlot," she said, so I did.

When I was done she said, "What is it you want from me?"

"Honestly?" I said. "For you to take us on as clients. Not just because of the problem we're having with the Merlot, but because we know you've helped a lot of other vineyards in the area and we've been impressed with your results."

Quinn poked me in the ribs because I'd said that *we* had been impressed. He pointed at me and mouthed *you*. I flapped my hand to shush him and stuck my finger in my ear so I could concentrate on what Josie was saying about the kind of commitment she expected from her clients.

"You're either all in or you're not," she said. "And y'all have got to agree to do what I tell you to do."

"Absolutely. No problem."

"And you've got to mean it," she said with emphasis. "That's the hard part. I usually don't take on anyone before we've had a chance to sit down and meet face-to-face. That usually happens here in Charlottesville in my laboratory. I'm leaving for Jamestown and Williamsburg for a few days, so maybe we could get together after that."

"Of course," I said. "Whatever works for you. We'll be there. Just say when."

Quinn made another face at me so I stuck out my tongue at him and turned away.

"Can I ask you something else?" I said. "It's not about our vineyard."

She hesitated, but then she said, "What is it?"

"Do you remember being in Williamsburg twenty-five years ago at an excavation in the Bruton Parish Church cemetery? You were attempting to determine whether a certain vault existed or not."

"Whoa." She sounded stunned. "Where in the world did you find out about that? It's ancient history."

"I came across a newspaper photograph taken at the site that day. You were there along with some people from the Colonial Williamsburg Foundation and Bruton Parish Church. Also a man named Prescott Avery."

"Prescott Avery," she said in a wondering voice. "He was found murdered in his home the other day."

"That's right."

"I read that his family are all suspects."

"I've read that as well."

"Did you know Prescott?"

"Yes," I said.

"Obviously well enough to know he was interested in whether the Bruton Vault existed," she said. "Just like his father."

"The Averys are neighbors. I also know about Jock being present at the other excavation."

"Is that so?" She still sounded amazed. "I'm curious how you came across that photograph and how you know about the Averys' interest in it."

"It's kind of a complicated story."

"I'm not surprised. It's kind of a complicated vault. Does Prescott have anything to do with your interest in this?"

"He does . . . did."

"I'd be interested in hearing your story," she said. "And I have an idea. What if we meet in Williamsburg instead of Charlottesville? I could show you the excavation site at Bruton Parish and you could tell me what Prescott Avery was up to, still looking for that vault."

"When and where?" I said.

"Tomorrow," she said. "Could you be there by ten-thirty?"

"We could. You also said you're going to be in Jamestown?"

There was another pregnant pause.

"I see," she said. "I'm guessing you want the whole story about the vault, or rather its supposed contents. Not just whether anyone uncovered anything in Williamsburg. Am I correct?"

"It would be helpful," I said. "Do you believe the vault existed?"

"I'm a scientist," she said. "I *know* there was no vault on the site we excavated. Before I got interested in studying grape growing and winemaking, I got my undergraduate and graduate degrees in geology. My interest at that time was in studying soil and mapping groundwater development in Colonial Virginia—specifically the Jamestown Settlement—and that was also the subject of my dissertation."

"How did you go from geology to being interested in making wine and growing grapes?" I asked.

I could hear her shrug through the phone. "Simple," she said, her drawl stretching the word into two long syllables. "Twelve years after the Jamestown Colony was founded, the Virginia House of Burgesses passed a law that required every adult male to plant and care for at least ten grapevines. You got in a heap of trouble if you didn't. The Founding Fathers—especially Washington and Jefferson—were desperate to produce American wines that could compete with the Europeans. Having an American wine industry was a big deal."

"I remember reading about that."

"Every winemaker in Virginia ought to know that story by heart," she said and it sounded like an admonishment. "Personally I've been a fan of Virginia wine—a believer—since the very beginning. Since Jamestown. Long before the Californians even thought about making wine."

I grinned. It was an old rivalry. We were first. They were biggest and best known. David and Goliath.

"Why don't we meet in Jamestown?" Josie was saying. "Not the Jamestown Settlement, but Historic Jamestowne. You know the difference, right? Historic Jamestowne is the excavation site on the river. Then we can drive back to Williamsburg and stop by Bruton Parish. Ten-thirty still work for you?"

"Ten-thirty sounds great," I said. "Thank you for doing this."

"You're welcome," she said. "And just so we're clear, I'll answer what questions I can, but I have a few things to ask you, too. Sounds like Prescott wouldn't let this go, even after the Bruton Parish excavation didn't turn up any evidence of a hidden vault."

She hung up and I remembered what she'd said. Unconditional obedience to follow orders if she took us on as clients. It sounded as if it applied to answering her questions about Prescott and the Bruton Vault as well.

I wasn't sure how I felt about that.

QUINN AND I DROVE over to the winery together after I told him about my call with Josie Wilde and the plan for us to drive to Jamestown and Williamsburg tomorrow morning.

I thought he'd balk since he wasn't totally on board with hiring her and ceding control of the vineyard. Instead he said, "I read about Jamestown in American history class in high school in California, all the usual stuff about Pocahontas, the Indian princess who saved the life of Captain John Smith, but I've never been there. Or Williamsburg, either. I'm looking forward to this."

"It won't take us long to get there, under two hours—it's only about a hundred miles or so," I said. "We can leave after breakfast."

Quinn parked the Jeep behind the barrel room where we had a few parking places marked STAFF ONLY and said, "Another exciting day of barrel cleaning and sterilizing for me."

I smiled. A lot of people have the misbegotten idea that owning a vineyard involves wandering around all day with a glass of wine in your hand benevolently supervising your workers happily toil in the fields and watching the grapes ripen on their own until they reach perfection thanks to nature's bounties and God's wondrous handiwork.

If only.

The reality is that it's not that glamorous and much of the work is backbreaking with a lot of heavy lifting and plenty of tedium. There's also endless cleaning, sterilizing, and sanitizing. Bacteria and contamination are the two biggest enemies in winemaking, so we clean and sterilize each piece of equipment every single time it's used. I don't mean at the end of the day, either. I mean every time we switch tanks or need to reuse a barrel.

We're also constantly inventing on-the-spot fixes for things that break or, in my case, since I don't have the upper body strength of Quinn or any of the men, finding easier ways to move heavy equipment or wine barrels—most of which seem to involve clever uses for our forklift and the pallets on which we store cases of finished wine. As for fixing the smaller stuff, you'd be surprised the wonders you can work with hair ties and duct tape. I'm particularly proud of figuring out a way to use bike pulleys to open the vacuum-sealed stainless steel tank lids so you didn't need superhero strength. Even the guys used it now.

"What's your plan?" Quinn asked.

"Persia left a shopping list on the telephone table in the foyer, just a couple of things, so I'll stop by the General Store and pick up what she needs," I said. "First I want to talk to Frankie about the 'Home for Christmas' party and all the other events we've got planned up until Christmas. I also haven't seen the Villa since she decorated it. I'll bet it looks amazing."

"Who is she going to get to be Santa Claus?" Quinn asked as we got out of the Jeep. "Noah Seeley?"

For the last few years, Noah, who owned Seely's Garden Center, had been the town's Santa Claus for Christmas in Middleburg after taking over from B. J. Hunt, who owned the funeral home. The first time Noah went to B. J. for help figuring out how to put on his Santa outfit, he said B. J. made him lie down on a table because he was more used to dressing people when they were in a horizontal position.

It was as good a time as any to ask Quinn. "Actually," I said, "she was hoping you'd be Santa. She asked me to ask you if you'd do it."

"Me?"

"Yes. You. Come on, be a good sport. You look good in red."

"I'll look like a furry tomato in that getup. What about Eli?"

"He's playing the piano for the caroling evening and he's already agreed to dress up. Knowing him and what a ham he is, he'll be an elf or one of Santa's helpers. Maybe even one of the reindeer."

Quinn shook his head and I could tell he was trying to imagine Eli dressed up as Rudolph. "I don't think so—"

"Oh, come on." I twined my hands through his. "*Please?*"

He hesitated. "Well, I guess I could—"

I kissed him on the mouth, silencing the rest of his words. "You're an angel. Thanks so much. You'll be great and the kids are going to love you. I'd better get over to the Villa and tell Frankie that you said yes. Talk to you later."

"Think about it," he called after me. "That's what I was going to say. I guess I could think about it."

I feigned deafness. "Frankie's got the suit. I'll bring it home tonight."

FRANKIE HAD MADE THE wreath hanging on the front door using grapevines from the vineyard and decorating it with the little silver bell and the ornaments she had borrowed from my mother's collection the other day. She'd also woven narrow red and green ribbons through the vines like lattice, added a hand-lettered sign that read HOME FOR THE HOLIDAYS, and finished it with a big loopy red satin bow.

The bell on the wreath tinkled as I opened the door; inside the Villa smelled of cinnamon, cloves, and nutmeg—the spices of mulled wine—mingled with the scent of fresh greenery. The room looked as homey and welcoming as it always did at this time of year, as if I'd arrived to stay with friends for the holidays and someone was going to appear and offer to whisk away my suitcase to a bedroom. Instead, Frankie looked up from behind the bar where she was busy working on something—probably more decorations—when she heard the door close. She smiled and I knew she was waiting for my reaction.

When Eli, Mia, and I were growing up my mother had impressed on the three of us that the true meaning of Christmas was not about material things or the gifts we received, but what we gave back. It was also about intangible qualities like kindness, friendship, generosity, a giving heart, and a helping hand. She'd explained that it wasn't always "the most wonderful time of the year" or a picture-postcard Hallmark movie for a lot of folks whose loneliness, hardship, and losses were especially hard to bear during the holidays. As a result we were expected to help with her many charities, whether it was collecting used winter coats for the people who slept in the street, gifts and books for children in the homeless shelter in Leesburg, or canned goods for the food pantry in Aldie—and then delivering them to their destinations.

But my most enduring memory of my mother at Christmas was how she seemed to effortlessly make our home and the winery into gathering places for friends and strangers, filled with laughter and music and happiness. I found out later that what had motivated her was her own loneliness after moving to Virginia when she married Leland, how homesick she had been for her home and family in France. Now that I was running the winery, I wanted these things, too—especially because the world seemed a harsher, more troubled, and angrier place than I remembered from my sepia-tinted childhood memories.

Fortunately, Frankie loved Christmas as much as I did and every year she threw herself into decorating the winery in a way that reminded me of the special touches my mother used to add. She had already placed red and green holiday-themed quilts and throw pillows on the sofas. A collection of nutcrackers—the three kings, drummer boys, toy soldiers—

sat on the fireplace mantel. More grapevines, sprayed with
gold and silver, were woven around the bases of the nutcrackers as if they were standing in an enchanted forest. On the
bar hurricane lamps filled with gold and silver pinecones had
chubby white candles set on top of them. Two halved wine
barrels at either end of the bar contained miniature Christmas
trees; one decorated with red bows, white lights, and silver
pinecones, the other with vintage tin baking molds, cranberry garland, and more white lights. Wine bottles painted
red, the necks wrapped in raffia, were each decorated with a
letter that spelled the word *joy*.

"It's gorgeous, Frankie," I said. "Every year you work your
magic and this place always looks so festive and Christmassy.
Just like my mother used to do."

"A high compliment. I'm glad you like it. You know me, I
love doing it and I plan for this for months."

I joined her at the bar, shedding my coat, unwinding my
scarf, and sliding onto one of the high bar stools. "What are
you making?"

"Christmas stockings," she said, "since your family is
growing in size this year. Quinn, Sasha, Zach . . . I thought
everyone needed a stocking."

I was flabbergasted. "How thoughtful."

She held up what she was working on. Quinn's, obviously,
since she was cross-stitching California poppies and bunches
of red and green grapes onto a cream-colored background.

"What do you think?" she asked.

"I think you're incredibly talented. Quinn's going to love
it. Thank you so much."

"I've already finished Sasha's and Zach's. I thought everyone could hang them when we decorate the tree. Don't tell them, though. They're meant to be a surprise."

I made a motion of zipping my lips and she grinned. "Once the trees and the garland are delivered after you and Quinn choose everything tonight at Seely's, we can finish decorating the rest of the place," she said. "We've already got a lot of reservations for the tree-decorating party and the caroling evening next week. If this keeps up we'll have to start a waiting list."

"I hope we don't. It would be nice to have a big crowd here," I said. "That's how it should be at Christmas."

"I know." She laid the stocking on the bar, securing the needle in the fabric and putting her embroidery floss in a quilted pouch. "Do you suppose Quinn would object to having decorations in the barrel room this year? The guys wearing reindeer antlers don't exactly count. I know it's his domain, but I was thinking one night we could serve mulled wine and cider down there and he could talk about this year's harvest. It would be nice to have the place look a bit festive."

"My mother always decorated the barrel room at Christmas," I said. "Nothing elaborate, but it was lovely. I remember red candles in hurricane lamps and a wreath she made out of wine corks and red berries that hung over the archway to the room where we keep the reds. She also wove ropes of white fairy lights and pine garlands around the wine barrels. And there was always a tree."

"I didn't know that."

"After she died, we didn't do anything that first year she was gone—she had always been in charge of Christmas and Leland didn't have the heart for it. For some reason, we stopped putting up any decorations down there altogether. I don't know why, but we—I—haven't done anything Christmassy ever since. Probably because Quinn's so utilitarian and he likes his workspace pristine and ship-shape."

Frankie's eyes softened. "Don't you think it might be a good idea to restart that tradition? It's your winery now. I bet your mother would really like it. She'd approve, Lucie. It's time."

I knew she was right. It *was* time.

"Okay," I said. "I'll tell Quinn. This year we decorate the barrel room."

"Great." She looked pleased. "Do you have any idea what happened to the old decorations? I've never come across a wreath like the one you described."

"It's been so long I don't remember," I said.

"Well, I can always make another one. Though it would be a shame not to have something your mother made. If it still exists."

"I'll take a look," I said. "Those things must be in boxes somewhere unless someone accidentally tossed them when we expanded the offices and renovated the barrel room a few years ago. In the meantime, I'll tell Quinn you're going to be fixing up the place a bit for the holidays. It's taking some time, but I'm getting him used to the idea that we do Christmas in a big way here."

Frankie grinned and came around from behind the bar. "I don't suppose you asked him about being Santa at the party?"

"You suppose wrong. I did ask him."

"What did he say?"

"Yes. Sort of."

She walked over to the fireplace and stood with her back to the crackling fire, hands behind her to warm them up. "Sort of?"

"He'll do it. Don't worry."

"Great. How did you manage to persuade him, if you don't mind my asking?"

"I didn't actually ask him. I sort of told him."

She grinned again. "Wish I'd been there."

The little bell on the wreath sounded as someone opened and closed the front door. Bianca Avery, glamorous in a black leather jacket, cherry-red cashmere pashmina knotted around her neck, and black stiletto-heeled boots over skinny jeans, stood in the doorway looking hesitant.

"I know you're not open, but I saw your cars in the parking lot so I thought it would be okay if I stopped by," she said in her soft accented voice. "I wanted to talk to you about Kellie."

"Come on in," Frankie said. "It's warmer here by the fire. Join us."

"Is Kellie all right?" I asked. "Is something wrong?"

Bianca crossed the room, pulling her long, dark hair out from underneath her scarf so it fell against one shoulder. Years ago when she was a teenager she had moved to the U.S. from Brazil to work for one of the top New York modeling agencies after being discovered while waitressing in a bar. Though she'd left modeling after she married Scotty and came to Virginia, she still moved with a self-awareness and grace that turned heads whenever she entered a room. Today, as always, she looked more like Kellie's sister than her mother, with one noticeable difference: the anxiety in her eyes and the dark circles underneath them had aged her. She looked around at the Christmas decorations as if she were in a daze and ignored my questions.

Frankie and I exchanged glances. Maybe Bianca was on tranquilizers, something to calm her nerves and help her cope with the news firestorm surrounding her family. She took a seat on one of the couches and Frankie and I sat across from her.

"Would you like something to drink? Coffee? Tea?" Frankie asked.

I was glad she didn't offer Bianca a glass of wine. Ten A.M. was too early to start day drinking. Especially if you needed the drink. Bianca looked as if she did.

"A glass of water would be great," she said.

I started to rise and Frankie said, "Sit tight, I'll get it."

She got a bottle of water from the refrigerator and a glass from behind the bar and set them on the coffee table in front of Bianca.

"Are you going to be okay?" Frankie asked.

Bianca started to nod as if a puppeteer were pulling a string to make her reply yes, and then shook her head. She stared at the bottle and glass without doing anything. Instead she reached for one of the throw pillows, white snowflakes needlepointed onto a bright red background, and wrapped her arms around it, hugging it to her.

"I came to talk to you about Kellie," she said. Though she'd spent most of her life in the U.S., the lyrical cadence of her Brazilian-accented Portuguese still came through when she spoke English and she softened her daughter's name to "Kayley."

"So you said," I replied. "Is something wrong?"

"She's going to need another couple of days before she's

ready to come back to work," Bianca said. "I hope that won't
be a problem. She would have told you herself, but she's not
up to facing anyone at the moment."

Bianca had been the parent who worried about Kellie's near
meltdown at Harvard, her desire to take a year off from the
pressure of Ivy League academics and the burden of what was
expected of her as the next generation of the Avery dynasty.
Still the fierce mother, a lioness protecting her cub whatever
was required, Bianca wasn't making excuses for her daughter.
She was laying down the law. *Back off. Give her time.*

"Tell her to take all the time she needs," Frankie said. "We
miss her—everyone loves her here—but believe me, we all
understand what she's going through. It's tough."

Bianca gave her a tight-lipped smile. "Thank you."

"I saw Scotty last night," I said. "He mentioned that Nico
went back to Brown, but he did say Kellie's having a hard
time dealing with what happened. I know she and Prescott
were close."

Bianca's eyes flashed surprise. Scotty obviously hadn't told
his wife we'd met. "That's right. The news stories about our
family are upsetting her terribly. I'm worried about her." As
if it were an afterthought she added, "Scott forgot to tell me
where you two saw each other, Lucie."

"Your father-in-law asked me to stop by the Castle. Scott
and I ran into each other as I was driving back to Mosby's
Highway."

No point telling her it had almost been a real collision.

"I see," she said. "I hope everything was all right with Clayton when you spoke to him. He's devastated about what happened to Prescott, just as Scott is. And then everyone in the

family being a suspect in his death. It's been a nightmare for all of us." She looked as if she were on the verge of tears.

"I know," I said. "I'm so sorry."

"The Sheriff's Office will get to the bottom of what happened soon," Frankie said. "They'll find out who really did it."

"There were over a hundred people at your party," I said. "That's a lot of suspects."

Bianca nodded and reached for the water bottle. Her hand shook as she started to fill her glass. Water sloshed on the needlepointed pillow.

"Look what I've done . . . I'm so sorry."

"It's only water," Frankie said. "Don't give it another thought."

Bianca moved the pillow to one side and picked up the glass with both hands, taking a long, deep drink.

"I don't know how this is going to end," she said, resting the glass on her lap, "but Scott didn't do it. He didn't kill Prescott. I know him. He just *didn't*."

"Do you have any idea who did?" I asked. "It had to be someone who knew their way around Hawthorne and was able to slip away from the party and find Prescott in his wine cellar."

"Plenty of people know their way around Hawthorne," she said. "It's also possible someone came in through the door on that lower level so it might not have been a guest who was at the party. I was in the orangerie that morning to pick a couple of oranges off the trees we have out there. You ate them with your feijoada. The door was already unlocked, so I left it that way."

"Who would use that entrance?" I asked.

She shrugged. "Anyone who wanted to be discreet or didn't want to be seen. The staff. Victoria. She still sneaks a cigarette every now and then, though she promised Clay she was going to quit. She slips out and smokes there. You can smell it. And my sister-in-law. She was in and out on Saturday, too."

Frankie frowned. "Your sister-in-law? You mean Alex?"

"No, not her. Celia. Celia Avery. Tommy's wife . . . widow. She's still very much part of the family after all these years. After Tommy was killed, Prescott named her CEO of the Miranda Foundation. She's also on the board of directors of Avery Communications. Prescott thought of her as another daughter after they lost Miranda."

Frankie's face cleared. "I forgot about Celia."

Bianca arched an eyebrow. "She's organizing the Miranda Foundation gala in two weeks so she stops by all the time to talk to Prescott. The Goose Creek Inn is catering the dinner. I've seen Celia and your cousin, Lucie, together a couple of times in the orangerie making plans."

"Was Celia at the party on Saturday?" I asked.

"Briefly," Bianca said. "Prescott told her she was expected at the board meeting on Sunday. I overheard them arguing. There was a rumor he was planning to replace her as CEO of the Miranda Foundation. She must have found out. She sounded really angry, so she left, slamming doors. I heard her car speeding down the driveway right after that."

"So she's another person who was upset with Prescott," Frankie said. "Wouldn't that make her a suspect as well?"

Bianca nodded. "Although she's not the only one who argued with him just before the party. He and Clay had words. Prescott objected to him wanting to marry Victoria. Told him she was only after his money." She paused and added, "Which she is."

"You don't like her, either?" I said. "Obviously."

"She's a troublemaker." Bianca flipped her long hair over her shoulder, an impatient, angry gesture. "Ever since she moved in, she's caused nothing but heartache in our family."

"I'm sure Bobby is looking at everyone who has motives," Frankie said.

"Even if Scott does have a motive, he *didn't do it,* Frankie. And that's what's upsetting Kellie. Bobby seems to be focusing on him."

"Why?" I asked.

Bianca stood up and walked over to the fireplace, holding her hands near the blaze for warmth, her back to us. She turned around and said, "I don't know."

She did know.

"Is it because he argued with Alex at the party?" I asked.

"He said some things he didn't mean. Taken out of context they sound bad."

"Whoever killed Prescott may not have wanted to do it," I said. "It might have been something that happened in the heat of the moment, a discussion that got out of hand. An accident because someone lost their temper."

Bianca gave me a weary look. "It's still involuntary manslaughter. Either way, you go to jail. If you want to know who I think did it, I'd bet it was Alex."

"Why her?" Frankie asked.

"She's the one with the temper. Everyone knows that." Her mouth twisted. "Plus she wasn't happy to be dragged home from New York. Or maybe it was Grant."

The conversation had strayed a long way from Bianca telling us Kellie needed a few days off from work. Now she was spilling family secrets to Frankie and me. I wondered why.

"Wait a minute. You mean Grant Lowry? The *Trib*'s managing editor? Why him?" I asked.

"I think he believed that with Clayton gone, he'd be able to exert more influence over the paper," Bianca said. "Except Prescott kept sticking his nose in and bigfooting Grant. He didn't like it and he wasn't shy about saying so and pushing back."

Nothing Bianca had said just now had exonerated any of Bobby's three principal suspects: Clay, Scott, or Alex. Not only that, but she seemed to have purposely added Victoria, Grant, and Celia Avery to the list.

She picked up her jacket and scarf. "I'd better go," she said, slipping on the jacket. "Thanks for the water and for understanding about Kellie. I'll tell her what you said. I know she'll appreciate it."

"No problem," Frankie said. "Please tell her we were asking about her."

"If there's anything we can do—" I said.

Bianca's eyes flashed again. "There is," she said and this time there was an unmistakable edge in her voice. "Pray for Bobby to find out who really did it. The *real* murderer."

She left, slamming the door and letting in a blast of frigid air. The fire jumped and danced as if the Ghost of Christmas Past had just departed, taking all the warmth and festive cheer out of the room.

"What was that all about? What just happened?" Frankie picked up Bianca's water bottle and empty glass and looked at them. "Was there something in her water to set her off like that?"

"She's worried about Scotty being found guilty, so she stopped by to plant a few seeds and add a few more suspects to the list of possibilities."

"Why tell us?"

"I have no idea. People are in here all the time. Maybe she's hoping we'll talk, get the rumor mill going after she convinced us there are others who ought to be considered suspects. Plus she knows I'm involved in the investigation since I was the last one to be with Prescott and Quinn and I found him."

"Did she convince you?"

"She got me thinking," I said. "Victoria, Grant, and Celia do have motives along with the rest of the family. But, to be honest, I think she was here trying to convince herself."

"Of what?"

I looked Frankie in the eye. "That her husband didn't murder his grandfather."

Sixteen

need a cup of tea," I said.

We had moved to the kitchen after Bianca's abrupt departure. I went over to the cabinet where we kept the tea and started pulling out boxes.

"Do *you* think Scotty murdered Prescott?" Frankie asked.

"I think Bianca spent a lot of time trying to cast blame elsewhere. Too much time, if you ask me."

"You didn't answer the question." Frankie took two mugs with the vineyard logo stenciled on them out of another cabinet.

"I know."

"So, do you?" she asked.

"I don't know. Do you think he did it?"

"I don't know."

"Well, there you have it," I said. "Green tea okay?"

"Yup. Fine." She filled the mugs with water. "That was a brutal conversation. Because if someone in the family, or even close to the family—Victoria or Celia or Grant, for example—

murdered Prescott, you can count the suspects on the fingers of one hand."

"I know. I feel sick every time I think about it," I said. "What a legacy after all the good the Averys have done, all the money they've given away. Research centers, hospitals, universities, museums. Plus signing the Caritas Commitment. Prescott told me the other day that Rose was the instigator behind that decision."

"It breaks your heart, doesn't it?" Frankie said. "All I can think of is *Hamlet*."

"*Hamlet*?" I frowned at her. "Really? The play?"

She nodded.

"Why?"

"Because in *Hamlet* nothing ends well for anyone in that family, either. Everyone dies: the king, the queen, Hamlet's friends, his corrupt uncle, the woman he loves. In the last scene Hamlet drinks from a poisoned chalice—on purpose—and then he dies, too." She plunked the two tea bags I handed her into the mugs, stuck one in the microwave, and slammed the door. "'*Now cracks a noble heart. Good night, sweet prince . . . and flights of angels sing thee to thy rest.*'"

I had read *Hamlet* in high school, but I didn't remember the play well enough to be able to recite lines from it.

"Do you really think everyone in the Avery family is doomed? That they're all going to die?" I asked.

"Of course not. Not literally, anyway," she said. "But in the play the downfall of the House of Denmark began when Claudius, Hamlet's uncle, killed Hamlet's father, the old king. Then Claudius made himself king and married Hamlet's mother, the queen, to solidify his position."

"This does not sound like the Averys."

"Clay was Prescott's son by adoption because Prescott married his mother. Look, *Hamlet* is a story about the downfall and destruction of a family because of Claudius's lust for power and Hamlet's desire for revenge. I think Prescott could have been murdered for the same reasons. One, so he would no longer control the family business and two, someone wanted revenge because he was threatening to sell the *Tribune* against everyone's wishes. The rumor going around is that Clay, Scotty, and Alex—especially Clay—thought Prescott had gone off the deep end with his spending sprees and they wanted to rein him in before he blew any more money. As for selling the *Trib,* every member of his family was dead set against it. No pun intended." She leaned against the counter and folded her arms across her chest. "Revenge and power. I think those sound like plausible motives, don't you?"

"When you put it like that."

If Frankie knew about Clay trying to control Prescott's spending and stop his pursuit of so-called "unicorns"—things that might not really exist—then it was common knowledge. The whole town knew.

The microwave beeped. I removed the hot tea, replaced it with the other mug, shut the door, and set the timer. "I didn't realize you knew your Shakespeare so well."

I handed her the mug.

"I should hope I do. Undergrad and graduate degrees in English Lit, specializing in British Literature during the Elizabethan era. I graduated summa cum laude. Twice."

"Look at you. I'm impressed."

"I wrote my master's thesis on the witches in *Macbeth*."

She blew on her tea. "Their mystical powers and the role of audience superstition at the Globe Theatre. I spent a summer at King's College at the London Shakespeare Centre working on it. Total bliss. Plus I practically lived at the Globe, watching every performance I could afford. I was so broke I had to stand in front with the groundlings. Even if it rained, which it did. Often. But it was worth it."

"How come you never mentioned any of this before?" I asked. The microwave beeped again and I took out the other mug of tea. "I never knew you were an English major."

"Do you have any idea how many job opportunities there are for someone whose skill set consists of being able to recite *Macbeth* by heart?"

"I'm guessing not many."

"You guess right. I didn't want to teach and my hoped-for career writing the Great American Novel stalled out after the first year." She shrugged. "So I went into Human Resources instead. But believe it or not, the Folger Shakespeare Library was interested in my *Macbeth* thesis. It's in their reference collection."

"That sounds like quite an honor. Congratulations."

"Thank you. And I still drag Tom to Shakespeare festivals all over the country," she said. "Or movie adaptations. I've seen his plays performed in more ways that you can imagine. Samurai Shakespeare, Roaring Twenties Shakespeare, sci-fi Shakespeare. You name it, it's out there."

I couldn't wrap my head around sci-fi Shakespeare. "Did you ever come across anything that said he didn't write his own plays?"

"Sure," she said. "The Folger has a fabulous research center they make available to anyone who thinks they might have new evidence about the plays or where they originated. Even the Folger admits it's still one of the great mysteries how one person—especially someone with Shakespeare's limited education—could have produced such an incredible collection of work. Though in all honesty, the consensus is that Shakespeare did write Shakespeare since no one has ever come up with irrefutable evidence that he didn't." She gave me a curious look. "Why are you asking about this?"

When I didn't answer right away she said, "Lucie? Do you . . . *have* . . . information proving someone else wrote Shakespeare's plays? Or *think* you have information?"

"I don't know," I said. "I came across something in Leland's papers recently." I wasn't quite ready to tell her about Prescott and the Bruton Vault. Which Josie Wilde had already debunked.

At the mention of my father's name, Frankie's expression changed from genuine curiosity to glazed-over polite interest. She had never met Leland, but she had heard plenty about his surefire-get-rich-quick schemes, his gambling, his profligate spending, and the laissez-faire upbringing of his children after my mother died. In short, I could tell she thought whatever I'd come across was probably just more of Leland's pie in the sky dreaming.

"I know the woman who heads up that research center," she said in a matter-of-fact way. "Her name is Tana Rossi. If you'd like to look into whatever it is he found, I can give you her email address." The expression on her face said she thought I was wasting my time—and probably Tana Rossi's—but I appreciated the gesture.

"That would be great. If you don't mind, I'd like to contact her."

"No problem." She set down her mug, pulled out her phone, and did some tapping and scrolling. After a moment she said, "Here you go. I just texted her information to you."

"Thanks," I said as my phone beeped. "I don't need to mention your name if you'd rather not let her know how I got her email address. I know this must sound like something out of sci-fi Shakespeare, especially if my father is involved."

She looked chagrined, probably because I'd read her mind, and her mouth curved into a guilty smile. "You'd be surprised the theories people come up with. But if you think you've got something, by all means get in touch with Tana." She picked up her tea and drank. "If anyone's heard 'em all—and they run the gamut—she has. And feel free to use my name."

"Okay," I said. "If you mean it, then I will."

I sent Tana Rossi an email when I was in the Jeep later that morning just before driving over to the General Store to pick up groceries for Persia. Since Frankie had given me permission, I used her name, hoping it would strengthen my case that I was a sane, rational person with a legitimate query, not some crank or crackpot with a wacky theory. I avoided mentioning the Bruton Vault, since that seemed to have been thoroughly discredited by the results of the two excavations, but I did say that I was interested in discussing the connection between the wreck of the *Sea Venture* and the plot of *The Tempest*. I also said I wondered whether the Folger had any information to substantiate whether Thomas Jefferson might have had access to the writings of Sir Francis Bacon, and finally, that I was curious about any information concerning Bacon's possible influence on Shakespeare's plays.

I hit send and drove over to Thelma's.

THE GENERAL STORE WAS located just off Mosby's Highway at the junction of Atoka Road and Rectors Lane, or as Thelma Johnson liked to think of it, at the pulsing nexus of the villages of Middleburg and Atoka, combined population 896 souls. A plain white clapboard building with a green tin roof, the store had a large picture window in which a pink neon OPEN sign had read OPE for years. With two gas pumps out front, four parking spots, three pots of different coffees, a showcase filled with fresh-baked breads and pastries, and an eclectic inventory that included everything from bait to hoof-polishing wax for horses, Thelma liked to brag that she had more to offer than the Safeway in Middleburg although not quite as much as the Leesburg outlet mall. Plus, as she always said, there was her legendary hospitality.

Like us, Thelma had also gotten an early start on her Christmas decorating. A wreath made with fresh woven greens, pinecones sprayed with fake snow, bright red berries, and a red bow edged in gold hung on her front door. The sleigh bells on the inside doorknob were there year round and jingled as I walked in. I knew from past years there would be mistletoe hanging from the ceiling just inside the front door.

I looked up. There was.

Thelma was big on romance, especially at Christmas.

The place smelled—as it always did at this time of year—of fresh-brewed coffee and the tang of wood smoke from a potbellied stove that was surrounded by rocking chairs in a corner of the room. Thelma had never been one for updating the place so it looked like a cookie-cutter 7-Eleven. She said her customers liked her little store the way it had always been, a throwback to a slower, gentler time when folks stopped in for a chat to go along with that quart of milk or loaf of bread they needed. And no one asked if she had free WiFi. My parents had come here for groceries; so had my grandparents. And her parents and grandparents had taken care of them.

If there were no customers, Thelma was invariably in the back room, the muffled sound of voices coming from a television she never turned off so she could follow her beloved soap operas. Today the store was empty, but I heard her reedy voice call out from the back, "I'm coming. Give me a minute. I'll be right there."

I picked up a basket and began my shopping as the swelling music at the end of one of the shows she adored sounded from the back room. A moment later I heard the clackety-clack of her heels across the floor as she emerged from soap opera heaven.

"Why, Lucille, how nice you stopped by. It's been a while since you've been in. And to think, the Romeos were here just this morning and we were talking about you." She sounded as delighted as a child peeking around the corner to see what was under the tree on Christmas Day.

You'd think the place had CCTV or maybe Thelma really had eyes in the back of her head because it was uncanny how she always knew who had walked in. Even if you couldn't see her because you were tucked away at the far end of one of the aisles.

I stepped out into the open. "How did you know it was me?"

She tapped her temple with a finger. "Aside from my extra-sensible psychotic perception which means I just *know* things, your Jeep's parked right outside the window where I can see it."

"Oh."

As for what she and the Romeos had been discussing that involved me, I'd find out soon enough. Thelma had a way of getting information out of you before you knew what happened, and doing it so effectively you didn't see the blood until it was all over. As Quinn liked to say, she'd be a great asset for any country's intelligence service.

She was somewhere north of eighty, or so everyone thought—her age was a more carefully guarded secret than the nuclear codes. Nevertheless she dressed with the saucy sexiness of a kid who intended to sneak out of the house before a parent could tell her to go upstairs and change into something respectable and not that low-cut, short, or tight, young lady.

Thelma didn't care; she wore her eye-catching outfits with va-va-voom verve and a refreshing effervescence. You couldn't help but admire her: makeup applied with a gardening trowel to cover wrinkles as deep as canyons, hair a shade of orange not found anywhere in nature, and as flirtatious as Scarlett O'Hara surrounded by her beaus at the barbecue at Twelve Oaks. Today she was dressed in Santa-suit red, a short, tight, long-sleeved shift with a wide black belt and white cuffs on the sleeves. Red stiletto heels and a reindeer antler headband to keep her carrot-colored hair off her face.

"So, tell me. What can I get for you today, Lucille?" She

propped her elbows on the counter next to her cash register, folded her hands together, and regarded me.

"I just stopped by for a few things," I said. "Actually, I've already finished shopping. I got everything I needed."

"I'm glad to hear that. With the big rush for Thanksgiving, the place was so picked over there was hardly anything left on the shelves come Friday. You know how much I pride myself on having what my customers need. Though I must say I'm surprised how many people wait until the last minute to do their Thanksgiving grocery shopping." She shook her head. "Especially the Romeos. Fortunately I still had a few turkeys left when the last of 'em came by. I only sell the hybrid ones these days, Lucille. You know, the kind that get to run around home on the range for free so they taste extra good. They cost a pretty penny, but people love 'em."

"I know. We bought one of your, er, hybrids. It was excellent."

She beamed. "Come sit a spell and tell me all about it. How about a nice cup of coffee? And a jelly donut. I've got an apple cinnamon left. On the house. I know you love them."

When Thelma resorted to bribery to get you to stick around and it involved donuts, it meant she planned to pump you for information. I already knew whatever she wanted to learn from me would involve Prescott Avery. Especially if the Romeos had been talking about me this morning.

"Thanks, but I really ought to be getting back to the vineyard. We have a lot to do just now with the holidays coming up."

"Is that so?" She placed her hands on her hips and gave me a stern up and down you're-not-fooling-me look. "That's not what Quinn said when he was in here the other day, missy. He told me harvest was over and you were finished for the year, so you could finally put your feet up a bit."

"Well, that's sort of true, but—"

"Lucille, you know I was close to your sainted mother, which is why I've always had mammary feelings about you and your brother and sister. And right now I think you ought to hear what I've got to say. To be honest, ninety-nine percent of me wants to spare you from telling you about this, but the other ten percent is saying *'that child ought to know.'*"

I was still trying to figure out her mammary feelings. "Know what?" I asked.

"How about we talk over a cup of coffee?"

She had baited the hook well. "All right. Maybe just a quick cup."

"I thought you might change your mind," she said, a glint of satisfaction in her eyes. "Today's Fancy is Java-Java-Doo. It's a new one."

I glanced over at the counter where Thelma had labeled her three pots PLAIN, FANCY, and DECAFFEINATED. The pot of Fancy was half-full.

"I'll try the new Fancy. And I will take that apple cinnamon donut." It seemed as if I might need the fortification of a sugar buzz.

Thelma poured two cups of Java-Java-Doo and let me add milk and sugar to mine while she got my donut. I left my shopping basket on the counter by the cash register next to her collection of Christmas snow globes and followed her over to the circle of rocking chairs.

She settled herself in her favorite Lincoln rocker. I sat in the bentwood rocking chair I'd come to think of as mine. Thelma took a demure sip of coffee and then plunged right in.

"There's talk that you and Prescott Avery were alone in his wine cellar just before he died."

There was a subtext in her words that made me squirm.

"That's right, we were," I said in an even voice.

"So what did you two talk about?"

At least she wasn't going to beat around the bush.

"Wine," I said.

"Wine?" She seemed surprised.

"Yes. Prescott wanted to buy some of my wine for a party he planned to throw. Which won't be taking place now. That's it. That's what we talked about."

That wasn't it by half, but at least it was all true.

"Must have been pretty special wine for Prescott to take you away from that party, so it was just the two of you having a private conversation." She gave me a sly look. "I'm sure you wouldn't mind telling me what kind it was, now would you?" She smiled, all guileless innocence and sincerity.

Thelma could be like a dog with a bone.

"He was hoping to buy some Madeira that my father used to own. Very old Madeira. Unfortunately, Leland must have sold it because I didn't know anything about it," I said. "That was the end of the discussion."

"Madeira?" She sat up straight, her eyes sparkling with interest. "Isn't that the wine you can practically boil and it still tastes good? Folks used to put it in wooden caskets and send it around the world on ships in olden times."

It was my turn to be surprised. "Ah . . . yes. They did. How do you know so much about it?"

"Because I know about that Madeira, that's how. Your great-uncle Ian told my daddy about it."

"He *did*? Why? When?"

"I was just a little girl, Lucille. But I remember because Daddy was so excited when Ian decided he was going to open a bottle so's the two of them could try it. Find out if it was as tasty as they thought it would be. Jock Avery had wanted to buy it but Ian wanted to hold on to it. First, though, he needed to make sure it was good."

"Your father and Ian Montgomery actually drank a bottle of that Madeira?" The napkin with what was left of my donut started to slide off my lap, leaving a trail of cinnamon sugar on my jeans. I grabbed it before it fell on the floor, but I couldn't take my eyes off Thelma. "*What happened?* You've got to tell me the story."

She leaned back in her rocker. "Funny," she said in a musing voice, "I haven't thought about that wine until you mentioned it just now. I'd kinda snuck into the back room and heard the two of them talking. Daddy and Ian swore me to secrecy—actually Daddy threatened to whup the daylights out of me if I told anyone—so I never talked about it again. But I guess everyone involved being dead and gone, it's okay to tell you."

"Tell me what? Do you have any idea what happened to it? Where is it now?"

"Why, wherever Ian put it, I suppose. Unless your father moved it."

"You don't think Leland decided to do what Ian did and drink it? All of it?"

She shook her head. "He mighta drank a bottle. Your father

did like a good bottle of wine. He especially liked the stronger spirits. But Lordy, child, that Madeira would be worth a fortune today. Lee was hanging on to it until he could sell it for a fine price at one of those fancy auction houses where people hold up padlocks because they want to buy something before anyone else gets ahold of it."

"I never knew anything about the Madeira until Prescott brought it up on Saturday. Leland never said a word. I don't even know if my mother knew about it."

"Maybe he wasn't going to say anything until he sold it and got the money for it," she said.

Our eyes met. We were talking about my father, after all. It was more likely he was going to sell it and *not* say anything about the money he got for it. Unfortunately when he died, the secret of where he'd hidden the Madeira died with him.

"I'm sorry, Lucille," she added.

"It's okay," I said. "Can you tell me anything else? Why did Ian decide to tell your father about the Madeira—and then open a bottle and share it with him?"

Thelma made a fuss of straightening her antler headband and I could tell she was stalling. "Oh, that," she said, reddening. "Well, you see, my daddy and Ian worked together from time to time."

She waited for the penny to drop.

"Your father was a Prohibition bootlegger, too? Like Ian?"

She blushed some more and nodded. "Not full-time like Ian was. He still ran the store out front, just like I do today. And then behind the curtain, he had a little side business going on."

"So the back room where you watch television used to be—?"

"A regular little roadhouse. Daddy even had a place to hide his liquor any time he thought he was about to get raided. It's still there, a false wall in the basement. Cleverest thing you ever saw. He never got caught, though I think that's because he bribed the Prohibition agents by giving 'em bottles of the good stuff."

"What happened when your father and Ian drank the Madeira?" I asked. "It was already over one hundred years old. What was it like?"

"They drank it long after Prohibition was over, so by then it was legal. They plumb enjoyed themselves, I can tell you that. Talked about the old days and the hijinks they got up to staying a couple of steps ahead of the law."

"How do you know?"

"I was there. Ian even gave me a sip from his glass."

"He did what?"

She smiled and nodded.

"What did it taste like?" I was floored.

She thought for a moment. "Cough syrup."

"Cough syrup?"

Lucille, I was seven," she said. "I didn't have the sophisticated paypal for wine that I have now. But Ian and Daddy thought it tasted like something the angels had made up in heaven."

"I wonder what it tastes like today."

"Probably just as wonderful, which is why Prescott Avery wanted to buy it," she said. "I suppose he told you what he was planning to do with it."

I said in a firm voice, "Drink it."

"Is that so?" She gave me another you're-holding-out-on-me look. "Some of the Romeos had been saying Prescott was acting awful peculiar lately. Seems he had some big secret, something real important that he wouldn't share with anyone. Not Clay, not anyone in his family. Maybe the Madeira had something to do with it?"

"I don't know."

"Now that," she said in a stern voice, "I don't believe."

I licked cinnamon sugar off my thumb. "Thelma," I said, "Prescott's murder was made to look like an accident. Everyone in Atoka knows that members of the Avery family are at the top of Bobby Noland's suspect list. It seems to me any so-called secret probably had to do with whether or not he planned to sell the *Tribune* and some of his other newspapers that were in trouble. And he certainly didn't share that with me."

She sat back in her rocking chair and crossed one leg over the other, rocking back and forth.

"You could be right," she said finally. "But I do believe you're wrong."

"What do you mean?"

"Prescott was a member of the Masons, Lucille. You've heard of 'em, haven't you? Not Mason like those special jars people use for canning fruit and vegetables. This is a club for men only—no women allowed. Everything they do is a secret—how they dress, what they talk about at their meetings, even their handshake is secret. They wear some peculiar getup for their ceremonies that reminds me of the characters from the Harry Potter movies, especially the ones who teach at Hogwarts."

The hairs on the back of my neck were standing up. Thelma always swore by her extensible psychotic perception. Did she really know something? Or was she just guessing?

"Of course I've heard of the Masons," I said. "What makes you bring them up and how do you know so much about them?"

"My father was a Mason," she said. "In fact, he belonged to the same lodge Prescott belonged to."

More surprises. "I didn't know that."

"Masons don't talk about being Masons. That's why they've got a secret handshake. So they know who's a real brother and who isn't."

"Your father never talked about what happened at his meetings?"

She shook her head and her antler headband wobbled. "He did not. You want a secret kept? Tell a Mason."

"I see." I hoped we were going to drop the subject.

"Jock, Prescott, and Tommy," she said, ticking them off on her fingers. "They were all so much alike, the three of them. Cut from the same bolt of cloth. Always looking for adventure, taking dares, trying something new. If it was dangerous, that was even better."

I nodded and waited for her to go on. Were we still talking about the Masons or had she moved on to something else?

"If Prescott was hankering to buy that Madeira from you, Lucille, I'm guessing he wanted it to celebrate something special. I heard tell he was planning to have a little party the same day as the Miranda Foundation's swanky holiday party," she said. "His lodge did a lot to help the Miranda Foundation, donating money and all, so I'm thinking Prescott's secret must've had something to do with the Masons." She folded her skinny arms across her chest. "I think he was keeping something to himself when he died. And I think you have some idea what it was."

"All he wanted to talk about that day was the Madeira." I stood up. "I ought to pay for my groceries and then I should be going. Thanks for the coffee and the jelly donut."

She gave me a we're-not-done-here look, but nevertheless she walked over to the cash register. She rang up my items while I packed them in a canvas tote with the vineyard logo on it. When she was done, she laid her hand on top of mine.

"Are you getting involved in this, Lucille?"

"Getting involved in what?"

She shook her head and gave me the look of disappointment my mother used to give me that always made me feel guilty as hell.

"Don't tangle with the Freemasons, child. They don't take kindly to folks butting in and exposing things that are private and sacred to them."

"Yes, ma'am. I know that."

She picked up one of her snow globes and shook it. Snow cascaded furiously over a sweet little white church with a steeple, lighted windows, and a manger scene in front of its open doors.

When the snow had finally settled, she looked up. "You've got your mother's beauty, but you're even more stubborn and ornery than your father was. Sometimes it's just best to leave things lay where Jesus flang 'em, child. I think this is one of those times. If you're getting yourself mixed up in something Prescott was involved in, you could be asking for trouble." She shook her finger at me. "Don't say I didn't warn you."

I said, "Yes, ma'am" one more time and got out of there.

Seventeen

found Tana Rossi's reply to the email I'd written to her earlier this morning in my in-box when I checked my phone for messages in Thelma's parking lot. She wrote that she would be willing to talk to me about the *Sea Venture* and its relationship to *The Tempest,* plus she said she'd be interested in any information I had challenging the authenticity of Shakespeare as the author of his plays.

I decided not to tell her that I didn't actually have anything concrete, no documents in my possession to show her that would make a case that Shakespeare might not have written Shakespeare. Then I figured she heard from people like me all the time that were convinced they'd made the discovery of a millennium—just as Frankie said—if only they had the evidence to prove they were right.

I wrote back and asked if it would be possible to meet with her in Washington later this week if she had time, possibly Thursday or Friday. She answered a few minutes later suggesting Thursday afternoon at one o'clock at the Folger. *Sign in at the front desk when you arrive and they'll find me,* she wrote. I replied that it was a date and that I was looking forward to it.

On the drive home from Thelma's I wondered whether to-morrow's meeting with Josie Wilde would yield any new information on the documents Hobson Banks had mentioned in his letter. If I were lucky, then maybe I'd have another arrow or two in my quiver when I met Tana Rossi on Thursday.

At the winery we had clients who worked in the intelligence world at the alphabet agencies in Washington and Virginia—though they never said anything overtly—so that over the years I'd heard an expression used in the spy business that always intrigued me: walking back the cat. It meant you retreated all the way to the origin or source to find out how a story or theory got started—tracing precisely where it came from. And that's what I wanted to do with Hobson Banks's documents: walk back the cat.

Because it seemed to me that walking back this particular cat led to Jamestown, where I hoped the documents Banks was referring to had first been hidden, and subsequently to Williamsburg, where, if I guessed correctly, they disappeared and had been brought to the White House by Thomas Jefferson. Josie Wilde had been one of the privileged few who had been present at the final excavation at Bruton Parish. Josie said they'd turned up nothing—but wasn't it possible, as some people claimed, they were digging in the wrong place?

There were also the theories I'd read about on the more controversial internet websites describing a conspiracy and a cover-up to make the story disappear once and for all by claiming Bruton Vault never existed. That there were never documents smuggled into Jamestown proving that a group of powerful Freemasons led by Sir Francis Bacon had laid out plans for the foundation of a government in the New World based on Masonic ideas and principles. And that later these plans and ideas had been incorporated into the Declaration of Independence and the Constitution written by Founding Fathers, who weren't Masons themselves, but were influenced by those Masonic ideas and principles. And finally, among the vault's most controversial contents was irrefutable proof that Bacon had had a hand in writing Shakespeare's plays, almost certainly *The Tempest*.

Far-fetched and crazy? Maybe. But wasn't it also true that where there was smoke there was fire? It seemed that Jock and Prescott Avery had thought so; and so had my father.

It was too tempting not to pursue what they had been searching for, especially after Prescott said he'd finally found the last clue to this treasure hunt. And now I thought I'd figured out what it was, too.

Or almost figured it out. But that was predicated on a very big *if*.

SEELY'S GARDEN CENTER WAS perhaps the only place in Middleburg and Atoka that could give Frankie's gorgeous Christmas decorations at the winery a run for their money. At this time of year Seely's was magical, every child's fantasy of what Santa's North Pole workshop looked like, except with a lot of plants.

The parking lot was busy when Quinn and I got there

around five o'clock, in part because folks were busily coming and going at the end of the work day, but also because some of the usual parking spaces were now filled with pines, firs, and spruces mounted on rows of one-by-sixes. Seely's was sprawling; a rambling conglomeration of pavilions, greenhouses, and gardens surrounding an enormous two-story building painted barn red. At this time of year the greenhouse overflowed with poinsettia, cyclamen, and mistletoe in addition to the other hothouse plants and flowers they usually had. A help desk, checkout counters festooned with pine garland threaded with white lights, a florist shop, and anything you needed or didn't know you needed for a garden occupied the two rooms inside the main building. My favorite, however, was the Christmas Shop, only open at this time of year and filled with ornaments, candles, potpourri, decorations, and trees arranged by theme: old-fashioned Christmas, whimsical Christmas, exotic Christmas, Nordic Christmas, woodland Christmas, under-the-sea Christmas. Any kind of Christmas your heart desired.

"Am I going to lose you to that Christmas room you love so much?" Quinn said, teasing me and taking my hand as we walked over to the tree-filled parking lot. "You'll be there 'til Easter."

"And what of it, buddy? I know I'll lose you to the homemade popcorn and mulled cider."

"Worse things could happen," he said, grinning. "That popcorn smells great and I'm starved. I'm definitely getting some before we go. Come on, let's go pick out our trees."

It didn't take long to find a sixteen-foot Fraser fir for the Villa and a twelve-foot Noble fir for the foyer of Highland House. Quinn stayed outside to chat with the crew who promised they'd put the trees aside and give them fresh cuts before delivering them tomorrow. I went inside to order the poinsettias and pine garland Frankie wanted for the Villa as well as what we needed for the house, plus pay for the trees and arrange for their delivery.

When I was done I found Quinn—as expected—at the popcorn-making machine talking to Noah Seely. Even without the Santa suit, Noah still looked the part: snow-white hair that curled over the collar of his plaid flannel shirt, bright blue eyes, bushy beard, and a little Santa belly that hung over the waistband of his jeans. He even wore suspenders with holly embroidered on them and black work boots.

". . . the suit gets hot so be sure you wear underwear that breathes," he was saying to Quinn. "The moisture-wicking fabric they make these days is great."

"I didn't think about the underwear," Quinn replied. "I'm not sure I'm cut out for this."

"Ho, ho, ho, you two," I said. "Any chance of a cup of mulled cider, Santa? I've been good."

Noah laughed and kissed me on the cheek. Quinn gave me a martyred look and said, "What have you gotten me into?"

"You'll be fine, Quinn." Noah reassured him as he passed me a cup of cider. "How've you been, Lucie sweetheart? I heard you two were the ones who found Prescott the other day."

Noah was one of the Romeos; he and my parents—especially my mother—had a long history together. Years ago when she decided to restore the gardens at Highland House after Leland had let them go completely to seed, she went to him for help tracking down the plants she wanted after poring over Thomas

Jefferson's *Garden Book* for inspiration. Noah had been indefatigable in researching and locating the more unusual plants
on her list. Afterward as a thank-you, she had surprised him
by painting some of the pretty vistas and scenes of the garden
center, presenting him with not only the paintings, but also
her rough sketches. Over the years, her art had been turned
into posters, greeting cards, even used in calendars. Most of
the paintings hung in the common room where staff meetings
and educational classes for the public were held. Noah's favorite, of the back lot where the trees and large bushes were kept,
had been painted in spring when everything was flowering
and in full bloom with the Blue Ridge Mountains as a backdrop. That one hung in his office.

It wasn't hard to figure out how Noah knew about us finding Prescott: Clay had probably told him.

"We were there," I said. "It was such a shock. Especially
afterward when Bobby announced it was murder and not a
natural death."

"Have you spoken to Clay recently?" Quinn asked. He had
helped himself to more popcorn and now held out the bag to
Noah and me.

Noah patted his ample stomach and wagged a finger at
the popcorn. "Thanks, but I'm trying to give it up. Not easy
around here. As for Clay, I haven't heard from him that much.
I've been talking mostly to Victoria about the funeral—we've
been asked to take care of the flowers at National Cathedral—
and to Celia, Tommy's widow, about the Miranda Foundation
fund-raiser at the orangerie since we're donating those flowers."

"I didn't realize they were still going ahead with the fund-
raiser," I said.

Noah nodded. "Everything but a small private party Prescott planned beforehand for his Masonic lodge. That's not going to take place anymore." He paused and added, "I know he really wanted to buy that Madeira Lee had put away, Lucie. Did you agree to sell it to him?"

I smiled through gritted teeth. "You must have heard about that from Thelma."

Thelma's information highway had been even speedier than usual. Unless you lived on another planet, probably a distant one, I'd bet by now everyone knew about Prescott wanting to buy the Madeira from me.

Noah seemed surprised by my question. "No, Prescott told me. He was keeping it quiet, but I figured you, of all people, would know."

It was my turn to be surprised. "Oh, uh, actually, no. I didn't sell it to him. I mean, I couldn't," I said. "I have no idea where it is, or if we even have it anymore."

"Lucie, are you serious?"

"Absolutely. The first I heard of it was on Saturday. Why did Prescott bring it up with you? I thought he was keeping it quiet, too."

Noah lowered his voice. "He wanted me to know about the party because I used to be a Mason—a member of his lodge, in fact. I haven't seen a lot of the guys since I left. He wanted to make sure it wasn't going to be awkward that he wasn't inviting me."

"I didn't think being a Mason was one of those things you could quit," Quinn said. "Aren't you a member for life once you sign on?"

"You don't have to be," Noah said, "though no one wants

to see a brother Mason leave. But if you decide you want to separate from your lodge, you just write a letter and say you want out. It's called a demit. If you're a dues paying member in good standing, that's it."

"Why did you leave?" I asked.

Noah looked around and crooked a come-with-me finger as if he were worried someone might overhear what he was about to say. All around us were the sounds of laughter and happy chatter and Christmas music, rambunctious kids who'd stuffed themselves with popcorn and cider as they played in the aisles, adults pushing carts laden with wreaths, garland, and poinsettias, and staff wearing floppy red-and-white Santa hats and CAN I HO-HO-HELP? buttons. It didn't look as if anyone was paying the slightest bit of attention to our conversation.

Quinn and I followed Noah to a niche off the main room that contained racks of vegetable and flower seed packets, watering cans, gardening gloves—all items for planting a spring garden and not a hint of Christmas. We had the little corner to ourselves.

"I left because it wasn't for me," he said, still keeping his voice low. "The time commitment and, to be honest, I wasn't comfortable with some of the rituals, the clothing you have to wear at the some of the ceremonies. Dressing up as Santa Claus is about the outer edge of my comfort zone."

I laughed.

"Me, too," Quinn said. "Maybe beyond the outer edge of mine."

I ignored him and he made a point of noisily crunching his popcorn.

"Plus," Noah went on, "I'm no good at a lot of memorizing."

"Memorizing what?" I said.

"Everything to do with being a Mason is passed on as an oral tradition," he said. "There are no rule books or documents or guides to explain the orders and ceremonies, the things you must recite. There's nothing written down."

"Nothing at all?" Quinn said.

Noah nodded and tapped the side of his head with a finger. "You keep it all up here. Each new candidate is mentored by a brother Mason. You've got to learn the catechism by heart. Memorize everything. Unfortunately I've got a mind like a sieve."

"What happened after you left?" I asked. "Were there any consequences? Were the others upset with you?"

"In my case, no. There's an understanding that you'll respect the privacy of your former brother Masons," he said. "That you won't betray their trust or reveal the things you learned in the sanctity of the lodge."

"It sounds a lot like a cult," Quinn said, "with all due respect."

"Plenty of people would agree with you," Noah said. "But it's not. Once upon a time they really were a guild of masons—stonemasons who were builders of buildings. Now they see themselves as builders of men. And there are two requirements for joining: you must believe in a higher power—whatever you want to call it, or him—even though they're not a religious group. Second, you must be a person of good character. They don't recruit—you approach them if you're interested and then there's a trial period before they agree they want you and you agree you want them."

"I didn't know that," I said.

"The Masons do a lot of good things, a lot of charitable work. They're just quiet about it. Unfortunately that secrecy is what's led to people thinking they're some kind of cabal trying to control the government."

"Has anyone ever talked about what really goes on?" Quinn asked. "Written a book or something?"

"Yes, and it didn't end well. Not just for him, but for the country," Noah said.

"What do you mean?" I asked.

"Back in the 1800s a man named William Morgan, who'd been a Mason for a while, decided he was going to write a tell-all book cashing in on the conspiracy rumors and fears going around. In those days anti-Masonic sentiment was a big thing. People wrote about it, talked about it." Noah finished his cider and crumpled his empty paper cup.

"As you can imagine, Morgan's book didn't go down well with the Masons," he went on. "His publisher was threatened, and William Morgan—who was going to go through with his project come hell or high water—was kidnapped." He snapped his fingers. "Vanished, just like that. Never to be seen again. The story was that a couple of Masons got to him and killed him, probably in upstate New York. That way they could shut him up for good."

"Did anyone ever find out what really happened to him?" Quinn asked.

Noah shook his head. "It almost didn't matter, because everyone just assumed the Masons were responsible. Guilty. There was a big public hue and cry because no one was being brought to justice, which only fueled the fire that the Masons were sinister, a secret society that needed to be reined in. The talk got uglier and eventually a third political party—called, to no one's surprise, the Anti-Masonic Party—came to be. That's how bad it was. They had one presidential candidate, William Wirt, in 1832 who lost. Abysmally. After that the party fell apart and died."

"Then what happened?" I asked.

"Nothing. Wirt had actually been a Mason and sort of defended the Masons at his nomination. He said George Washington never would have belonged to the kind of organization the Anti-Masons were describing. So after he lost the election Wirt faded from view."

"That's a hell of a story," Quinn said. "At least it happened a long time ago."

"Maybe so, but you can still find plenty of stories right now—especially on the internet—about the Masons being run by men who still secretly want to control the government, or that they were infiltrated by the Illuminati centuries ago in Europe. Then there are the conspiracy theories about Masonic symbols being hidden in government buildings in Washington and that the city was built based on a pentagram, which is sacred to the Masons. Or that All-Seeing Eye on the back of the one-dollar bill is a Masonic symbol of power."

"I've heard some of that," I said.

"So have I," Quinn said.

"The irony is that talking about politics or religion is forbidden at Masonic meetings," Noah said. "And though it's true George Washington and Pierre L'Enfant were Masons, they didn't design the city based on some secret hoop-de-doop. L'Enfant was in love with Paris. That was his inspiration." His paper cup was now a tight little ball.

For someone who had left the Masons, he sounded almost too defensive, and I wondered why.

Quinn nudged me. "We should probably be going."

I nodded. "Yes. We should let you get back to . . . everything, Noah. And thanks for delivering the trees and all the greenery tomorrow."

"For one of my best customers, anything," he said, adding with a rueful smile, "I'm sorry I got a bit wound up just now. Don't mind me. I don't usually talk about this stuff."

"You seem to have some strong feelings about the Masons," Quinn said. "For someone who dropped out."

Noah gave a dry laugh. "I suppose you're right. I also have some strong feelings about what happened to Prescott. I hope whoever killed him gets exactly what's coming to them. God knows they deserve it."

To look at Noah just now was to see Santa without the red suit, a gentle soul whose two favorite lines at this time of year were usually "Ho-ho-ho" and "Were you naughty or nice?" Instead he was talking about vengeance and murder.

"Do you think the murderer was a Mason?" I said.

"No," he said, "but I think Prescott's death had something to do with him being a Mason."

"The Sheriff's Office suspects it's someone in the family," Quinn said.

"The two aren't mutually exclusive."

Quinn and I glanced at each other. "No one else in the family belongs to the Masons," I said.

"I didn't say the killer was a Mason," Noah said. "Prescott intimidated a lot of people. At ninety-five years old, he was still someone to be reckoned with. He played hardball and he played to win. As a result, he alienated people."

"I'm not following you," I said.

"Prescott and Rosie did a lot of good for a lot of people during their lives," Noah said. "But he made enemies over the years. Especially when there was something he wanted—a work of art, a rare jewel, an item no one believed could be found. Pirate's treasure. Evidence of the existence of Noah's Ark. It was all about the quest. Always about the quest."

"Indiana Jones," Quinn said under his breath.

"The thrill of the hunt," I said.

"Exactly." Noah nodded. "The more elusive, the better. Cost was no object."

And it infuriated his family. I wondered if Noah knew about that. And I wondered if he had known Prescott just bought James Madison's copy of the Declaration of Independence, written out by Thomas Jefferson.

"So someone killed him because of something he was looking for?" Quinn asked.

"Possibly," Noah said. "Or maybe it was to stop him before he found it. Whatever 'it' was."

"Any idea?" I asked. How much had Prescott confided in Noah about what he was searching for, his lost treasure?

Noah shook his head. "I'm afraid not. Only that it was something worth killing for."

Eighteen

On the drive south to Jamestown on Wednesday morning, Quinn and I tried to parse Noah Seely's theory about why someone had murdered Prescott: because of what he was searching for or because someone didn't want him to find it.

"Noah said he had no idea what *it* was," I said. "So how did he know Prescott had angered someone enough to make him—or her—commit murder?"

"Prescott must have told Noah he pissed someone off," Quinn said.

"You'd think Noah would want to know why. Or what. And especially *who*."

"Not necessarily. First of all, Noah doesn't seem like the type of guy who would ask," Quinn said. "You're the one who told me he worked in intelligence before he retired. He kept secrets for a living. Second, Prescott might not have made a big deal about it."

I thought about it. Quinn could be right. Prescott could have just come out with some off-the-cuff remark. Taking risks was part of the thrill of the hunt. Maybe even a prerequisite.

"I guess so," I said. "Noah is the kind of guy who believes in 'need-to-know,' and perhaps he thought this wasn't one of those times. Maybe Prescott mentioned it in passing because—as Noah said—it's not the first time he's alienated someone when he's been on the trail of whatever it is he wants. Noah probably didn't think anything of it, either—until Prescott turned up dead."

"Plus you've got Bobby who believes someone murdered Prescott because of money and the fact that he was threatening to sell a big chunk of Avery Communications. Specifically the *Washington Tribune*," Quinn said. "Do you think he's wrong?"

"Who? Bobby or Noah?"

"Take your pick."

"I don't know. I wonder who else knew about the lost treasure Prescott was looking for."

"You do."

A shiver ran down my spine. I didn't want to end up like Prescott.

"I have an idea what it might be. Only because Prescott asked me to sell him Ian's Madeira and then suggested the clue to where I might find it was in Leland's 'secret' safe-deposit box. Without Hobson Banks's letter and those newspaper photos of Jock and Prescott at Bruton Parish when the graveyard was being excavated, I would have had no idea about any of this," I said.

"I still think someone else might be looking for the same thing, darling." Quinn gave me a look that didn't do anything to quiet my uneasiness.

"Look, the official reason we're driving down to Jamestown and Williamsburg today is to meet with Josie Wilde. Talk to her about getting her to help us at the vineyard. No one has a clue we're also going to talk to her about Bruton Vault and whether it exists or not."

"Fair enough. But depending on what we find out today," Quinn said, "I think it would be a good idea to talk to Bobby when we get back to Atoka."

"Are you kidding? I already told him when he questioned me the other day about Prescott telling me he was on the verge of solving a puzzle that's baffled people for centuries." I twirled my finger next to my temple. "Bobby thinks that's nuts. He thinks *I'm* nuts. Don't forget, Clay's trying to make a case that Prescott wasn't mentally competent when he died. That he wasn't capable of making sound financial decisions because he was living in his own imaginary little world."

Quinn groaned. "What a mess." He reached for his to-go coffee mug and took a sip. "This has gone cold. Want to stop for another coffee?"

"Not just now," I said, an edge of excitement creeping into my voice. I pointed to the exit sign next to the highway. "This is where we turn off to take the back road to Jamestown. We're almost there."

IT HAD BEEN A dozen years since I visited Jamestown—both sites—the living history exhibition where visitors could explore a replica of the colonial fort, see a Powhatan Indian village, and tour replicas of the *Susan Constant, Godspeed,* and *Discovery*—the three ships the settlers had sailed on in 1607—and the actual site of the original fort where archaeologists were still making new discoveries.

In the 1950s a scenic twenty-three-mile road known as Colonial Parkway had been completed that connected the Jamestown Settlement, the American Revolution Museum at Yorktown, and Colonial Williamsburg in what was known as the Historic Triangle.

America started here.

The site of the Jamestown fort, known as Historic Jamestowne to distinguish it from the Jamestown Settlement, was located off a spur of Colonial Parkway. We drove across a bridge that led to what had once been a peninsula but, thanks to rising water levels and changes in the topography of the James River, was now Jamestown Island.

"I didn't expect it to be so remote," Quinn said as we drove along a desolate stretch of road surrounded by nothing but forests of pine trees and bare deciduous trees. We hadn't seen a car for a couple of miles.

"The fort is located on the banks of the James River," I said. "Not so far inland that the settlers couldn't easily sail back out to the Chesapeake Bay and the Atlantic Ocean. Plus, the land belonged to the Powhatan Indians. The English were encroaching on their territory, so they stayed near the water on purpose."

Quinn pulled into a parking lot where fewer than half a dozen cars were parked. A red-and-white Mini Cooper that reminded me of a car I used to own had a Virginia license plate from the Jamestown quadricentennial—a picture of the *Susan Constant,* along with 1607—JAMESTOWN—2007 written across the bottom. The tag read VAYNDOC.

"Vain doctor? A medical narcissist? Vein doctor? What do they call those people—phlebotomists?" Quinn started guessing as we parked next to the Mini and got out of the Jeep.

"Phlebotomists are the people who draw your blood for lab tests," I said. "Phlebologists are vein doctors. Personally, I think it stands for V-A Wine Doc. Virginia wine doctor. As in Dr. Josephine Wilde. I bet that's her car."

He laughed. "Good call. I bet you're right."

The Visitor Center was a long, low gray-blue building with a row of windows and reminded me of a large shed. It sat on the edge of the parking lot and looked as if it were meant to blend unobtrusively with the scenery. A sign out front announced we had arrived at America's birthplace.

I recognized Josephine Wilde the moment we walked inside the building. For one thing, her photo appeared regularly in all the major wine industry and vineyard management journals. For another she was also frequently featured in glossy magazines like *Wine Spectator, Saveur,* and *Food and Wine.* Last but not least, she was drop-dead gorgeous.

She had been speaking with a woman behind the ticket sales counter, but she turned around and smiled when Quinn and I entered the large, airy atrium. It was deserted except for the three of us and the ticket sales person; the place seemed to echo.

"You must be Lucie and Quinn." Josie Wilde came over and put out her hand. "Nice to meet you. I'm Josie."

She had the flaming red curls of a Botticelli angel, wide

violet eyes, and a dusting of freckles across the bridge of her nose. Dressed in a bright red down jacket, a navy turtleneck sweater, jeans, and work boots, Josie Wilde looked like the person you wanted with you if you were ever lost in a forest in the middle of nowhere or stranded on a desert island. She had the calm, unflappable demeanor of someone who would know how to start a fire without matches, build a shelter using a Swiss Army knife, and find food using her wits.

Quinn and I shook hands with her as she sized us both up. Her eyes lingered on Quinn, who I hoped would be on his best behavior. He wasn't still totally sold that we needed her. I was.

"Nice to meet you, too," I said.

"Absolutely," Quinn said. "A pleasure."

He wasn't sold on her. The look in her eyes said she knew it, too.

"Come on," she said, "let's walk down to the fort. It's so cold and raw today I think we're going to have the place practically to ourselves."

"Thanks for doing this," I said. "We appreciate it."

Josie led us to a door at the back of the Visitor Center and we followed her outside. It was even more hauntingly desolate than the drive along Colonial Parkway had been. Dead trees poked up out of a marshy swamp covered with dry, straw-colored weeds. We walked across a pedestrian footbridge that looked as if it led nowhere.

"You're looking at the Pitch and Tar Swamp." Josie gestured to the bleak landscape on either side of us.

"Seems like an appropriate name," Quinn said.

"Look," I said. "The fort."

A crude, uneven fence built with spindly-looking logs rose in the distance. Beyond it, a British Union Jack flew atop a flagpole. It looked both defiant and somehow inadequate in the lonely surroundings.

"Where's the river?" Quinn asked.

"On the other side of the palisade fence," Josie said. "Archeologists found stains in the clay soil from the original fence, so the one you're looking at is located exactly where the settlers built it, although part of it's now under water in the James. It's triangle-shaped so it completely surrounded the fort."

The James River came into view just then, wide and gleaming, the color of dull pewter. The shoreline on the other side was a long, low, dark smudge. Proper grass had been planted in this area and gravel paths with benches lining them criss-crossed each other leading to the fort and down to the river. A map under glass showed the full fort, the Visitor Center, a picnic area, a cafe, and a building called the Archaearium.

We stopped in front of a tall gray obelisk.

"What's this?" Quinn asked.

"It was erected for the tercentennial in 1907," Josie said, giving him a puzzled look. "A monument to Jamestown when it was a shrine to old Virginia. To what we wanted our history to be."

"What you *wanted* your history to be?"

"You'll have to excuse him," I said. "He's from California."

Josie's face cleared and she grinned.

"It's a rather large state on the West Coast," Quinn said. "Of America. Although we're big enough to be our own country."

Josie laughed. "Obviously this is your first time here?"

He nodded and she turned to me, "You've been here, Lucie, of course?"

I said, chagrined, "Yes, but it's been a while. The last time was for the quadricentennial, in 2007."

"Honey," she said, giving me a severe look, "that's a lifetime. You're not going to recognize the place. They've been making discoveries that put Jamestown on the list of top ten archeological finds in the *world*. Twice. That means what they found here was significant enough to be on a par with ancient sites like Athens and Cairo."

She caught my look of surprise. "You didn't know that?" she asked.

"No," I said in a faint voice.

"So why is this monument a shrine to old Virginia?" Quinn asked.

Josie turned back to him. "That," she said, "is the million-dollar question. And the answer is that until archeologists started finding remains of the old fort and of colonial life here, Jamestown was a place to commemorate Virginia's British heritage, to celebrate our accomplishments and achievements in establishing the first permanent English colony in the New World. Also it was the first place a representative government existed in America." She waved a hand like she was shooing a fly. "We sort of glossed over that pesky old conflict with the Indians and the fact that slavery also began here. The first African slaves arrived in Jamestown in 1619. Sort of by accident, but still, it happened. All of that makes for a very different narrative."

"The fort wasn't discovered until the mid 1990s," I said

to Quinn. "Before then, everyone assumed it had disappeared into the river because of shifting tides and erosion." I gave Josie a sidelong glance. "I do remember some history."

She grinned again and Quinn said, "Wait. Do you mean until about twentysomething years ago no one knew where the Jamestown fort really was? You thought it was in the river somewhere? For almost four hundred years?"

Josie and I looked at each other. "More like three hundred," she said.

"That's still a long time to lose a valuable piece of American history, Virginia people," Quinn said.

"Point taken, Mr. California," I said. "Except it wasn't lost. It was more like a miscalculation about where it was."

"A miscalculation? Really?"

"However, we are making up for lost time." Josie said in a bright voice. She pointed to a roped-off rectangular area that was about twenty by thirty feet. Inside a tarp covered what was clearly a pit; sandbags placed around the perimeter of the tarp kept it secure. "As you can see by all the tarps and fenced-off areas around here, this is still an active archeological site. For obvious reasons everything is covered up now to protect it from the weather. But if you come back in the spring you get a chance to watch the archeologists doing their work."

"You said a lot of new things have been discovered since the quadricentennial," I said.

Josie looked around as if she were trying to conjure a list. "That's right. Since then they've uncovered the foundations of a couple of buildings that were inside the fort . . . the original church, the kitchen, the well. They also found structures in what was known as New Town." She gestured behind us. "Plus they uncovered a couple of dump sites."

"What's a dump site?" Quinn asked.

We were heading toward a fretwork structure of slender logs located inside the perimeter of the triangle fort. It looked like the skeleton of a large building.

"Just what you think it is," Josie told him, "Dump sites or trash pits, if you prefer, are an archeologist's treasure trove. One of the things archeologists learned from them is that the Virginia Company in London bought provisions for the set-tlers on the cheap. The dump sites are full of the junk people threw out. The stuff that didn't work. They even found hel-mets, breastplates . . . armor. Not a good sign."

She watched us absorb that information. What must it have been like for the colonists to realize halfway around the world that they had been suckered into a deal made by a com-pany motivated by profit rather than their well-being? That the owners wouldn't be there to watch this colony fail? Their lives wouldn't literally depend on it, so tough luck.

"The other thing they learned," Josie went on, "is that the men who risked their lives to come to Jamestown weren't lazy good-for-nothings who refused to work as some people had thought. Instead they discovered that this place was a hellhole and the men who came here weren't prepared for what they found. It's practically a miracle anyone survived."

"Why was it a hellhole?" Quinn asked.

"A lot of reasons." Josie started ticking them off on her fingers. "The worst drought in the last six hundred years co-incided with the first six years of Jamestown. A lot of people starved to death. Then you've got the James, a salty tidal river that becomes even saltier in summer. That meant no digging deep wells. Anyone who didn't starve probably died of dysentery or typhoid. Last but not least, two-thirds of the colonists who came here had never done manual labor before in their lives. The sailors from the three ships that brought them to America stayed on for six weeks and built their fort before they returned to England."

"I didn't know about the sailors building the fort," I said.

"The Virginia Company of London didn't send the cream of the crop," she said. "The men who came were hustlers. Scrappers. Children. Servants. Second sons who had no hope of inheriting anything in England."

"This building must be where they lived," I said, indicating the open wooden structure surrounding us.

"The barracks. You wouldn't have seen it in 2007," Josie said. "When John Smith became governor he made the men build it so they weren't sleeping outside in trenches as they had been doing. He also made the rule that anyone who didn't work didn't eat. It was pretty effective."

A frigid gust of wind blew in off the river as she spoke. I pulled up the hood of my jacket and jammed my hands into my pockets. Quinn tugged on his knitted cap so it covered more of his ears and Josie zipped up her down jacket. No one else had joined the three of us the entire time we'd been here. The fort, which already seemed a grim, desolate place, looked increasingly bleak as dark clouds across the river scudded toward us.

"How did they survive in weather like this?" I said. "It must have been brutal."

"It was," Josie said. "The summer wasn't much better."

We left the delicate-looking barracks and walked over to an area that had been marked off by unfinished walls that appeared to be made of packed earth and came up to about the height of my waist. Wooden benches faced an area separated by a railing. Four crosses commemorating graves stood inside what must have been where the minister preached his sermons and led his congregation in prayer. This had to be the original church.

Fifty feet away—outside the walls of the fort—was a brick church that had been here on my last visit. In fact it had been here for more than a century and I knew it had been built on the site of several churches, including one that Nathaniel Bacon the Rebel burned down when he torched Jamestown in 1676. The only part of that church to survive the fire was the bell tower, the remains of which I was looking at right now.

According to what I'd read over the last few days, Nathaniel Bacon the Elder, a distant cousin of his rebel namesake and kin to Sir Francis Bacon, had buried the documents he brought over from England under that very bell tower. Later they had been moved to a vault at Bruton Parish in Williamsburg. The answer to Prescott Avery's search for a lost treasure could have had its origins a few feet from where I stood.

". . . you're standing on the site of the earliest church erected in Jamestown," Josie was saying to Quinn. "This was the church where Pocahontas married John Rolfe."

"Are you serious? Pocahontas?" Quinn sounded awed.

Josie nodded. "Please tell me you're not thinking of the cartoon version of a willowy girl with doe eyes and a feather in her long, dark hair. The real Pocahontas moved to England where her name was changed to Rebecca Rolfe. She died there and was buried there. In Kent, actually."

Quinn gave her a guilty smile and she said in exasperation, "I should have guessed, Mr. California. The land of Mickey Mouse. Of course you're imagining a Disney character."

He laughed and I said, "As long as we're on the subject of fantasy, what about Nathaniel Bacon the Elder burying documents he brought over from England under that bell tower over there?" I pointed to the church. "Supposedly they were moved to Williamsburg during the fire set by the other Nathaniel Bacon when he burned Jamestown. Or maybe even earlier."

Josie raised an eyebrow and turned to look at the bell tower. "I've heard all those stories. No one really knows precisely when the documents were moved to Williamsburg. Or, to be honest, if there were any documents to move." She held up the index and middle fingers of both hands to put quotation marks around "documents."

"You don't believe there was anything to the story?" Quinn asked.

"In all this time, no one has found proof that there *was* anything to it. Just a lot of theories. Some of them crazier than others. I'm a scientist. I deal in facts." She looked over and gave me a wry smile. "I can see you're disappointed, Lucie."

"Is it possible you were digging at the wrong place at Bruton Parish?" I asked. "What if the documents had already been moved?"

"You mean moved from Bruton Vault?"

I nodded.

"For one thing, we didn't find a vault," she said. "Even an empty one."

I shivered and she said, "Come on, let's walk over to the Archaearium. We'll be warmer inside. There's an exhibition on the *Sea Venture* I know you wanted to see. It wasn't there in 2007, either. You can have a look and then we should head over to Williamsburg. I'm afraid I've got a two o'clock appointment at William & Mary that just came up this morning."

"We appreciate you giving us this time here," I said. "And we haven't even spoken about the problems at the vineyard."

"I looked both of you up," she said. "And your vineyard. Now that I've met the two of you, I might be willing to take you on. It's a close working relationship so I've got to like my clients or it doesn't go well. My only condition, as I've told you, is that you have to be willing to go along with what I advise if I'm going to put in the kind of work I intend to do for you. I want you to make good wine. Actually, I want you to make great wine. Wine that wins national prizes, maybe even international prizes. That's the plan."

She hadn't said anything about us liking her. I wondered if the jury was still out with Quinn.

He started to say, "We'd—"

I elbowed him before he could finish. I wanted her to work with us. She was the best and she knew what she was doing.

"Love to," I said. "That would be terrific, Josie. Thank you so much."

"Lucie took the words right out of my mouth," Quinn said and I caught him protecting his ribs from another dig.

"You both need to be one hundred percent on board," she

said with a knowing look at Quinn. "And you need to come to my lab in Charlottesville to see what I can do for you. Then I want to see your vineyard. On my own. Without either of you with me."

"It's a deal," I said and Quinn nodded.

"All right," she said. "After you visit me and I visit you, let's see where we are. Okay?"

"That sounds fair," Quinn said. "What do you think, Lucie?"

"I think I'd really like Josie to work with us," I said. "So I hope the next two meetings are smooth sailing."

"You have an interesting vineyard and a long family history of owning your land so I know how personally important this is to you, Lucie." Josie hooked a thumb in Quinn's direction. "However Mr. California here is not completely sold on the idea. That's why I'd like you to come to the lab. We need to talk some more."

This time she did see me elbow Quinn. "Mr. California," I said, "will see the light by the next time we meet. You have no worries."

We had been walking past rows of metal crosses with no adornment and no names—a large graveyard on the edge of the James River. Next to it was a larger-than-life weathered bronze statue of John Smith, his back to us, proud and defiant, as he looked out over the James River. I already knew that the inscription on the front of the statue read GOVERNOR OF VIRGINIA, 1608 along with his coat of arms: *VINCERE EST VIVERE.* TO CONQUER IS TO LIVE. He'd returned to England under arrest, just as he'd arrived in Jamestown. Eventually he died there without ever returning to Virginia, though he'd written books about his adventures in the New World.

Who were the men buried in the graveyard next to his statue? Had he known many of them and led them as governor? Years ago when I visited the American cemetery in Normandy with my French grandfather, he told me that all the graves of the American soldiers buried there faced west, toward the Atlantic Ocean. Toward home. I wondered if any of the dead buried here at Jamestown had wanted to face England, their home—or did they not want to go back, whatever the consequences?

A small sign indicated the site of Confederate earthworks as Quinn, Josie, and I continued walking toward a long, low building made almost entirely of glass and set up off the ground on short, stubby blocks: the Archaearium.

"Jamestown was a Civil War fort, too?" Quinn pointed to the sign, changing the subject smooth as silk, so we weren't talking about us working with Josie anymore.

She nodded. "The Jamestown settlers picked the perfect strategic location for their fort. Not only were they worried about the Powhatan Indians, they were also afraid the Spanish—who believed Florida extended all the way to Virginia—might sail up the river and attack them. The fort was so well situated the Confederate Army used it as a base to prevent the Union Army from reaching Richmond. Even now the U.S. military still brings troops here to study its strategic importance."

"There must be ghosts that haunt this place," I said. "Spirits of people who died at Jamestown under such horrible conditions."

Josie gave me a startled look. "There are," she said. "I feel them as I walk around these grounds. It's as if the sadness and tragedy never left. It's still here—in some places more than others—but it's real."

"All right, you two," Quinn said, holding the door to the Archaearium for us. "Can we talk about something else besides Jamestown being haunted?"

After the cold, sharp wind that had buffeted us outside, it felt good to be somewhere warm.

"Sure," Josie said. "Welcome to the Archaearium. The museum of Historic Jamestowne."

"I've been here before," I said.

She nodded. "Right after it opened. Now it holds more than four thousand artifacts. It's expanded a lot in the last decade. One of the things I especially like is the fact that because the museum is located right here at the settlement, whatever has been discovered in the field is integrated into the exhibits almost immediately. It's rare to have a museum that's so current and up to date."

A sinewy map of the James River was painted on the floor in the lobby where we stood; a mural in shades of brown and tan depicting London in the early 1600s as a hurly-burly city with the Thames flowing behind it proclaimed THE VIRGINIA COMPANY in bold white letters with a description of how a group of investors decided to take a chance on establishing a colony in Virginia.

England. Where it all began.

"There are eight galleries laid out chronologically," Josie said. "We'll follow them clockwise through the museum."

"Are we the only people here?" I asked.

"We might be," she said. "Though there will be at least one person from the museum staff in the gift shop. It's the last stop."

Though the floor-to-ceiling windows on both sides of the building let in plenty of natural light as we walked through the exhibits, on this gloomy, overcast day the somber exhibitions looked especially stark and sobering. Our footsteps seemed to echo; I was certain we were alone.

The Jamestown Settlement's Archaearium—the repository of artifacts from a fraught, violent, and tragic past—reminded me of a warehouse with its muted browns and grays and twinkling spotlights shining on Plexiglas display cases. It also seemed to be a place where you whispered or spoke quietly so as not to disturb what was preserved here.

"The *Sea Venture* exhibit is nearly at the end," Josie murmured, confirming my suspicion of library silence.

We had gone more than halfway around the museum when Quinn stopped so abruptly that I ran into him.

We were at an exhibit called *Survival*. Quinn leaned forward to read the explanation inside the Plexiglas cabinet. "What the . . . oh, Jesus Christ."

In front of us, the lifelike bust of a beautiful young girl with unblemished skin, full lips, and wavy golden hair partially covered by an embroidered cream-colored cap stared sightlessly into the distance.

"This," Josie said, "is one of the more recent developments that the archeologists working here have managed to confirm along with the help of the Smithsonian. It's . . . unfortunately . . . proof of cannibalism. Survival cannibalism."

"Survival cannibalism," Quinn repeated. "You mean they ate each other because they had to?"

"That's right."

"They ate . . . her?" I asked. "This girl?"

"You didn't know about this?" Josie asked. "They call her Jane."

I wished Josie hadn't given her a name. "No," I said in a faint voice, placing my hands over my stomach. "Somehow I missed it. Though I don't know how."

"The winter of 1609 and 1610 was called the Starving Time," Josie said. "By the time the *Sea Venture* landed in Jamestown a year and a half after it was wrecked off the coast of Bermuda—in the spring of 1610—the men who arrived found only fifty people out of the entire population of Jamestown. They looked like walking skeletons."

"How did they—the researchers—find out about the cannibalism?" Quinn asked.

"Another trash pit," Josie said in a matter-of-fact voice. "They discovered her remains. Bone fragments. Part of her skull. She'd been hacked to death with a cleaver and then eaten. I'll spare you the details—it's more gruesome than you want to know; there were a lot of blows and failed attempts to crack her skull—but scientists from the Smithsonian and Jamestown archeologists were able to reconstruct her face using CT scanning and computer graphics. They were also able to determine where she came from in England and that she was approximately fourteen years old."

"Good God," Quinn said.

I remained mute.

"Are you sure about the cannibalism?" Quinn asked.

Josie nodded. "Absolutely sure. Believe me, everyone did a lot of research and double-checking before putting out something like this to the public. Come," she said, "let's go find the *Sea Venture*. To this day it's called 'the shipwreck that saved

America.' At least that story has a happy ending. There are a lot of what-if theories that if the *Sea Venture* hadn't been shipwrecked and had arrived with the other supply ships instead of a year and a half later, the British might have given up any idea of establishing a colony in the New World. Everyone at Jamestown almost certainly would have died—or disappeared like the lost colony of Roanoke."

No one spoke as Quinn and I followed Josie until we reached the display depicting the wreck of the *Sea Venture* on the island of Bermuda. Knowing what we knew now about the cannibalism that had preceded the arrival of the two smaller boats built out of the salvaged remnants of the *Sea Venture,* it seemed even more astonishing that the passengers had found anyone still alive in Jamestown that spring. Had the Jamestown survivors hidden what they'd done from the unsuspecting colonists who arrived with fresh supplies and an improbable story of their own survival on an island that everyone had believed was enchanted?

"There's a quicker way back to the Visitor Center than walking through the fort and across the bridge," Josie said. "It's used by staff and the researchers, but it's so cold and windy we'll take it, since it's more protected."

We were still subdued as she led us to a path that took us into the forest behind the museum and the fort.

"Where are we?" I asked.

"The staff buildings are back here," she said as the path widened into a dirt-and-gravel road.

The fort, the river, and the Archaearium had disappeared. We came to a fork in the road where two moss-covered stone pillars looked as if they'd once marked the entrance to the settlement. A wrought-iron gate with ivy curling through it was propped against one of the pillars.

Quinn and I exchanged glances. The woods surrounding us were completely silent. No birdsong or the scrabbling noises of squirrels or other animals anywhere.

"Come on," Josie said, as we left the road, "this path will take us back to the parking lot."

"It's even spooky here," I said.

"I know what you mean," Josie said. "You don't want to be walking through these woods alone at night . . . are you all right, Quinn?"

"Just thinking," he said, "about the Donner Party. They ate their dead when they got stranded in the Sierra Nevadas on their way to California back in the Gold Rush days."

"The Donner Party," I said. "I forgot about that. My God, how bad does it have to get when people do something like that?"

"Pretty bad," Josie said. "What happened at Jamestown didn't happen to any of the other early American colonies—Plymouth, the Quakers in Pennsylvania, the Dutch in New York. At Jamestown they were so desperate they ended up killing each other for food after they'd eaten everything else—including their shoes—that they could find to eat."

The view opened up in front of us and suddenly we were back in the parking lot.

"Sorry to end on such a gruesome topic," she added.

"It's okay," I said. "Thank you for the tour. It was unforgettable."

Her face cracked into a small smile. Then she added in a sober voice, "The tercentennial was a celebration of the first

English settlement in North America. By the time the quadri-centennial came around and we knew what really happened here it was more of a commemoration. Everyone should visit this place. It's important."

She hit a button on her key fob. Two quick beeps sounded as the parking lights flashed on the Mini. "Why don't you follow me to Williamsburg?" she said.

On the fifteen-minute drive along Colonial Parkway, I kept thinking about *The Tempest,* which I'd just finished reading, and how it had a happy ending as everyone prepared to leave the island: Ferdinand and Miranda about to get married and Prospero giving up his library of magical books and asking the audience's forgiveness for causing the shipwreck and controlling the characters in the play so that they would do as he wished.

The story at Jamestown—starvation, death, a fire set by one of their own consuming the settlement like a funeral pyre—had been so different I wondered how much Shakespeare had known about what awaited the survivors of the *Sea Venture* after they reached Virginia.

I'd learned more than I bargained for at Jamestown and Josie had said there was nothing to find at Bruton Parish. Yet Jock and Prescott Avery both seemed to think, to the contrary, there was something to Bruton Vault—that it had existed. Prescott hinted before he died that he might even know where the contents were now located.

I would have nothing new to bring with me to the Folger Library tomorrow proving that Shakespeare might not have written Shakespeare. And now that I knew about the cannibalism that had taken place at Jamestown, the memory of the young girl named Jane would haunt me for a long time.

Nineteen

The weather had changed for the worse as we arrived in Williamsburg and it looked and felt as if snow was on the way. Josie parked in a commercial lot near the Wren Building at the edge of the William & Mary campus. Quinn pulled in next to the Mini.

The three of us walked down Williamsburg's main street, affectionately known as Dog Street to the students and locals, and Duke of Gloucester Street to everyone else. Bruton Parish was a few blocks away on the edge of the commercial district and the beginning of the restored eighteenth-century village.

Williamsburg at Christmastime is a magical place. The highlight of the season is the Grand Illumination, an evening in early December that ends with spectacular fireworks and features a torch-lit parade of the Fife and Drums down Dog Street, Christmas music and readings on the Palace Green, and, most famously, more than two thousand five hundred handmade wreaths, swags, and garlands made from pine boughs, magnolia leaves, dried rushes, vines, or feathers and decorated with pinecones, clove-studded oranges, pineapples, berries, dried fruit, flowers, cinnamon sticks, and ribbons. If you could attach it to a wreath and it was faithful to the colonial era, it was probably hanging on a wall, door, window, column, or fence.

We had just missed the Grand Illumination by three days.

"Were you here on Monday?" I asked Josie.

She shook her head. "I was at a vineyard in Orange."

"What happened on Monday?" Quinn asked.

"The Grand Illumination," I said. "We'll come here one year so you can see it."

We crossed Nassau Street and left the commercial district behind. "So is this place the Disney version of Colonial America?" Quinn asked as a woman wearing a long skirt, a heavy cape, and a bonnet walked past us.

Josie and I exchanged glances.

"No," I said. "A lot of these buildings were actually here in the 1700s."

"It's a historic restoration, not a theme park," Josie said. "In the 1920s, the rector of Bruton Parish Church—a man named W.A.R. Goodwin—convinced John D. Rockefeller that Williamsburg was an important colonial town that ought to be saved. The story goes that after Goodwin talked to Rockefeller, Rockefeller took a midnight stroll by himself and when he returned, he agreed to take on the project."

"The rector of the church we're going to visit?" Quinn asked.

"That's right," she said.

"I read that one of the reasons John D. Rockefeller took on

restoring Williamsburg was to keep the documents in Bruton Vault from ever falling into the wrong hands because they were so controversial," I said.

Josie gave me a stern look. "Look, for years Goodwin tried to find a wealthy patron to buy Williamsburg. He started with Henry Ford and then worked on other members of the Ford family after Henry turned him down. He got an "absolutely not" letter from Henry's brother that included a Detroit newspaper article headline: 'Henry Ford Asked to Buy Ancient Virginia Town.' So, I'm sorry, Lucie, but I can't go along with your Rockefeller conspiracy theory. It was a stroke of luck that the Rockefellers happened to visit Williamsburg and Goodwin got a chance to talk to John D."

Quinn reached for my hand and squeezed it. So far Josie had successfully knocked down everything I'd read about Bruton Vault. Plus she'd been here the last time anyone tried to find it. If, against all odds, Prescott had discovered what happened to the documents everyone said didn't exist, it would be a very big deal.

We reached a long low wall enclosing the redbrick church and its small graveyard. A sign next to the entrance announced that Bruton Parish Church, established in 1674, had been an active church continuously since 1715.

"Let's go see the graveyard—the churchyard—before we go inside," Josie said. "That's where we found the foundation of the old church. If the Bruton Vault existed, it was supposed to be there, underneath the original church."

We walked around the back to a tree-shaded enclosure of weathered gravestones and a row of small stone markers lined up in the middle of a bed of ivy.

"Do y'all see those paving stones over there?" Josie pointed to a line of rectangular gray stones bordered by an ancient pine on one side and a magnolia tree on the other. "They mark the perimeter of the old church. We discovered the original foundation on the second excavation when we were searching for the vault. The Colonial Williamsburg Foundation and the Rector of Bruton Parish were fed up to their back teeth with stories and rumors that they were covering up the existence of a secret vault and they swore this was going to be the last damn time the place got dug up. Believe me, Lucie, if there had been a vault hidden there, we would have found it. I can tell you that the soil hadn't been disturbed in a very long time. No vault had been dug. Nothing had been filled in, either."

I stared at the weedy grass and three large tombstones in the middle of the old church boundary. It had just started to snow, fine as mist. But definitely snow.

Could Josie be right? Had I read too much into what Prescott said to me that last day in his wine cellar?

"What if the documents were moved a long time ago?" I asked.

I could almost hear her mentally count to ten. "Where and by whom?"

"Thomas Jefferson supposedly was the last person to see them," I said. "There's a story that he sealed the vault for good and that was supposed to be the end of it."

"That's a lot of supposing." Josie drawled the words in a flat, emphatic voice.

"I know. But what if instead of sealing the vault with the documents inside, Jefferson took them instead? What if he removed Sir Francis Bacon's papers?"

"Well, if he did take them, he didn't take them from any vault located over there." She hooked a thumb in the direction of the old church boundary. *"Because there was no vault."*

"Okay," I said, "maybe it was somewhere else. It's not impossible, is it?"

"Where?"

"I don't know."

"Nor does anybody else."

"But if there *were* documents, is it so impossible to imagine that Thomas Jefferson might have decided they were safer with him than in a vault in the ground?"

She let out a noisy sigh. "Okay, Jefferson was a huge fan of Sir Francis Bacon, I'll give you that. I'm over at Monticello a lot, talking to them all the time about Jefferson's vineyards. And in his study I can tell you there are portraits of the three men Jefferson called 'his trinity of the three greatest men in the world.' John Locke, Sir Isaac Newton, and—" She paused for effect. "Sir Francis Bacon."

"Okay," I said. "There you go. Don't you think that if Thomas Jefferson came across papers that were actually written by Sir Francis Bacon himself, one of Jefferson's three greatest heroes, and they were papers no one had ever seen or knew existed, that a man of Thomas Jefferson's intellectual curiosity would want to take them and keep them someplace safe? Why risk leaving them for someone else to find?"

"If there were papers," she said, "maybe."

"Plus Bacon was one of the investors and founders of the Virginia Company in London. He'd certainly be really interested in everything that went on in the new colony he was helping to finance, right? How far-fetched would it be to imagine that one of his relatives might bring some of his papers—a book that laid out his ideas for how the new government should be set up—to Jamestown itself?" I said. "I'm talking about a completed version of *New Atlantis*—his Utopian novel—as well as proof that some of Shakespeare's plays were actually written by Sir Francis Bacon and not Shakespeare. Say, maybe *The Tempest,* which is probably based on the wreck of the *Sea Venture,* something Bacon would have known about firsthand."

"Lucie," Josie said, "I've heard all this before and you make a convincing case. But no one has found anything—any evidence, any vault, any *anything*—in three hundred years."

I folded my arms across my chest and gave her a stony stare.

"Wait a minute," she said. "Prescott . . . found . . . something? Is that what this is all about?"

"Possibly. I'm not entirely sure."

Her eyes narrowed. "Does this have anything to do with his murder?"

"The Loudoun County Sheriff's Office believes he was murdered because he threatened to sell off the family business—specifically the *Washington Tribune*—against the wishes of everyone in his family and his employees."

She tilted her head and stared as if she were seeing me for the first time. "What do you think?"

The snow had begun falling more heavily, dusting the three of us so we looked as if we were coated in powdered sugar. Three snow angels.

I don't know for sure," I said. "That's what I'm trying to find out. That's why we came here."

I didn't want to tell her about my speculation that the documents had ended up in the White House thanks to Thomas Jefferson and that Dolley Madison had them moved the night the British burned Washington during the War of 1812.

"Did you find what you expected?" she asked.

"You're doing your best to convince us the Bruton Vault didn't exist."

"I could have told you it didn't exist and saved you the trip."

"We needed to see everything for ourselves."

Josie glanced at Quinn. "We? So you also go along with the theory there was a vault and some secret documents, Mr. California?"

Quinn gave me a pained smile. "Sweetheart, you know what Clay said. Prescott was starting to lose it, having trouble separating reality from fantasy." To Josie he added, "You're very persuasive that there was no vault. And there's the fact you were here the last time this graveyard was dug up."

"Prescott was adamant about the Madeira," I said. "That was no fantasy. A lot of people in Atoka knew about it. Thelma Johnson even tried it."

"That's different," Quinn said. "One has nothing to do with the other."

"What Madeira?" Josie asked.

"Ladies, can we discuss this inside the church?" Quinn asked. "My feet are going numb."

Josie started to open her mouth.

"Don't go there," Quinn said. "Just because I'm from California."

She grinned as he held the door for us and we walked inside Bruton Parish Church. Quinn dropped a twenty-dollar bill in the collection box and we said hello to a church volunteer sitting in the vestibule. She thanked Quinn and handed him a brochure on the building's history and architecture.

Since my student days I had always loved the peaceful simplicity of this little church. Though I'm not religious, it had been the place I used to come to get away for a while and just sit in one of the pews. I always felt calmer when I left.

Natural light that was now dulled by snow filtered through the large windows on both sides of the church; lighted wall sconces gave off a golden glow. Just as at Jamestown, we had the place to ourselves. Josie and I watched Quinn walk down the main aisle, pausing to read the signs on the doors to each pew.

"He'll be impressed," I said to her. "Wait and see."

He was. When he came back he said, "General George Washington, Thomas Jefferson, James Monroe, Patrick Henry . . . did all those guys really go to church here?"

"All those guys really did," Josie said.

"Williamsburg was the capital of Virginia after it moved from Jamestown," I said, "and it was the law that you had to attend services."

"Not to change the subject," Josie said, "but what about this Madeira?"

We sat side by side in George Washington's front-row pew because Quinn wanted to, and I told Josie what Prescott had told me about it.

"You have no idea where it is?" Josie asked.

"None," Quinn said.

"Just like everything else we've talked about today," I said.

Her smile was rueful. "If you do find it, you've got to let me know. Madeira was the wine of choice in America for two hundred years—it's all anyone drank. The British saw to that when they taxed everything else. Plus it was a sign of wealth. People used to have Madeira parties to show off their collection—they even rented pineapples, which were also a sign of wealth, for the parties. I would have given anything to be at one of them, just to see a rented pineapple. And try the Madeira, of course."

"Me, too," Quinn said. "Maybe not so much for the pineapple, but definitely the Madeira."

"The Founding Fathers drank it when they signed the Declaration of Independence and toasted the Constitution with it," Josie said. "Madeira used to be a very big deal."

Which explained why Prescott had been so adamant about having Ian's Madeira: James Madison planned to drink it at a July 4 anniversary celebration on Capitol Hill, just as his friends and colleagues had done in 1776.

Josie checked her watch and stood up. "I'm sorry, but I've really got to go. It's a quarter to two and I'm going to have to run to get to the college for my appointment."

"Thank you again for meeting with us," I said as Quinn and I stood and shook her hand. "And for all your help."

"I'll be in touch about a date when you can come see me in Charlottesville," she said. "If I were the two of you, I'd focus on looking for that Madeira. If you find it, it will be worth a fortune."

"Believe me," Quinn said, "we're looking."

"As for the documents in the Bruton Vault . . ." She rubbed her fingers together and then snapped them open to show there was nothing there, her eyes fixed on me. "In three hundred years, no one has been able to prove they existed. We know for a fact there was no vault here at Bruton Parish where everyone said it was supposed to be. In spite of what Prescott Avery may have told you, I'm sorry, Lucie, but as a scientist, I've got to go with the facts."

We heard the click of the church door as it closed behind her.

"She could still be wrong," I said.

"Let it go for now. And let's go home, sweetheart." Quinn glanced out the window. "It looks like it's starting to blizzard."

I nodded. Quinn was right.

The bigger question, though, was whether Josie Wilde was right as well.

"YOU'RE AWFULLY QUIET," QUINN said as we pulled onto the final stretch of highway on our way back to Atoka in the steadily falling snow.

The pristine landscape illuminated by our headlights looked peaceful and serene. Traffic on I-95 heading north had slowed because of the slick roads and limited visibility. Every so often a snowplow passed us and trucks lumbered by dispersing liquid snowmelt or salt. Inside, the Jeep was a comforting cocoon; the heater blasted warm air and my feet had finally thawed. I'd found a satellite radio station playing Christmas holiday classics and Bing Crosby was crooning "I'll Be Home for Christmas." The windshield wipers swishing back and forth kept time like a muted metronome.

"I'm thinking about everything we saw today," I said, "and all the reasons Josie gave us why there was no secret trove of documents that Nathaniel Bacon smuggled into Jamestown. And no hidden vault under Bruton Parish."

Quinn put on his turn signal and changed lanes to let a car pass us. "Yes, but in spite of those reasons you still believe the documents exist," he said. It was a statement, not a question.

"I think Prescott believed they did. And Hobson Banks's letter in Leland's safe-deposit box talked about something of value Banks removed from the White House before the British showed up to burn it."

"Sweetheart, Banks could have been referring to anything. Everything in the White House is valuable, isn't it? And I wasn't asking about Prescott." He gave me a meaningful look. "I was asking about you."

"I know you were."

"So?"

The song changed and the display on the radio read *Doris Day . . . Have Yourself a Merry Little Christmas.*

"I know Clay thinks Prescott was starting to lose it and that he was becoming mentally unstable, but I don't believe it. First, Clay has the best reason of all for wanting to prove he's right—so he can challenge Prescott's decisions, like his plans to sell the *Trib*. Second, I think Prescott was as sharp as a tack. He knew exactly what he was saying, hinting about the final missing piece he'd discovered so he could find a hidden treasure," I said. "He also said it was time to shine a light on something that had been hidden in the darkness for too long. And then he said something that's been stuck in my brain—a proverb. 'Truth is the daughter of time.'"

"What's that supposed to mean?"

"That was only part of it . . . I don't remember the rest." I reached for my phone, flicked it on, and started searching. A moment later, I said, "Here it is. 'Truth is the daughter of time, not of authority.' And you'll never guess who it's attributed to."

"Thomas Jefferson?"

"Sir Francis Bacon."

His eyebrows went up. "Maybe it's a coincidence."

"Seriously?"

"Okay, it's not a coincidence. Then what was it? A hint? A clue?"

"Possibly. But not a coincidence. And after everything we've seen today, I think what Prescott meant was that sooner or later the truth always comes out. No one can stop it forever. That's what he was planning to do—finally reveal the truth about those documents, even though, as he told me, there were people who didn't want anything about them to be known."

Quinn seemed to consider that for a while. The music changed again. *Dean Martin . . . Winter Wonderland.*

Finally he said, "You could be right."

"Why, thank you."

He grinned. "So what's the plan now?"

"Tomorrow I'm meeting a friend of Frankie's in D.C. at the Folger Shakespeare Library."

"Do you still need to do that?"

I nodded. "I'm curious whether she believes *The Tempest* was based on the wreck of the *Sea Venture* and what she can tell me about it. And even though I don't have any proof that Sir Francis Bacon might have written some of Shakespeare's plays, the Folger has a research center available to anyone with new information on him or the plays. Frankie's friend is in charge of it."

"Do you need me to come along?"

"You have that deer-in-the-headlights look as if I just asked you to come clothes shopping with me. No, you don't need to come. Anyway, I'm going to try to have lunch with Kit before my meeting."

"In Leesburg?"

"In Washington. Things are in such turmoil at the *Trib* they asked her to work in D.C. She figures she'll be there until the Sheriff's Office arrests someone for Prescott's murder. According to her it's like being in a European royal court a couple of centuries ago when the king or the queen and some heir apparent were plotting against each other and everyone was trying to figure out who was going to win and what side to be on. She says the place is full of spies and intrigue. It's making her crazy."

"I wonder how long that's going to take."

"Until she goes crazy?"

"Until Bobby finds out who did it."

"Somehow I don't think it's going to take long at all. I'll bet Bobby's already circling the wagons around a suspect."

"Who?"

I sucked in my breath. "I don't know. I try not to think about it because of who the most likely possibilities are."

"It must be hell living at Hawthorne Castle these days."

"Or working at the *Trib*," I said.

He turned onto Mosby's Highway. Almost home.

"I have an idea," he said. "We forgot to have lunch and I'm

starved. The snow's tapering off. Why don't we go to the Inn for dinner?"

We hadn't forgotten lunch. Neither of us had wanted to think about food after we left Jamestown earlier today.

"The Inn sounds like a good idea," I said. "I'm hungry, too."

THE GOOSE CREEK INN sits in the curve of a bend on Sam Fred Road on the outskirts of Middleburg. When you come upon it on a snowy night as we did, it looks like a life-sized sugar-dusted gingerbread house tucked away all by itself in the middle of a forest. The fairy lights strung through the surrounding trees were snow-frosted and the windows glowed with the golden light of crystal chandeliers and candles on tables, making the place seem enchanted.

The parking lot, however, was jam-packed and anything but peaceful.

"Why the hell is this place so crowded on a Wednesday night? Who's crazy enough to eat out when it's snowing?" Quinn asked in a growl.

"Well, we are."

"We're different . . . hey, I think there's going to be a spot. That couple's leaving. I'm following them back to their car."

"You're stalking them. Be careful you don't hit them . . . it's slippery."

"Do you want to drive?"

"How much snow did you get in California?"

"I didn't do too badly getting us here, did I?" He zipped into the parking place right behind the other car as it pulled out. "Look, not a scratch."

We got out of the Jeep. "I'm sorry," I said. "I'm just hangry."

He pulled me toward him and wrapped his arm around my waist. "I love you. And I'm hangry, too."

He held the front door for me and we stepped into another crowded space. The congested lobby was filled with people waiting for tables, occupying every available seat, or perusing the recipes in the *Goose Creek Inn's Best-Loved Recipes Cookbook,* which was on display on an antique sideboard. As always, the place smelled of something wonderful for dinner.

Hassan, who had been the maître d' for as long as I could remember, stood at the front desk in his usual dark suit and a floppy Santa hat, charming a grumpy-looking party of four.

"This wasn't a good idea," I said to Quinn. "We should go home."

"Lucie?" Hassan gestured at Quinn and me to join him as the foursome followed a waiter into the dining room.

We made our way through the crowd to his desk. "I'm so sorry, but there's truly no room at the Inn tonight."

"We'll find a stable," Quinn said. "No worries."

Hassan burst out laughing.

"Seriously, we're going home," I said. "We should have called, but we were on the road for the last couple hours driving in the snow. It was an impulsive decision to come by."

"Wait a minute, don't go," he said. "I have an idea. You might help me with a . . . situation. Your cousin is dining with a guest just now in the green dining room. I can assure you that she'd welcome your company. If you wouldn't mind, that is. . . . Give me a quick second."

He pulled out his phone and started to text.

The green dining room was the most private and secluded

room in the Inn. Dominique usually kept it available for VIP guests—a former president and First Lady, a Supreme Court justice and a spouse or friend. A senator and his much younger female . . . aide. Anyone who required discretion. There was also an unobtrusive exit to a side parking lot.

"Who's her guest? Ebenezer Scrooge?" Quinn asked.

Hassan's mouth twitched and he lowered his voice. "Celia Avery. She's here to talk about the Miranda Foundation gala and we're catering it. Dominique already made a quick trip to the kitchen on the pretext of checking something and told the chef she was like 'a tiger at the end of her tail.'"

Though my cousin had lived in the U.S. for the last twelve years and was now a citizen, she still wrestled with English—especially our idioms. Usually, though, you knew exactly what she meant.

I grinned. "It doesn't sound good."

His phone beeped and he checked it. "It's not. Care to join them?"

"Maybe we should just go home and leave Dominique to it," Quinn told him, as I said, "Of course we would."

The two of us looked at each other. Quinn sighed and shrugged, turning to Hassan.

"You heard the lady. We'd love to."

Hassan picked up two menus and handed them to a waiter. As we were leaving I heard him say under his breath to Quinn, "A wise decision, Mr. Santori. Very wise."

"Somehow," Quinn said, "I think I'm going to regret this."

On the way to the green dining room he said to me, "Why would we love to have dinner with Dominique and Celia Avery when it's not going well?"

"To bail out my cousin," I said. "Why else?"

I heard him mutter, "Should have ordered a pizza" as we walked in to the small green-and-gold jewel of a room and Dominique caught sight of us. Her eyes registered gratitude and relief.

Celia Avery was a cool patrician beauty with fine-boned features and silvery-blond hair she wore in a sleek pageboy. She was originally from Boston and had an East Coast aloofness that could come across as snobbish or haughty—though over the years I grew to think it fit in well with the polished patina of the Avery family's reputation as old Southern aristocracy. Whenever I saw Celia she always looked perfectly pulled together in expensive tailored clothing and as if nothing got under her skin. Tonight, based on her body language, something definitely had gotten under her skin. I took a wild guess: the Miranda Foundation gala.

Dominique stood up as we joined them. Today my petite cousin's auburn hair looked as if she'd hacked it off herself with pruning shears and it stuck up in wild tufts. She was dressed, as usual, with the innate style and confidence every Frenchwoman possessed, wearing offbeat clothes no one else could get away with and looking smart and stylish. Though she'd given up smoking a few months ago, she flashed an SOS at me that I knew meant she'd kill for a cigarette just now.

"We don't mean to intrude," I said, "but Hassan said there are no more tables available until later tonight and—"

"*Pas de problème.* He texted me, so I knew you were coming." She was smiling but her voice sounded strained. "Celia and I just finished our business conversation. Please join us."

She cast a look at Celia, who gave a stiff nod and started to rise.

"Actually, I should be going," Celia said. "Nice to see you, Lucie, Quinn."

"Celia," Dominique said, "you just ordered coffee and dessert. Please stay."

Celia's lips tightened and she sat down. So did Quinn and I. A waiter appeared and we quickly glanced through our menus and both decided to have the carbonnade. Quinn asked for a beer; I ordered a glass of Willamette Pinot Noir.

Quinn broke the silence first. "So how's everything going with the gala?"

Dominique looked like she wanted to strangle him for asking and I found his foot under the table and gave it a kick. I caught his eye as he realized belatedly that he had just waded into a swamp of alligators.

"Awful," Celia said immediately. "Worse than awful. I've been telling Dominique all evening that we really ought to cancel it. With this criminal investigation hanging over everyone's heads, no one wants to go through with it. Guests are backing out and canceling left and right."

"And I've been telling Celia," Dominique said as if she were still struggling to hold on to her patience, "that canceling will be the worse option of the two because the foundation will forfeit so many deposits at this late date. It's Christmas, the busiest time of year for entertaining. We've been planning this evening since August. People will still come. The Miranda Foundation does a lot of good in the community. We've made our bed, now we just have to find it."

Celia's hands fluttered like a pair of nervous birds. A diamond solitaire on the third finger of her left hand flashed in the candlelight and she began twisting it around and around.

"Is that an engagement ring?" I said. "It's beautiful."

Dominique looked as if I'd thrown her a lifeline. The waiter arrived with our drinks, an espresso for Dominique, and a coffee and tiramisu for Celia.

Celia gave a faint smile and said, "It is. Jack finally got down on one knee and proposed the day before Thanksgiving."

Celia had never remarried after Tommy's death, but five or six years ago she fell in love with her personal trainer at the gym. Eventually he moved in with her and they had been together ever since.

"Congratulations. How wonderful."

Quinn lifted his beer. "Great news. To the two of you."

"Yes," Dominique said. "*Félicitations.*"

Celia stopped fiddling with her ring. "Thank you, all of you. Unfortunately not everyone is happy for us. I stopped by to tell Prescott the news on Saturday before the party."

"What do you mean?" I asked.

"He was upset. Actually, he was angry."

"You're not serious." This from Dominique.

"I am."

"Why?" Quinn asked. "Jack's a great guy."

"I know he is. But Prescott blew his top. He told me he's cared for me as a member of the Avery family ever since Tommy died, treating me as if I were his and Rose's daughter. Financially, personally . . . plus he gave me a job running the foundation," she said. "He made it sound as if I were being disloyal. He's always thought Jack was unworthy of me because of what he does for a living."

"That's unfair," I said.

"After I told him about the engagement I found out he'd just had a huge battle with Clayton over him wanting to marry Victoria." Celia picked up her spoon and toyed with her tiramisu. "Prescott said he didn't care if Jack and I lived together, but if I remarried and made it legal he was going to remove me from the Avery Communications board of directors and I was done running the Miranda Foundation."

"Why would he do that?" I said. "That's awful."

"Jack is good at what he does, but he doesn't make a lot of money. It's no secret that I'm supporting both of us with my income." She shrugged. "He thought Victoria was a gold digger. Chasing after Clay because of the Avery family fortune."

"He said the same thing about Jack?" Quinn said.

"Prescott told me if I marry Jack, I'm also out of the family will. Even though Tommy and I didn't have children, after Miranda died, I became the only link they had to Tommy. And running the Miranda Foundation almost seemed as if I took Miranda's place in their lives."

"What are you going to do?" Dominique asked.

Celia set down her spoon. "Prescott's dead and the will he had in place at the time of death still stands. There's really nothing to do—anymore."

"In other words, you're still in it?" Quinn asked.

Celia nodded. "I am. But because I was at the Castle the day Prescott was murdered and we argued, I'm now a suspect. And I have no alibi for the time he was killed."

"Isn't Jack your alibi?" I asked.

"Unfortunately not," she said. "Jack was so upset when I came home and told him what happened, he drove over to

Hawthorne right after that to have a talk with Prescott. So guess what?"

"You're both on Bobby Noland's suspect list for the murder of Prescott Avery?" I said.

She nodded. "We are. I wish I could alibi Jack but I can't. When he left he was so angry he said he was ready to kill someone. I hope he didn't mean it."

Twenty

When Quinn and I came downstairs the next morning the Fraser fir that Seely's Garden Center had delivered to Highland House while we were away yesterday scented the house so it smelled like Christmas.

"When do you want to decorate it?" Quinn asked as we stood in the foyer admiring the tall, fragrant tree.

"I don't know. I'm having lunch with Kit in town before my meeting at the Folger. I'll probably be gone most of the day. Maybe tomorrow? Or else after the weekend when Christmas in Middleburg is over."

"If I get a chance I'll bring the ornaments down from the attic. We can put the boxes in the library so they're out of the way until we get around to the tree," he said.

"That's a good idea." I walked over to the library and opened the door. "What the hell . . . what happened here?"

He sprinted across the room and peered through the doorway. "What's wrong?"

"Leland's documents. I left the envelope Seth gave me next to the computer. Now those papers are scattered all over the desk." My voice rose. "Did you . . . ?"

"Do that? No."

I felt the color leave my face. "Someone's been here looking through these papers."

Quinn put an arm around my shoulder. "Calm down, sweetheart. It was probably Eli. Or maybe Persia moved the envelope when she came in to clean and they fell out."

"If it was Persia, you know she'd put them back where they belonged."

"All right, then, Eli."

A quick call to my brother who I woke up and got the tetchy reply that the only room he'd been in yesterday was the kitchen to make himself lunch.

"And you're welcome for setting up your Christmas tree and getting it in the stand," he said, still grumpy. "I got pine-sap all over me."

"Thank you."

My next call to Persia, who was still in her apartment above Eli's studio in the carriage house, confirmed two things: first, she hadn't touched anything on my desk, either. Second, when Quinn and I had been in Jamestown yesterday, she had left the house for about an hour to run errands, but left the front door unlocked for Eli who had misplaced his keys. I thanked her and hung up.

"Someone's been here," I said to Quinn. "Someone who knew about Leland's papers."

"Why didn't they take them?"

"He—or she—probably took photos. Maybe Persia or Eli

showed up and whoever it was didn't get a chance to clean up."

We both went quiet. Then Quinn said in a tense, worried voice, "Is anything else missing?"

"Check the gun cabinet," I said. "I'll check upstairs in the bedroom."

My mother's jewelry, the pieces I'd inherited after she died that meant so much to me. For years I'd been promising myself I would get around to having the more valuable items appraised and properly insured. Then there was my beautiful antique engagement ring—Quinn's Spanish grandmother's ring—that I didn't wear on days when I knew I was going to get my hands dirty at the winery.

Please. Not them, too. I climbed the grand circular staircase in the foyer as quickly as I could and flew into the bedroom.

I didn't realize I'd been holding my breath until I opened the burgundy leather jewelry case my father had bought my mother as a birthday gift on a trip to Switzerland. Everything was where it belonged. I said a silent prayer of thanks, vowed to photograph and insure all of it, and at the top of the stairs leaned over the banister and called down to Quinn.

"Everything's here."

He stepped into the foyer and looked up. "Same with the gun cabinet."

I came downstairs and checked my purse, which I'd left on a chair in the foyer next to Leland's bust of Thomas Jefferson. "Wallet, credit cards, keys. They're all here. That envelope seems to be the only thing that anyone touched."

"Maybe you should call Bobby."

"And get a lecture because someone walked into an

unlocked house and looked at some papers, but didn't take them? Plus no jewelry, money, credit cards, or guns are gone? No thanks. He'll never believe me, you know that."

"Are you absolutely one hundred percent sure you left the papers in the envelope?"

"Yes."

"So who, besides you, me, Eli, and Seth would know about them?"

"I don't know . . . nobody."

"What about when you left the bank? Did you run into someone?" he asked.

"Nope. But even if someone saw me, I was carrying an envelope. Big deal."

"Someone must have seen you. Or found out you had those documents."

"The only person who would be interested in them is searching for the same thing Prescott was."

"Do you mean whoever killed him?"

"Maybe," I said and then thought about it some more. "Very likely."

"In that case, you should definitely call Bobby."

My phone dinged with a text message and I slid it out of my pocket. "It's from Kit. She's stuck at her desk and wants to know if I'd mind eating in the newsroom. Or, as she calls it, the shark tank."

Another ding.

I shook my head. "And would I mind bringing lunch."

"What are you going to do?" Quinn asked.

"Pick up something to eat, have lunch with her at the *Trib*, and go to my meeting at the Folger."

"I meant about calling Bobby."

"We can't prove any crime was committed." I twirled my finger next to my ear. "Bobby already thinks the idea Prescott might have been murdered because he was looking for a hidden treasure is nuts. If I tell him about this, he's going to say I jumped into the same crazy boat."

Quinn shrugged, but in the end he agreed I was probably right.

"I'll make coffee," he said. "Why don't you clean up in here? Maybe you should lock the envelope in the file cabinet this time."

"The horse has already left the barn," I said. "There's no point locking up anything."

We had breakfast then he kissed me good-bye at the front door.

"Text me when you get to D.C. And when you leave. I hope nothing goes wrong."

"I'll be fine. The meeting at the Folger is at one. I probably won't be there more than an hour or an hour and a half, tops."

"I wasn't talking about the Folger," he said. "I was talking about the shark tank. The *Trib*."

I STOPPED IN MIDDLEBURG before driving into Washington and got sandwiches at the deli—pastrami and cheese on rye with extra pickles for Kit, a veggie wrap for me. I also bought cow puddles, her favorite cookies, from The Upper Crust. I very nearly brought a bottle of our wine because it seemed as if she could use a drink, but figured it probably wasn't the best idea if we were dining in the newsroom. So I bought two waters instead.

I paid a usurious fee to park in a garage half a block from the *Trib* headquarters on Farragut Square and walked to the imposing granite building with its huge glass entrance and THE WASHINGTON TRIBUNE in enormous Gothic brass letters above the door. At night the *Trib*'s Art Deco tower, a well-known feature on the Washington skyline, was lit up—usually the lights were white, but on the Fourth of July, they were red, white, and blue, green on St. Patrick's Day, and so on. I'd heard that the year the Redskins went to the Super Bowl the lights were burgundy and gold. No one I knew expected to see those colors again during their lifetime, though, as they say, hope springs eternal.

The *Trib*'s Loudoun bureau, on the other hand, was a sweet little house on Harrison Street in Leesburg with a white picket fence out front, a front porch where Kit and her staff ate lunch in warm weather, and a graceful magnolia tree that shaded the front yard. I wondered if anyone from D.C. had been out to Leesburg to see the bureau in the hinterlands. Night and day.

I pulled open the heavy front door, which had another *Tribune* logo in Gothic gold lettering stenciled on it, and entered the lobby. More granite, at least an acre of it, and highly polished teak walls. Framed photographs of iconic moments in history when a *Trib* reporter—or an Avery—was in the thick of it. A long, sleek guard's desk, a metal detector, two no-nonsense well-armed security guards who eyed me as I came in, and an enormous screen with the *Trib*'s website displayed, all of which looked a lot more formidable than the motherly lady who sat at the front desk in Leesburg answering phones and calling visitors "dear" or "sugar."

I had to show my license, have my photo taken, and Kit had to come to the lobby to escort me upstairs. I put our lunch and my purse through the security machine and waited for them to emerge. She leaned over and swiped the badge hanging around her neck on a lanyard on a security pad at an entrance gate. It opened and we walked to a bank of elevators.

The Metro desk was at the back of the newsroom on the third floor.

"I didn't expect it to be so big," I said.

"You've been here before," Kit said.

"Nope. First time."

Floor-to-ceiling glass windows ran along one side of the airport-hangar-sized room. They looked out on an interior courtyard below filled with benches and tables that I suspected got a lot of use when the weather was nicer. The newsroom itself consisted of rows and rows of open cubicles where reporters and editors worked at computer screens, watched television news, and talked quietly on the phone. Offices and a conference room lined the side of the room opposite the windows; all the walls were glass, meaning everyone could watch what was going on.

Most of the televisions had the sound turned off and conversations—whether on the phone or between journalists and editors—were muted. We could have been in a library.

Kit had already pulled an extra chair into her cubicle for me. Except for a wilted-looking cactus on a shelf above her desk and a plain vanilla wall calendar, it was bare.

"Whose office is this?" I asked.

"No one's. I stole the plant to make it look more homey."

"It's quieter than I expected. And you don't have much privacy."

"It's a goldfish bowl," she said. "See those offices up there?" She pointed to two large glass offices one floor above us that were cantilevered out over part of the newsroom. "Those belong to Scotty and Alex. She took over Clay's office after he retired. Even though they're upstairs and partially screened off, those of us with desks at the back of the room can see them arguing. It's not much fun. And the glass isn't entirely soundproof when they're shouting."

"That must be awful." We sat down. "Whose office is that?" I pointed to a large glassed-in room across from us. The vertical blinds had been pulled to one side. The office, which was strewn with papers, books, piles of newspapers, and a couple of Starbucks cups, was empty.

"Grant Lowry's," she said. "Fortunately he's the kind of managing editor who has an open-door policy. The only time those blinds are pulled is to give one of us privacy with him when we need it. He also believes in management by walking around, so don't be surprised if he appears over your shoulder."

"Thanks for letting me know." Instinctively I looked over my shoulder before taking our sandwiches out of the deli bag. "Hazel knows you like extra pickles. She says to tell you hi."

Kit's face lit up. "You went to the Middleburg deli? And The Upper Crust for cow puddles? Aw, Luce, thanks."

"I figured you could use comfort food. How are you doing?"

She shrugged. "It's like living in a snake pit. I can't wait to get back to Leesburg. For the time being I'm staying in a boutique hotel off New Hampshire Avenue during the week so I don't have to commute every day. Anyway, Bobby's working flat-out trying to solve Prescott's murder, so he's not home much, either."

"I hope he finds out who did it soon."

"You and me both." She bit into her sandwich and closed her eyes. "I'm in heaven. And homesick." When she finished chewing she said, "What are you doing in town? You didn't mention why you were coming."

"I've got a meeting on the Hill." The Folger was only two blocks from the Capitol, so it was mostly true.

"Lobbying on behalf of farm wineries again?"

I hadn't told Kit anything about Prescott's claim that he'd found the last clue in the search for a lost treasure and how I'd gotten involved. Not only that, I *believed* Prescott in spite of all logical evidence to the contrary. And then there was my ransacked office. Kit would give me a fair hearing if I told her what had happened—and I could trust her. But the besieged newsroom of the *Washington Tribune* was not the place to start spilling information.

"It's not about farm wineries," I said. "It's a story that should be told over a bottle of wine at the Goose Creek Bridge. Not here."

Her eyes widened. The Goose Creek Bridge had been our private hangout since we were teenagers. Built more than two hundred years ago, it had been abandoned after Mosby's Highway was widened in the 1950s. Now the local garden club cared for it because it was of historical interest as a Civil War battle site. The two of us liked going there because most of the time it was deserted.

"At least tell me what's going on."

I lowered my voice and leaned closer to her. "Prescott claimed he had made an important historical discovery before he died. It's a long story, but I'm trying to find out if he was right."

"So you're going up to the Hill?"

"I'm going to the Folger Library."

"The Shakespeare Library? Why? What for?" Her voice rose.

"Shh." I laid a finger over my lips. "More than likely just chasing a unicorn."

"What are you talking about?"

"I'll explain. Word of honor. But not here."

She dropped her voice to a whisper. "Does this have something to do with Prescott's death?"

"It might. And before you ask, I already told Bobby about it. He doesn't believe there's a connection."

She sat back and folded her arms, absorbing that information. "But you do."

I nodded. "What's going on with the investigation, anyway? Is he any nearer to finding out who did it?"

"My husband is incredibly tight-lipped, as you know, but they're still taking a close look at the family. Grant ended up on the short-list of suspects, so he's taken himself off the story and our senior Metro editor is handling it. That's why I'm here in D.C.—I'm off it as well because Bobby is the lead detective on the case."

"Quinn and I had dinner at the Inn last night. We joined Dominique and Celia Avery," I said. "Celia and Jack—her new fiancé—were also at the Castle on Saturday. Apparently they both have motives as well."

Kit chugged water from her bottle. "I heard. Prescott was going to kick her out of the will if she married Jack."

"Word gets around fast."

"Small town."

"So who did it?" I asked.

"I don't know." She crumpled her sandwich paper and stuffed it in the deli bag. "They all have motives. And means and opportunity. If you ask me, I think there's a good possibility that—"

"Kit. So sorry to interrupt what appears to be a private conversation, but there's a staff meeting in my office in fifteen. I thought I'd drop by to tell you in person." Alexandra Avery, dressed in a black turtleneck, black sweater, and black wool pants, stood behind me. Her shoulder-length blond hair was pulled back into a ponytail and tied with a black ribbon. She looked so pale and tense that her bright red lipstick could have been a slash of blood across her face. She also didn't look sorry to have interrupted anything.

She gave me a cool look. "Hello, Lucie. What brings you here?"

How long had she been standing there? We wouldn't have seen her over the other side of the partition. How much had she overheard?

"Hi, Alex. A meeting on the Hill. I stopped by and brought lunch since I was in town," I said. "My condolences again on your grandfather's death."

"Thank you. How very kind. I suppose Kit told you there's

an office pool, betting which one of us in the family killed Prescott?" She arched an eyebrow in a way that made me think of the White Witch who froze Narnia for a hundred years.

I threw Kit a shocked look. "No, she didn't. Of course not."

Alex swiveled her gaze to Kit. "Am I still the pool favorite, the guilty one? What are my odds? Maybe I should bet, too."

"Alex, stop," Kit said. "Don't."

"Then don't underestimate me," she said. "Nothing goes on around here that I don't know about sooner or later." She eyed both of us. "*Nothing*. And believe me, once this all shakes out, the troublemakers will find themselves out of jobs."

She swept out of the cubicle. Kit and I looked at each other. Now she was the one who was as pale as chalk.

"Do you think she overheard us?" I mouthed at her.

She shrugged.

"I should go," I said.

"I'll escort you to the lobby." She sounded chastened.

At the elevator she said under her breath, "I told you it was bad here. I didn't realize she's been keeping a naughty-and-nice list like Santa. Jeez. What do you bet I'm on the bad list? Where's your car, by the way?"

"The garage down the street."

"I wouldn't drive to the Folger if I were you. Parking's a misery. You'd be better off taking a cab or Ubering and leaving your car here."

"That's a good idea."

"When are we going to talk?" she asked.

"Are you coming home for Christmas in Middleburg this weekend?"

"Of course. I'm bringing my mother. She's still such a kid about Christmas."

Faith Eastman, Kit's mother, had been like a second mother to me after my mother was killed when her horse threw her in a riding accident. I adored Faith. Now she lived in a nearby assisted living home.

"We'll find time to talk over the weekend. Somehow," I said.

"Good."

The elevator arrived and we stepped in. In the lobby downstairs she hugged me and took my badge. "I'll sign you out. Good luck with your meeting."

"Thanks. Hey—is there really a betting pool?"

She hesitated. "There is. Journalists are the worst cynics in the world."

"Who's . . . I mean, is there a . . . ?"

Her smile was lopsided. "Who do you think it is?"

"Alex?"

"You didn't even hesitate." She pointed a finger at me. "Bingo."

I LEFT THE *TRIBUNE* building and walked to the corner of Farragut Square where Connecticut Avenue, K Street, and 17th Street intersected and where it would be easy to hail a cab and probably faster than Uber. A black Lincoln Town Car pulled up alongside me as I put up my hand and someone powered down the rear passenger window.

"Lucie?" Grant Lowry looked out of the window. "I thought I recognized you. Heading somewhere?"

"The Hill," I said.

The car door opened. "In that case, hop in. That's where I'm going. I've got a meeting in the Capitol."

I did not feel like getting in a car with Grant Lowry and having to explain to him where I was really going.

"I don't want to trouble you. I'll just catch a cab . . . thanks, anyway."

"It's no trouble at all," he said, smiling and opening the door wider. "Besides, you look like you're freezing out there."

As if on cue a stinging blast of wind blew the hood of my coat so it flew up and whipped my hair into my face.

"Come on," he said. "Get in before the next wind gust blows you away completely. It's cold."

He moved over and waited for me to climb in. I let him take my cane as I slid in and closed the car door.

The driver turned left on K and left again at 17th, heading past the White House to Constitution Avenue. The quickest route to the Hill.

"Thanks for the lift," I said. "I don't want to make you late for your appointment."

"We're going to the same place. Don't worry. What brings you to town?" He was wearing a navy wool overcoat with a Burberry scarf knotted around his neck. A smart-looking gray suit, pale blue shirt, and paisley tie were visible under the coat. A leather satchel lay on the seat between us. I could smell his cologne, something sophisticated, traces of lavender, musk, and cedar.

"Lunch with Kit Noland and then a meeting."

"On the Hill," he said.

I nodded and didn't elaborate.

"It's a big place," he said, sounding amused. "Where can my driver drop you?"

Of course he had to know. "The Library of Congress would be fine," I said. "I don't want to take you out of your way."

"There are three buildings," he said. "Which one?"

"Jefferson."

Grant leaned toward the front seat. "Orlando, we're going to drop Ms. Montgomery at the Jefferson Building. Then you can take me to the Capitol."

Orlando stopped as a traffic light turned red and said, "Very good, Mr. Lowry."

"Thank you," I said again.

Grant waved a hand. "Well, it gives us a chance to talk, doesn't it?"

I could feel him transform from chivalrous gentleman to flinty interrogator. He was going to grill me about Prescott.

"Talk about what?"

"Come on, Lucie."

"You want to know about my meeting with Prescott," I said. "That's why you offered me the ride."

"My dear," he said and it sounded as if he were chiding me, "you were the last person to see him alive."

"Second to last."

He didn't even blink. "Why did he bring you downstairs to his wine cellar to ask you about buying wine? He could have done that in his study, or any place else in the house."

"Maybe because he wanted privacy." I shrugged. "It didn't matter because I didn't have the wine he was interested in. So that was the end of the discussion."

Grant crossed one leg over the other and picked at an

imaginary piece of lint on the knife-sharp crease in his trouser leg. "Clay said it was bottles of a rare Madeira."

"That's right."

"Did Prescott say why he was interested in it?"

"He wanted it for a party."

Grant smiled. "That sounds like him."

It was my turn to push back. "I read your stories in the *Trib* about the murder investigation. You're very thorough. Do you have any idea who did it?"

He didn't seem surprised by the question. "I do not. As I'm sure you know, I'm a suspect just like everyone else in the family. Consequently I've taken myself off the story."

"I heard. Still, you must have some suspicions?"

"The Avery family is my employer. No, I don't have any suspicions. Except I know it wasn't me."

He wouldn't tell me if he did suspect someone. We had been making good time getting across town, but Constitution Avenue suddenly filled with stopped cars and we were no longer moving.

"The British prime minister is in town, Mr. Lowry," Orlando said. "I think we're blocked by a motorcade."

"Then take Independence," Grant said. "I'm meeting the Speaker of the House in twenty minutes. I can't be late."

"Yes, sir." We turned right at the Washington Monument, cutting across the Mall.

"Bobby Noland will figure out who killed Prescott," I said as we turned onto Independence Avenue. "I'm sure it won't take him long."

Grant gave me a cool look. "No doubt," he said. "I also heard you were the first to see Prescott's copy of the Declaration of Independence before any of the family knew about it. Obviously he trusted you quite a lot to keep a secret, taking you into his confidence that way."

"Can I ask why we're having this conversation since you apparently know all the answers to the questions you're asking?"

He shot right back. "Because I wanted to hear what you had to say, if you had anything to add."

"And did I? Have anything to add?"

His dismissive look said no, I hadn't. "What is the relationship between the Madeira and the party Prescott was planning?" he asked.

"Thomas Jefferson wrote out that copy of the Declaration by hand for James Madison," I said. "Madison was planning to toast the anniversary of the signing of the Declaration at a ceremony in the Capitol on July 4, 1809—which was during his presidency, as I'm sure you are aware—with that Madeira he believed my family had. Unfortunately I have no idea where it is."

"So Prescott was going to show off his acquisition and have his own toast with bottles of two-hundred-year-old Madeira that James Madison never got around to drinking?"

"That was the plan."

"Mr. Lowry?" The driver spoke up. "We're coming up on the Library of Congress. I'll pull in and drop Ms. Montgomery under the portico."

"Thank you, but you can just leave me in front of the building," I said.

Grant gave me a curious look. "As you wish."

The Town Car pulled to a stop at the curb. Grant reached

for my cane to pass it to me. As he did a gold-and-blue cuff link peeked out from under his cashmere coat. Etched into the enamel were a compass and a carpenter's square. Masonic symbols.

I looked up and we locked eyes.

"You take care of yourself, Lucie," he said in an even voice. "You hear?"

Twenty-one

The Town Car pulled away and I started walking down First Street toward East Capitol, away from the Library of Congress. The Folger was the next block behind it on East Capitol and Second. Grant Lowry was a Freemason, just like Prescott. Had he known anything about Prescott's search for the documents hidden in Bruton Vault, or supposedly hidden there? Did Grant believe Prescott, or, like Clay, did he consider Prescott's search to be an expensive wild-goose chase?

It felt, all of a sudden, as if I were running out of time to find the Bruton Vault documents. If there was something to find. My heart was still pounding as I walked into the Folger Shakespeare Library a few minutes later.

"Can I help you, dear?" A middle-aged woman standing behind a counter in the small dark-paneled entryway gave me a concerned smile. "Are you all right?"

"Yes . . . I'm fine, thanks. I have a meeting with Tana Rossi at one o'clock," I said. "I'm Lucie Montgomery."

The woman made a call and Tana Rossi appeared before I'd finished signing in. She looked as if she were about Frankie's age, in her early fifties, with short, curly, salt-and-pepper hair, a pair of knee-high suede boots worn with faded jeans, a turquoise-and-lavender knitted turtleneck, and an eye-popping fuchsia scarf around her neck. Elaborate turquoise earrings that looked Southwestern dangled from her ears and she wore scholarly-looking oversized tortoiseshell glasses.

We shook hands and she said, "Won't you come with me? We need to leave your coat and purse in my office before we do anything."

Her office was a small rectangular room off a hallway on the main floor that made me think of a repurposed coat closet. I shed my winter coat, scarf, and gloves and set them on a chair.

"Your purse will be perfectly safe here," she said in a faint English accent. "I'll lock the office. You may bring a notebook and your phone, if you want to take photos without a flash, but all notes must be taken in pencil. Help yourself to one from that pencil holder on the table over there."

I did as I was told and followed her back down the corridor after she locked her door. The building, I knew, dated from the 1920s, but inside it seemed more like a place where Will himself would feel at home, with its subdued lighting, dark, heavy oak paneling, and carved wood.

"I'll show you the Great Hall and the library later," she said. "Plus if you'd like to visit the vault and see our manuscripts—I presume you'd like to see a First Folio—we can do that as well.

For now, I thought we could talk in the Founders' Room, where we'll have some privacy."

She opened a door and I followed her into a dimly lit room with more carved paneling, a stained-glass window, and an enormous stone fireplace with a large oil painting of Queen Elizabeth I hanging above it. A long table with a dozen or so high-backed chairs on either side of it like a dining room table in a palace or a grand English country home occupied most of the room. It felt like a place where we might drink mead from golden goblets, minstrels would play, servants would bring platters piled high with roast pheasant or wild boar for us to dine on, and candles in tall silver candelabra would gutter if a draft of air swept through the room.

"Please have a seat," Tana said, moving to the other side of the table and pulling out one of the chairs. "You've never been here before, have you?"

"How did you know?" I sat down across from her.

"The awed look on your face. We may be off the beaten path for a lot of tourists," she said, "but the Folger contains the preeminent collection of material on Shakespeare in the world, thanks to the foresight and generosity of Henry and Emily Folger. And, yes, I know, it's like stepping back to the 1600s in here—always a surprise after the Art Deco exterior, especially if you don't know what to expect."

"Busted." I smiled. "Thank you for seeing me."

"Not a problem. Anything for a friend of Francesca's. And now tell me more about what brings you here."

I told her as much as I could without bringing Prescott into the story. She listened attentively but I could tell by the spark in her dark, intelligent eyes that she'd heard this story before. And more than once or twice. Shakespeare didn't write Shakespeare.

When I was finished, she folded her hands and leaned toward me. "There have been Shakespeare doubters for years, Lucie. Centuries, even. Among the more notable were Mark Twain, Nathaniel Hawthorne, and James Fenimore Cooper, so you're in excellent company."

"Thank you," I said. "I think."

She grinned. "Are you familiar with what a First Folio is and why it's so important?"

"It's a book containing all of Shakespeare's plays," I said, "that he had published by members of his company. I do know that these days a copy sells for a fortune."

"Not exactly," she said. "The First Folio, which was put together by John Heminges and Henry Condell, two of Shakespeare's colleagues, was published in 1623. Shakespeare passed away in 1616. He didn't know about it and he certainly couldn't have vetted the contents. Although a number of his plays had been published before 1623, what makes the First Folio so important, perhaps the most important document in the English language, is that it is the first time all of Shakespeare's plays—*that we know of*—appeared in a single bound book. The exceptions are *Pericles, Prince of Tyre,* and *Two Noble Kinsmen*. Then, of course, there are the two 'lost' plays: *Cardenio* and *Love's Labour Won*."

Frankie had sent me to the right place. But surely Prescott knew all of this, even if I didn't have my facts completely straight. Jock had contributed financially to the Folger when it was being built. Prescott had done considerable research here.

"You need to remember that in those days, members of the cast weren't given a script containing the entire play the way they are now," Tana went on. "Everything was handwritten and what an actor got were his lines—*only* his lines—with the last few lines of the previous actor's part and the first lines spoken by the next actor. The plays were written out on long rolls of paper and then each part was torn off and handed to the appropriate actor. It's is where the word 'role,' as in role in a play, comes from."

I had been making furious notes with my new Folger pencil in a notebook I'd brought with me. Now I sat back and stared at her.

She smiled. "I know. It was a different world."

"Clearly."

"So," she said, "do you have any idea what happened to these 'rolls'—rolls of paper—when the play was finished? What each actor did with his individual part?"

"No," I said, but I had a feeling I could guess what her answer would be.

"They were thrown out as scrap paper or the paper was reused, perhaps for the binding of a book," she said. "Which is what makes the First Folio so important. Because in it we have thirty entire plays in one place. If it weren't for the First Folio we never would have known that *The Tempest, Macbeth, As You Like It,* and *Twelfth Night* even existed. Can you imagine?"

The Tempest. The last play Shakespeare wrote on his own and supposedly based on the wreck of the *Sea Venture.* Without the First Folio no one would have known about that play.

"Are you saying that anything in Shakespeare's

handwriting—all those different papers for each actor in each play—didn't survive?" I asked.

"Not only his plays," she said, "but *anything* in Shakespeare's handwriting. Do you know where we get most of our information about his life?"

I shook my head.

"Not from his plays. From court records," she said. "It was a very litigious age, believe it or not, and we have many court records from the sixteenth and seventeenth centuries that document Shakespeare's business life as well as his real estate assets since he was a businessman and an investor. We learned the most about him when the family applied for a coat of arms."

"So how was the First Folio put together if no one had the pages from the plays?" I asked.

"More than likely from prompt books. And there were what are called 'fair copies' of the plays that existed." She stood up and took off her glasses, cleaning them absentmindedly on her scarf. "Would you like to see a First Folio? And I can give you a tour of the library as well—especially the Tudor Great Hall."

"I would."

"Come with me."

We took a tiny elevator down one level to the basement where the vault was located. The anteroom had more dark paneling, glass cabinets containing figurines from Shakespeare's plays and busts of the Bard that were no doubt collectors' items, along with a couple of antique chairs tucked in corners, and a beautiful Oriental carpet. It looked as if it could be the waiting room of a Fortune 500 company CEO. The substantial-looking exterior door to the vault was open.

"It's going to be cool in here," Tana said as she swiped her badge to unlock the interior steel door. "We keep the temperature at fifty-nine degrees with fifty-five percent humidity to protect the manuscripts and documents. In case of a fire, we have a system that removes the oxygen from the air—literally pushes it to the ground—to give the fire nothing to feed on. If you're ever caught in here when that happens, you need to crawl out of the place if you want to live. And be fast about it."

"I'll try to remember that," I said.

She grinned and led me into a room filled with rows of book-lined shelves that went from floor to ceiling. We walked down a narrow corridor to the back of the room.

"Are all these books about Shakespeare?" I asked.

"No," she said, "our collection is much broader. It dates from 1475 to 1714—the period of the reign of the Stuarts in England. That said, we own more First Folios than anywhere else in the world."

"How many are there?"

"Between five hundred and seven hundred and fifty were printed. Of those, two hundred and thirty-five are extant. The Folger owns eighty-two."

"Eighty-two? That's more than a third of the number of copies still in existence. Why does a private American library own more First Folios than anyplace else?" I asked. "More than a British library or, say, the Globe Theatre in London?"

"Because Henry Folger bought them during what we call the 'Downton Abbey' years in England," she said in a matter-of-fact voice. "After World War I, many once-wealthy English families were selling off their copies because they needed the money."

"So he picked them up on the cheap?"

"Let's just say he did all right." She brought me over to a counter where an open book rested in a cradle. "Here you are. One of Shakespeare's First Folios. This is copy number fourteen."

I held my breath as I looked at it. Bound in rust-colored leather with gilded trim, First Folio number fourteen looked as if it were in pristine condition. In the last four hundred years, how many people had owned it, turned its pages, read it, recited the words of a favorite passage?

"It's beautiful," I said.

"It is. As you can see, it was bound in Moroccan leather—which was a decision made by the individual who originally bought the unbound pages, which were basically stacks of sheets folded in half. Hence the name 'folio.' Each copy is different, some more elaborately bound than others. Gilded pages, different choice of leather, some people just bound the pages as they received them with no cover . . . the decision was up to the owner."

Tana walked around the counter so she was facing me. "I'll turn the pages for you so you can have a look at the book. Stop me if there's something you particularly want to read."

"Don't you need to wear gloves?"

"At the Folger we believe it's better for the books to be handled without gloves. You can't really feel the paper with gloves on and we think there is less wear and tear if the pages are turned by hand. Plus there's no harm to the paper from the natural oil from one's fingers—as long as they're clean, that is."

The book was already open to the title page. Above a fa-

miliar engraving of Shakespeare—the one everyone knows—
the publishers had printed:

Mr William Shakespeares
Comedies, Histories, & Tragedies
Published According to the True Originall Copies

Tana began turning pages. Just as in Quinn's copy of
Shakespeare's plays, *The Tempest* was first. Comedies, then
tragedies. I read the opening lines.

A tempestuous noise of thunder and lightning heard
Enter a master and a boatswain

And so the story began when Prospero used his magical powers to cause a ship that had left North Africa after
a wedding and was bound for Italy to be wrecked on his
island.

"Do you think *The Tempest* was based on the wreck of the
Sea Venture?" I asked.

"There's plenty of evidence that it could have been,"
she said. "Shakespeare would have known members of the
Virginia Company and he could have read the diary or the
letters that were sent back to England by one of the men who
was stranded on Bermuda."

"What about Sir Francis Bacon? Couldn't he have written
some of the plays? He *was* a shareholder in the Virginia Company so he definitely would have known about the *Sea Venture*. There are accounts that claim that Shakespeare wasn't
educated enough to have written them, couldn't write well

enough . . . he was just the front man, to speak for others in power to express their political opinions anonymously."

"Without proof," Tana said, "at the Folger we believe Shakespeare wrote Shakespeare. So far, no one has come forward with anything to the contrary. *Definitive* proof, that is."

I nodded and she continued, "Look, I'm not saying something's not out there. But after all this time it seems doubtful."

"I get it," I said.

In the elevator back to the first floor, she said, "Of course, there's always Project Dust Bunny."

"Project what?"

She smiled as the door opened and we stepped out. "The technical name is 'proteomics,' which is the study of proteins and their interactions to learn about the past."

"Sorry, I'm lost."

"Do you remember a news story a few years ago when the body of Richard III, the British king who also happened to be one of Shakespeare's great villains, was discovered under a parking lot in Leicester, England?"

"I do."

"The archeologist who identified the body as King Richard came to Washington to talk about it. Her visit started a conversation about whether there might not be an easier way to get DNA samples than digging up bodies buried under parking lots," she said. "And what we at the Folger specifically wondered was whether or not there might be DNA traces left behind in old books. After all, people lean over them, turn pages, handle them—meaning they deposit skin and hair on those pages, right? And then they put the book away, usually in a cool place where that DNA remains intact and essentially in the dark. It can be left undisturbed for centuries."

"You're saying you can find DNA in old books?"

"Actually we did find it," she said. "We took a four-hundred-year-old Bible and used a Q-tip to swipe the gutter, which is the seam where the pages come together. Then we sent it off to the National Institutes of Health in Maryland. And guess what?"

"They found something."

She nodded. "It was incredible. Not only did the scientists at NIH manage to sequence the mitochondrial DNA of two individuals, they were also able to discover their haplotype, which means the region they were from—in this case, northern Europe. They even managed to find bacteria that suggested those two people had acne."

I knew my mouth was hanging open. "Do you mean you might be able to find out if Shakespeare had acne? Although if it's true, I don't think I'd want to know. It would ruin some of the magic and the aura around him."

Tana laughed. "Worse than finding out Santa Claus isn't real."

"Something like that."

"As it happens, the Folger owns one of his property deeds— Shakespeare, not Santa Claus. So if he did leave any proteins on that deed, we might be able to identify his DNA by getting a sample from a living member of his family and seeing if there's a match. It wouldn't need to be a direct descendent— but it would work as long as it was someone traced through his mother's lineage." She saw my hopeful look and held up her hands, palms out. "Whoa. Hold on there. We're a long way from that happening. It's true the possibilities are really exciting, but for now we're just trying to collect more dust bunnies from the gutters of books that go to our Conservation Lab to be restored. In the next few years, we'll see what happens as biologists study those samples. But mark my words you'll be reading more about it."

BY THE TIME WE finished our tour of the library, it was nearly three o'clock, which, Tana explained, was teatime at the Folger. I declined her invitation to stay, thanked her for her help, and managed to hail a cab back to my car at Farragut Square as soon as I stepped outside the front door because someone was just getting dropped off.

Leaving Washington at rush hour was another story. Traffic was a nightmare as usual, but at least the crawling pace heading west on Interstate 66 gave me time to think. I had learned plenty yesterday at Jamestown and Williamsburg about the history of the Bruton Vault and more today about Shakespeare writing Shakespeare. Josie Wilde and Tana Rossi had humored me and my questions, but neither of them believed any documents existed, even if I did.

Unfortunately I was no nearer to finding out where they might have disappeared to—that is, *if* Thomas Jefferson had brought them to the White House from Williamsburg and *if* Dolley Madison had given them to Hobson Banks to hide somewhere for safekeeping the night the British burned Washington in 1814. And of course, *if* they existed.

I also didn't know whether Prescott had actually known

where they were hidden or if he merely had a good idea where they might be and was still looking for them. Either way, it no longer mattered. His secret had died with him.

Unless.

What if he'd been forced to reveal that information to his killer? Someone who was after the same thing he was—who believed the documents in Bruton Vault really existed and were still hidden away. Someone who wanted to find them as badly as he did. The same person who had walked into my home yesterday and gone through the envelope with Leland's documents.

Which meant I probably ought to mind my back so I didn't end up like Prescott.

Dead.

Twenty-two

F riday, the first day of Christmas in Middleburg weekend, didn't start well. Quinn and I were about to leave
for the winery after breakfast when his phone chimed
that he had a text message. He pulled it out of his pocket, read
the text, and said, "Damn."

"What?"

"Antonio says one of the barrels in the room where we
store the older reds apparently sprang a leak. There's wine
everywhere. Dammit. We'd better get over there."

A barrel of wine was worth anywhere from eight to ten
thousand dollars of bottled wine—on the higher end if it contained one of our older reds.

"Let's go," I said. "This isn't going to be good."

BY THE TIME WE got over to the barrel room, Antonio was si-
phoning wine from the defective barrel into another oak barrel.

There was still the matter of cleaning up what had leaked onto the floor. The good news was that the leaking barrel had been on the bottom of the rack so wine hadn't dripped over other barrels. The bad news was that it had been in the very back row in the deepest alcove where we stored our reds, meaning it had taken a while before the leak had been spotted. We couldn't just take a hose and rinse the spilled wine into the floor gutters, either; there were environmental regulations and a protocol that we needed to follow.

"There's something else you ought to know, Lucita," Antonio said.

His jeans and a light gray sweatshirt were splattered with red wine as if he'd been shot. A knitted Andean *chullo* covered his head and ears. It was always chilliest back here in this far alcove, but in December the cold could go right through to your bones in no time.

"What is it?" I asked him. "Not another barrel leaking."

"Nothing like that." He shook his head. "I found a door in the wall behind those barrels. About the size of a crawl space. Come over here where you can see it."

Quinn and I followed him and crowded into the tight space. Antonio turned on a flashlight and used the beam to pick out the edges of a small wooden door with a rusty ring attached. I caught my breath.

"Jesus H.," Quinn said.

The Madeira.

"Did you open it?" Quinn asked him.

"I figured you'd want to do that." Antonio picked up a crowbar that was leaning against the barrel stand. "I brought this. It looks like the door might be stuck."

"You want to open it?" Quinn asked, passing me the crowbar.

"I do. I had no idea this storage place or whatever it is existed."

"You think the Madeira might be here?" he asked.

"Why not? It's the perfect place to store it." I couldn't keep the excitement out of my voice.

Quinn backed out of the way and Antonio shone the flashlight over my shoulder so I could see what I was doing. I slid the crowbar through the ring and leaned on it using my weight as leverage. It didn't budge.

"I'm afraid I'm going to break the ring off," I said. "The wood is sort of rotted."

Quinn tried next and finally Antonio yanked on it so hard the ring broke off, but the door opened with a groaning creak. The momentum knocked Antonio off his feet and he crashed into Quinn and me.

Quinn grabbed the metal barrel rack and hung on, catching me before I went down, but Antonio sat down hard on the concrete floor, letting out a sound like the wind had been knocked out of him.

"Are you all right?" I asked him.

"My pride and my butt hurt," he said. "I hope I didn't break the flashlight. Or my tailbone. What's in there?"

A cold, damp gust of stale air that smelled as if it had been undisturbed for a long time assaulted us. Quinn sneezed and picked up the flashlight off the floor. The beam was weaker, but the light still worked. He shone it inside, on something dark and substantial.

"Boxes," he said.

"The Madeira," I said, in an exultant voice. "I knew it."

"Someone's going to have to crawl in there and get those boxes," Antonio said. "They're too far to reach."

"Do you want to do that?" I asked.

"Because you're worried about dead mice maybe?"

He knew I hated mice. Alive or dead. "Maybe."

"Quinn?" Antonio said.

"It's all yours."

Antonio grunted. "Yeah, thanks. Okay, hand me the flashlight so I can see what I'm doing."

Quinn passed it to him and he crawled in on his hands and knees. The flashlight beam bobbed around. "This place isn't very big," he said.

"What about the boxes?" I asked.

A moment later he said in a muffled voice, "I don't think it's bottles of Madeira."

"It has to be," I said.

"Nope." Less muffled.

"What is it, then?" Quinn asked.

Silence and some scrabbling noises as he seemed to be opening one of the boxes. "Hang on."

A moment later he appeared, crouching in the doorway, a smear of dust across one cheek.

"Christmas decorations."

THE LITTLE CRAWL SPACE held four boxes of my mother's Christmas decorations, the ones she'd used to decorate the barrel room. That was it. Nothing else. Frankie, who joined us from the tasting room as soon as she found out, was overjoyed.

"I'm sorry it's not your Madeira," she said, "but these are beautiful. Your mother was really talented, Lucie. I think we should put them up now and enjoy them. It would be the perfect tribute to her."

I realized with a lump in my throat that no one had seen or touched these decorations since my mother's last Christmas with us.

"You're right," I said. "We should."

In the end everyone pitched in, including Quinn, and by the time we were finished, the barrel room looked as magical as I'd remembered from when my mother was alive. Quinn hung her wreath over the arched doorway to the room where we stored the reds. Antonio helped Frankie weave lights and greenery around the wine barrels in the main room. I decorated the live tree Frankie had already brought here with my mother's handmade ornaments and all of us tied red ribbons on the wall sconces and wound more greenery and lights through the mezzanine railing. We put on Christmas music—rock and roll—through the sound system and eventually everyone loosened up enough to dance or sing along, which helped because it was so cold.

"I pronounce this place terrific," Frankie said when we were done. "I'm so glad you found these decorations, Lucie. We'll have to arrange a few wine tastings down here so everyone can see the place."

"Thank Antonio. He's the one who found them," I said.

Antonio smiled and Quinn's eyes met mine across the room. He smiled, too, but not before I caught the unmistakable look of disappointment in his.

It wasn't the Madeira. Maybe it was gone forever. Maybe Leland really had drunk it. Nor was I any closer to figuring out where the Bruton Vault documents might be hidden—at a place where George Washington and James Madison had met.

". . . is that okay, Lucie?" Frankie was asking.

"Is what okay?"

She gave me an exasperated look. "I just said that we ought to close early so everyone can go home and get ready for caroling and the Christmas tree lighting tonight in Middleburg."

"Sure," I said. "Good idea."

"You two are coming, aren't you?"

"Of course," I said. "We'll be there."

But on the way back to the house Quinn said, "Maybe we could just skip the tree lighting this one time?"

"I wouldn't mind, but you know we'll feel better if we go."

"I wish we'd never known about that damn Madeira," he said. "It's going to eat at me."

"Let it go," I said. "We need to move on. Besides, it's Christmas. And no town celebrates Christmas like Middleburg does."

"That," he said, "is for sure."

CHRISTMAS IN MIDDLEBURG, ESPECIALLY the celebration on Saturday morning, is tradition-filled, charming, horsey, small-town-hospitable, festive, and everyone's Hallmark-movie idea of exactly what "the most wonderful time of the year" ought to be like. The whole town turns out to celebrate and thousands of visitors join us. The Methodist Church sets up a sidewalk stand and passes out hot chocolate to keep folks warm, the community center hosts an all-day craft fair, and a deejay across the street from the Red Fox Inn plays Christmas music you can hear the length of Washington Street. Noah Seely dresses up as Santa for a family pancake breakfast and a "visit with Santa" for the kids at the community charter school. Food trucks behind Blue Ridge Federal catch the business that restaurants and cafes are too crowded to handle. No one starves at Christmas in Middleburg.

Quinn and I arrived early enough Saturday morning to find a parking space in a large meadow off North Pendleton Street—the only parking area within walking distance to town.

"It's cold," Quinn said, picking up a program from a pile of newspapers lying next to an old oak tree as we left the parking lot and stuffing it under his arm.

"I know, but it's going to be a gorgeous winter day— sunshine, blue skies, perfect weather," I said. "I've been here years when it poured rain or blizzarded. We're lucky."

"What do you want to do?" Quinn asked.

"Get some hot chocolate and then stake out a good viewing spot from the parking lot so Hope and Zach can see the hounds and horses as they canter up the street to the Red Fox," I said. "I promised Eli and Sasha we'd save them a place."

Until a few years ago, watching the Hunt and Hound Review meant lining up on either side of the street and waiting until the Goose Creek Hunt's Huntsman, resplendent in his pinks and black helmet, appeared with a joyful pack of forty or so tail-wagging foxhounds, followed by over a hundred beautifully turned out horses and their riders dressed in their best attire. Unfortunately one year the crowd got too close to the hounds, which promptly got the dogs overexcited. Before the Huntsman or Whippers-In could regain control of the situation, the hounds had made their way onto the sidewalk and detoured through the open doors of some of the shops. A wagging tail can do a lot of accidental damage to fragile French china or a jewelry display. The resulting pandemonium changed the parade set-up in perpetuity: now there were barricades on either side of Washington Street with a few designated places for crossing from one side to the other.

By nine-thirty, plenty of folks had already staked out front-row places next to the barricades and set out camping chairs. The review started at eleven o'clock; by ten there wouldn't be many front-row spots that hadn't been taken. The new way of doing things.

"Sasha's going to wait somewhere along the barricade once the kids finish seeing Santa at the school to try to save a front-row spot," I said to Quinn after we'd gotten our hot chocolate and were walking back to the parking lot behind the Red Fox Inn. "Eli will bring them to the parking lot with us so they can pet the hounds and see the horses up close. They'll leave early and join Sasha so they can be in place to watch the review. We'll catch up with them after the Master of Foxhounds gives the Christmas toast."

Eli, Hope, and Zach found Quinn and me standing on a grassy knoll with a good view of both the parking lot and the street below where the Goose Creek Hunt would gather before arriving at the Red Fox for their annual pre-parade Christmas greeting to the town. My sweet, dark-haired niece, whose cheeks were flushed pink with excitement, wore a bright red winter parka, a hat with ears, whiskers, and a face that looked like a cat, bright green leggings, and knee-high boots. Zach was dressed in camouflage pants, a navy jacket, and a bright yellow hand-knitted hat with a smiley face that Sasha had made for him. Quinn and I got hugs and kisses from both of them before they abandoned us to join friends who were also waiting for the hounds.

The folks who turn out for the gathering of the Goose Creek Hunt at the Red Fox before the parade starts are a fairly intimate group of friends of the Hunt, townspeople who know about the charming annual tradition, and a few out-of-towners who have stumbled upon it by accident and return year after year.

"Hey," Eli said, nudging me after he finished off my now-tepid hot chocolate. "Look who's here."

"Who?"

"Victoria Barkley and Bianca Avery. Across from us."

"Probably because Clay and Scotty are riding in the review like they always do," I said.

"No Alex or Kellie," he said.

"Maybe they have other plans," I said. "And Victoria and Bianca obviously have the hearing of bats because they're staring at us as if they know we're talking about them." I raised my hand and waved.

Bianca waved back. Victoria gave me a hard stare and turned to her future daughter-in-law.

"She doesn't look very happy," Eli said.

"Half the town thinks her fiancé killed his stepfather," I said. "Would you look happy?"

"Hey," Quinn said, "here comes the Huntsman with the hounds."

Eli pulled out his phone. "I gotta go take pictures. And videos."

The hounds formed a semicircle around the Goose Creek Hunt's Huntsman as the children who had been waiting descended on the dogs to cuddle and pet them. The rest of the one-hundred-plus riders crowded into the gravel parking lot behind them. I watched Victoria as she went to Clay's side, pulling him down for a long, deep kiss. It seemed jarring and out of place among the lighthearted atmosphere and the crowd of families with children, friends, and admirers who wanted to talk and ask questions about horses, hunting, families, and holiday plans.

"Come on," Quinn said. "Let's go watch the kids. And stop staring at Clay and Victoria."

"I'm not staring."

"Yes you are."

He tugged my arm and for the next fifteen minutes we watched Hope and Zach and the other children petting and hugging the foxhounds until waiters from the Red Fox showed up carrying silver platters with finger sandwiches for the members of the Hunt, followed by stirrup cups—small glasses of port—for the toast.

The crowd quieted down for the Master of Foxhounds to raise his glass and thank the town of Middleburg for its hospitality to the Goose Creek Hunt and for a good year. "Merry Christmas, everyone," he said.

Eli came up to us holding the children's hands. "We're going to take off."

"I thought you were leaving before the toast," I said.

"I couldn't get them away from the hounds," he said.

The Huntsman had already left with the hounds and the other riders were slowly filing out of the parking lot onto Marshall Street. The crowd melted away as well, heading toward the parade route.

"Uncle Quinn," Hope said, "will you give me a horsey ride?"

He knelt down. "Of course I will. Climb on, sweetheart."

"Where's Sasha?" I asked Eli.

"She just texted me. It was too crowded at the intersection of Washington and Madison. So she moved up farther, across the street from the antique emporium," he said as Quinn left the parking lot with Hope. "We'd better go."

Zach tugged on Eli's hand. "I want to see the horses and puppies again."

"Be right with you, buddy. Luce? You coming?"

"In a minute," I said. "There's something I need to do."

"The porta-potties are down by Safeway."

"Not that."

"All right," he said as Zach pretended to strain as he pulled Eli toward the street. "Don't be long or you'll miss everything."

"I won't," I said. "I just need to check something."

Where President Washington and President Madison met. Could that also be a street named for each of them—as in the intersection of Washington and Madison *Streets*? *Right here in Middleburg?* If the Constitution and the Declaration of Independence had been hidden in Leesburg for safekeeping, why couldn't the Bruton Vault documents be hidden here in Middleburg?

Washington and Madison Streets met at the lone Middleburg traffic light in front of the Red Fox. I looked around the nearly empty parking lot. The Red Fox Inn was the oldest continuously running inn in America, established in 1728. So it had certainly been here and well known almost a century later in 1819 if Banks had come to town looking for a place to hide his package.

The parking lot where I stood backed onto a gated outdoor garden where hotel and restaurant guests could sit outside for drinks in the warm weather. I went over and checked it out. Nothing looked like a potential hiding place. Maybe I needed to look closer to the actual intersection of the two streets. I left the parking lot, walked down Madison, and stopped to watch two giggling girls who had stuffed themselves into a small opening underneath a fieldstone staircase that led to a side entrance to the Red Fox. I waited until another friend took photos and they left.

I must have walked past that staircase hundreds of times over the years. Now I took a closer look. The reason for the opening was to provide light for a small window for the Tap Room, a restaurant that had once served as a Civil War hospital to care for wounded Confederate soldiers. Between the window and the brick sidewalk there was a small square area underneath the stairs covered by what looked like mulch.

I went over and sat down on the stone ledge like the girls had done, took off my gloves, and pulled out my phone as if I wanted to take a selfie. Then I took my cane and shoved it behind me, moving it back and forth to dig up the mulch. A moment later it hit something hard. I reached back with my hand.

A handle, something strong and round, probably made of

iron. Underneath surely lay an opening of some sort, possibly one of the hidey-holes Mosby's Rangers had used under houses throughout our region when the Yankees had come to town.

There was definitely something under this staircase. I brushed dirt off my hand and pulled myself up. A few feet away Victoria Barkley stood watching me.

Our eyes met and hers gave her away. Victoria, whose perfume I had smelled in the elevator when I returned to the wine cellar for my phone. I'd been right all along.

Now here I was staring at Prescott's killer and the other person who, like me, had been searching for the lost treasure: the contents of Bruton Vault. More to the point: she knew I'd just figured out the truth.

That she was a murderer.

Twenty-three

Victoria Barkley was by my side at once. "I need to talk to you, Lucie," she said.

"I'm meeting my family to watch the review," I told her as I got up. "We can talk some other time."

"I don't think so," she said and jammed something hard into the small of my back. The barrel of a gun. "Walk with me, keep your mouth shut, and nothing will happen. If you do or say anything, I'll make sure your adorable niece has an unfortunate accident and doesn't make it home from the parade today."

"You're bluffing." My voice shook. Was she working with a partner? Clay? Would he harm an innocent child?

"You don't want to find out," she said. "Now move."

"Where?"

As we walked down Madison Street away from the crowds and the parade, there was no one around where a few minutes ago hundreds of people had gathered. Even the police officers and sheriff's deputies who had been here had moved to where the action would be happening when the Hunt and Hounds Review paraded down Washington Street.

"We're going to the horse trailers," Victoria said. "We can talk there."

"What do you want?" I said.

"What's legitimately mine."

"What's that?"

"Don't play dumb." Her voice was harsh. "You were in Williamsburg and Jamestown the other day. And you went to the Folger."

How did she know that? How long had she been stalking me? "Who told you? Were you following me?"

"I didn't need to follow you. In my business you make plenty of contacts, especially people who work at museums, libraries, and historic sites. And some of those people owe me favors."

"You killed Prescott," I said.

"Prescott." She practically spat his name. "He wasn't going to give me any credit for the work I did for him. Finding him that copy of the Declaration of Independence. And, as a bonus, the correspondence that came with it. I helped him figure it out. Instead, it seems he confided in you."

"So you killed him."

"It was an accident. But he was being obstinate and greedy. Now get going."

"You went through my father's papers," I said. "You broke into my house."

"Your front door was unlocked. I walked in."

"How did you know about the papers?"

I wasn't sure she would answer, but she seemed only too pleased with herself, how clever she'd been.

"I was at the bank. You were so absorbed in that envelope you were holding—like it was the crown jewels—you never even noticed me. Seth's secretary accidentally spilled the beans about why you were there. Of course, she didn't realize I knew it was you she was talking about."

We had reached a meadow across from the field where Quinn and I had parked the Jeep; this place was filled with horse trailers and cars. A copse of trees near the street blocked the view so no one would see us—and even if they did, probably wouldn't take much notice. Still I was surprised that no one else had hung around, stable lads, maybe, waiting for their horses to return.

Victoria pulled a key fob out of her jacket pocket and hit a button. I heard the sound of the trunk of a car popping open.

"Come on," she said. "We're going to Hawthorne."

Clay's car was an old Ford Taurus and it was hitched to a horse trailer. Victoria marched me over to the car and indicated the trunk. "Get in."

"You've got to be kidding me. No. Besides, Clay will wonder where the trailer is. You can't leave."

"Of course I can," she said in a nasty voice. "He's going hunting after the review. I'm meeting him with the trailer at the polo grounds in a couple of hours. Now don't make me tell you again to get in."

"No." I raised my cane to swing it at her but she was faster, raising the butt end of her gun.

Then everything went black.

I DIDN'T WAKE UP until she opened the trunk. She'd put the kind of adhesive wrapping tape vets and stables used for the horses over my mouth, and my hands and feet were trussed like a Thanksgiving turkey. Hot pink. Thoughtful choice of color.

My head hurt like hell and I blinked in the sudden brightness. If we were at Hawthorne, I'd been out for a good ten minutes. By now Quinn and Eli would be looking for me. Quinn would alert Bobby or else he'd find the Middleburg police chief, whose car always rode first in the 2 P.M. parade. The Loudoun County sheriff was second.

They were going to find me. Hopefully in time.

But first, I had to deal with Victoria, who was standing over the trunk looking down at me. If I could have spat on her I would have.

"I'm going to cut the tape binding your feet," she said. "Try anything and I'll shoot you. I can bury your body in the woods where no one will find you."

She cut the tape with a pocketknife and maneuvered me so I could get out of the trunk. I held out my hands and jerked my head in the direction of my cane, which she'd thrown into the trunk, thank God.

"Mpf, mpf, mpf."

"What?" She looked exasperated. I repeated myself. "Oh, what the hell." She ripped the tape off my mouth. It felt as if skin had come off with it.

My face stung and my head throbbed. "I can't walk without my cane. So you'd better free my hands or you can carry me."

I sounded half-drunk. She must have figured I wasn't much of a threat in my condition because she leaned forward and slashed the tape binding my hands. Her gun, a little nine-millimeter Glock, made a return appearance.

"Now get out."

She had parked near the orangerie and the back entrance to the Castle that was near Prescott's wine cellar. At least I knew where I was.

I obeyed her with difficulty, climbing out of the trunk and managing not to fall flat on my face. Except for the sound of the whistling wind, the place was as silent as a graveyard. I looked up, hoping to see a face in the window above us.

"Don't bother," Victoria said. "Everyone's gone. Open the door. It's unlocked."

It hadn't worked last time, but I tried again, jamming the end of my cane into her ribs before she realized I'd done it. I heard the clunk of the gun as it hit the ground and stepped inside, shutting the door. She managed to pull it open, but as she entered I clubbed her again with my cane handle.

She went down hard, but this time she didn't loosen her grip on the Glock. I took off as fast as I could. Two shots whizzed past me. At least she was a lousy shot. She had three, maybe four more bullets in the clip until it was empty. I turned a corner. I could continue straight, which was the way back to the elevator, but I probably didn't have enough time. Turning left would take me to Prescott's wine cellar. I wouldn't make it there, either.

A few feet ahead of me I spotted a recessed alcove. Probably—knowing the Averys—displaying a piece of sculpture. Instead it contained a beautifully decorated Christmas tree. A string of white lights lay coiled on the ground. Someone hadn't finished the decorations. I slipped between the tree and the wall as Victoria's footsteps grew closer.

My timing was going to have to be perfect. I held my breath and shoved the tree. It fell onto her and she yelped with surprise as she went down among the branches and ornaments.

She was still clinging to the Glock, fighting to regain her balance. I grabbed her wrist, snapped it, and the gun clattered to the floor lying between the two of us.

"Hold it right there."

I spun around. Kellie Avery, in a shooter's stance, held a rifle pointed at Victoria and me.

"Kellie," I said, "listen to me. Victoria killed your great-grandfather."

It was a mistake to have turned my back on Victoria. Before Kellie could warn me, Victoria reached over and grabbed the Glock, aiming it at me.

"Put down your gun, Kellie, or I'll shoot her. Lucie's the one who killed Prescott."

"No," I said. "She's lying."

It happened fast. Kellie aimed at Victoria as I dove behind the tree. Kellie's shot hit Victoria, who screamed and grabbed her shoulder. By the time Kellie reached the two of us, I had gotten the gun away from Victoria once again and put on the safety.

"Where were you?" I asked her.

"Pop-pop's wine cellar," she said. "I've been going there to get away since he died. I came out when I heard the shots. Thank God he kept a loaded gun in that Masonic room of his."

"I need medical help." Victoria spoke through clenched teeth. "I'll bleed to death."

"Do you want to go outside to call 911?" I asked Kellie. "I can handle her."

"No, you do it. I can manage just fine." She looked down at Victoria. "Move and I'll shoot you in your other shoulder. Understand?"

Quinn was my next call after 911. He and Bobby arrived in Bobby's unmarked car just as Victoria was being lifted into an ambulance on a stretcher.

"Clay's expecting Victoria to pick him up after he finishes hunting," I told Bobby as the ambulance pulled away.

"I'll tell him," Kellie said.

"I need to handle that," Bobby told her. "I need to find out how much Clay knew about what Victoria was up to. Whether he was involved or not."

Kellie turned pale, but she nodded as another car pulled up and Scotty and Bianca got out. Kellie ran into her mother's arms and Scotty embraced them both.

"Let's get you home," Quinn said. "I want Doc Turnbull to look at that bruise."

"I'll be all right. It's over, Quinn. Victoria was the one who helped Clay purchase the Declaration of Independence. She knew everything, including what he was looking for," I said. "And there's something else."

"What's that?" he asked.

"I know where the Bruton Vault documents are."

Twenty-four

t took two days to get permission to dig under the staircase at the Red Fox Inn and bring together everyone I thought ought to be present when the site was excavated—Tana Rossi, Josie Wilde, two historians from Colonial Williamsburg and Jamestown, two archeologists from the Smithsonian, Kit, Bobby, and, of course, the entire Avery family.

Clayton Avery had known nothing of Victoria's involvement with Prescott; he had not even been aware that she found the Jefferson copy of the Declaration of Independence for Prescott since he swore her to secrecy. Then the day of the feijoada Prescott had made it clear he thought she was wrong for Clay. Victoria had visited him in the wine cellar after I left, furious because she believed Prescott owed her in more ways than one. She claimed she didn't mean to kill him, but once he fell and hit his head, she realized the blow was fatal. So she left by the back entrance, rejoining Clay who hadn't been aware that she'd been downstairs with Prescott.

Clay was the last to arrive at the Red Fox Inn. He came with Scotty and Alex, who, for once, stood on either side of their father as if they were giving him not only physical support but also badly needed emotional support. I thought he looked awful, still devastated by the knowledge he'd welcomed a viper into the midst of his family, and that his adoring fiancée had been his stepfather's killer. The rest of the Averys had come separately, including Celia and Jack who, I was glad to see, were welcomed and greeted by the others.

"Maybe there's hope for that family," I said under my breath to Quinn.

"I heard Clay is talking to his lawyers about restructuring the Caritas Commitment so they can hang on to the *Trib*. They want to keep Hawthorne intact for now, but they'll sell the other homes and donate the art and jewelry and furniture as Prescott and Rose wanted," he said.

"Well," Kit said as she came up behind the two of us. "Here we are. I guess all's well that ends well."

"Wrong play," I said and she grinned.

"Lord, what fools these mortals be?"

"Quit while you're ahead."

She laughed. "Seriously, you've assembled quite a crowd, Luce. I just finished talking to Tana Rossi and the historians from Colonial Williamsburg and Jamestown. Plus I did some research at the Balch Library in Leesburg and found a death record for Hobson Banks. He died in August 1814. The date of death had a question mark beside it but it must have been soon enough after he hid his package here that he never came back to retrieve it."

"*If* he left it here," I said. "I'm nervous as hell. I could be wrong. Or it could be some piece of White House china that Dolley Madison especially loved."

"Oh, ye of little faith," Kit said. "I bet you're right."

"Where's Grant?" I asked her. "He was invited to this."

"The newsroom. The *Trib* comes first with him. He sent me to cover the story." She leaned in closer. "You didn't hear this from me but Alex is leaving. She wants to move to London and Clay's fine with that. Scotty's going take over as publisher and run the place solo. The staff is so pumped we're ready to light up *Trib* tower like the Eiffel Tower at night."

"I'm glad."

The Inn had been closed for the morning for "a special event" and the Tap Room was once again going to be used as a triage site as it had been during the Civil War to examine anything the two archeologists dressed in hazmat suits found. Opening the heavy metal lid turned out to be a chore that required yet another crowbar, the strength of both men, and about twenty minutes of pulling and tugging before it finally came loose.

One of them shone a flashlight into the opening. "It's not that deep," he said, "and there's something down there."

I squeezed Quinn's hand so hard he winced as the archeologist lowered himself into the opening. A moment later he emerged holding a dirty, shapeless lump in both hands as if it were the Holy Grail.

"There's something inside this sack," he said. "It feels like papers."

A few people gasped.

"Congratulations, sweetheart," Quinn said in my ear, "you were right."

But was I?

The sack hadn't been waterproof and Hobson Banks had probably expected to return for it not long after he hid it underneath the Red Fox Inn. Instead it had remained in that small vault for more than two hundred years.

What had I been expecting? A swashbuckling Indiana Jones–like ending to a centuries-old mystery? Proof that Shakespeare was not really the genius the world believed he was? And that Francis Bacon had masterminded the plans for the government of the United States, plans Thomas Jefferson hid in the White House after borrowing Bacon's ideas to write the Declaration of Independence?

Life is never that simple, nor is it black-and-white. The papers had suffered water damage and were mildewed. The ink had run, smearing words and seeping through to other pages, staining them like Rorschach blots. It would take time to dry them out, analyze the handwriting, and test for DNA. Today there would be no answers.

Almost none.

"Wait a minute," one of the archeologists said, "take a look at this. It was still inside the sack, not with the other documents."

We crowded around the table. It was a letter, heavily mildewed except for the signature of the correspondent at the bottom of the page. In script as large as the signature on James Madison's copy of the Declaration Independence, Thomas Jefferson had signed his name with a flourish in his distinctive handwriting.

"Then these documents really did come from the White House," I said. "Maybe Thomas Jefferson did remove the contents of the Bruton Vault and bring them there for safekeeping."

Josie glanced over at the historians from Jamestown and Williamsburg. "What did we miss?" she said. "There was no vault."

"Dust bunnies," Tana said. "The answer is in the dust bunnies."

QUINN TOOK ME TO dinner at the Goose Creek Inn that evening. By now what had happened at the Red Fox was all over town. Thelma and the Romeos had outdone themselves in getting the news out.

"Faster than a video gone viral on YouTube," Quinn said as my phone rang all afternoon.

Hassan gave us a table in the green dining room because he figured we'd want privacy. "I'll let Dominique know you're here," he said.

"Don't tell anyone else," Quinn said, half-joking. "We'll be mobbed."

But after we sat down he turned serious. "However it turns out, I think whatever is in that package was a hell of a find. Now we just have to wait."

"Do you really want to find out that Shakespeare didn't write Shakespeare?" I asked.

"Do you?"

"I guess I want to know the truth. But a lot of people went to a lot of trouble to keep a secret. For centuries."

"The truth will set you free," he said.

We had finished dinner and were waiting for the bill when my cousin walked into the dining room holding a tray with two balloon glasses. "Madeira," she said, setting the tray down. "A twenty-year-old Malmsey. On the house. I had the sommelier go down to the cave to get it. It's a good Christmas wine. I thought you might enjoy it after everything you've been through lately."

"Can you join us?" I asked.

She smiled and shook her head. "Unfortunately not. One of the chefs called in sick, so I'm in the kitchen tonight. Plus I got a call today from Celia Avery. The Miranda Foundation gala is on and they've had a flood of people buying tickets. So I'd better get busy."

After she left I said to Quinn, "You know, my mother's Christmas decorations were hidden behind a wall. Prescott's 'sanctum sanctorum' was behind a wall and Thelma's father's hiding place for his Prohibition booze was, too."

"What are you saying?"

"We've never really examined every single inch of wall in Leland's wine cellar."

"Do you think it could be there?"

"It's worth a second look," I said.

"I'll take the word of someone who figured out where Hobson Banks's package was."

"Let's go home."

WHEN WE HAD NEARLY given up I found the first loose brick. It didn't take long to dismantle the rest of the hiding place— the mortar was poor and most of it had turned to pebbles and dust. When Quinn finally shone a flashlight inside, the beam caught a couple of rows of dark, gleaming, dusty bottles.

For a long moment we were both speechless.

"We found it," I said. "I don't believe it."

"Let's make sure."

He had to crawl partway into the hole before he could reach one of the bottles. When he reemerged there were cobwebs in his hair and on his clothes.

The label on the dusty bottle was handwritten in old-fashioned spidery penmanship.

For the celebration of the 4th of July 1809 with President James Madison at the United States Capitol

"There are a lot of bottles back there," Quinn said.

"Worth. A. Fortune."

"I know." He looked at me. "What do you want to do? Auction them off? Keep some back?"

"I can't even think I'm still so stunned."

He leaned over and kissed me. "I'll tell you one thing we're going to do. We're drinking a bottle at our wedding," he said. "Okay?"

"Our wedding? And when would that be?" I asked, smiling.

"When would you like it to be?"

I caught my breath. We hadn't talked about this at all. Until just now.

"May," I said. "The vineyard is beautiful at that time of year. We can toast our marriage with the Madeira and share it with family and our closest friends."

"Then we'll get married in May," he said and kissed me again.

Acknowledgments

If you search the words "Bruton Vault" or "Bruton Vault Williamsburg" on Google, you'll be rewarded with dozens of websites to explore—some validating the existence of the mysterious vault, others debunking it, and each with a different version of what was or was not buried there. For my own purposes, *Mystery at Colonial Williamsburg: The Truth of Bruton Vault,* an ebook by David Allen Rivera that I found on the internet, was my most helpful and comprehensive reference source on that subject. Whether or not you believe the vault existed, the idea that Thomas Jefferson removed its contents and stored them in the White House is something I invented. There is also no such thing as the handwritten copy of the Declaration of Independence that Jefferson gave his good friend James Madison. R. S. Brazil's blog, *1609 Chronology,* provided helpful information on the wreck of the *Sea Venture.*

As you might imagine, I had a lot of help researching this book and, as always, all mistakes are mine. Rick Tagg, winemaker at Delaplane Cellars in Delaplane, Virginia, answered questions and offered advice as he has done for the last dozen years. I also confess to stealing the idea for using bicycle pulleys to open the lids of vacuum-sealed tank lids (and the ingenious idea of using hair ties to fix anything) from Kiernan Slater of Slater Run Vineyards in Upperville, Virginia, after her husband, Chris Patusky, told me Lucie's fictional vineyard is located almost exactly where Slater Run is located on the banks of Goose Creek.

Lucie Morton, one of the leading viticulturalists and vineyard consultants in the United States, gave me an engrossing tour of her state-of-the-art laboratory in Charlottesville when I was in town for the Virginia Book Festival and allowed me to use her as the inspiration for Josie Wilde—finally rectifying the long-standing rumor that she was actually the doppelganger for Lucie Montgomery.

I am grateful to Abby Yochelson, Reference Specialist in English Literature at the Library of Congress, for organizing a fascinating meeting at the Folger Shakespeare Library with Dr. Georgiana Ziegler, Associate Librarian and Head of Reference Emerita, and Rachel Dankert, Learning and Engagement Librarian, where we discussed whether Shakespeare really wrote Shakespeare (the Folger believes the answer is yes), Project Dust Bunny, the wreck of the *Sea Venture* as an inspiration for *The Tempest,* and, of course, paid a visit to the vault to see their world-class collection of First Folios.

Enormous thanks to Mark Summers, Public Historian at Historic Jamestowne, for an absorbing, informative, and passionate private tour of the fort on an afternoon where we had the place to ourselves while the sky across the James River grew progressively darker as Hurricane Florence made its way toward Williamsburg and news bulletins began urging people to evacuate low-lying areas (like Jamestown).

Thanks to members of the Freemasons who willingly answered my questions about their organization; for obvious reasons, they have requested anonymity—but you know who you are and that I appreciate your time and candor.

My Brazilian neighbors—and dear friends—Mario and Neide Winterstein have hosted a feijoada at their home for years on the Saturday after Thanksgiving and it has become one of our favorite holiday traditions. No one was ever murdered, but their warmth, hospitality, and good food—plus those lethal caipirinhas—were the inspiration for the party Scotty and Bianca hosted.

At Minotaur, thanks and love to Hannah Braaten, my wonderful editor; her assistant, the indefatigable Nettie Finn; as well as to Kayla Janas, Joe Brosnan, and Megan Kiddoo. Dominick Abel, my agent, is simply the best.

My husband, André de Nesnera, is my first and best cheerleader and sounding board—the love and lodestar of my life. For anyone who knows me, he and our three amazing sons, two beautiful daughters-in-law, and—the best Mother's Day gift of all—an adorable new granddaughter, are the center of my world. For all of them, I am eternally grateful and blessed.